The Swindle

Stuart McLean

Australian Self Publishing Group
P.O. Box 159, Calwell, ACT Australia 2905
Email: publishaspg@gmail.com
http://www.inspiringpublishers.com

 A catalogue record for this book is available from the National Library of Australia

National Library of Australia The Prepublication Data Service

Author: Stuart McLean
Title: The Swindle
Genre: Fiction

Paperback ISBN: 978-1-923449-94-7

Acknowledgements

Thank you to everyone who took the time to read my manuscript. Your encouragement gave me the motivation to see this through to the end.

The following people deserve special mention as they gave me the confidence to see my story from a much wider perspective. My neighbour Tony and his sister Jenny who willingly gave my manuscript its first professional review. Your final words 'keep going, there's something in this,' stayed with me till the end. Irina Dunn my editor and advocate, thank you. Hidden within my poor writing you saw a story that needed to be told. Panda, thank you for being my sounding board. Your emotional response to characters, especially Victoria reassured me that the story I wanted to tell was on the right track.

Finally, to my family, thank you for giving me the time and encouragement to see this through. This story sat in the back of my brain for years. Then, while I was driving somewhere between Lithgow and Mudgee, my wife turned to me and said, 'you need to stop talking and write this.' Thank-you Bren, without those words this story would have remained untold.

Contents

1. Unexpected opportunities 1

2. More than a race...8

3. Behind the gates...15

4. Consequences...25

5. Darkness...34

6. The shoebox..42

7. A different life..51

8. Demons and angels...56

9. Behind the scenes...67

10. Total commitment...73

11. Welcome additions...76

12. Tata (father)..80

13. Tenterfield 91

14. The day after 103

15 Road trip...107

16. Cooee 110

17. The fall 118

18. Mates..130

19. Surfside 138

20. Maryborough..153

21. Heatwave..162

22. Murray River..168

23. Dene 174

24. Manipulation..178

25. Gateway 183

26. Nothing to chance 196

27. The Golden Gift 201

28. The proposition 207

29. Goldfields 211

30. Coronation...218

31. Complications 224

32. Round one 232

33. Round two 241

34. Sunday...245

35. Day of days 249

36. The Gift...258

37. Payback 270

38. Scotch on the rocks 276

39. Atone..281

40. Thunder 289

41. Redemption 293

42. Serenity 301

CHAPTER 1

Unexpected opportunities

Autumn is a delightful time to live in Sydney, with balmy temperatures throughout the day followed by cool serene comfort in the night. Today had been one of those quintessential harbourside days you appreciate just that little more because you are mindful winter was only a matter of weeks away.

Descending behind the Blue Mountains, the sun gathered its last vestiges of warmth, leaving a jacket-worthy chill in the air.

Defying the laws of meteorology, the atmosphere under lights at the Homebush Athletic Centre was febrile. For the first time since the confinement of Covid, the grandstand was full. Each bay was congested with private school girls attired in full dress uniform and their parents in the latest high street fashion.

The floodlit arena was alive with competition. Schools against schools, staff against staff and the most competitive of all, parents against parents. The toxic undercurrent of scrutiny was overwhelming.

This was the IGAA athletics carnival, the oldest and most distinguished event in the independent girls' athletic association calendar.

Gillian Hardy strode boldly, as only a proud mother could. With Scott and Jack by her side, she felt the best she had in years. In a scant moment of self-indulgence, she allowed her thoughts settle on herself; *Everyone is afforded one Cinderella moment in their life, and tonight is mine.*

Ascending the stairs, her cherished rags to riches fairy-tale shifted unpleasantly. Moving across the row to her seat, she struggled to identify the origin of the discomfort. Her only point of reference was an emotion that had remained dormant since her own days at school.

Sitting among this throng of overt affluence, Gillian finally put her finger on it. Casting her eyes left and right, she concluded; *What was I thinking, K-Mart can't compete with casual couture.*

Unable to move, her thoughts turned to Jayde. *What have I done? I was the one who pushed this, but maybe I should have listened to Scott.* Her deeply protective maternal instinct was now aroused, and it wasn't giving her positive vibes.

The bright arena was heaving with activity. The crack of the starter's gun repeatedly captured the crowd's attention, while the extensive assortment of field events provided a more composed distraction.

The organising committee only had a few hours to deliver what would normally take an entire day. Juvenile girls at the beginning off their high-school journey competed in the same space as young women savouring this last event in their beloved school colours.

Embedded deep within this over-crowded program was a race like no other, the solar flare to the evening's heat and tension; the Betty Cambridge Cup. This single race held the gravitas to force the program into a temporary hiatus.

This modest, yet highly decorated, ninety-eight-year-old piece of tarnished silverware would be awarded to the winner of the open 100m dash. Hidden beneath the hallowed stains of patina, etched in private school immortality, were the names of former Olympic greats – eminent businesswomen and several political trailblazers who kicked doors off their hinges as they challenged the halls of post-federation misogyny.

In keeping with its custom, only young women in their matriculation year were permitted to compete.

Heats and semis whittled the field, leaving the eight fastest runners. Jayde Hardy, a newcomer in this private school setting, was relieved to be one. Until recently, there was no circumstance that would place her in the company of these private school elites. Not unless they were lost or diverted off the motorway that linked the coast to their weekend getaways in the elevated wilderness of the Blue Mountains.

Her home, St Marys, a wage-dependent suburb on Sydney's greater western fringe, was a place they most likely had heard of, but never visited. Being fast, extremely fast, was her ticket into their world; accepting a generous scholarship to the Mackenna Anglican Girls School elevated her to be an associate to Sydney's gentry in waiting.

Embracing her opportunity, Jayde took full advantage of the offer. Under the careful guidance of the school's coach, her technique refined, opening access to speed she never knew she possessed. Working equally as hard with her tutor, tertiary opportunities that were once optimistic dreams became attainable considerations.

Winning the Betty Cambridge Cup would ensure a sporting scholarship, providing the necessary finances to break away from the pay cheque poverty generations of her family had already endured.

Separating Jayde from this dream? A mere 12 seconds.

* * *

Barbara Cockington-Hardy, the frumpy, stoic, old-school principal, first laid eyes on Jayde at the state school athletics championships last year. Ordinarily, there was no way she would be witness to a public-school event, not a person of her station.

The lure was her adored niece, Stephanie.

Sitting high in the grandstand, Barbara had absorbed the conundrum which was Jayde in full flight. Mesmerised by her raw and unrefined technique, she muttered to herself, '*I need her.*'

Trusting her *think quick, act quick* mantra which underpinned her ascension to the pinnacle of education leadership, Barbara hastily compiled an ad hoc plan. She unquestionably had the discretion to express an interest. However, advancing this to a full-blown offer was a prosecution none of her predecessors had the audacity to engage.

As a matter of due diligence, affairs like this were referred to the sports selection committee and the board of directors. Faithful to her instincts, Barbara was prepared to violate this trusted process.

Moving forward, the voice inside her head demanded information; *'Where is she from?'* Shooting a quick glance towards the scoreboard, her confidence grew. *'St Marys, just under an hour away by train, well within the grasp of MacKenna Anglican.'*

Fumbling for her phone, her fingers barely kept pace with her brain. Searching several athletics sites, the empty screen affirmed her most fanciful whim. *'Unbelievable, this is her first big race!'*

Barbara's heart was pounding with excitement. However, she knew this wasn't a closed event. Rival IGAA principals, including Celeste from Swinton House, may be watching online via the sports unit's YouTube channel. If they saw Jayde, they would have the same ambition; secure her signature.

Inherently frugal, she would advocate for their partially subsidised scholarship before having to begrudgingly retire to her best offer; a fully subsidised scholarship with extras, including proper top-notch coaching in sport and academia.

Either way, what she was about to offer would significantly alter the direction of this young woman's life. Jayde would undoubtably become both faster and smarter. *'My pitch must highlight this win-win opportunity.'*

Her eyes remained fixated on Jayde as she left the track, continuously sending vital data to her frontal lobe while she profiled this enigmatic bolter from the west. *'Where was she sitting? Who was she with? Were they working or middle class?'*

The answer to each question informed her approach. Their partly shared surname would be the icebreaker needed to initiate her plan.

Abandoning the medal ceremony, Barbara strategically positioned herself on the far side of the concourse behind the grandstand, adjacent to the only exit gate. Hearing the final wrap-up by the ground announcer, she knew her wait wouldn't be long before Miss J. Hardy and the old grey-haired man would appear.

From this vantage point she obtained a more illuminating perspective of the pair. Judging by the iPhone 8 Jayde was bringing down from her ear and the decade-old running spikes in her hand, combined with the worn clothing and footwear on the old man, she determined disposable income was an issue for this family. *'Forget the partial, its either full or full with extras.'*

Falling back to a safe distance, she shadowed the two as they slowly followed the blue transit dots to the train station. Recognising the importance of catching them before they passed through the opal card barriers, Barbara uncomfortably increased her pace.

Between several heaving breaths, she boldly initiated the process to procure Jayde's speed. 'I just wanted to congratulate you on that outstanding performance. Truly amazing, I was given the impression my niece was the favourite, but you certainly had her measure.'

Flattered, Jayde said, 'Thank you'.

Directing her attention to the old man, Barbara continued. 'You must be very proud.'

'Too right I am!'

Not fazed by his response she continued, 'Sorry, I should introduce myself. I'm Barbara Cockington-Hardy, Principal of MacKenna Anglican Girls School.'

Her purposeful pause lured his retort. 'You're a Hardy?'

'Yes, it's my maiden name. My lineage dates to the Clan Mackintosh from the lowlands of Scotland. Contrary to popular belief, Hardy isn't Scottish, it's French, where it ended with an i. It is the embodiment of bold and courageous.'

Not the least bit daunted, the old man rebutted, 'Jayde's a Hardy, I'm not, I'm a Hill, Jack Hill, and my origins are Lidcombe; here in Australia, a mile or so over there.'

Barbara swiftly appreciated this old man's disposition; it was clear he didn't suffer fools, especially sharply dressed strangers who aim to impress with their intellect.

With no room to manoeuvre, she paid homage to her heritage, boldly going all in. 'I would like to offer Jayde a full fee-paying scholarship to my school.'

The cold shoulder she was receiving was fed some much-needed warmth.

Softening his stance, Jack gave Barbara permission to continue. 'Under the terms of this offer, my school is willing to cover the cost of tuition, coaching, and after hours tutoring, as well as all ancillary expenses. I estimate the value of this to be somewhere in the vicinity of forty-thousand dollars. I am supremely confident my school will have a positive influence on Jayde's speed and grades, opening opportunities well beyond her final year.'

Stunned into silence, Jack and Jayde shared the same bamboozled expression.

Not wanting to conduct anymore of this business in public, Barbara presented her card before placing a morsel of judicious insurance on her offer. 'My proposition will stand for one week. I look forward to hearing from you soon.' With that she again assumed her pompous stride and headed back to preside over her sanctum of affluence.

Lurking beneath the altruistic nature of this scholarship, Barbara had more hedonistic motives. She was fed up with losing the customary bet to her rival, Celeste Ferguson, Principal of Swinton House, the most acclaimed girls' school in the country.

This bet had remained a quiet wager between the two schools since the cup's inception. Tradition dictated the stakes: a bottle of red wine. Like the egos of those who presided over this quiet flutter, the wager had grown.

This year's bounty, a 61-Grange, valued well beyond their monthly salary.

In her six-year tenure, Barbara had not once tasted the rich, velvety, smooth spoils of victory. Celeste always managed to find an unknown speedster to ensure she would be the one to pop the cork.

This chance encounter gifted her the opportunity to beat Celeste at her own game.

CHAPTER 2

More than a race

Parents abandoned the various coffee karts and food stalls scattered throughout the concourse to return to their seats. Principals and dignitaries topped their glasses and staked their place on the narrow terrace. The finalists were about to enter the arena.

Barbara and Celeste acknowledged the occasion with a terse glance, both convinced they held dominion over the outcome of the cup.

Standing in the athletes call room, Jayde couldn't avoid feeling intimidated. She was not like them. They were styled within an inch of private school acceptability. Subtle toned make-up, lightly painted nails, delicate spray tans, and stylishly braided hair. The cost of their vogue was well beyond Gillian's weekly wage.

Their polish was on point, but looking at her reflection in the glass, she felt ashamed. Ashamed of who she was and where she came from. She barely had any polish at all. Luminous white skin, no highlights or accents on her face, and hair that was pulled back into a tight short ponytail. Vanity like this was something she'd never really considered. Trying her hardest to push this distraction aside, she reminded herself, *'Tonight is about winning, not all this other bullshit!'*

Victoria Livingstone was the antithesis of Jayde. Born into opulence, wanting and sacrifice were abstract constructs in her world. She had the best of everything. She was enrolled in the finest school, tutored by eminent scholars, possessed all the latest equipment, and all wrapped up within a cover-page model appearance.

To the private school 'toffs', she was their poster girl.

The undisputed race favourite, she had won each age division since entering high school, inscribing her name in IGAA history with several records along the way. However, this year unlike those before, Victoria had competition, real competition.

This unknown bolter with the unorthodox style moved comfortably through the heats and semis to enter the final only one-one-hundredth behind her. For the first time in six years, she was going to be seriously challenged. Would she hold or fold, no-one really knew.

Alex the Carnival Convener and Track Referee scanned the room before making the time-honoured call; 'Ladies, track positions please'. Each quietly stationed herself in lane order, from one to eight. Unsure of what to do, Jayde strategically lingered until all positions were filled.

Happy with the order, Alex stepped forward and thrust the doors open. A high-pitched roar erupted; a cacophony of sound greeted the precession, and chants and war-cries echoed throughout the arena. Young ladies screamed at the top of their lungs, doing their part to dominate this pre-race pandemonium.

Proudly marching at the head of the pack, Alex led the procession into position for the athlete's call. As the name of each finalist rang throughout the packed stadium, it was muffled by the unmistakable shrill scream of teenage girls.

Following their introduction, protocol demanded each athlete step forward and shake the hand of the great granddaughter of the event's namesake – Lily Cambridge.

As the formal party moved down the line, each young lady was afforded a brief juncture to acknowledge the crowd before assuming their position back in the line. Competition protocols dictated Victoria and Jayde were placed next to each other, in the blue-ribbon lanes, four and five.

Victoria revelled in this moment. She had rehearsed her wave in front of the mirror for weeks, emulating other famous athletes and how they acknowledged the crowd.

As her name rang through the stadium, *Victoria Livingstone, Swinton House*, she reverently followed protocol. Pausing to allow the official precession to pass, Victoria raised her hand to wave to the crowd. Accentuating this movement, she gave a subtle, yet appreciable, hip and boob shimmy, adding the obligatory sass social media required.

Somewhere between her last shimmy and shake Victoria's eyes left the crowd, shifting upwards to the dignitary's box. Celeste willingly caught her gaze, and rather than encouragement a significantly different message was sent.

After the semis, Victoria had been summoned to a private conference with Ms Ferguson. As a form prefect and now head girl this was not peculiar, either here at the track for a last word of encouragement, or at school to check on her progress.

These special privileges were in recognition of the exalted positions she held, and the influence her family had within this entitled school community. The Livingstones were one of the last foundation families enrolled at Swinton House; generations of old girls proudly wore the colours, but most importantly, they always made the largest extra-curricular contribution each year. With money, comes influence and power.

However, this meeting did not follow the protocols of the past. Celeste's usual affable demeanour was replaced by a serious and indignant manner. During their conference she gave Victoria a sinister, vile, and un-becoming instruction. Her plan? Remove Jayde before the starter called the field to their marks.

Taking advantage of Victoria's innate arrogance and sense of entitlement, she was a marionette in no time.

Celeste's eyes reinforced the obligation Victoria had to both her principal and school. Hidden within her enthusiastic wave and surreptitious hip and tit movements, Victoria reassured her with a careful faint nod of her head.

Refraining from emulating the new precedent, Jayde stepped forward and lightly shook Lily's hand. Her acknowledgement to the crowd was quick and tentative before she briskly retreated to the safety of the line-up.

Barbara witnessed the connection between Celeste and Victoria, and tried hard to mimic their silent, powerful connection. Her message of obligation never found its mark. Jayde's eyeline barely rose above the lower concourse.

After the last of the lower ranked qualifiers were introduced, the finalists were paraded to the end of the track.

Regally coloured track suits and running tights emblazoned with school crests and Latin mottoes were discarded, starting blocks were carefully set and start sequences meticulously rehearsed. As expected, there was a mass of uncoordinated, confusing movement, ideal conditions in which to execute an obscene, unladylike act.

Like most sprinters, Jayde had her own unique start process: she seated her feet into the blocks before looking down each arm as she settled her hands. Rising into the set position, and waiting three or so seconds before exploding, she drove her legs in powerful chopped strides with her head down. After fifteen metres, she cut her stride and rolled out to a gentle stop, exactly how her coach taught her.

Feeling strong and powerful, she affirmed her positivity; *'let's go!'*

Looking back towards the start line, she saw Victoria pointing and remonstrating about something in her lane.

With her limited experience on the track, Jayde never considered she could be in trouble. However, this could not be any further from the truth. When she returned to the start line, Trevor, the chief track marshal, stopped her and told her to look in the right corner of lane four.

Sitting there, glistening under the bright stadium lights, was a sizeable glob of spit. Before he could say anything further, Jayde knew she was about to be accused of this horrendous act.

In her submissive, timid voice she proclaimed, 'That's not mine.'

Not satisfied, Trevor said, 'Well, whose is it?'

'I don't know.'

Although apprehensive in her response, Jayde could feel the warmth of anger building in her veins. Celeste's audacious plan was beginning to take effect.

An uneasy silence fell over the crowd as the race ground to a halt.

As Alex hastily exited the athlete's tunnel, those who understood the formalities of athletics recognised the seriousness of the situation. Once a track referee is required at the start line, someone is about to be sanctioned or ejected.

Striding out onto the track, Alex cast a quick gaze towards the VIP box. It was amazing how much Celeste could say with just her eyes. The outcome to resolve this situation had already been decided. Unknown to all in the stadium, he and Celeste were enjoying a relationship that extended beyond the track. Unaware of the plan, he was not about to throw away his first promising liaison since his divorce.

Favourably for him, the scene descended into unprecedented mayhem. The team of start line officials packed around Jayde, each offering Trevor an embellished recollection of what they saw.

Jayde tried in vain to affirm her innocence, but with no willing ears, her proclamations became louder and more aggressive. Pacing within earshot, Victoria knowingly kept tensions high, relentlessly offering her opinion about the disgusting nature of spitting, especially in the wake of the pandemic.

Finally, as Jayde's inflection revealed desperation, Victoria leant into the group, and cast the catalyst needed to initiate an incorrigible reaction. 'I don't care how much you clean it, I'm not putting my hand there. Who knows what I will catch.'

Piercing the uneasy silence within the stadium, the unmistakable words 'It's not fuck'n mine!' escaped Jayde's mouth. With rage in her eyes, she lunged between the shocked officials, right first clenched. A glancing blow brushed Victoria's forehead, and clutching her face, Victoria fell to the ground.

Only the quick actions by Trevor and the starter prevented Jayde from landing more. The slightest of movements in Celeste's mouth and cheeks gave the hint of a smile. Victoria had executed her plan to perfection.

This outburst gave Alex no choice. Due to her violent actions and offensive language, Jayde would be instantly removed from the track.

Aware his actions would hand Victoria the cup made him excited. Casting his eyes above the pandemonium, he saw the hotel suite they would share later. For a conservative private school principal, Celeste was the complete opposite once her tailored power suit hit the bedroom floor.

By the time he reached Jayde, her rage was too far gone to listen to reason as she continued her tirade against Victoria, the officials and the whole event. The unmistakable word 'fuck' continued to echo throughout the stunned stadium.

This was a side of her that no-one, not even her parents, had ever seen. The normally quiet, timid girl had been replaced by a foul-mouthed firebrand.

After much coercion, Alex and Trevor finally ushered Jayde off the track. The deafening silence of the deserted call room reinforced the isolation she was afforded on the track. Battling to suppress her rage, she tossed anything that wasn't fixed around the room.

Barbara was quickly summoned to calm her student, and as she entered the room, it was difficult to tell who had more anger in her eyes. *Your unconscionable, scandalous behaviour is going cost me a small fortune, and another year of crowing from that woman,* she thought.

As she approached Jayde, the potential career-ending confrontation was interrupted by a massive cheer erupting from the grandstand above. Both froze as the opening verse of the Swinton House school song heralded Victoria as the victor.

Dropping her head, Barbara took a deep breath and resumed her standing as principal. Straightening her jacket she looked directly into Jayde's eyes. 'You will leave the event right now, your parents will meet you at the front gate. We will discuss this further back at school.'

This proclamation was delivered in the darkest, most chilling tone Jayde had ever heard. There would be no discussion back at the school; Barbara already knew what needed to happen come Monday.

*　*　*

Meanwhile, back on the track, Victoria was lapping up the trappings of her success. Holding the cup aloft, she shook her body in a way that again blurred the lines of acceptable private school behaviour. Her thoughts were far from the historical significance of her achievement, or the impact her actions were going to have on Jayde; instead, she was thinking about how many likes, hits and forwards she would have this time tomorrow.

Insta and Snap were going to go off. The increase in her online profile would be just another reason why any of the major running brands would want to sponsor her. This race reiterated that she had talent, and combined with her looks and a growing profile, *brand Victoria* was now developing into a tradable commodity. For Victoria, the pieces were beginning to fall into place.

CHAPTER 3

Behind the gates

In the dignitary's box, Celeste lapped up the obligatory congratulations. Cognizant of the politics of the room, she was measured in her comments. She avoided engaging in the pre-race post-mortem, mindful that a misdirected remark had the potential to expose the farce she had created.

The fallout was inconsequential; Jayde was just collateral damage. Chiefly, she would again be able to impress the Board of Directors at the Foundation Day Dinner with her prized glass of red. It was amazing how, regardless of the academic, sporting and cultural excellence she oversaw, this little tipple in the recess room to Keelor Hall kept her in favour.

Remaining on the good side of the board was Celeste's highest priority. Despite being a Swinton House old-girl, and growing up in the harbourside epicentre of Sydney's rich and famous, she was never truly accepted as a genuine eastern suburb's blueblood.

Growing up with only her mother, who was a live-in housemaid in the renovated servants' cottage on an expansive harbourside estate, she, like almost everyone else on the estate, was unaware of who her father was.

This all changed suddenly when she was thirteen. Without any warning signs or symptoms, her mum collapsed while vacuuming. She was gone before the ambulance arrived, the coroners finding acute myocardial infarction.

Charles Ferguson and his wife Rosemary generously provided a small out-of-hours service in the Swinton House Chapel before discreetly laying her to rest a few days later in the newly established Forest Lawn Memorial Park, forty odd kilometres away on the southwest fringe of the city.

To Celeste's knowledge, her mother hadn't made post-life plans, effectively leaving her without any assets or legal direction. Assuming she would be forced under the care of her mother's only sister, Beth, she began sorting through their paltry possessions.

Buried deep in the bottom drawer of the dressing table she stumbled upon her birth certificate, where it clearly named Charles Ferguson as her father.

Things that had seemed strange now made sense. These included the unused family trust that enrolled her in Australia's most esteemed girls' school, the raft of gifts at Christmas, and the added attention she received whenever he was around.

Still in shock, she marched up the forbidden path to the main residence, the incriminating piece of paper tightly clenched in her right hand. There was so much she needed to know.

Rosemary opened the door. For a raft of reasons, she had never taken to Celeste. Speaking in her usual condescending manner, she said, 'What do you want?'

'To see my father'.

Quick with her wit, she mocked, 'Well, that could be anyone, you know, your mother never told us who he was'.

Thrusting the incriminating piece of paper forward, Celeste firmly stood her ground.

A decade or more of unconfirmed suspicion was suddenly legitimised, there in the box next to the name of the father, *Charles Ferguson*. There was a loud thud as Rosemary's limp body crashed into the side table, shattering the crystal vase as it hit the hard tiled floor.

Charles, enjoying his nightly scotch and cigar in his sanctum, begrudgingly rose from his favoured dark leather chair to find out what had interrupted his evening musings.

Scanning the lobby, he observed Celeste standing in the open doorway, piece of paper in her hand, and his wife rising to her knees. Water, broken crystal, and flowers were strewn across the nineteenth century Glasgow patterned tiles.

'What on earth happened here?'

Rosemary now on her feet, straightened her dress and hair. 'That!'

His carefully guarded secret was out of the bag.

The ingrained silence of this house was swiftly broken by a volley of screaming and shouting. 'How could you do this, with our housekeeper for goodness' sake!'

With nowhere to manoeuvre, Charles mercilessly purged years of frustration. 'It was easy, Rosemary, when you showed no interest in me, Margaret did!'

In her late-thirties, Rosemary joined the unfortunate small percentage of women enduring premature menopause. This unexpected termination of her cycle not only eliminated her ability to have children; it also destroyed her desire for intimacy.

Coming from old money, discussions about sex or menstruation were taboo. Considerate of this etiquette, Rosemary chose not to mention she had gone through the change with Charles or her doctor; like many women of the time, she quietly bore it as part of her lot.

To the gilded eastern suburbs community, Charles and Rosemary had just about everything. Plenty of money, both old and new. A beautiful, generational, historic house with spacious gardens on the harbour. Fancy European cars and a live-in housemaid. Their only blemish, no successors, no children to carry their family legacy.

Rumours circulated throughout this fickle community that they were unable to conceive due to Charles' heavy workload. Long days and late nights gave them no time to make babies. For most part this was true.

The deeper truth was Charles took on more work to avoid Rosemary. If he desired intimacy, he could call on Margaret, or take a slight detour home from the city, up Darlinghurst Road into the heart of Sydney's red-light district.

When at home, Charles would be in his chair in the drawing room enjoying a cigar, a single malt, and the rich textures of the Duke and his big band. The whisky was for him, it helped him relax; the cigar was for Rosemary, it kept her away. She hated the heavy smell of tobacco that was left on both his clothes and his breath.

Retreating to the safety of the lounge room, Rosemary spent her nights watching television boozed up on her drink of choice, Martinis on the rocks.

Behind the heavy wrought-iron gates and six-foot sandstone, life was far from the utopian illusion they portrayed. Their marriage was now founded on convenience and alcohol; both had far too much to lose should they accept their circumstance and divorce. Charles would lose his family estate, and Rosemary her influence in the Sydney socialite scene.

Love and affection had long disappeared, replaced by silence, alcohol and separate bedrooms.

Standing silently in the doorway, Celeste revelled in the melodrama.

Now that the genie was out of the bottle, Charles didn't hold back. 'We went from having a healthy sex life to nothing overnight.'

Retorting with ferocious venom, Rosemary bit back. 'You know I went through the change early.'

Devoid of sympathy, Charles fiercely countered. 'No I didn't!'

Letting his denial hang just a little longer than needed, he added, 'As my dad taught me, if you leave a gap in the market, something, or in this case someone, will always fill it. Margaret was more than happy to fill the void.'

Shocked he could be so callous, Rosemary fought hard to keep the welling tears at bay.

Finally, after years, their dirty laundry was now exposed. An awkward silence fell over the room.

Conveniently ignoring the emotional carnage she had just sustained, Rosemary looked towards Charles, and for the first time in years, she dropped her usual condescension and spoke with vulnerability. 'We both know how and why we got here, so we need to drop the hostilities and find a way to sort this out.'

Realising there was nothing more to gain by purging anymore frustration, Charles nodded in agreement.

'Go back down to the cottage, girl, my wife and I need to have an adult conversation.'

Celeste silently turned and headed down the dark path, pondering where she would be this time tomorrow.

Retreating to the neutrality of the kitchen, Rosemary strained two cups of coffee from the pot.

As she was topping up the second cup, Charles cut to the chase. 'What do you suggest we do?'

'Send her to Beth, you support her financially, and we keep everything else the same.'

There was no way she would let this news reach their social group and the wider eastern suburbs community. *We would be the talk of the town. Imagine the comments, especially since I was so outspoken about Yvonne's marital problems last week,* she thought.

Celeste was Charles's only child, his successor in blood. Without any prospect of having more children, he was never going to entertain sending her away. Having sat through numerous high stakes negotiations, he knew this wouldn't be a one-sided affair. The question he was asking himself was, *'How much will I have to give to get what I want?'*

After several hours of toing and froing, Celeste was summoned back to the house.

Each step was full of apprehension as she walked back up the path, her anxiety building the closer she came to the imposing mansion. Without consultation, her fate had been decided.

Waiting by the door, Charles was proud to announce 'After a long discussion, we have decided that you will stay here. But there are some conditions. Come in and I will fill you in.'

'Publicly, we will declare that we adopted you after the unfortunate death of your mother. You couldn't go to Beth's because of her Parkinson's disease.'

This gifted Rosemary with a probable story for her capricious friends.

'Under this arrangement you will take your true surname, Ferguson.'

Changing her surname from Wilson to Ferguson was a large reason why Celeste remained illegitimate in this heritage-rich community. Her claim to patrimony was considered through title, not blood.

'As it has been, you will remain unwelcome in the main house. You will continue to live in the servants' cottage.'

Like Charles standing his ground on keeping Celeste, there was no way Rosemary was going to accept this bastard child into her home. Domestically mature beyond her years, Celeste had the knowledge and skills to be self-sufficient.

'A retail domestic cleaning service will be employed to take care of the main house. To keep the charade, you can make up one of the spare rooms to look like it's yours.'

Each day Rosemary roughed the bed and threw clothes on the floor to maintain the illusion.

'You are by no means permitted to unveil any detail of me being your natural father. The prefix *adopted* must be used before mother or father.'

Even with this fraudulent prefix, Charles was thrilled to finally be acknowledged as her father. Now his secret was finally out, life would change for the better. No longer did he have the need to maintain his long hours; his junior partners could take up the slack and start earning their keep.

He had years to catch up. His priority each night would be the cottage, not the drawing room. He pictured telling her the origins of her name, Celeste, a proud old Ferguson family name. Three others carried her name, the closest a great aunty whom he had known only for a few years before she passed.

To Charles, Aunty Cel was the kindest, most loving woman he ever knew. Widowed early, she lived on the estate. Every day she made time for him. Making up stories, playing in the garden, their time together was always an adventure. Throughout his childhood and teenage years, he cherished her memory and the special time they spent together.

Entering adulthood, he decided that if he was ever blessed with a daughter, she would carry her name.

Rosemary's last vengeful insistence condemned Celeste to the social fringe of Swinton House.

'You are forbidden from bringing anyone onto the estate. No-one can know about the living arrangements that exist behind our sandstone walls.'

Having no capacity to contest these conditions, Celeste had no choice but to accept her fate.

* * *

Now the principal of their most coveted school, holding the power to accept or deny their daughters, she finally had the status to match her surname.

Associates of the past now coveted her attention. Presenting themselves as friends, they introduced their friends, hoping to elicit some privilege to advance their cause. In this community, she wasn't the richest in monetary terms, but she was one of the most powerful.

Her ego happily feasted on this superficial attention, acutely aware that one day the feast would turn to famine. Her appetite for prominence remained strong; of course, she would do everything in her power to keep her job.

* * *

Concerned with limiting brand damage, Barbara remained in the call room, doing her best to quickly return it to its previous order.

As the last chair was carefully placed, Alex entered the room. 'You need to leave; the carnival has to resume.'

Short of breath, she mustered up. 'Thank you, Alex, I think everything is back in place. Please accept my sincerest apologies.' With that she did her best to hold her head high as she exited the room.

Heading down the corridor she was conflicted. *Duty dictates I should go back upstairs, but if I do, there's going to be endless questions and comments, or I could leave, giving me the benefit of time between this fiasco and my community.*

As she approached the point of no return, the real Barbara stood up. From the moment that hideous song penetrated the reinforced concrete, she had no intention of going back to the VIP room. *How could I possibly explain Jayde's behaviour, or worse, suffer the inevitable postulations about the values and virtues of private school education.*

Most of all, she did not want to be anywhere near Celeste. *I've endured her smug smile and condescending condolences repeatedly for six years. This year was supposed to be different; this was the year where I was supposed to be the swindler.*

There was no way of avoiding it; she had made the captain's call, bypassing the sports selection committee and the board of directors. *It's only a matter of time before this debacle is brought up at my next performance and review meeting. What do I say?*

The culpability of her arrogance would be measured by loss, both financial and reputational. *At best I can expect an official reprimand, at worst it could be my job.*

Barbara slipped through the main doors and into the night. During the short walk back to her car, she sent a text message to Anne Williams, her Assistant Principal. *Have a migraine, need to leave immediately.*

Anne knew that the only migraine Barbara would have was going to be on Saturday or Sunday morning after she had drowned her sorrows with her liquor of choice, aged Irish Whisky, delivered as it should be – neat.

Working under Barbara for the past two years, Anne had been witness to this spineless behaviour, this was her 'go to' when under pressure. In front of the staff and students, Barbara was Thatcheresque, tough and intimidating. However, when pitted against those with real power, she quickly lost her hard and heavy persona, continually shifting her position to avoid criticism or judgement.

Anne knew there would be repercussions from tonight's debacle. Power brokers at the school would not stand for Jayde's reprehensible actions; Barbara would be in line for some very hard and direct questions.

She knew Barbara would struggle to have the answers. Anne recognised this was her time to step up and impress. Moving up and down the rows she cunningly informed the parents she was now the most senior staff member at the event. Giving extra attention to those who were members of the Parents and Friends Association, she knew their endorsement would go a long way in moving her up the leadership ladder.

Anne always saw herself as a principal, and if there was to be a move on Barbara's job, she wanted to be first in line. At only forty-one, she would be the youngest principal ever appointed at MAGS. Despite being several years ahead of her career path, she knew opportunities like this were extremely rare, so she needed to position herself swiftly and tactfully.

* * *

As predicted, Victoria's post-event social media ratings exceeded expectations. Her Insta and snap accounts received an astronomical increase. Likes were coming in from all over the world. Comparisons were being made to other famous athletes, pampering her already inflated ego.

There were tens of thousands more hits for the pre- and post-race celebrations compared to that of the race itself – proving what she already knew, that sexy sells and she was sexy. Slender well-defined legs, a shapely bottom, tight yet subtle six pack, toned arms and a nice rack. Of course she was a hit on the internet. Brand Victoria was on the rise.

* * *

The social network among the young elite throughout the country was alight, and it was difficult to determine which was more popular, Victoria's win or Jayde's disqualification. Victoria had more likes and shares, while the comments about Jayde were astronomical. Popular national and international social media influencers bought in on the controversy, fearlessly providing and inviting opinions and judgements on Jayde's outburst.

* * *

Jayde spent the remainder of the weekend in the safety of St Marys.

Whenever she checked her phone the notification bar informed her there was a new vile message in her inbox. Parents, students and even staff vented their sentiments with no filter or shame.

No matter how she looked at it, Monday was going to be bad day.

CHAPTER 4

Consequences

Jayde woke well before her alarm, jittery with apprehension. She dug up the courage to climb out of bed. Following her morning routine, she showered quickly before pulling on her school uniform.

Scott, her father, decked out in his faded tradie outfit, caught her in the kitchen. Appreciating the torment that would be heading her way, he suggested, 'Why don't you stay here today with Poppy, I'm sure he'd love the company.'

On most other occasions, this would be met with an emphatic *yes*, but today it was an appreciative 'No'.

Jayde knew this was only holding off the inevitable. Whenever she returned, Ms Cockington-Hardy and the MAGS community would hold her accountable. *A few days of shit and then it will disappear.* This tended to be the attention span of the MAGS gossip cycle.

The west gave her the internal fortitude to withstand these private school princesses. After all, she had already endured their derogatory glances and surreptitious snide comments when she had first arrived. The only difference now was that the entire school community knew who she was.

Judgemental eyes and overt whispers greeted her as she walked from the train station to the grand, ornamental front gates. Parents in luxury European cars beeped their horns, extended the middle finger, and even hurled obscene abuse as she trekked the normally peaceful leafy streets.

Paradoxically, she found satiric humour in their actions. *Where's their moral compass now, adults hurling abuse at a teenager, like that's acceptable.*

The alienation continued as she moved across the primary and middle school playgrounds. Girls far younger brashly fired disparaging comments towards her, echoing their parents' thoughts and sentiments about this unrefined, blow-in westie.

Keeping the brim of her straw boater low to avoid eye contact, she hastily made her way towards the safety of the senior area, hopeful Petra and Georgia would be waiting to meet her.

As she rounded the corner of the newly renovated Science block, a warm feeling of relief flowed throughout her body. Her friends welcomed her with open arms. Jayde drew strength from their embrace. Acknowledging the awkwardness, Jayde professed her innocence. 'I didn't spit in her lane. I think she did it to get me disqualified!'

Supporting her hypothesis, Georgia offered a sullen, 'I know'.

Sharing the same piano tutor when they were seven, Georgia had her own story about the princess of Swinton House.

It was the end of year recital and she had been rewarded with the last and most challenging piece. Relegated to the penultimate position, Victoria was incensed. Retribution saw her commit a piano sin – playing with sticky fingers. The hard peppermint lolly she said was for her breath ended up as a fine tacky film over the keys.

Georgia sat to play, and although it wasn't enough to stop her, the sticky sensation on the keys destroyed her feel. Struggling to find the rhythm she hit her first bad note; soon after one became two, and her performance was ruined.

Before her piece had the opportunity to reach its colourful crescendo, she ran from the stage, tears streaming from her eyes. Georgia knew all too well a vile act like spitting was well within the boundaries of Victoria's morality. Before she could offer her uncomfortable memory, the familiar harsh beeping sound blasted across the campus; period one was about to start.

Like subjects from Pavlov's classical conditioning paradigm, the girls immediately halted their conversation, hoisted their overloaded school bags onto their shoulders and joined the morning migration to re-engage with the MAGS education production line.

Sadly, they were spread across the entire senior campus. Once again, Jayde would be alone and vulnerable. She moved in her usual way, head down, diffident steps.

Despite her head and hat being lower than normal, she could still feel the sharpness of the stares which were not isolated to the student community. Unknown to Jayde, all staff had been summoned to an impromptu meeting in the common room before the period one bell.

Barbara, nursing the after-effects of a heavy weekend, informed the staff, 'Despite the disgraceful behaviour on Friday night, you must continue to accept Miss Hardy into their classroom. However, all her additional support has been terminated. Any further sanctions directed towards Miss Hardy will come directly from my office'.

As most of the teaching staff were up for contract renewal, there were no objections.

*   *   *

Sally Morrison sat patiently behind the teacher's desk in room 22. Her day's lessons were meticulously planned, learning intentions carefully mapped back to syllabus outcomes, while the success criteria gave instant feedback on the effectiveness of her tutelage.

Staring at her laptop, Sally was conflicted by a message that popped up on the internal messaging system. *Ms Cockington-Hardy requires Miss Jayde Hardy to report to her office immediately.*

Judging by the strident directions provided earlier, Sally knew Jayde was in serious trouble. Never in her six-year tenure at MAGS had she seen Ms Cockington-Hardy be so open and indignant about a student under her care.

As her teacher/mentor, it was Sally's responsibility to help Jayde achieve her best. During their meetings she was expected to set goals, review assessment tasks, and provide advice on revision techniques while checking in on her social and emotional wellbeing.

This whole of student approach was an important element in the pastoral care program at MAGS. Mentors begin their journey with their students from the day they arrive at MAGS.

As a late entrant, Sally had a lot of catch up to do with Jayde. Utilising the school moto, *Scientia omnia vincit*, knowledge conquers all, she was able to create an environment that acknowledged Jayde's past, but most importantly gave her hope for the future.

However, after this morning's meeting, Sally thought Ms Cockington-Hardy should proclaim a new moto – *Perficiendi imago*, performance and image – as it was patently clear these were the metrics that really counted. Unfortunately for Jayde, she was found wanting on both.

As a teacher she had felt the same pressure. Performance was the only metric that counted and band sixes in the higher school certificate were the gold standard. Fortunately, Sally had the emotional and intellectual intelligence to meet this challenge.

In her short tenure at the school, Sally had become a band six highflyer, with most of her students achieving this meritorious outcome. Not only did these results provide her with status within the school; the performance bonus offered by the board of directors gave her a welcomed holiday bounty.

Sally knew Jayde's name would never make this esteemed list; at best she would scrape into the band below. However, given her starting point six months ago, the value add on her was likely to be astronomical. Jayde was the type of student that inspired teachers. Her effort was always commendable. She listened intently and although her work was not at the highest standard it was by no means anything less than her best.

While her pre-frontal cortex was sympathetic to Jayde's situation, her pragmatic right hemisphere was reviewing her own circumstance. Signing mortgage documents only a matter of months ago, Sally, like many other Australians, was bound by heavy, yet controllable, debt.

She needed this job; her pay was well beyond industry standard, and the performance bonus provided the means to be indulgent when she desired. Taking a stand against Ms Cockington-Hardy on behalf of Jayde could put her employment and all its perks at risk.

It was only a year ago her mentor Donna Smith courageously stood up to Ms Cockington-Hardy at an executive meeting. The fallout from this altercation was atrocious, and Donna was hastily dismissed on nefarious grounds, her name smeared to the extent she became unemployable in the independent education sector.

Emotionally broken, the fallout nearly cost her marriage, while financially, she lost the security and lucrative benefits MAGS provided. Finding employment in the public sector, her pay was appreciably less. Although she wasn't married with children, Sally still had a lot to lose; her pragmatism was too strong.

Jayde presented her ID card to the reader and entered room 22. Sitting in her allocated seat, she opened her bag and took out her geography book. Miss Sally Morrison waited patiently for the last of her class to sit before resuming their investigations into urban dynamics. Although the practical, right side of her brain won the battle, her empathetic cortex was allowed a small victory.

Rather than send Jayde immediately, Sally, in her own small act of defiance, begun her lesson as planned. Only when the class was quietly engaged in their own work did she discreetly approach Jayde. Carefully handing her a toilet pass, she was able to create a credible subterfuge for her to leave the room, minimising any additions to what she presumed was an overcrowded rumour mill.

*　*　*

Following Miss Morrison's instructions, Jayde presented herself to the Executive Secretary where she was promptly ushered into Ms Cockington-Hardy's office. She remembered her last visit to this room. It was filled with excitement and promise, not to mention the distinct smells of freshly baked pastries and barista coffee.

However, this time the smell in the room was vastly different. Jayde knew this smell – ugly brown liquor. This smell reminded her of dad when he had the time to get drunk. For the next two days he carried the same smell, a smell that told Jayde to stay away. This smell always made her nervous.

The secretary closed the door. Jayde was now trapped and alone. Barbara, in her terrifyingly calm tone, instructed Jayde to 'Sit down'.

Reluctantly she sat. Internally, Barbara was deriving sadistic pleasure from Jayde's anxiety. However, she was a busy woman, she had a school to run; more importantly she had to mitigate the damage from Friday night.

She knew her meeting with the board of directors would be scheduled soon, where it would be her turn to be under the blowtorch. Barbara's eyes locked onto Jayde. 'Look up!'

Once she caught and held Jayde's eyes, in the same calm, evil voice she had exposed on Friday night, she said, 'You failed to meet the conditions of our contract. Even though I could expel you, I won't. I want to keep you here and remind you each day; you owe me.'

Terrified, Jayde tried hard not to breathe, fearing this may insight further admonition.

Resting deeper into her high-backed brown leather chair, Barbara continued. 'Your academic adviser, Miss Morrison, tells me that your marks have improved, well done! She also informed me you're now considering university; primary teaching I believe.'

Holding this comment, Barbara took a long contemplating breath before folding her arms across the top roll of her belly. 'I have decided to withdraw all your extra-curricular services and classroom support. From now on, you're on your own. Good luck with becoming a teacher now.'

Maintaining her callous eyes, Barbara leant in. The distinctive cracking sound of upholstered leather being unloaded provided Jayde with a welcome distraction.

Resting her elbows on the deep reddish-brown mahogany desk, her left hand cupping a softly clenched right fist, her voice lowered, and her eyes held a merciless glare, Barbara said, 'You cost me, and I will not forget it. Now get out!'

Barbara didn't even bother to tell Jayde to keep this meeting quiet. She had no means of taking this further anyway. If her self-esteem wasn't low enough already, this meeting made a bad day even worse.

*　*　*

The following days and weeks were like a rollercoaster ride. The anticipated shift in focus didn't abide by her predicted timeline. Just as interest in her start line fiasco began fading away, a new meme or edit would emerge online to spark everyone's interest. The main offenders were *The Sprint Princess* and another account titled *#BCH61*.

In the classroom, Jayde spiralled out of control. Ms Cockington-Hardy's decree was stridently observed; she was afforded no support. Ignored during class discussions, her notes were only sporadically reviewed, and assessment tasks were returned with nothing but a grade.

Miss Morrison was placed on a curriculum review team which just happened to coincide with their scheduled conference time. Academically, her results followed the same path as her self-esteem – downwards at unconscionable speed.

Jayde was in free fall. Petra and Georgia tried their best to support her, using break times as tutoring sessions. However, for this to work effectively, it required Jayde to match their effort. Unfortunately, these brief moments of positivity were overwhelmed by the negativity inflicted over the other five or so hours of the school day.

Jayde would never discuss this disgraceful treatment with her parents, especially with her dad. When she was offered the scholarship, her parents had vastly different opinions about the merits of the offer. Gillian championed the proposition. 'This is a golden opportunity for Jayde to break away from the pay-to-pay cycle we have suffered our entire life.'

Grateful for everything she had, Gillian knew this was not the life she had hoped for. Circumstances beyond her control had landed her in this position and she was adamant that Jayde was not going to endure the same in her life.

Scott, on the other hand, was much more reserved. He was a hardworking man who laboured through two mediocre jobs to make ends meet. During the day he was a sheet metal fabricator in a small family business, and after hours he drove a taxi.

However, with the recent introduction of ride share this was not as profitable as in the past. To make the same money, he drove more hours and further from home. He investigated becoming a rideshare operator, but his near twenty-year-old Falcon was well below the expected standards and there was no way he could afford an upgrade.

'I've witnessed first-hand the attitude of these young elites when Santo sends me into the city.'

He was happy to take their money, but at the same time he was grateful Jayde was sheltered from this capricious world. Now his precious daughter was invited to associate with the segment of society he readily despised. He knew there was so much of her life that would not fit into this affluent new world. Scott fought the good fight, before concluding, *This is an argument I'll never win. Gillian's never going to change her mind.*

Jayde was always within earshot of these heated conversations and knew exactly how each of her parents felt. She also knew her father could be very short-tempered. Maybe that was the origin of her outburst.

She knew if her dad found out about the bullying and abuse, he would quickly make time to confront Ms Cockington-Hardy. At best, this would be fodder for a new round of abusive memes, at worst, it would end with him fronting a magistrate.

Either way, no good would come from telling her parents. This included Poppy Jack.

CHAPTER 5

Darkness

Weeks turned into months and there was no abatement from the academic isolation. With her confidence in tatters, Jayde was under no illusion she was anywhere near ready as she walked into her first HSC exam. The simplicity of the situation was undeniable. She was significantly underprepared, but as she had done each day since that fateful evening, she mutely faced the demon the best she could.

At the conclusion of her last exam there were no celebrations, no invitations to formals or graduation dinners. Walking out the gate for the last time, Jayde was grateful to farewell the private school experience.

She would miss Petra and Georgia, but she was optimistic their friendship would remain now the curtain was drawn on their time at MAGS.

Her results were released and, as expected, they were underwhelming. Even with bonus points due to her postcode, she would struggle to scrape in as a last-minute, second-round candidate. Her only option; a pathway program. Even with deferring the tuition costs, the other incidental expenses made this impossible.

Rather than dwell on what could have been, she took a casual job with her mother, working as a teacher's aide at the local long day care centre. Although it wasn't teaching, it did involve working with children and for the most part she was happy. Finally, the fiasco of the past twelve months appeared to be fading.

Jayde was at the beginning of the life that Gillian had wanted her to avoid, a life that revolved around acceptance of circumstance. Unfortunately, she was on the path to join the ranks of the overworked and underpaid.

Over the holiday period and into the new year, Jayde remained in contact with Petra and Georgia. Either as a catch up in the city, or online, mindful about protecting herself, she insisted they utilise the private setting. Even though her meltdown had fallen out of favour, it remained dormant somewhere out there in cyberspace.

* * *

In contrast to Jayde's experience, Petra and Georgia had jostled for the coveted accolade of dux as they entered the examination period. Pushing each other, they both received mentions in the meritorious Premiers honours list. In the tightest of contests, Georgia proudly stood at the alumna dinner with the famed royal blue and white silk ascot of academia adorning her black academic gown.

With an abundance of options, both girls accepted offers to pursue their tertiary studies at Sydney University, Petra in Pharmacy and Georgia with a double degree in Science and Doctor of Medicine. While attending Orientation Week festivities, they arranged for one of their usual coffee catchups with Jayde. Today's venue was an off-beat establishment they discovered just outside campus at the head of Glebe Point Road. Rostered on the opening shift, Jayde finished early and caught the train direct from work to Central Station.

Strolling down Broadway, she felt relaxed among the sights and sounds of the south-western fringe of the city. The three girls were happy to sit outside on the wooden stools, catching the cooling mid-afternoon breeze. Two of the three were excited about the new directions their lives were taking.

Despite her positive demeanour, Jayde was jealous, resentful of their opportunity. Although there was satisfaction working with the pre-schoolers, it wasn't teaching; it wasn't where she thought she would be.

As was the way with Jayde, just as life was settling and she was beginning to feel grounded, something, or in this case someone, tears her stability apart. Once again, it was Victoria.

Jayde spotted her first, and the cold rush of adrenaline flooded her veins. Not wanting to be noticed, she shifted on her stool, tilting her head down and away. Unfortunately, this wasn't enough to protect her. Recognising the fresher's packs and then Georgia, Victoria stopped for a chat.

With no point of escape, Jayde had to turn and face her nemesis. Inside, the cold rush had turned boiling hot, and her hypothalamus was in overdrive. Less than two metres away was the bitch who destroyed her only opportunity to be here, studying with her friends. Right here, right now, she could finish what was started on the track so many months ago.

Her mind raced, assessing all the variables. *There's a clear path, a quick lunge forward, right fist cocked; without seeing it, she will be lying on the ground with a broken nose and shattered teeth. I'll go for the nose and teeth, that will fuck her gorgeous, angelic face up the most.*

Revenge would be swift and sweet.

Before launching, common sense kicked in. *An unprovoked attack will surely see me escorted away by police before fronting a magistrate on assault charges. There's no way I can work with kids with a conviction.*

She had had some experience with the law after her father had an altercation with a neighbour over a barking dog. Although he didn't start the fight, he certainly finished it. Scott was given a good behaviour bond for minor assault.

Thankfully, her mum's calm DNA kicked in. *The skanky bitch isn't worth it!*

Now, in the calming parasympathetic phase, she resumed the timid, quiet, insecure demeanour that saw her survive those torturous months of high school.

With her cover blown, she was forced to reluctantly acknowledge Victoria's presence.

Standing tall, Victoria took a moment to appreciate post-school Jayde. *Clearly, she's not running, look at those thighs and boobs.*

Continuing her critique, she took careful note of the logo on Jayde's shirt before turning her attention to Georgia. 'I noticed a public piano in the Fischer Café. We must get together and tinkle the ivory, just as we did with Ms Valerie.'

'Scrunch up girls, I need a selfie.'

Walking away, she looked over her shoulder and gave Jayde a chilling smile.

* * *

The following day started just like the day before and the day before that. Jayde woke to the abrupt blast of her alarm, ate breakfast, and prepared herself for the mid-morning shift. Planning her day early, she ironed her uniform before going to sleep, giving her those precious extra minutes of blissful morning sleep.

Kissing Jack on the cheek, she left with time to buy herself a small coffee on the way. Since starting work, she looked forward to her little cup of joy each day.

She pushed through the front doors with time to spare. With a few sips left she could read the board and prepare herself for the day. Still on probation, she was constantly moved between rooms. Dealing with babies is very different to managing four-and five-year olds with way too much attitude.

While assessing the roster, Claire,, the director came into the staffroom. 'I need to see you in my office.'

Jayde's heart raced. Aware there was a full-time position available since Donna quit two weeks ago, she believed this was going to be the offer she had been waiting for. Rushing her last sip, she threw the cup in the bin.

Once in the office, Jayde sensed this meeting was not going to go as she thought. Claire now seated looked across the desk and bluntly asked, 'Where did you go after work yesterday?'

'I met some school friends at Glebe for coffee.'

'Were you wearing your uniform?'

'Yes. Why?'

'Well then Jayde, we have a problem. This surfaced last night across a range of social media platforms.'

Claire pushed her phone across the desk. On the screen was the selfie Victoria insisted on taking before she left. However, it had been heavily edited, focusing on Jayde from the boobs up, in the bottom left corner – the Poplar Park LDCC name and logo. Below the caption read, *What do you teach them first, swearing or punching?* followed by the footage of Jayde's infamous meltdown.

Fuck, I knew she was up to something.

'This was sent to me by Isaac, the owner of our centre. It popped up in his feed through his daughter's Swinton House connections. He's very protective of his business and its brand.'

Taking a deep breath, she delivered his decree. 'He has instructed me to dismiss you immediately.'

Expressionless, Jayde rose from her chair, collected her belongings, and headed towards the front door. The toddlers from the middle room were returning from outside play when they saw her about to pull on the handle. They adored her, she was fun; they all competed for her attention. Hearing their calls was the final straw, with tears streaming down her face she pulled on the handle and ran away as fast as she could. Only stopping when her lungs were on the verge of collapse.

The remainder of the walk home was a blur. Thoughts raced around her head; none could be reconciled. *What did I do that was so bad to deserve this? Why won't she just leave me alone? It was just a race! I'm not threat now; I don't run anymore! Will this ever go away?*

With the dark cloud of self-loathing billowing, she saw a solution that could remedy her unfathomable pain for good.

Holding a bottle of rum and a length of rope she snuck quietly through the side gate. Grabbing the hidden key, she slipped silently into the garage through the side door.

* * *

Returning some tea towels to their drawer, something caught Jack's eye. *For shit sake, who left that unlocked?*

The rickety, dishevelled, fibro structure housed his only prized possession, a Harley Davidson motorcycle. Since he caught a local junkie trying to steal it a few years ago, he was fastidious about the doors being locked.

Grabbing the metal bar stashed near the backdoor, he went to investigate.

Crouching in the corner, Jayde was typing a message on her phone when the door burst open. Instantly recognising the scream, his eyes darted to find its origin.

He could see from the expression on her face, along with the noose hanging above her, that she was about to commit a heinous, inconceivable act.

Tossing his makeshift weapon, he rushed to her side. Dropping hard on his knees, he hugged her tighter than ever before. Secure in his arms, months of torture come flooding out in her tears. Looking up at the macabre loop dangling over his head, he thought, *Thank God I got here in time.*

She was safe for now.

Where did this come from?

Jack needed to move, kneeling on concrete was possibly the worst position he could be in. 'Let's go to the kitchen where I can make us a cup of tea.'

Helping Jack, they rose together.

Entering the house, her emotional pendulum swung well past centre and was now in the opposite arc. Pacing around the kitchen, she was rambling. 'That fucking bitch, I knew she was up to something, why else would she want a selfie with me. I should have punched her when I had the chance; the charge would have been worth it. Now she's given me the time, I should use it wisely by smashing her pretty face in!'

Mad and irrational were not traits Jack readily associated with his granddaughter.

Rambling and blowing off steam was healthy; she needed to purge. Sprinkled throughout her incoherence were small snippets of important information, helping to frame the picture that nearly took her away.

The sharp click of the kettle cutting off was enough to halt her rant.

Dropping the tea bags into their cups, he gently inquired, 'Why are you home so early?'

This simple question initiated another tirade. 'Because Poppy, I was stupid enough to let a fucking bitch who shit on me once to do it again; fucking social media won't leave me alone. The preppy vindictive moll got me fired. For fuck's sake! I didn't do anything and I'm still paying for it!'

Confused, he spoke before thinking, 'You were what? How?'

'Didn't you hear me, I WAS FIRED! I went into town yesterday after work for a catch up with the girls. When we were having our coffee, I got caught in a selfie with Victoria who edited everyone else out of it. The fucking bitch then posted it, along with the video of my cup meltdown. Isaac the owner saw it and demanded Claire give me the boot.'

Catching herself on the last few words, Jayde realised this was the first time she snapped at her Poppy. Ashamed she leant on her elbows before cupping her face.

'Isn't Victoria that missy from Swinton House?'

Gaining more composure Jayde gave a muffled 'Yes!'

Conscious more questions about Victoria had the potential to set her off again, Jack tried to piece together why she would do such a heinous thing. *What did she have to gain from doing this? It wasn't likely they would ever cross paths as competitors again.*

However, no matter how much he tried, he could not land on a reasonable answer; he had no choice, he had to ask more questions. Jack knew sitting and talking wasn't the way to get her to speak. She loved his motorcycle, and she also loved cleaning it, making sure it was immaculate, making it the envy of all his mates.

Knowing this, he strategically proposed, 'I've been lazy after my weekend ride with the boys, how about we go outside a give my bike a good clean.'

'I'd like that.'

Busy hands gave her a clear mind. Jack could now get the answers he desperately needed.

Together they cleaned every inch of his bike. The paint and chrome were polished to a mirror finish. The leather seat and tyres were also given the proper treatment. Suitably distracted, she willingly divulged everything that occurred after the IGAA carnival. The internet trolling and abuse, the abandonment of the school, her poor HSC results and now Victoria taking and posting the picture.

Jack was speechless; how could all of this occur right under his nose. He understood how it slipped past Gillian and Scott; they worked so hard there was precious little time for them to pick up the subtle signs of trouble. But he was her constant, the most significant adult in her life. Since the day she was born he swore he would always protect her.

He missed the signs of trouble; his conscience painfully declared he had failed his assignment.

CHAPTER 6

The shoebox

As males do, Jack immediately went into fix-it mode.

His own encounter with the black dog gave him a profound appreciation of how it impounded your thoughts, enforcing its will on your every action. His brush with the dog would be categorised as self-inflicted, hers on the other hand came from uncontrollable outside influences, ones that could rear their ugly heads at any time.

Jayde needed redemption; it was imperative she square the ledger. Violence, although immediate, was not the solution; it would only deepen the problem. He needed a point of coincidence, an unlikely point of intersection where she would cease being the victim, rebuild her self-esteem and regain control over her life.

He needed to know more, much more about this nasty piece of work.

'Bring up her socials?'

'Why?'

'I want to see what you're dealing with.'

Jack knew this would be an anthology of her life. If there was any point of coincidence, it would be hidden among her pictures and posts. It was only a matter of seconds before he saw it; it was so extraordinary he had to take a second look for confirmation.

This is perfect, in fact, this is more than perfect. This was the point of coincidence he was looking for, and the best thing;

he already had the blueprint to work from, after all, he had done it before.

*   *   *

Victoria was contesting the Grampians Gift, the oldest and most sought-after professional running race in the country. The beauty of this event was it's not a standard match race, it's handicapped, and handicaps can be manipulated. With the right strategy what seems impossible can become possible.

Nothing in this world happens by chance; you need brains more than brawn if you want to succeed.

When Jayde was born, Jack made a promise to Gillian and Scott to never speak of his life before she entered their world, and till now he had solemnly kept his word. But today was a game changer; to save her he needed to introduce her to the man he used to be.

Triggering this shady plan would involve resuscitating dangerous elements of his personality, ones which possessed paralysing seduction along with a ravenous appetite. Walking back down these dark corridors of regret could see this master resume its dominance and veraciously claim its prey. Petrified he pondered, *Is it better to let sleeping dogs lie?*

Taking a deep breath, he contemplated the ramifications. Standing with confidence he strode the best he could down the hall to his bedroom.

Jayde could hear rumbling and after a short time, Jack returned holding an old shoebox. Positioning himself on the stool next to Jayde, he said, 'Before I open this, you need to understand, once the lid is off, we commit to the journey which is my past. There is joy and sadness; there are parts I'm not proud of and there are others you may find confronting. But I cannot just let you see what's inside without giving you the story behind it.'

Nervous and intrigued Jayde carefully lifted the lid.

Inside was an old pair of soft white leather running spikes lovingly wrapped in tissue paper, a brilliant red silk sash and a yellow tinged newspaper clipping with the headline GIFT INVESTIGATED. In a large picture of men in white running shorts and dark bibs, there was one man clearly out in front and lunging through some funny looking gates.

Looking closer at the picture, Jayde recognised the facial features of the lunging man. It looked like a younger version of her Poppy. Reading his name in the bio underneath confirmed this was him.

Jayde's eyes moved across and down the page. Without any real foundation, the article accused Jack of cheating. An impromptu meeting of the Stewards and race committee had been convened, and all finalists were required to report and give evidence.

The most critical person, Jack, had vanished. Deepening the conspiracy, the bookies were caught with large bets at long odds. Three additional unknown males were suspected of being a part of this coordinated sting.

Once she lowered the article, Jack took another deep breath. There weren't any more newspaper articles that could explain his story, the rest had to come from him.

Jack began. 'Back in the day I was a very good sportsman. Cricket, football, and running were my specialties. Running was my favourite, I did it for money. I was what they called a pro or professional runner in the athletic league, and I raced in events known as "gifts".'

Early in his teens, Jack was spotted playing football by Earl Impey, a gnarly, wiry old bloke. In the winter months, Earl occupied much of his spare time scouting junior football, while in the spring and summer he coached and mentored young sprinters in the Professional Athletic League.

Impressed by Jack's natural speed and power, Earl approached him after a game and suggested he quit football and join his squad of runners. At fifteen, Jack was introduced to his first professional race, the Murrumbidgee Gift in Gundagai. From that moment until Earl's demise, summers were filled with trips up and down the highway, racing in Gifts and country carnivals.

Earl was old school; a hard task master who quickly taught Jack professional running was not based solely on how fast you could run. It was more about how you planned your run. You had to target an event and work carefully for months or years to ensure you had the best mark.

In professional running, not everyone runs the same distance. Marks or handicaps are given as a head start from the full race distance, and if set correctly everyone should cross the finish line at the same time. Every yard you didn't have to run counted. This allowed small variables like the quality of the grass in a lane or the direction and velocity of wind to be the difference between a win or loss. However, when you add in the influence of money, other motivations come into play.

Athletes and their coaches continually tried it on to manipulate the result. Should the Stewards, or Magpies as they were affectionately known, determine an athlete was running dead, or as they called it "sandbagging", their mark would be pulled, adding an extra yard or two to their remaining races.

'In professional running, you run full steam from gun to gate, anything less is against the rules. However, when there is prize money up for grabs all sorts of deception occurs. Athletes and coaches try all sorts of tricks to get an advantage. Lead lined spikes, filing spikes and drinking gallons of water were just a few of these unscrupulous methods. Add to this, bookies, with their self-interest, and it was a recipe for trouble or, for me, opportunity.'

Jack was comfortable in this world. He had a clear understanding of his station in society; working-class, from his heavy denim work pants and laced black leather work boots.

On the weekend he would travel around New South Wales and Victoria, chasing professional running events. Gifts in small country towns were a great way to make extra money. Betting and playing the odds was an easy way to make cash and when you understood how the system worked.

Delving deeper into his past, he said, 'My dad, your great grandad Harry, was the bag man for an SP bookie. As a boy, I worked in the backroom of the local pub, scribing odds on a chalk board. Pieces of paper would be passed from the bar through the waiter's window. Odds would change quickly, and it was my job to keep up with the call. My payment was a few shillings and a glass of lemonade.'

Taking a relieving breath, Jack continued. 'In my early teens I moved away from the chalk board, moving up the ranks I become a runner, moving quickly between the different pubs in the area collecting bets to take them back and be processed. Through this I was able to see how bookies and betting worked, how odds could be manipulated, how and when bets should be made and, most importantly, for how much. Big bets attract attention. Small frequent bets in this world stay under the radar. Good money can be made when you're not greedy.'

When at the track Jack would get some money on, but never directly from his hand. Instead, he would rely on a trusted friend. Sometimes this would be a mate, others it would be lady friend, either way their job was to follow his instructions to a tee. He very rarely bet on himself. And another gift from these devious days was, he learnt how to read form. He could predict when runners were peaking for a win.

No race was a random event, runners would plot and plan to peak at just the right moment. With his knowledge, Jack could read this ascendency, allowing him to get on at the right time.

He also learnt to never kill the goose that laid the golden egg. Make what you need and no more. Small wins give you longevity. In this business, greed will wipe you out quickly. Bookies are skittish, and if they suspect they're being played, they will shut you down.

Jack continued. 'Earl and I were able to make a tidy sum, but I never flaunted it. Fancy cars and clothes were another way that they can tell something was suspicious. My money was squirreled away in biscuit tins and glass jars hidden or buried under the house.'

When he had a win, he would always leave a few bob on the kitchen bench for his mother. Like all working men he paid board, but this extra made a difference. It helped to keep her afloat, especially since the car accident that took Harry well before his time.

Sipping tea to moisten his mouth, Jack moved on with his walk down memory lane. 'There was one race that was the hardest to predict, it was like the Melbourne Cup of professional running. The Grampians Gift, or "The Gift" as we knew it. The oldest, most celebrated, and highest paying race in the country. Winning this race put you in rare company. Always run at Easter it was the final event on the professional league calendar. The prize, a red silk sash and your name on the honour board in the Stewards' room along with the money. On the track, the prize money was good, off the track, if done right, the bookies money could set you up for life.'

Breaking her silence, Jayde interrupted him. 'Isn't that the race Victoria's running in?'

'That's the one.'

Through his days of working with his dad, Jack knew if this off-track amount was a fortune, then it was the end of his days as a runner. Bookies don't take kindly to paying out huge sums of money; they're in the business of taking it, not dishing it out.

However, this year, Jack was going to take them for all he could.

Getting back to his past, Jack continued. 'It was 1966 and my birthdate just dropped in the national service ballot. I was a fit, strong twenty-year-old, and there was no way I could avoid fighting in Vietnam.'

'I knew I was fast leading into The Gift. Several semi-finals and one final in Maryborough throughout the mid-season forced a review of my handicap. With no wins or places in the calendar year, and only a few wins over my whole career, the League kindly gave my handicap a lift. That half yard gave me the edge I needed.'

Like all the runners on the circuit, Jack had his own unique approach to fool the magpies. However, his didn't involve the traditional means of added weight or water. His was more cunning. He would never get pinned for weight or equipment discrepancies; his method was based around fatigue. You never run your fastest when you are fatigued, and it was how he brought this on that was the genius of his plan.

When at a Gift, Jack never strayed too close to town. He was always on the outskirts in a small shitty motel or pub that was the cheapest around. Given the state of his car, kit, and coach, everyone on the circuit assumed he was a battler, always short of a penny, let alone a pound.

Truth be told, he had more than enough to stay in the ritziest joint any town had to offer. But that would have made things harder. Staying out of the spotlight gave him anonymity, providing freedom to move without being seen. This was another critical element of his plan.

Fascinated, Jayde listened intently. 'I arrived in Stawell as I had done for the past three years. Staying in my favourite dump. The only difference, my clapped-out FJ had three passengers, not the usual one. Cleaning out all my jars, each of my mates carried a sizable wad of my cash which was to be dropped on me at very specific times. Initial bets were modest, then as I moved through the rounds the size was to increase substantially. No-one could make multiple bets with the same bookie. They were not to stand together; bookies had spotters. My plan even detailed where they would be dropped off and collected at the beginning and end of the day. Every element was under my control.'

Another change this year which went largely unnoticed was his FJ didn't roll silently out of the hotel carpark at 5am. This year Jack remained in bed, peacefully sleeping for as long as he could, controlling his fatigue. In fact, he wouldn't be fatigued at all. He was ready to go, and no one had picked it.

'Everything went to plan. Thankfully, I wasn't the un-backable favourite as the finalists were introduced to the waiting crowd. Typically, the outcome of the race was now almost predictable, the odds so small it made betting worthless. A pompous dickhead, Bill Paterson held this honour. His stride exiting the finish gates and up to his mark was one of supreme arrogance. Knowing I was viewed as an outsider gave me confidence. The starter called us to our marks, and the rest was history.'

'I won by two yards, which in professional running is contemptuous. Handicaps by design should give a blanket finish. This resounding victory raised eyebrows. The other finalists led by Bill Paterson instantly protested, they claimed I was a sandbagger. Bookies caught long on their bets were forced to pay out. My mates moved quickly and strategically through the betting circle or, as we knew it, the bull pen, collecting my winnings. Bookies looked at each other with astonishment; they knew they had been played, and they were pissed off.

'I took the sash and the winner's cheque. Quickly stood for the obligatory photos before moving off to collect my old beaten-up blocks, I was able to escape to the colour tent, then the athlete's room. In this quiet sanctum, I could hear the commotion spewing from the Stewards' room next door. The bookies bagmen competed with Bill Paterson and Ernie Bellamey to be loudest in their protest.'

Wetting his mouth with sip of lukewarm tea, he was able to speak without tacky resistance. 'From what I could piece together, this tirade was directed at Bill's father Reg, the Chairman of the Professional Athletic League. Above the other commotion I clearly heard Ernie bellow, *this was supposed to be Bill's year, that was the arrangement.*'

The delegation of athlete and coach demanded an immediate enquiry. They had invested too much to be taken by a roughie journeyman.

'Hearing the ruckus on the other side of the wall was magnificent. However, I knew it wouldn't be long before they would come looking for me.'

With a wry smile he said, 'I quickly changed and headed for the usually locked backdoor. My mates under the cover of darkness cut a hole in the wire fence and broke the rusty old padlock. Using fishing line, they strung the wire chains back together, and with a single swipe of my pocketknife I was free.

'As planned, my friends picked me up one street away from the track. Although we were booked for another night, we headed straight out of town. Knowing the bookies would be calling in their muscle we headed northwest to Dimboola, before making our way up to Mildura and then across to Hay. It was the long way around, but it kept us clear of any unwanted company.'

Captivated, Jayde sat in silence. *What the ...? This is not my Poppy; this is more like Netflix.*

'Jerry cans of fuel in the boot kept my old FJ running throughout the night. With each of us taking turns behind the wheel we were well beyond the clutches of any bookies or magpies. Arriving in West Wyalong, the boys filled the tank and cans, and I went to the bank to cash my winner's cheque.'

Stopping to take another sip of cold tea, Jack realised this was the first time in over fifty years the full details of his swindle had been aired. *I can't believe I got away with it!*

Convinced there was treachery at play, the Stewards upheld the protest and called for an immediate enquiry. All remaining finalists were interviewed, and records were scrutinised. Nothing out of the ordinary was found.

The only anomaly came from the owner of the hotel. Traditionally, it would be Jack plus one, but this year it was plus three. The hotelier also noted he didn't hear Jack's car leaving before daybreak each day. Changes to his usual routine weren't enough to implicate him in a conspiracy.

'Vanishing before the formal enquiry, I arrived home to a telegram petitioning me to report back to Stawell. Naturally, I ignored it; I had the sash and already collected the cash. Anyway I couldn't, I had to report for my nasho service.

'As I expected, after the medical, I was off to basic training. Twelve weeks at Puckapunyal, then up north to Canungra and Shoalwater for jungle training, then on the plane and off to war.

'That's where my speed came from!'

Raising his eyebrows, Jack nodded and said, 'You know your funny arm action, that's from me'.

CHAPTER 7

A different life

Jack needed a bit of time to compose himself for the next instalment of his past. 'Give me a moment, I need to get rid of that tea.'

Standing in the bathroom, taking a deep breath, he was trying to figure out how to talk freely about the darkest period of his life. Apart from his service and Gillian, there was nothing else about this time that gave him pleasure or pride.

After some quick, deep consideration he concluded, *The only way to do this, is to present it as it happened.*

Returning to the kitchen, he took one last thoughtful breath. 'I need to warn you, it gets a bit rough from here.' Reaching down to his special drawer, Jack placed his sacred pack of Butterscotch on the table.

Wow, Poppy never shares his butterscotch. Jayde knew this was going to be a bumpy ride.

'Before I left, I needed to get my affairs in order. After all, I was going to war, there was a chance I may never return. I gathered my prize money and winnings and went to meet one of my dad's old mates. I needed to exchange my old pounds for new notes.'

I remember this, we covered it in Modern History.

'I could have done this at the bank, but how could I explain that an apprentice boiler maker had just over a thousand pounds.

So, Lenny was my man. I knew I would lose a bit, but most importantly there would be no questions. He counted the pounds, converted them to dollars, minus his fee and I walked away. I gave it to your Nan Shirley; this would keep her going if I didn't come home.

'It was my last night before leaving. To honour the occasion me and my mates tied one on at the local. For the first time in my life, I splashed my winnings about, shouting my mates drinks and a slap-up Chinese feed.'

Jayde appreciated the significance of this night. The Poppy she knew was always tight with his money, so hearing how he spent it with such abandon was almost unimaginable.

'Linda Smith, my nosey neighbour, was in the Ladies Lounge. I think she heard me talking to mum about heading down there. She was always somewhere near the fence when I was out in the yard.

'She cornered me as I left the public bar and inviting me into the Lounge for a drink. Preparing for the encounter, she popped the top two buttons on her dress. Hypnotized, I followed her into the quieter, more civilised area of the pub. After a few more drinks, we disappeared into the carpark, into the backseat of my old FJ, where your mother was conceived.'

Despite the boorish nature of its delivery, Jayde didn't blink an eye. It was a reasonable assumption that her mum was conceived during a one-night stand.

'I woke the next day with a splitting hangover. I gave Nan Shirley a hug and left for war.'

Shit, how do you do that, one last hug and leave.

'I breezed through basic before heading up north for jungle training.'

His exploits as a boy and teenager taught him a thing or two about fighting, and his time with Earl, tenacity; vital traits when preparing for war.

With a noticeable quiver he said, 'I deployed with Uncle Bert and the other Piggies in the 7th RAR. We were based with the

6th and then the 2nd in Nui Dat. Early operations kept us away from the serious action. Tasked with security meant long days of walking or sitting and watching. We went out on a few search and destroy missions, but I was generally held in the reserve unit, ready to engage if needed.'

Jack was taught by his dad and Earl, who both served in New Guinea, that the safest place in a war is anywhere but where the bullets are flying.

'While I was in country, I would receive the occasional letter from home. Nan Shirley loved giving me a recount of events in the neighbourhood. For the first time in years I enjoyed reading, and for the briefest of moments I was back in the streets of Lidcombe. However, one letter in mid-67' rocked me; I was a dad. Accompanying the letter was a picture of a beautiful baby girl named Gillian, born in January to Linda Smith.

'I studied every feature of the baby in that small black-and-white photo before showing it off to everyone in my hooch. Eventually, I got back to the letter, and it turned out Gillian was with my mum. It was the 60s and single mothers were frowned upon; getting up the duff was a blight on both Linda and her mother Norma.'

Hearing the term *up the duff* made Jayde uncomfortable; although she knew that's how pregnancy was referred to back then, it still felt horrible and crass. For the briefest of moments, she felt compassion for Linda; after all it wasn't entirely her fault.

On a roll, Jack continued. 'Noticing Linda was spending more time in her backyard, Nan Shirley became suspicious. She was always up for a bit of neighbourhood scuttlebutt, but the protruding bump gave it away. Keen to know more, she was always near the back of the house when Linda was getting some fresh air.

'Early on, she discovered they weren't keeping the baby; it was going up for adoption. But when she heard it was mine, her thirst for the scandal changed.'

Understanding this might be her only chance of having a grandchild, Shirley gritted her teeth and took matters into her own hands.

'Not having a bar of this adoption business, she grabbed a fistful of cash before storming around to the backstreet and knocking on Norma's door. Despite being small in stature, Nan Shirl could be very persuasive when she wanted.'

Jayde had only seen a few pictures of her Nan Shirley. Even with the shadowy resolution, she could see toughness in her eyes.

'A cup of tea later, along with several orange and yellow banknotes for their trouble, it was agreed; as grandmother, Shirley would take the baby. Shortly after, Linda and her family silently moved away. No forwarding address or contact details were left behind.'

Jayde sat there amazed; her strange family now made sense. *I wonder what happened to Linda. How did her life turn out after walking away from her baby? Does she ever think about her hidden family?*

Jack continued. 'In August of 67, I saw my first and only real action. It was during Operation Ballarat in Hat Dich, where the battle of Suoi Chau Pha occurred. This was where we took the fight to the VC. Our mission; find and engage them. The intel was our boys in Long Tan weakened them, our job was to force them out of the province.'

'"A" company headed the mission, and when fresh footprints were discovered, we were ordered to get set for an ambush. Soon after, two enemy soldiers walked into our killing zone. Fearing they weren't alone, "2" platoon was sent up the track to investigate. They found what we were looking for, running directly into the 3rd Battalion of the 274th VC Regiment. We were now engaged in an encounter battle, and that's when shit got real, really quick.

'I was in "1" platoon. We were sent on a flanking mission. The VC had the same idea, and we were caught at close range. Bullets raced through the air; like flies in summer, mortar rounds were quickly zeroing in on us. One of my buddies, Neil, took several hits to the chest and was bleeding out quickly. Unable to help, the rest of my fire team – Don, Jimmy, and myself – continued to provide supressing fire. A mortar round exploded behind me, and I wore several pieces of shrapnel in the back of both legs, bum, and groin. With my ears ringing and my legs and bum bleeding, I kept fighting, popping rounds at the flashes in the thick jungle.'

With sadness in his eyes and a heavy quiver in his voice, Jack soldiered on. 'Neil was lying motionless. Jimmy kept firing while Don quickly applied field dressings to my legs before doing the mandatory stocktake in my pants. Barely getting to two, he gave up and packed my groin with a thick dressing. My adrenaline was so high that it was only when the dressings were applied that my brain recognised the pain.'

Jayde knew of his service, but this was the first time she had heard it in such intimate detail. His recount put much needed perspective on her problems.

With a lump in his throat, Jack ploughed on. 'I propped myself against a mound of dirt, and emptied my magazine. They were getting the upper hand. Bruiser our FO radioed *Danger close, fire for effect*. Those bloody shells were dropped on our heads. In his forward position, Bruiser, god rest his soul, took one of ours direct, but his quick thinking and bravery saved us. What VC survived bugged out, and a few bodies and a shit load of blood told us we had done our job.'

There was a renewed sense of pride in his delivery.

'Unable to walk I was stretchered back to the LZ. When the count came in, three more of my company joined Neil and Bruiser occupying a body bag, while another eighteen accompanied me in the hospital. Initially, I was evacuated to the triage unit at Nui Dat where it was determined I needed an immediate air lift to the 8th Field Ambulance in Vung Tau for more intensive treatment.'

It was only through the quick action from the CMF doctor that saved his leg and what was left of his wedding tackle. Flesh and bone can be repaired; nerves on the other hand cannot. From now on Jack would be resigned to a life without physical intimacy and walking with a very noticeable limp.

Also, his time as a professional athlete was over.

CHAPTER 8

Demons and angels

Not having spoken about this in such detail, Jack needed several minutes to get himself centred. Recognising the difficulty he was experiencing, Jayde stood from her stool and gave him a hug.

She could feel the stress in his body; he was tense, his breathing shallow with a distinct shake. Appreciating her gesture, he held her arms, gaining composure from her affection.

Finally, he nodded his head. There was no way of avoiding the reality of the next chapter in his life.

'After spending a year going through a bunch of repat hospitals, I was finally discharged. Returning home I finally met my daughter, your mum. She was coming up to her third birthday and was understandably frightened by this strange man with the funny limp. However, over time she got used to me being around and within a year began to call me "dad". Nan Shirley had spent most of the money, and the nest egg I had left was now under a hundred bucks. Even with my service pension, I needed to get a job. My old one was long gone, and there weren't a lot around. The recession took away most of what I could do.'

Visibly aggravated he continued. 'For a while I struggled to blend back into society. Unlike previous soldiers, me and my mates who flew in weren't welcomed home with applause and parades. We were unwanted soldiers who fought an unpopular war, not by choice, but because our government made us. I heard the stories and saw the pictures of soldiers marching up George St in their lines, people crowding the footpaths clapping and cheering. I had none of that. I was angry and frustrated; life as I knew it had been turned upside down. It became far too easy to find comfort at the pub looking through the lens of another empty beer.

'Eventually I found a job that accounted for my gammy leg – driving a taxi. It was good work; I enjoyed the company of my customers. Through the day I would drive, then after the pm changeover I would drink and gamble. Stumbling in the door sometime after dark, I was not bothered that your mum and Nan Shirley had barely eaten.'

Dejected, he continued. 'Looking back, I was a selfish son and a bad dad. I abandoned your nan and raised your mum in poverty.'

Not wanting to linger too long in this moment, Jack forged on. 'Your mum was now in high school and beginning to rebel. Life with no mother, a gambling alcoholic father and a frail grandmother was difficult. When Nan Shirley passed, she really went off the rails. I wouldn't see her for days, then she'd come home, eyes hanging out of her head, reeking of grog or dope. That was until she fell pregnant, then it all stopped. Not long after, your dad moved into the home first occupied by your great, great grandmother Heather over seventy years ago.'

Bullshit, there's no way my mum was wild.

'The expectation of being a grandfather gave me what I needed, a sense of belonging. I was able to get some control over my afflictions. Scott and I prepared the nursery that welcomed both your mum and me. Things were going well, everyone was in a good place, until one morning Gill, not far from the end, woke to a strange feeling in her belly. The baby was unusually still and heavy.'

Clearing his throat and blinking heavily he struggled on. 'Knowing something was wrong she called an ambulance. A monitor was placed on her bump. No heartbeat. Your mum lost her baby. Later that day she was given some medicine which forced her to deliver a beautiful, sleeping baby girl they called Hannah.'

He pointed towards the assortment of pictures in the large frame. 'That baby in the middle,' he said, softly shaking his head. He mumbled the last words. 'She's your mum and dad's angel.'

Sitting in shock, Jayde struggled to absorb what was just said. She had never considered herself to be anything but an only child. *I had a sister. How did they keep this quiet for so long?*

Giving Jayde time to digest what he had just said, Poppy took a calming breath before continuing. 'As much as the excitement of having a baby brought me out of my drinking and gambling, losing one sent me the other way. I began drinking earlier and earlier in the day. It was only a matter of time before I was caught drink driving. I was sacked on the spot. Apart from losing my licence for six months, I would never be allowed to drive a taxi again. At just over forty and a rotten alcoholic, I was again on the hunt for a new career.'

'Out of work with a small service pension, I had just enough money to fund my addiction. Betting with the new owner of the book at the pub where I worked with dad, my poor choices hurt the people I loved the most.'

Exhuming this festering skeleton from his past, Jack pressed on. 'This bookie who I only knew as Alf offered a line of credit. I began betting money I didn't have. This was dangerous, and before I knew it, I was in trouble, serious trouble, and the more I tried to get out of the hole, the deeper I went in.'

Jayde knew these words were difficult for her Poppy. His head was slumped, and the shame he bore prevented him from looking her in the eye.

In a soft, remorseful voice he said, 'The problem with debt is it must be paid back. No bookie, especially those acting on the other side of the law, carries bad debt. Once it reaches the limit, credit is cut, and the money owing paid.

'Savvy, Alf did his due diligence on me; I was the benefactor of my family home, an oversized block in Lidcombe, close to the train station. Prime real estate for his legitimate business; property development. So, early one Saturday morning, Alf sent his representatives over for a quick chat.'

'Coming out of this business as a child and teenager, I'd been witness to this one-way negotiation. Within a minute, my only asset, mum and dad's home was gone. Apart from some old worn furniture, my only other assets were a beaten-up Holden and my motorcycle.'

'I sold the car quickly. Your mum refused to let me sell the motorcycle. She knew it was too important. Picking it up as a repairable write off, Bert and I rebuilt that old thumper so I could join him at the Vets. That bike gave me connection to the mateship I needed to keep me alive. She was adamant, the bike had to stay.'

Struggling, Jack took one last trembling sip of his now stone-cold tea. 'The problem was the house and car didn't cover all the debt. With no savings of my own, your mum and dad gave me theirs. They had just enough to keep me safe.'

This last part was the hardest for Jack, this was his rock bottom. He pushed this horrible reality to a dark recess of his conscience. The culpability of his selfishness would be measured through sacrifice from those he loved the most. From this moment on, his days held the shadow of this shame. What capacity did he have to ever repay what he owed his daughter?

'Needing return on a house he just acquired in St Marys, Alf arranged for the three of us to move in. Our rent, including the extra bit for the remaining debt, was always paid in cash. Well outside his redevelopment belt, and with my debt still owing, this arrangement stood for years.'

'Is that this house?'

'Thankfully no, we got out from under the bloodsucker just after you were born. Those ugly yellow brick townhouses over on Lethbridge Street is where that shithole used to be. We still rent, but it's all above board through a proper agent.'

Through saving Jack, Gillian and Scott sacrificed their dream, life in the shire near Cronulla beach.

This stretch of white sand and surf was Jack and Gillian's special place. Staying off the grog, he would wake her before the sun blessed the new day. Walking hand-in-hand through the early morning light, they would watch the suburbs wake as the train guided them to Central and then to the last stop on the Cronulla line.

Arriving before the crowds then leaving after dark, their day was loaded with adventure; swimming in the shallows, splashing on the sandbars, sandcastles on the beach, swings, and slippery dips in Dunningham Park. Those few Sundays in summer were the only time she didn't share Jack with the other lady in his life; Victoria Bitter.

Pretending he found a couple of twenty cent pieces on the ground, he would give her the two large silver coins and let her walk across the park to Joe's Milk Bar for a milkshake or Paddle Pop.

If he had had a win, it was treat-time – fish and chips on the beach.

Not wasting a minute, she would be fast asleep before they joined the main line at Sutherland. These precious few days in summer were by far the fondest memories from her childhood. Gillian never abandoned her dream; her optimism allowed it to reside in every new year's resolution.

This wasn't just his story. It became the story of her family. Jayde hung on his every word.

'After losing so much, your parent's marriage was put to the test. The stress I created, combined with their ongoing grief, made it near impossible for them to conceive.'

'Your dad was flogging himself with two jobs. Despite getting the arse I still had contacts in the taxi game who trusted me. After a phone call or two I got him his late afternoon and night shift, while your mum picked up some extra work behind the bar at the Bowlo. For years they were like two ships in the night.'

Stopping to consider the ramifications of what he had just said, he spoke with insight only reserved for those with the lived experience. 'I think working so hard saved their marriage. They were either too busy or too tired to have the time or energy to fight.'

Finding more confidence, Jack's head rose. 'Although I continued to struggle, I tried hard to clean myself up. Several stints in AA slowed my drinking down, and my bets were now dropped on at the TAB, where there is a clear no money no bet policy.'

'Pete, one of the boys from the club saw I was on the mend, vouched for me, and got me a job putting water metres together at Davies, all the way over in Taren Point. It was process worker money, but it allowed me to sit for most of the day. Travelling two hours there and back on a train and bus gave me less time to drink or gamble. After work I would still call into the pub for a few with the boys, but it wasn't the dozen or more that I was used to. Things were starting to look up.

'Having a job gave me purpose, something to wake up to each day.'

Jayde knew this was a beacon of light in what was a dark period of his life.

'This was our routine for more than a decade; your parents worked two jobs, and I managed to keep mine. My problems were generally under control, and we were slowly clawing our way out of the shit I put us in.

'Money wasn't the biggest concern in the house, pregnancy, or the lack of it took its place. Your mum was becoming desperate in her quest to have a baby. With tensions high, major fights would spark over minor issues.'

'Under the advice of her doctor, your mum began IVF. Treatments took time and were expensive. Each month hopes would build while the bank balance would fade. With only enough money for one last try your mum came home from the doctor with the most exciting news; she was pregnant.'

Even now, just under twenty years on, trepidation could still be heard in his voice. 'The following months were tense. Every precaution was taken. Gill gave up her bar work and had regular check-ups at the hospital. Your dad and I did what we could at home to make things easier. He kept his two jobs going to keep the money coming in.

'Everything was going well until about the seventh month. Your mum had just finished up at the day care centre. The doctors told her to leave earlier than normal just to be safe. I rolled up to work, ready to start a new week, only to find the company that had kept me on the straight and narrow had been sold, and all operations were going overseas. By the end of the month, I was back on the scrap heap.

'Restructuring was occurring throughout Australian manufacturing. Cheaper overseas options were viewed as better for the company bottom line. Once again, my heavy drinking sparked up along with its buddy, gambling, this time the pokies. I was back on my ragged path of self-destruction.'

Jayde could hear the helplessness in his voice. There was no bitterness in his tone. He reconciled long ago, and this was his fallback position when things got rough.

'Thankfully, before this debilitating habit took control, I was stopped in my tracks. I rolled into the club ready for my daily ritual of lunch frothies and a slap when Ruth the bar lady called me to the phone. Sometime between leaving home and arriving at the club, Gill went into labour, and you came into the world like a bullet out of a gun.'

Nearly two decades on, Jayde could feel the pleasure this news brought him.

'Putting the phone back in its cradle, I abandoned my beer and credits. I had to get to the hospital. Stopping at the entrance to the maternity ward I straightened my hair and shirt before entering the room. I didn't want to enter your life as a dishevelled old alcoholic.

'Nothing could prepare me for what I saw. Your mum sitting upright in bed cradling the most gorgeous baby. I stood in the doorway frozen. The delightful, infectious sounds of your tiny voice penetrated my soul. Standing there, caught between the corridor and you a tear rolled off my cheek.

'I can remember this next part like it happened yesterday. *Dad, come and meet Jayde*. Awkwardly, I moved forward and stood next to the bed, breathing as shallow as I could so you couldn't smell the beer. Never experiencing this I didn't know what to do. Scott directed me to a chair and ushered me to sit. Although moving, I was still struggling to find words. My brain and body lost their unity.'

'Once seated Scott took you from your mum's arms and invited me to hold out my own. As I cradled you, staring into your tiny eyes, Gill again had to call my name several times before she could get my attention.

'Looking directly at me she said, "Dad, I need you to listen carefully. Jayde needs you to straighten up. You need to stop the drinking and gambling. If you don't this will be the first and last time you hold your granddaughter. If you come home smelling of booze, then you're out. I'm not bailing you out again. Scott and I have waited too long for this. Jayde is not growing up in a house where getting smashed every night is considered normal. She deserves better".

'Mesmerised, all I could do was nod in agreement. I knew those days were behind me. From now on, my future would revolve around you. For all the assistance and tools that AA and gamblers' support gave me, this ultimatum of all or nothing rocked me. I swore an oath that from that moment I would never touch another drink or place another bet for the rest of my life.

'In an instant I was clean. It was as though a switch was flicked in my brain.'

Jack's walk through his troubled past was working. Jayde was getting some perspective on her own misery.

'My redundancy from Davies kept me going until my service pension finally hit the full rate. Your mum's maternity leave was almost done, and with her earning more than me it was decided I would stay home with you. Your mum went back to work, working like she does now with other people's babies.'

Pausing, Jack pondered these last words. His only daughter missed out on being a mother so she could be a daytime mum to strangers' children. The enormity of this sat heavy on his conscience.

Reflecting on the impact this must have had, he deliberated on why he hadn't tried harder to get another job. The reality of this question was undeniable. *I needed Jayde,* he thought. *The more I was with her, the further away I was from my vices.*

'I was your daytime parent. I heard your first word and saw your first steps. I took you to your first day of school. All these milestones you shared with me instead of your parents.'

Jayde could see from the expression on his face he was tormented. Although he cherished every one of these precious moments, they really belonged to Scott and Gill. After waiting so long for their child, the quest to regain what he had taken away cost them memories, memories that could never be recovered.

'Aware my poor choices took so much away from your mum and dad, I made sure I had somewhere to go whenever they had time with you. Every day when your mum came home, I would slip next door to Vince and Rose's for a cuppa.'

Jayde distinctly remembered this afternoon ritual. 'We called it "mum time".' It was the highlight of her day.

'On the weekend I would ride with Uncle Bert and the fellas.'

Jack was a member of the Veterans Association Motorcycle Club. The guys he rode with were not only his mates; they were his brothers in arms.

Some were fellow piggies, others a mixture of one to nine RAR, armour or artillery regiments. Many like Jack were conscripts, while others were regular servicemen. There was everyone from commissioned officers to regular grunts. Newer recruits were servicemen and peacekeepers who were deployed throughout the Indo-Pacific, Middle East and Africa; their common bond was action in the service of their country.

Organised rides were Jack's favourite, rolling down the road in formation, the thunderous gurgle was breathtaking. A tank of fuel, a coffee and a bite to eat were achievable on his meagre income.

This recount of Jack's previous life was not quick. It started with the sun only a few hours into its daily descent and was now concluding after it had disappeared behind the sandstone curtain that hemmed Sydney's west.

Returning from work, Gillian could hear Jack talking in the kitchen. Intrigued, she took a moment to stop and listen. Captivated, she stood silently out of sight. In the quiet corner of the loungeroom she traced the complexity that framed her life. Quiet tears streamed from her eyes as Jack recounted that horrible day baby Hannah was taken away.

Unable to keep her anonymity anymore, Gillian tried in vain to wipe her tears/ She needed to hug her dad and daughter. This walk through their past reinforced how fortunate she was to have her family. These were her special people.

Jack froze, wearing the expression of a child with their hand caught in the cookie jar. Before he could find the words, Gillian settled his ever-increasing anxiety. 'It's alright Dad, Jayde is old enough to hear this. Everyone has a history.'

Unaware of the catastrophic circumstances that founded this exploration into his forgotten years, Gillian was more concerned about Jayde and her job. It was her day in the toddler's room. These delightful little people were not babies, nor were they children. They existed somewhere between.

This room was organised chaos. Between stopping arguments, changing nappies, getting sleeping mats out, putting them back, cleaning toys and helping the teachers with paperwork there was little time for anything else.

Work for Jayde and Gillian mirrored their life. They were in the same building but never quite crossed paths. It was only when Claire caught her at the end of her lunch break that she had any idea of what had happened.

Seeing she was calm, Gillian figured there was a logical explanation. Before she could ask, Jayde offered an abbreviated version of the one she gave Jack hours ago, including the noose.

Gillian was numb. *I did this. I pushed her into that world.*

Breaking the uncomfortable silence, Jack offered a glimmer of hope. 'I know how we can bring her down, it's there on your phone. The Gift, we can beat her at the Grampians Gift. She won't have any idea how to be a professional runner.'

His plan would give her redemption without violence. However, it would not be immediate. It would be a long, slow burn, with a lot of hard work. But hard work and this family fitted together like a hand in a glove.

Knowing this was their only option, Gill gave her father a nod of approval. Her precious daughter was not going to be another silent, lifeless victim to the cesspool that is social media.

CHAPTER 9

Behind the scenes

Two years of national service succeeded by decades of self-abuse slowed his body, but by some miracle, his mind remained razor sharp. Looking at the picture and post, Jack became emboldened. *This is too good!*

The picture; the finish gates at the Surfside Gift in Glenelg. The post; *Won first pro final. Fastest chick on this track. Thanks Matt Bellamey. Best coach in the country. Bring on The Gift.*

Matt Bellamey was undeniably the son of Ernie Bellamey, Bill Paterson's coach from back in the day; they shared the same distinctive eyebrows and chin.

He hoped the apple hadn't fallen far from the tree. Ernie was an outstanding coach; he had techniques that could make anyone run faster. However, this was his Achilles heel when it came to professional running. He assumed a pro-running handicap was like a golf handicap, the lower it was the better you were. Although essentially true, this approach always guaranteed his runners a short mark and ultimately a longer race.

Jack remembered another of Earl's pearls of wisdom. *Amateur runners who try to run professionally are always at a disadvantage. Their intuition is to match race, but they don't understand the difference between being fast and the fastest. In handicap racing you are both the hunter and the hunted; match racers lose their shit when they are hunted.*

Despite vanishing from running, Jack maintained a keen interest in The Gift, quietly catching the coverage in his bedroom on his transistor radio or portable television. His highlight, the commentators recount of the controversy in 66. Their favoured verb, *disputed*, highlighted his deceptive acquisition of the illustrious sash.

Like all good urban myths, fact and fiction morphed into outrageous furphys.

Fact, he pulled a swindle; you don't win like he did, then scarper out of town with everyone's money without leaving a mess behind. Fiction, he was juiced or linked to underworld crime organisations. Truth or tall tale, the 66 race would always hold infamy in the rich tapestry of The Gift. Honoured to be a fabled footnote, Jack was content to leave these conspiracies undisturbed.

Through keeping a keen eye on the event, he intuitively knew the time Jayde needed to run; 12.1 seconds would guarantee the winner's sash. His job, get her off a mark inside this time. Considered planning and precision in execution would be fundamental to her success. Traditionally it would take years to get a competitive mark. Jack's plan, do this in just one.

The strategic left side of Jack's brain was hungrily engaged, demanding intelligence about the current climate of pro-running. Seconds after Jayde hit search on her phone, Jack felt another tingle of excitement.

The New South Wales arm of the Professional Athletic League had fallen on hard times and was now under the management of its Victorian counterpart; VPAL. *This works, distance will aid her anonymity.* More importantly, when she raced in Victoria, her full mark would stand. Traditionally, interstate athletes had their mark pulled a quarter metre or two when they competed out of their jurisdiction. Mistrust was a stable in this world.

Swiping down the VPAL page, the second catch tag caught Jack's attention, a dedication to Bill Paterson who, after three decades as chairman, then CEO, was stepping aside. He was praised as a visionary leader who continued the progressive work of his father, reforming The Gift into a true open event. In appreciation for his years of service, Bill was awarded life membership.

Reading on, Jack paid close attention to his concluding quote. *'I'm not ready to watch from the grandstand; I'm returning to my original role as a keen observer at the edge of the track.'*

This crusty old magpie is a dangerous link back to 66. As an on-track steward he could pick the connection between Jayde and me. The first red flag of caution cast a shadow of doubt on the resurrection of his fifty-year-old plan.

The Paterson family were stalwarts of the Victorian Professional Athletic League. They had held at least one seat of power since its inception. Self-appointed custodians, they maintained the balance between the present and the past. With foundations steeped in conservatism, tradition was a powerful entity within this sport.

Early into Reg's tenure he was confronted with the tsunami of social reform; 1960s feminism. Offering a racing program across several minor country Gifts, he hoped this beneficence would be enough to appease the needs of this ravenous juggernaut.

The winds of change were blowing; the stifling construct of male tradition, a prized target. His piecemeal offerings did nothing to alter their course; they wanted a place at The Gift. Only when the threat of legal action and event stalling injunctions entered the narrative did women's racing at The Gift shift from a proposition to a scheduled event.

Aware resistance would play out in the court of public opinion, the Reg and the VPAL hierarchy publicly embraced the expansion, ponying up a tantalising purse from their own coffers to lure a field of well-known national, and international, women sprinters.

Starting with the traditional one thirty yards, the appetite for equity forced further expansion, and race by race the women's program progressively grew. Within a decade, popularity provided opportunities for women across every event.

Publicly Reg was supportive, but behind closed doors he held a considerably different opinion. 'Women at The Gift will be a tit and ass sideshow that we'll have to support. I can't see a naming sponsor jumping on board.' His executive minions collectively nodded in agreement.

Corporate sponsors were vital to The Gift. Heritage and prestige provided romance, but romance was soft currency, one which was difficult to trade. Prize money, on the other hand, was hard and tangible. While small and medium business covered the support program, big corporate was needed for The Gift.

Return for their investment was naming rights that would feature nationally through network prime-time news. There was no way the committee was going to kill the goose that laid the golden egg. Those twenty plus seconds were the cornerstone to any negotiation; each additional second of exposure was measured in value of return.

The half-hour smash and grab live coverage bounced around the free-to air networks. Placed mid-afternoon on a public holiday, the ratings were underwhelming; a bonus to any suiter, not a tangible point to negotiate.

The maths was simple; public interest secured coverage which sat patiently behind higher profile football codes. Adding another race into this precious third drop slot would undoubtedly have a devaluing effect, one that would be reflected in the number on the cheque the winner presented to the bank teller on Tuesday morning.

Surprisingly, support for the women's Gift grew. Regular sponsorship removed the financial burden. Occasionally, if there was limited content, or a recognised name, they would get a splash in that most valued prime-time slot.

At pace with popularity, Reg's view on the women's Gift tempered. He appreciated the revenue women brought to the VPAL coffers. He also enjoyed the spectacle they brought to the track. *I can't think of anything finer than a toned female sprinter.* He always made time to venture onto the track for the women's final, his favoured position directly behind the blocks.

Believing the winds of change had tempered to a zephyr, Reg foolishly presumed VPAL was now immune to the push or pull of social influence.

That was until a new and powerful paradigm, gender fluidity, shunted the parameters of male and female sport. Administrators tiptoed along a razor's edge to find a palatable balance nestled within the moral, biological, and legal arguments.

Bill appreciated it was only a matter of time before his sport would be called for their response. When that day arrived, he knew any profession against change would be futile, validating the affirmative – the handicap. Handicaps by design negate imbalance, ensuring pre-determined equity.

Bill's only consideration was whether it was better to be proactive and go early, or quietly celebrate the final fling of tradition.

Appreciating the political and commercial mileage available, the Board endorsed his proposal for gender neutrality. The press release announced the upcoming VPAL season would be contested with non-gender open races.

Aided by his dad's decades old blueprint, Bill had a pre-worked model at his disposal. He watched in awe as his father danced with the media, his charm and charisma swaying them to his favour. A raconteur, Reg intuitively knew what to say and when to say it.

Inheriting some of his dad's wit and charm, Bill knew how and, more importantly, to whom, he should speak to announce this new direction. *If I do this right, VPAL will come out a winner.*

He also knew what could be said in the sanctum of the board room around his tight five. 'The Gift has been what it is for over a hundred years, and it's going to be that way for another hundred. They may have forced us to change, but they will never win.'

It was amazing what half, or three quarters of a metre could do.

Stridently aware of the rules and regulations, Neil, his trusted ally and handicapper, offered his advice. 'We can't play with marks, there's too much scrutiny.'

Thinking aloud, Bill continued. 'There are other ways races can be influenced. There's always a yard or two difference between lanes and then there's us on the side of the track.'

Country Gifts were contested on ovals curated for Cricket and Australian Rules Football. The type and quality of grass often changed from one side of the track to the other. Consequently, some lanes wore in faster than others, providing any lucky recipient a subtle advantage. Others had infrastructure like sheds, grandstands and toilets that could shield an athlete in a headwind or provide a virtual wind tunnel in a tailwind.

Lane allocation was always a random process, traditionally drawn from the handicapper's hat. Leading into the semis and final it became the hottest topic in the paddock, and titles could be won or lost on the condition of a lane. More than a few times the element of chance was reduced during this process.

The last and most subjective consideration were the Stewards. Placed at specific positions around the track, like magpies ready to swoop, they stood in their black and white sports jackets observing the effort of every runner. Should any of these maggies suspect anything less than full effort, they could recommend a pull. Minimum penalty, immediate loss of half a metre for the following three events.

Jack knew the system was rigged, but he didn't know exactly how or where. However, his years with a piece of chalk in his hand taught him wherever there was gambling there was manipulation. His time racing taught him you had to be at least two to three yards faster than your mark if you had any chance to beat their system.

His mission: coach her to run faster than they expect.

CHAPTER 10

Total commitment

Jayde woke to Jack nudging the end of her bed. He was ten minutes earlier than her alarm.

'You've got 15 minutes to be in the car.'

Complying with his stern instruction, Jayde immediately climbed out of bed and stretched high before pulling on her variety store active wear and running shoes.

The distinct smell of rich exhaust fumes greeted her as she bounded off the concrete-topped step. *Good, I made it out before the old girl is ready to go.*

An amateur apprentice to her dad and Jack as they worked on their cars, she instinctively knew by the heaviness of the odour that the carburettor was functioning on full choke.

Satisfied the temperature gauge had moved far enough to the right, Jack hastily pulled on the T-bar, engaging reverse. Jayde barely closed the passenger door before the wheels were heading backwards towards the street.

Bringing the car to a whiplashing halt, Jack momentarily held his hand on the shifter. He needed reassurance before engaging "drive". 'Jayde, for this to work you must be one hundred per cent committed. I need you to do what I say, when I say it. I'm going to be a different Poppy when we're at the track. I'm going to train you as hard as old Earl trained me.'

Listening carefully to each word, Jayde nodded her head in agreement. She only hoped her body could match his expectations. Looking deeply at her image in the mirror the previous night she knew she was in for a few rough months.

* * *

Bradfield sports ground was ideal, a top-flight AFL and cricket ground as well as the location for the local Little Athletics Club. It was a showpiece ground that emulated a Gift track. The perimeter of the complex housed a fitness track with exercise stations. A free grass track and gym was precisely what Jayde needed.

Jack was very particular about training on grass. Earl had taught him that hard track athletes rely too much on the rebound effect, and *no matter how good the preparation was, grass is always softer and less responsive*. Hard trackers would invariably lose their hips and shoulders, altering their stride and ultimately their speed. Earl always said, *you don't train a horse on the road to then race on the grass*.

Jack also wanted her to stay out of view. He didn't want other athletes or coaches to see her; anonymity was critical to his plan. Observation is a powerful tool in athletics. Fit, toned athletes demand attention.

That was his end goal. His granddaughter would be powerful, toned and running like the wind, but that was a long way down the track. For now, he was content with her holding extra weight.

Standing at the finish line, like a sentinel in the post-dawn light, his trusty old fob stopwatch ticking away in his hand, his eyes focused on the fluency of her style. As she came off the bend, he could see she was fatigued. Her form was deteriorating quickly; her elbows dropped, pulling her shoulders low and forward.

Not caring for the early hour he bellowed, 'Elbows, pick up your elbows!'

Her body immediately straightened, returning to its strong, settled position over her hips.

Struggling through the finish line, Jack's thumb halted the distinctive ticking sound. Looking down at her buckled over, gasping for breath, he tilted his eyes lower. Catching the frozen clockface he shunned her unmistakable distress. 'Three more, same pace. Hold your form.'

He knew she was deep in the hurt locker, but this was right where she needed to be. These painful repeats will not only give her a solid base; they will empower her, building a protective barrier around her self-confidence, making it impervious to doubt and distractions.

Although he wouldn't tell her, he was happy; very happy. There was drive behind her training. She had fire in her belly, and it was burning bright and strong. Fire was good; it drove her to train harder, push through the pain, train in the wind and in the rain, do the extras required to win.

She was also an angry young woman. One moment of madness could incinerate his cunning plan, mutilating her opportunity for redemption. It was evident she had a temper, and when it was activated, the outcome was explosive. At the track he would make her faster, at home, emotionally smarter. He needed to prepare her for Victoria.

CHAPTER 11

Welcome additions

Jayde maintained her focus throughout the winter, training in weather that would drive the toughest of athletes inside. All her hard work was starting to pay off; the reflection from the mirror was beginning to emulate an athlete.

Jack anticipated this change, but the speed at which it was occurring was cause for alarm.

At this rate her performance won't match her physique, the magpies will be all over this. She's a rookie, so they'll already be suspicious. She can't stop training, but I need her to keep the weight on.

Perplexed by this conundrum, Jack racked his brain for a solution.

* * *

Away from the track, Jayde could be found working behind the counter at the Grey Ghost Café. Studying Hospitality and working in the school pop-up coffee shop gave her experience behind a coffee machine. Kahlil, the owner and chief barista, could see she had talent; her timing and technique were good and with his guidance she could be a real asset in the months and years to come.

Established well before coffee had become trendy, his philosophy was simple; your first coffee from him won't be your last. He took pride in offering a superior product and paying overs to his staff he demanded superior service.

He had a plan for Jayde. First, she needed to earn his customers' trust at the counter. They needed to know her name as much as she needed to know theirs. She needed to know their orders. His regulars were very particular; anticipation reinforced their value.

After years of experience and dozens of employees, Kahlil knew once Jayde had earnt their trust, he could finally step back and give her the critical role behind the coffee machine.

Interaction at the counter was good for Jayde as it forced her to come out from under the safety blanket of shyness. She enjoyed her work, especially the fuss the oldies gave her each day.

Complimenting her on her weight loss, some of the more brash ones suggested she should get ready; the boys will come calling soon. This comment always made her blush; till now she never really had much interest in boys. Not like that, anyway.

There was, however, one young man who called in every day to get his coffee and muffin. His was one of the first orders she memorised; medium flat white with regular milk and a blueberry muffin warmed for 30 seconds.

That half-minute provided enough time for a quick chat. She knew his name, Thomas, and could see he worked at the hardware warehouse across the road.

Over the next few days, she discovered he was on a management program that would eventually see him in charge of his own store. However, that was years away; for now he was required to work on the floor with the service staff and the section managers.

Kahlil and the oldies looked forward to their quick flirtations. To them it was like a soap opera playing out in front of their eyes. They could sense the increasing level of tension and nervousness as their attraction grew stronger.

Clumsy with romance, it was clear that neither of them had any idea about what to do next.

That was until Thomas walked in and changed things up. Today, he asked for a latte, vanilla slice, and Jayde's phone number. Writing her number on a small white paper bag, she couldn't hide her excitement. It was written all over her blushing face.

Thomas took the paper bag and his morning tea, giving Jayde a smile before heading back to work. Kahlil and the oldies were more excited than Jayde. Their in-house love story just went to the next level; now things had the potential to become more interesting and complicated.

Later that day Jayde's phone pinged. It was Thomas asking if she would like to catch up on the weekend. Of course, she accepted.

Like most things in spring, their relationship blossomed.

Doing anything to impress, he joined her for a session at Bradfield Sports Ground. Not a natural track athlete he did his best, quickly appreciating she was a different person when in this space. She trained with steely determination.

More than once, he was left behind, buckled over and gasping for breath as she ran off to complete another rep. Standing by the finish line, Jack struggled to hold back his laughter, muttering to himself, *Careful don't break him. We need him.*

Thomas was the solution to the weight conundrum.

It was obvious Jayde was smitten with Thomas; their connection was growing stronger by the day. It would only be a matter of time before they would test the bounds of their physical attraction.

Fiercely protective of his granddaughter, he wanted assurance she would be safe. Hidden within this ruse of protection was the resolution to his problem, the pill. This tiny tablet would not only give him piece of mind, but it would also hold her body shape through the first few events.

Now that body shape wouldn't be a pressing issue, it was time to strengthen her mental and emotional intelligence. There wasn't much time before her first race, and there was plenty to cover.

Like her seasons at the track, Jack had to carefully position how and when information was delivered.

Training entered the house.

When at home, running dominated their conversations; tactics, performance, and the logistics of professional running, simple processes like collecting your bib from the colour tent, through to the complex; how blocks are set to a mark.

Jack focussed on reversing her indoctrination of match-racing. He had to make her understand that *Losing is ok, it's times and place that count. Losing at the right time will set the mark we need.*

Strategically, he discarded any mention of Victoria. He knew they would cross paths sometime before The Gift, but he expected it would be much later in season. There was nothing to gain by preparing her now; her focus was needed elsewhere.

CHAPTER 12

Tata (father)

Victoria's season following the Betty Cambridge Cup announced her as a star in waiting. A blistering performance at the nationals gained her automatic qualification to the world junior championships. The next stamp in her overloaded passport; Ukraine.

A potential medallist with runway model looks, she became the nucleus of this small elite team. Days before boarding the plane, her opportunity to be authenticated on the world stage evaporated as Russian threats of invasion escalated from rhetoric to war.

As thirty-five million Ukrainians rallied to defend their nation, just over a thousand athletes selfishly grieved.

Victoria's response was more subdued, her reaction more disappointment than devastation. Although prestigious, these championships were just another stepping stone before she accepted more permanent options overseas.

Unlike many of her teammates, she was already more than just a name or a clip on Tic Toc or YouTube. Embracing sister school opportunities, Victoria strategically established her presence.

While her friends spent their mid-year break on the slopes of Perisher or Thredbo, Victoria was training and competing against the highest profile athletes in the American private school system. A guest from down under made her a novelty, while matching them on the track made her noteworthy, especially to any scouts sitting in the stands.

World juniors or not, Victoria was confident her name was already shortlisted.

Returning her clothes to their hangers and drawers she came across her competition kit. The deep green and yellow crop top and bun-huggers were the perfect cut for her, accentuating her toned, powerful, feminine profile.

Standing in front of the mirror, her reflection was enchanting; *this is too good not to share*. Grabbing her phone, she knew how to give the shot a bit of spice.

Since leaving Swinton House, restrictions on her socials disappeared. No longer was she constrained by the school's strident social media policy. Selfies could now be more provocative; targeted teasers gave her discerning followers something extra to enjoy.

It was amazing what a bit of subtle nipple or hungry bum could do for her socials. Each flirtatious pic and post expanded her views, forwards and follows. Brand Victoria was no longer muted.

A pleasant by-product of being accepted into the junior national team was promotion into the state's elite athlete performance program. Matt, whose careful guidance brought her here, had to be dropped as his certification fell short of the institute's requirements. Her new mentor became Romanian Gregore Zugravescu.

In his early thirties, he was impressively young for such an esteemed position. Credentialed well beyond this state role, he was biding his time, patiently waiting for that special athlete, the one that would carry him to a top-line international program.

* * *

Migrating to Australia a month short of his seventh birthday, Gregore Zugravescu prayed this would be the last stop in his gypsy lifestyle following his father Marcu around continental Europe as he rebuilt his coaching career.

Marcu Zugravescu, the eighteen-year-old boy bronze medallist from the Moscow games, returned to Ceausescu's Romania a national hero. He, along with the other medallists, instantly gained privileges usually reserved for ranked party officials. In a country burdened by poverty and despair, he lived and trained in a microcosm of entitlement and opportunity.

A year later, Marcu was in the Netherlands contesting his final European Junior Championships. Positioned comfortably in first place, he started down the runway, gathering speed. Leading into his penultimate stride, the agonizing whipcrack declared that this and any future championships were lost. No triple jumper ever returned from Achilles surgery the same.

Cashing in the last of his political credit, he coerced his way into a coaching role within the state program. Cutting his teeth through the juniors he was able to widen his scope of influence, moving out of the sandpit and onto the track.

*　*　*

Working with the next generation of sprinters, he crossed paths with a young attractive Nadia Popescu. At just over sixteen she was a late entrant to this elite program. The niece of the First Minister of the Interior, she came with credentialed influence.

Their attraction was immediate. Marcu found himself uncomfortably distracted whenever Nadia was near, his thoughts extending to places beyond the track.

For her part, Nadia sought any opportunity to be in his company.

Constantly reminding himself that this was forbidden, he did his best to push against the desires of his heart. At the institute he was safe; watchful eyes kept them apart.

Contesting championships throughout Europe removed his safety blanket. Routines and protocols shifted to accommodate the logistics and scheduling of the host city. Crossover was inevitable. As he entered the makeshift physio room, he caught a glimpse of her through a small gap in the curtains. Semi-naked, her body was tantalizing.

Unable to erase her image, passion assumed the balance of power in the battle for his heart. Emotionally, he was gambling with a loaded deck; the enchantment of that moment was the house, and the house always wins.

Considerate of the inherent danger he was now in, Marcu pushed harder against his desires. Suppressing feelings is like using a finger to stop water flowing from a tap; pressure will progressively build until it becomes too great to hold.

On the eve of her eighteenth birthday, Nadia created a moment of rare privacy. Procrastinating through her warm-down stretches, she was able to walk alone with Marcu as they left the track.

With only a few strides of solitude, she chose her words carefully, '*te vreau*;' I want you.

Aware of suspicious eyes, he didn't break stride, '*curand*;' soon.

Not long after attaining her right to vote, Nadia took advantage of life without a chaperone, venturing into the previously restricted areas of the institute. Finding Marcu alone enjoying an afternoon coffee she courageously sat and joined him.

Free from persecution, Marcu remained mindful of the optics. Playing it calm he welcomed her to his table. Athletics was not the focal point of their conversation. Using this liaison as his litmus test, Marcu concluded, 'there's too much noise around here for our interest to be noticed'.

Athletes, coaches and administrators were distracted by the twenty-fourth incarnation of the summer games, while the late teens interest was aimed directly at the newly formed world juniors in Sudbury, Canada.

A week before boarding the plane, Nadia, along with the other juniors, was summoned to a meeting in the gymnasium. Bogdan, the Director and his usual array of government officials, stood tall on the weightlifting platform.

Without mercy he announced, 'The team for Sudbury has been reviewed and revised and athletes will be advised of their status for this championship. Omission from the team will also result in suspension from the athletic program.' With that, he and his pack of silent observers turned and stepped down from their makeshift stage.

Anxiety replaced excitement. Years of dedication and pathways to more prosperous futures were in jeopardy. The root cause was money or the lack of it. Ceausescu's adoption of a fiscal policy saturated in Stalinist economics obliterated the national economy.

Nadia packed her bags. She was fortunate, sent to her uncle's house. Her furloughed teammates found themselves on buses heading to the farmlands, joining thousands forcefully donating labour for their country. Agriculture was critical to Romania's economic recovery; without it there was no way back.

Positioned behind the driver, Marcu stared blindly through the windscreen; cost-cutting wasn't limited to athletes. At the start of the decade, he, along with the other medallists from Moscow, enjoyed the trappings of state receptions, rubbing shoulders with the communist elite.

Eight years on, that medal and those connections were no longer tradable commodities. Athletics was his way out. His parents' were entrenched in the post-war industrial class and were slaves to the machine. Living and working at the Institute, he had risen above their day-to-day grind.

Rolling out of Bucharest, resentment filled his veins.

Working sunrise to sunset, Marcu felt like a prisoner. His crime had been to represent his country with distinction. Resentment rapidly deteriorated to indignation.

Following a horse and plough, harvesting potatoes by hand was a menial, cumbersome process. Looking at the never-ending ridge of churned dirt, a forbidden word rose to prominence in his brain; *defection.* He knew there were athletes and coaches that went overseas and never returned.

Allowing this thought to fester and ferment he stumbled on his way out; *Bulgaria is the next major junior event. If I go, I never come back.*

* * *

Long after the cauldron in Seoul was extinguished, Marcu and the other interned athletes and coaches returned to the institute, each bringing with them the discontent that was brewing throughout the nation.

A noxious undercurrent of division obliterated trust; political affiliation replaced performance as the most critical aspect of institute life. Adding to Marcu's bitterness; Nadia was not there. The gap between her potential and her uncle's political sway became too great. Like the rest of her family, she was given a job deep within the communist bureaucracy.

Disgruntled, Marcu channelled his anger and frustration into coaching, masking it behind intolerance of under-performance. Fearful of the repercussions, his athletes rose to his new expectations, setting new performance metrics, allowing them to soar in European and World rankings.

The unexpected consequence for over-performance; promotion. Constantin his coach and mentor was thwarted in his attempt to abandon his country while in nearby Budapest. Tyranny affords no trial. Once on Romanian soil he was transported to Gherla Prison for savage re-education.

Walking out of Bogdan's office, Marcu was now in charge of the national sprint program. With promotion comes privilege, perception altering privilege.

Standing in what was Constantin's lounge room, Marcu scanned the room. Apart from the furniture, any trace of his friend had been removed. This two-bedroom apartment was a palace compared to the single room he called home.

Closing his eyes, Marcu wanted to absorb this moment. In the quiet solitude, he heard his future. Opening his eyes, he stared down the small hall. There was Nadia cradling their baby. *Este timpul sa-mi clarific intentiile* – it's time to make my intentions clear.

Interrupting his romanticism, an emergency broadcast crackled over his beaten old Grundig. Riots in Timisoara spread nationally; central Bucharest was besieged; revolution was in the air and violence filled the streets. Drowning the reporter's words was the defiant chant, *Jos Dictatorul,* down with the dictator.

Thirsty for more information, Marcu switched on Constantin's grainy black and white television. '*Grabiti-va!*' hurry up, the old tube struggled to comply with his command. As the pixels finally blended, a cold shiver ran through his veins. Magheru Boulevard was the epicentre of the uprising, and this was in the same precinct as his future wife.

Rushing to his office, he needed to hear her voice. '*Verni, verni,*' come, come, every ring compounded his anxiety, '*buna ziua,*' hello. '*Vin sa te iau,*' I'm coming to get you.

Moving swiftly through the moving mass, Marcu dodged and weaved his way towards Nadia. The unmistakable pops of automatic gunfire did nothing to stifle his or the crowd's intent. Glancing to his right, he saw a pack of five young men splinter off and charge towards a man standing in the recess of a doorway. Shouting, '*Securitate, securiate,*' secret police, secret police. their assertion was validated, as the man raised his pistol and fired. The leader of the pack froze before collapsing limp onto the cold ground. Jumping over their compatriot they overwhelmed their target. The second bullet to leave the chamber reduced the influence of the secret police by one.

Disoriented by the overt violence, it took a while for Marcu to gather his bearings. He had missed his target. Moving against the swarm of people was almost impossible. More than once, he wore a heavy bruise, '*dezertor,*' desertor, stumbling he fought to keep his feet.

Seeing her building gave him the strength for a final push. Reaching her door, he thumped the heavy wooden panel in his normal rhythm. The door moved inwards just enough for Nadia to squeeze through the gap before it was abruptly shut. Pulling her close he grabbed her hand and ruck sack, '*nu da drumul,*' don't let go.

Moving across the angry mass was far easier than moving into it. Away from the Boulevard the crowd progressively thinned. Acutely aware that the streets were not safe Marcu hollered '*nu te opri,*' don't stop.

Marcu was never happier to see the post-war brutalist architecture that he now called home. Collapsing onto Constantin's old lounge, overcome by exhaustion and relief it was only minutes before both they both fell into a deep contented sleep.

The deep resonate thwip, thwip, thwip of helicopter blades whirling with a heavy pitch rudely woke Marcu. Looking out his window he saw the shadow before the mechanical bird thundered by. He had seen helicopters before, but never this low and in this part of the city.

Supporting Nadia's head with his only cushion, Marcu leant forward to switch on his television. In their hours of slumber, the protest had escalated to an uprising, powerful divisions of the government pledged their support to the rebellion. The future of his country was playing out before his eyes.

Mesmerized he could not turn away; the dictator who shook his hand was now a fugitive. Fleeing the city, he left his ministers to answer to the masses. One by one they were rounded up and placed under military guard. As the Minister of the Interior, Nadia's uncle Mihai was at the top of this list. Pulled from the communist headquarters he was paraded past the cameras for all to see.

A muffled gasp announced Nadia was awake. Her uncle, who was like her second father, was now at the mercy of the revolution. Breaking news cut the report on Mihai's arrest short, Ceausescu had been captured and was on his way back to Budapest.

* * *

Proceedings against the former leader were swift. He was convicted on all charges. The sentence, death. Nadia shook as the sound of several guns firing at once escaped from the speakers. Fearfully, she contemplated whether her uncle would be forced to stand in front of a firing squad.

Arrests were being made across the capital. Auntie Yetta and her cousins were under house arrest. Fearful she was next, Nadia pleaded with Marcu to leave. Uncertain about their future, they grabbed what they could and headed for the border. Looking at the fuel gauge, Marcu estimated there would be enough to get them there.

Arriving at the border under the cover of a moonless sky, Marcu used their first piece of crisis currency to bribe their way across the border. Prior to pushing Nadia out the door, Yetta had handed her a small jewellery pouch full of gold coins; '*asta te va salva,' this will save you.*

Granted asylum, they were free from persecution, free to move through Yugoslavia and Western Europe, free to start a life together. Freedom and the opportunities it provided was an aphrodisiac, it was also an enlightenment; with freedom comes responsibility, one that takes nine months to gestate.

Trading on his reputation, Marcu was able to secure work at schools, universities or provincial academies, he didn't care. He was a mercenary; power, prestige and most of all money was his motivation, he knew what he was, a foreigner with three mouths to feed.

* * *

Exhausting his European options, Marcu accepted a position on the other side of the world at WAAS, West Australian Academy of Sport.

Like many new Australians, the Zugravescus' struggled to adapt to their new country. Gregore felt this the most, especially at school. Having no previous contact with formal education and a limited understanding of the English language Gregore struggled to meet minimum cohort standards.

Ignorant of these hinderances, Marcu demanded results, good results, and fast.

With the intent to please, Gregore devoted hours to his studies. Recess and lunch were spent in the library. In class he needed to be focussed, and ignoring the other students made him a prime target for bullying.

For the most part, Gregore ignored their barbs, but occasionally one would get through his defences. His reaction – not to follow the talk, walk, squawk policy, but go straight to his fists. These altercations would lead to formal school interviews, suspensions and even one expulsion.

Gregore had one sanctuary, a place where he was not bullied or harassed, the WAAS track with his dad's athletes. Although not officially a member of the elite program, he would train as though he was part of the squad. Stemming from Olympic blood he had potential, but it was clear that no matter how hard he trained he was never going meet both his own and his father's expectations.

What he did have was a keen eye for technique. He could pick up small inconsistencies in style that even his father missed. These micro-adjustments had a compounding effect and often made the difference between being a finalist or medal winner.

* * *

Gregore expanded his studies at university. Moving across the country to Wagga Wagga, he forged his own career in coaching. Linking with the local athletics club he started his own sprint squad.

In the four years of his degree, members of this squad went on to win several country and state titles. From this small squad he created his own hallmark in coaching. After graduation he accepted positions in Tasmania, then New Zealand.

With each new appointment he would abandon his athletes, never feeling guilt or sorrow for moving on. Each was just another rung in the coaching ladder.

He deliberately kept his athletes at a distance emotionally, never fully investing in them. They sensed this; he was a dictator on the track who demanded performance. Failure to meet his mark would result in merciless castigations in his hybrid Romanian-Australian dialect.

Having no emotional investment, Gregore didn't care for his athletes' feelings. He was all about business. That was until Victoria joined his squad.

CHAPTER 13

Tenterfield

A plethora of vital information could be derived from Victoria's social pages. Jack quickly and confidently determined there was no chance she would be at any of the Athletic League's opening events. They were not prestigious enough for her consideration. He expected she would limit her pro-season to the three headline events, Surfside, Yarra and The Gift.

With her Institute responsibilities she was committed to undertake hard track racing. By only running the glory events, her handicap would be reviewed. All races, whether they are part of the Athletic League or for club, state or country, count towards a handicap. As a funded elite athlete, Victoria was committed to a full season of high-performance racing. As old Earl prophesised, *fast runners have the longest to run in handicap racing.*

Jack was convinced; this was the first chink in Victoria's armour.

* * *

The time arrived for Jayde to start her official journey to The Gift. In Jack's Day, the season opened in Southern Queensland an hour or two over the border. Small country towns celebrated their annual festival with heats in the morning and semis in the early afternoon, with the final closing of the carnival under the last natural light of the day.

Betting at these events was strictly forbidden; the only money legally exchanged was for first, second and third place. That was unless of course you knew the right, or in this case the wrong, people to speak to. Arriving in town a day or two early, combined with a bit of chat with the locals in the pub, always allowed Jack to find an underground bag or two. He knew from growing up around pubs and bookies who to look for, and what to say. Bets were always taken on the sly, and any winnings were returned the same way.

Southern Queensland was always a good start to the season. Warm weather provided fast tracks. Looking at the schedule now, many of the events he enjoyed had disappeared, swallowed up by costs, insurances, economic dips, and a decline in runners.

Only two events remained; Warwick and a new one in Toowoomba. Warwick was the one event up north that Jack didn't enjoy. He always lost on and off the track. In his last year, one of the locals suspected he was up to something and confronted him. Like most disagreements, it ended with fists in the carpark. Jack lost the fight, spent a night in a cell, but most importantly had his integrity questioned.

Even without social media, news like this travelled quickly through the circuit. Jack was always careful to stay out of the limelight. Accusations like this quickly put you in a place you always tried to avoid – on everyone's lips. Thankfully for Jack, it was his accuser who was discovered to be the cheater.

At the next event in Goondiwindi, a flattened lead slug dropped out of one of his spikes as he was taking them off after his race. The Chief Steward, standing only a few metres away, gave him a look that told him this would be his last race for quite a while.

Despite the vindication, there was no way he was going to send Jayde up there.

The other event in Toowoomba was a hard track event. This was another change that had been introduced since Jack had left the scene. To lure new runners, some events were now on synthetic hard tracks, contested over a non-Sheffield distance of

100m. Given his stance on hard and soft tracks, his planned early start was scratched.

After Toowoomba, the Queensland season moved north. The decision was easy; *entering these made no sense, they're too far away for our limited budget.* Instead, Jayde's introduction would need to wait another fortnight and follow the events as they migrated south through New South Wales.

Back in the day, you needed eleven events to become an established athlete. This year, because of the after-effects of Covid, the Athletic League made an emergency resolution to reduce this to seven. Looking at the calendar, Jack plotted a schedule that would see Jayde competing off her correct mark before The Gift.

With southern Queensland scratched, Jayde's first event would be the Thunderbolt Gift or, as Jack knew it, the Tenterfield Gift, renamed to pay homage to the infamous bushranger Captain Thunderbolt, who pillaged the region in the 1860s.

Jack knew through his Vets rides that bushrangers were now their own industry. The Kelly Trails in Victoria were popular with the biker community. A good mixture of open roads, tight mountain terrain and classic country pubs made it a bucket list ride for any club or enthusiast.

Most country towns that could were now actively promoting their bushranger past. Profiteering from their infamy, Jack found funny irony in the renaming this Gift *thieves and fraudsters competing for clean money.*

Tenterfield was one of Jack's favourite events. There was always a positive buzz around the town and a great atmosphere at the track. The local brass band entertained the crowd and the runners between events. Each of the small grandstands were full, local clubs manned barbeques, cake stalls and makeshift bars. It had all the necessary ingredients for a successful event.

Jack lost himself in this walk back through the happy times of his past. Returning to 1965, he could clearly hear the crowd cheer as his chest broke the tape, recalling how he spilt beer all over himself as he raised the loaded victory cup.

He vividly remembered his victory night. The publican refused to take his money; 'winners of the Gift don't pay'. The beers tasted better that night. This last memory made his stomach retch.

Back in the now, it was time to enter Jayde into the Thunderbolt Gift. In his day, entries were posted along with a cheque or money order weeks prior to the event. Assuming this antiquated process would have been rationalised, he scanned the screen to find the link.

Jayde found it first, but before she could enter anything she had to join VPAL. Coming from the pen and paper era, Jack was astonished at how easy and fast this process was. Type in her details, provide some previous race results, and pay. Within seconds she was registered as a novice, with a nominal mark of 5.25m.

Next step, enter the Thunderbolt Gift. This was faster than joining VPAL; enter your name, select the race and pay. Jack knew that once this process was complete Jayde's name could be seen on both the Athletic League and Tenterfield Gift websites.

Jack appreciated the potential danger Jayde was now in. *Victoria can now see she is competing again. How will she react? History tells me not well. I don't think she'll be on the League website until at least Surfside. By then Jayde should be a recognised face.*

The final step – book some accommodation. Following his days on the circuit, this would be cheap and out of town. Much like the entry process this was easily achieved online. Jayde had so much to be excited about. This would be the first time she went anywhere overnight with Thomas, and it would also be the first time she ventured to the other side of the Great Dividing Range. But most of all she was looking forward to driving. Despite obtaining her learner's permit several months ago, she was struggling to get any time in the driver's seat.

Scott's car was nowhere near suited for a beginner driver. Both foot controls required careful finessing to make them work effectively. Jack's old Cortina wasn't an option; to save money he converted it to historic plates which prevented her from driving it.

Thomas, with his later model car and an open licence, took the responsibility of teaching her how to drive. He was happy to fulfil this role, and Jayde was an excellent student. She listened carefully and respected the opportunity he was giving her.

Scott was embarrassed and ashamed. Again, he was on the wrong side of another rite of passage moment.

* * *

The drive to Tenterfield was long. Concentrating on the road, Jayde wasn't up for talking. Even when Thomas took the wheel, Jayde remained silent, her thoughts focussed on Jack's instructions for the race.

Over the past month, Jayde was set the task of intimately knowing her speed, especially under fatigue. Jack wanted her to run 11.6 seconds for 100m which equated to 13.3 for the 120m Gift distance.

This opening time would be critical to her entire campaign. Run too fast, too soon and people take notice. Especially the Stewards. His target was to move her mark out; times and places were critical to this process.

Jayde was also anxious about the logistics of the event. The colour tent, the bibs, where to place her blocks, how to retrieve these after the race and returning your bib would be new processes, and like all teenagers Jayde didn't want to look foolish.

* * *

Jayde and Thomas weren't the only ones with Tenterfield entered into their satnav. Three generations of the Patersons were also travelling up through the interior of NSW. This trip was important to Steve; as the new CEO he wanted to touch base with each organising committee.

This road trip held other official duties. As the official opener to the VPAL season, Steve had to be the Chief Steward as tradition dictated. It would also allow Bill to appreciate his new role. He was the living link to the past; his presence was there to remind everybody of the rich history and traditions of professional running.

Unknown to Bill, this would be the extent of his duties; any of his observations on the track would be considered but ultimately dismissed.

For Adam, the Thunderbolt Gift would be his first as a sanctioned steward.

* * *

Thomas and Jayde checked into their accommodation. Too hungry to worry about their room, they collected the key and headed straight into town for dinner. A pub style schnitzel would sort out their hunger in no time.

After dinner, they walked the stiffness of travel away, wandering around the town. There were Thunderbolt Gift signs in just about every shop window and a huge banner stretched across the main street. Strolling through the town where her Poppy had won so many years before gave her a special feeling. She knew that this was the start of her own path to glory.

* * *

Returning to their accommodation they were able to appreciate the off-track simplicity of Jack's plan. A single room with shared bathroom facilities. The overwhelming theme was country style, everything from the curtains, carpet and bed – gawdy country.

The bed was a traditional wrought iron frame with an old-style expanded mesh base. Jayde and Thomas had never shared a bed, and an awkward silence fell over the room as they prepared to sleep.

Once under the covers, sleep became the furthest thing on their minds. Their first night together was filled with passion and the constant sound of creaking with every move. Thoughts of the next day's event were forgotten many times throughout the night.

Thankfully, Jayde set an alarm or there was a real chance she would have slept through and missed The Gift altogether. She woke quickly as she always did. Thomas, on the other hand, rolled over and remained sleeping. Jayde was thankful; he appeared to be a heavy sleeper.

Before heading to the shower, she did a series of high intensity exercises, stationary sprints, lunges and squats in the small space between the bed and door. The intensity brought her to a sweat, and her face was noticeably red.

At the completion of her routine, she quickly grabbed her toiletry bag and headed off to the shower. Comfortable during the day, Tenterfield in spring can be brisk through the night and into the morning. Cold showers in these conditions are not comfortable. If her breasts weren't tender enough from last night's romp, then a cold shower in cold conditions made them want to explode.

When she arrived back in the room Thomas was awake and preparing breakfast. Nutra grain with warm long-life milk, a culinary displeasure. More focussed on the energy it provided, Jayde ploughed through hers. Thomas was never more thankful when he heard, 'Put it down, it's time to go'.

*   *   *

As they walked through the gates into the showground, Jayde appreciated why Poppy was so attracted to this event. Everything was just as he described it. The track looked amazing; beautiful freshly cut grass, traditional knee-high white ropes dividing the lanes, tall proud finish gates and the starting grid. Runners in their coloured bibs, the starter in his traditional white coat and the Stewards in their black and white striped jackets and straw hats.

As they moved further into the ground Thomas noticed a change in Jayde's demeanour, her face becoming stern and serious. 'I've got to go to the colour tent.'

The what? Thomas had no idea what she was talking about. With his stomach grumbling and the distinct smell of bacon and eggs in the air he really didn't care.

Using her phone and the QR code posted on the side of colour tent she checked in. Scanning the start times she still had about 45 minutes before her heat. *Perfect, just enough time to warm-up.*

With only a few minutes before her race, Jayde moved back to the colour tent where she was handed a green bib, reminded of her mark, and told to go onto the track and line up behind lane six. Looking down the track, the first ten metres looked like a massive ladder. Forty incremental lines, each a quarter of a metre apart, allowed runners to quickly find their mark.

Not wanting to catch the attention of the Stewards or starter, Jayde quickly set her blocks, remembering what Poppy said; *left block on the back edge of the line*. The starters' marshal walked past and raised his white flag, signalling to the crowd and starter that Jayde was clear to run.

Jayde intuitively knew her time; it was deliberately on the slower side of her current mark but close enough to the times she nominated at registration. As this was her first race, Jack was confident this wouldn't raise the interest of the handicapper.

The field was called to *dig in*. After that fateful night, Jayde no longer stuffed around wiping her hands or settling her feet. Her process mirrored her life; no mucking about, just get down and get on with it. *Set*, she raised her hips, allowing her shoulders to roll slightly forward.

Finally, the sharp crack of the gun set her off down the track. Powering out of the blocks, head down with short low crisp strides, out of the power phase, she lifted her head and opened her stride. It was here Jayde appreciated the nuance of handicap racing.

She could see runners in front and hear those closing from behind.

Before she knew it the race was over, and she was placed somewhere between fourth and fifth. There were no times or places given at the finish line; these were traditionally provided outside the colour tent. Jayde followed the lead of the other athletes, stepping off the track before walking back to collect her blocks.

Back at the colour tent calmness replaced the usual chaos. In the past there would be a constant precession of athletes collecting and returning their bibs, as well as coaches and athletes mingling around the constantly updated results board.

However, due to Covid, this process had been significantly overhauled. Bibs were converted from reusable cotton to a single use recyclable fabric which was returned in a bin adjacent to the opening of the tent.

Results were now livestreamed via ProRun. This free app eliminated the traditional print and post method, removing the need for athletes, coaches, and the public to crowd around a pinboard.

For some, the requirement of Covid safe protocols and social distancing was an annoyance, while for others it provided an opportunity for profit. This app messaged athletes at the conclusion of each round, letting them know if they could stay and play or if it was time to go and prepare for another day.

Athletes and coaches were now in their own space, heads down constantly checking their phones. This was the process the Patersons had really come to see. Steve, the founder, owner and principal code writer of the company responsible for its development had a vested interest in its success.

Now on the other side of the fence, Jayde searched for Thomas. A quick scan of the crowd didn't reveal his location. As she was about to ring him, her phone pinged, and ProRun told her to get ready for round two. Not anticipating progressing into round two, she had to call home. Thomas could wait.

Jack was expecting her call. 'I placed fourth, that's pushed me into round two. Is that ok?'

Moving through the rounds was never really discussed this early in the plan. Jack was more concerned about her time; place at this stage was irrelevant, 'What time did you run?'

'13.4.'

'Good, well done!'

Jack's reassurance was the antidote to her adrenaline overload, 13.4 gave her more wriggle room in the next round. Thinking on the run, Jack recalibrated her target; his last words ensured she wouldn't progress to round three. 'Don't forget when you're getting ready, load the legs.'

Touching the red call end button on her phone, Jayde felt composed. She knew exactly what to do, and more importantly, how to do it.

Scanning the crowd, she finally found Thomas, who was settled under the shade of a cork tree not far from the Rural Fire Service BBQ. Finishing his last bite of the best steak sandwich he had ever consumed, he wiped the remaining sauce from his mouth before giving Jayde a well-done kiss.

'Better than Nutragrain and warm milk?'

Rubbing his tummy he nodded in agreement.

The time came for Jayde to move back into the warm-up area and prepare for the second round. Jack warned her that rounds two and three were generally the fastest of the day. Appreciating this, he narrowed her target to between 13.2 and 13.3. With the race speed up, it would be impossible to keep hers down.

Confident with the process, Jayde began her warm-up routine, carefully adding the desired heaviness. Walking back from each drill, she noticed curious eyes following her every move. Jack had warned her; newcomers are always treated with suspicion. One old bloke in a black and white steward's jacket on the edge of the track wasn't having a normal look; there was something deeper occurring behind his eyes.

Feeling uncomfortable, Jayde quickly finished her warm-up and moved to the safety of the colour tent to get her bib.

* * *

The race was uneventful. Starters gun, run, dip at the gates. As expected, the finish was much tighter, the gap from first to last was just over a metre. Casting her eyes left and right Jayde knew she wouldn't get the ping calling her up for round three.

Walking back to collect her blocks she noticed the old bloke staring at her again, the same deep thoughtful expression on his face.

Jayde and Thomas hung around till the end of The Gift. She wanted to see what happened during the semis and finals. The final was just as Jack had described; the runners blasted through the finish gates in a bunch. However, there was one runner's chest that just crept forward as they all lunged.

The crowd cheered and as tradition dictated, the sash and victory cup were immediately presented on track for him to hold aloft. The only difference to when Jack held it above his head is that the victory cup was not brimming with beer.

*   *   *

That night the town was full of cheer. Locals and visitors crowded the restaurants and pubs, drinking, laughing, and having a good time. As always, the runners and officials adjourned to the Royal for the post-event celebrations.

Jack made it clear; it was important for her to attend. As she was not much of a drinker, he knew she wouldn't be around when things got loose later in the night. But being there, quietly sipping a drink in a corner, she would be noticed and, more importantly, accepted.

As protocol demanded, the Patersons were also at the pub. They were holding court with the organising committee and other self-proclaimed dignitaries on the opposite side of the bar. As the CEO and Chief Steward, Steve was the king of this court.

Pre-Covid this was Bill. He was the man, the one whose titillating stories kept everyone amused. For more than 20 years he never stood in line to buy a pot or schooner. Now he was forced to join the plebs and wait his turn.

Most were getting through their drinks at a reasonable rate. Bill, on the other hand, was downing them at almost double their speed. This wasn't unusual for Bill; he had a reputation of ripping in once racing was done.

However, this time was different. He wasn't drinking to be social. He saw a ghost today and Jayde Hardy was her name. There was something about her that didn't sit well with him, a reminder of something in the past. What it was he didn't quite know, but something was telling him, she is dangerous.

He needed to catch Steve and warn him. Stopping him on the way to the toilet, Bill twisted his shoulders towards Jayde. With slurring words, he gave it his best go. 'That girl over there, there's something not right about her, we need to investigate, I've got a bad feeling in my guts about her.'

Desperate for a piss, Steve said, 'REALLY, you stopped me for that. Come on, you get crook guts after a glass of milk. We need newbies. Look at her, she could barely run out of sight on a dark night. Take it from me, she won't win a Gift, let alone The Gift!'

These were the ramblings of an old man well past his prime. This was his time now, and there was no way he was going to start his tenure investigating an overweight female rookie who decided for some reason that she could run.

Jayde and Thomas were about to leave when a stumbling, mumbling Bill approached. Pointing his finger at Jayde he said, 'There's something about you. I've seen you before.'

Old, slow, and drunk are not a good combination. Tripping on his own feet, Bill fell hard. Without any thought for self-preservation Thomas lunged forward, protecting the old man from hitting his head on the corner of their table.

Both Bill and Thomas ended up on the floor. The commotion caught the attention of everyone in the pub. Steve, not wanting to squander his moment in the sun, gave Adam a clear instruction; 'Get him out of here!'

Adam arrived to help his grandad to his feet. Thanking Thomas, he quickly removed the gibbering old drunk.

CHAPTER 14

The day after

Sunday was leaving day. Runners, coaches, spectators, and officials exited the town to return to their regular lives. The carnival of running would reconvene again in a few weeks further south in Gilgandra.

Unlike most, Jayde woke fresh and ready for the trip home. With a full day of driving, her brain demanded coffee and a snack before heading off.

The coffee shop was the place to be. Everybody needed their coffee fix before hitting the road.

Eventually reaching the counter she placed their order, before retreating to the footpath to patiently wait with Thomas for their cups of joy to arrive. As they were standing, lost in their own thoughts, a stunning jet-black Discovery pulled up beside them. Adam exited the car to join the line.

Recognising Thomas from the night before, Steve stepped out from the front passenger seat. 'I'm terribly sorry about last night. My father can get a bit loose when he's had a few. I'm Steve Paterson the CEO of VPAL.'

Looking at Thomas, he added, 'Thank you for catching my dad in time, he could have done himself a real mischief if he'd hit that table'.

'Not a problem, how is he?'

'Apart from a bruised ego and a heavy hangover, ok.'

Interested in knowing a bit more about these two newcomers, Steve invited Jayde into the conversation. 'Are you both runners?'

Answering before Jayde could muster up the words, Thomas replied, 'No, Jayde is the only runner here.'

'Yes, I saw your heat, well done.'

In her usual timid tone, she replied, 'Thank you.'

Just as the conversation was about to dance dangerously close to the details regarding her motivation to become a member of the Athletic League, their names were called from the pick-up window.

'Excuse me, that's ours.' Jayde went to collect their coffees and breakfast snacks.

Returning, she gave Thomas the look. *It's time to go.*

'Thanks for letting me know about your dad. We've got a long drive, so we should hit the road.'

As they were leaving, Steve, as always, had the final word. 'I'll look for your name on the start list for the Cooee.'

Jayde took a sip of her coffee before starting Thomas's car. She had been excited to arrive in Tenterfield; now she was happy to leave it behind.

Soon enough the urban sprawl of the greater Sydney basin would once again be in the rear-view mirror. Jayde's next event was the Cooee Gift in Gilgandra. Since VPAL took ownership of NSW, a strategic decision was made to compress what they called the northern season into few early season months. Apart from the Denni Dash and the Golden Gift in Temora, NSW was dusted by late-December.

* * *

With their own coffee and treats, the Patersons made a bee line for home. The GPS set its course directly through the central west. It would be a solid twelve hours to the border then a few more to their front doors.

Contrary to the manufacturers' promise of a comfortable ride, there was no way this trip was going to meet that expectation. The first few hours were driven in uneasy silence, the post-mortem on ice until Bill's hangover was more under control.

After a fuel stop and another coffee, it began. However, the direction of this tirade wasn't father to son, it was the other way around. Steve's comments were swift and direct, underpinned by Paterson family values and VPAL standards.

Bill had had the same one-directional conversation with his dad decades before. Tradition was a powerful entity in Paterson household.

Bill despised being on the receiving end. This confirmed his glory days were behind him. He knew his status and opinion would progressively fade to insignificance. This was a bitter pill to swallow; this was his life. Without VPAL he had nothing. His wife Emma gave up fighting for his attention, walked away, and never looked back. That was over twenty years ago.

Holding the mantle of chairman, then CEO, Bill had plenty of attention to distract him. He willingly let his marriage go, rationalising it by telling himself, *she knew what she was getting into when they first met*. Only now did the implications of that decision become patently clear.

Bill, switched off from Steve's tirade, turning his mind to more important matters, namely Jayde. *Why has this newbie got under my skin?* He tried to break the problem down. *Is it her name, her face, her style?* Normally strong with his memory, he ran each through the database of the past; nothing. *This is going to bug the shit out of me.*

With his frustrations purged Steve's thoughts moved on. He had a 9am meeting scheduled with Dave McPharland, the state's most successful country bookie. Dave spent Saturday on his computer testing a bookies extension he wrote for ProRun.

PVAL money covered some of the set-up costs. Steve had been required to make his own investment, one that he couldn't afford to lose. His CEO salary wasn't enough to cover the mortgage, car payments, university and private school tuition combined with the weekly expenses of his wife. Manicures, pedicures, facials, massages, spray tans, yoga classes and an exclusive gym membership left nothing but red in his account at the end of each fortnight.

This bookies extension had the potential to yield a quick return, giving him some desperately needed liquidity.

Unlike New South Wales, the Victorian Government allowed on-track betting for Athletic League events. The basic feature was a real-time data link, allowing them to react quickly and frame early markets the minute after registrations closed.

If they paid a bit more, they could access a range of data about recent performances. Marks, times, places, track grades, and wind influence was all available. Further to this, each of these was combined in an algorithm which indicated if an athlete was on the improve, stagnant or going backwards.

The full program utilised AI to provide a predicted finish list with suggested odds for the entire field. A provision like this should ensure they were never caught long on their bets.

Access would only be granted once the relevant fee was paid. In the betting game, information equals power, and this information, especially the last element, was the power that would equal profit.

Initial feedback from Dave gave him confidence. Apart from some minor alterations, the bookies section appeared to work as planned. Projecting forward, Steve anticipated that schools and clubs would be his bread-and-butter, and this bookie function would be the cream on the top.

In the driver's seat, Adam pretended he was concentrating on the road, but mentally he was taking notes. One day it would be his turn to dethrone the king.

CHAPTER 15

Road trip

Jayde returned to the Grey Ghost and her training, Thomas to his traineeship. For the next few months, he was rostered on the trade desk and timber yard. Bulk hardware was where the rubber literally hit the road. Utes, cars, and small trucks took the place of shopping trolleys.

Customers carefully navigated the moving maze with lengths of timber or sheet product. Wall and drop saws squealed as they ripped and docked timber and boards into manageable sizes.

Forklifts danced between the customers and cars, dropping fresh pallets of concrete and cement or moving timber packs from up high into the lower racks to keep the customers' insatiable appetites fed. Thomas sensed this was going to be the hardest part of his traineeship.

The most intense day was Saturday, when tradies mixed with home renovation warriors, so it was all hands on deck. Next month's roster was posted, and he saw he was supposed to be working the weekend of the Cooee Gift in Gilgandra. New to the section, he didn't possess the leverage to request time off.

Taught by his parents not to dwell on a problem, he spoke with Jayde as he ordered his coffee and muffin. Her pragmatic disposition allowed her to appreciate the conundrum he was in.

keeping a straight face, she was able to mask her disappointment. This trip would have pushed her over the minimum hours needed for her provisional licence. She also wanted her time with Thomas. The last trip allowed their relationship to deepen physically and emotionally, and she wanted more.

For the remainder of her shift, Jayde's mind continually wandered. She knew it was impossible for Jack; he had made it patently clear. *'There was no way I can go to any events. If I'm recognised, then your showdown will disappear.'*

There was no way Scott or Gillian could do it. Both were far too busy and she wasn't convinced the car would make it.

Not having the luxury of a training squad, her last option was Petra and Georgia. Maybe one or both would like a trip out into the country. With nothing to lose, her thumbs rapidly typed the message; *Anyone interested in a road trip out to Gilgandra?*

Soon after her phone buzzed; the girls were heading west.

Relieved his plan was still alive, Jack wanted to finish the Thunderbolt debrief before bringing up the tactics for Gilgandra. Times and tactics took care of themselves, but he wanted to hear how she felt running in a Gift.

'It's just like you said. The town was buzzing, and the track, it was amazing, the bright green grass and white lane ropes. The brass band and stalls, it was just as you described. Thomas is still banging on about his steak sandwiches. I think he ended up eating three by the end of the day.'

Knowing what was ahead, Jack thought to himself, *Wait till you walk through the gates at The Gift.*

With a noticeable shift in her expression, she continued, 'There was an old bloke, that official we saw on the website, he kept staring at me, then he had a crack at the pub.'

'What do you mean, he had a crack?'

'Just as we were about to leave, this pissed old fart stumbles over from the bar, spilling his beer, pointing at me and mumbling *There's something about you.* When he got near us the stupid old bastard tripped over his own feet. Thomas jumped forward to save him from smashing his head on our table. Then someone came over and picked him up, then we left. The next day, when we were getting coffee, his son, some bigwig, apologised for his dad's behaviour last night.'

Pondering the implications, Jack carefully processed what she said. *Clearly the old fart was Bill Paterson, the only link to his swindle in 66. He's the only one that could throw an old spanner in our new works.*

Catching Jayde's eye he said, 'Keep a keen eye on that old bugger'.

'If he gets too close, report him to another magpie.' No organisation wants to be known for harbouring an old pervert in their ranks.

* * *

Working, training, catching up with Thomas, the days evaporated, and before she knew it the girls were pulling into her driveway. Bags and blocks were quickly stowed, and they were off. Georgia did the hard part up and over the Blue Mountains.

Open roads gave them a chance to do more than touch base. Each had their own story to tell, but what they wanted to hear about the most was Thomas.

By nature, Jayde wasn't someone who willingly divulged intimate details. Remaining aloof until pressed on whether they had gone all the way, she couldn't conceal the red blush that flooded her face. The girls were like a seagull on a hot chip, demanding more details.

Products of a Christian childhood, they were indoctrinated in the belief that sex before marriage was a sin. Living this moment vicariously would be the closest Petra would get before a ring slid over her finger. Georgia on the other hand could waver if everything was right.

Jayde did her best to move the conversation, and only when it shifted to Victoria was there some clean air after her exploits in Tenterfield.

CHAPTER 16

Cooee

As documented by her socials, Victoria was preparing for the first round of the Aussie Track Classics. This elite invitational event worked its way through each capital city, following a similar format to the headline diamond event in Europe. Enticing prize money and substantial bonuses for the grand slam lured big name local and international athletes. In her first year on this circuit she was an outsider; things would have to fall heavily in her favour for her to win the slam.

The first event in Perth was only weeks away. To get her ready, Gregore planned a couple of hit outs in the local A grade competition. As predicted, the Surfside Gift in Adelaide would be Victoria's first look at a rejuvenated Jayde.

Surfside was the first of the four category one Athletic League events. Since removing the differentiation between professional and amateur athletes, both bodies fostered a symbiotic arrangement. Deliberately scheduling the track classics to align with three Gifts, the fourth, The Gift, always stood alone.

The swag of pictures and posts highlighted her body. The balance between muscle and tone was supreme and she knew it. So did her agent Bethany, quickly arranging photo shoots and promotional gigs. She knew it was imperative to strike while the girl was smoking hot.

Beyond her socials and endorsements, Victoria was also working hard on her coach. She knew he had connections, either his own or through his father. Her plan was to start tertiary studies in Australia, then finish Ivy League in the States. Using the fundamentals of marketing – product and placement – her sales pitch was beginning to have an effect.

Whenever possible, she ensured he was privy to some special views of her body. Her go to, tightness in her legs. Hamstrings, glutes and quads always worked the best. During these one-on-one moments she would wear the most revealing knicks and crop tops – the ones which require careful waxing and leave very little to the imagination.

Gregore, with his impassive approach, was typically immune to these types of advances. Like his father, he was all about business when at the track. However, each flirtatious encounter expanded the fissure she was exposing in his emotional barrier. He was in trouble; his thoughts were becoming more and more conflicted.

*   *   *

Back on the road, the girls were having a fantastic time. Chatting away and singing songs took away the monotony of long straight country highways. Even a near miss with a kangaroo didn't dampen their spirits. As they were nearing their destination, Petra asked Jayde, 'Why are we driving so far for a running race?'

'I need to race here to become an established athlete.'

'A what?'

'Professional racing isn't like a normal track race. Everybody starts from a different position, but they should finish together, that's the handicap. Because I'm new, I don't have my real handicap yet. Once I run enough races, I'll be given one.'

'How many do you need?'

'Seven, I need seven before the Grampians Gift.'

'What's the Grampians, aren't we going to Gilgandra?'

Using Petra's love of horses she explained, 'the Grampians, or The Gift as it's known, is like the Melbourne Cup of professional running. It's not till Easter, but it's where I'm going to give it to Victoria!'

'What, how?'

'Poppy Jack and I have a plan; we might need your help.'

Excitement filled the car; the girls were now fascinated about professional running and couldn't wait for tomorrow. Arriving under the late afternoon sun the girls checked into their three-star motel out on the fringe of town.

Jayde didn't think twice when she had to give the door a bit of a nudge to make it open. Petra on the other hand was beginning to feel anxious; she had never stayed in anything under five-star.

To her surprise the room was neat and clean, styled in the more traditional country motel minimalist fashion. A double and two single beds with navy blue covers, a simple three-seater lounge, and a basic toilet, shower, basin combo bathroom.

Jayde woke before the sun, changed, and went to walk outside. Georgia, a horribly light sleeper, woke to Jayde's movements. 'Go back to sleep, I'm just going for a walk to settle my nerves.' Her instruction was met with instant compliance, rolling over, Georgia was back asleep in no time.

Jayde quietly left the room. There was some truth in what she said, she was going for a walk, about five hundred metres down the road to a park. The ideal venue for her pre-race routine, ten incline sprints – all done very quietly.

By the time she returned to the room, the sun had risen above the horizon and the early morning chill was beginning to evaporate. She needed to shower. Any evidence of this activity needed to be quickly erased. Cold showers in the country seemed to have an added bite. The initial shock of the cold water on her warm body took her breath away. Within minutes, her complexion returned to its normal colour.

Once again, Jayde tucked into her horrendous mixture – cereal and warm long-life milk. Having no desire to join her in this culinary nightmare, the girls were unanimous, they could wait till they drove back into town. There had to be a coffee shop with something more palatable.

Just like Tenterfield, there was positive energy throughout the town. Runners and townspeople alike were about preparing for the day ahead. Coffee was the beverage of choice. Fit toned bodies shared space on the pavement with locals in their denim jeans, Ariat farm boots and checked shirts.

Jayde left the girls sharing the biggest bowl of bircher muesli they had ever seen. She had to get to the track and start warming up again. Her first race was early, and she still needed to get her colours. The track was only a short walk, and the girls knew her start time. As they were finishing the last spoonful, a couple of locals came over and offered to buy them another coffee. Flattered, they agreed.

The brief interlude between order and arrival gave provision for a few getting-to-know-you-style questions. *What do you do?* brought unexpected commonality; all were studying at the same university. Nick, the taller of the two, was enrolled in the same degree as Georgia. In his third year he had plenty to share.

Unfortunately, Andrew and Petra couldn't find the same common ground. On campus, Andrew spent his time in the Engineering Faculty, on the annexed Darlington side while Petra's timetable had her in the Pharmacy Building on the opposite Camperdown side. As their contrived conversation was becoming excruciatingly painful, Petra exposed her complete disinterest by checking her phone. 'Fuck me, we're going to miss the race!'

Andrew was stunned and strangely excited by this outburst. Petra pushed her chair back and headed off towards the track. Rude or inappropriate, she didn't care, she was frustrated; once again, Georgia had the attention of the best-looking boy.

The other three quickly caught up to her, and silently they all broke into walk-run combination. Georgia had seen this look from Petra before, although they were best friends, they could crack the shits with each other from time to time.

Thankfully Jayde hadn't noticed the girl's absence. She was more focussed on her performance. Jack again set very defined parameters for this event. Gilgandra was traditionally a hard, fast track, with many season bests set at this venue.

Jack warned her she needed to keep her pace close to the time set at Tenterfield. Consistency would go a long way to setting a competitive mark for The Gift. Appreciating this she upped the intensity during her pre-dawn session.

The girls and their new companions arrived to see Jayde take her marks. Pissed off at Georgia, Petra paid extra attention to the race. Things Jayde explained now began to make sense. The sharp crack of the gun made her jump.

Jayde was away, not thinking, just running. Letting her body do what it did best. As is the design with this type of racing, the field drew level close to the line. Jayde and one other athlete pushed in front of the pack as they crossed the line. Petra and Georgia hugged and cheered; for a moment their hostilities were forgotten.

Jayde followed the League protocol, quickly removing herself and her equipment from the track. By the time she reached the colour tent, the result pinged on her phone; she had progressed into round two, her time, spot-on Jack's insistence.

Once clear of the official area, she called Jack. 'Good news, I'm into round two, the time was competitive.' This last word was their code for 'exactly to plan'. She deliberately kept the call short and to the point. To anyone within earshot, it sounded like general chitchat between an athlete and their coach.

Petra left the group to go and find Jayde. Despite the brief cessation of hostilities, she needed time away from Georgia. There was a liberal amount of bias in the way she explained what happened prior to her race. Nevertheless, for now they were a group of five.

Jayde could see why Petra was so annoyed. Nick was without doubt the more handsome of the two. He stood at about six foot two, solid physique, neat country style hair and a voice that was deep and engaging. Andrew, on the other hand, was shorter, unshaven with dishevelled hair and a noteworthy muffin top.

Introductions were made, after which Georgia and Nick slipped straight back into their isolated two-way conversation. Petra showing her total distain for Andrew, turning her back on him to talk to Jayde. This was the final straw; a wingman can only take so much. For Andrew, his exit plan was simple. 'I'm off to the BBQ for some gut luggage, anyone want some?'

Dropping a bitch shot across his bow, Petra mumbled, 'I hope there's enough on the grill'.

* * *

It wasn't long before Jayde had to begin her warm-up for round two. Petra noticed her demeanour changed as she picked up her blocks and headed to the track. She watched Jayde go through her routine. Everything she did had a purpose. Petra had never seen Jayde like this before.

The starter gave the call; 'Runners dig in.'

Jayde stepped into her blocks, settled her shoulders, and lowered her head. Rising on 'Set', she was ready to go. Instead of one crack there were two. Anticipating the first crack, Jayde was up and away. It was a beautiful clean start. Almost too good.

Hearing the second crack, her body went onto autopilot and shut down. Walking back to her mark, she noticed a red flag in her lane. Jack had made it clear. *Never false start! It instantly costs you a metre.*

Jayde had 30 seconds to reset her blocks, or she was out of the race. Although her body was calm, her mind was racing. She had trained off this mark for two weeks. Now she was a metre back.

What's the strategy now? I was never given the instructions on how to handle this. How could Poppy overlook this. Should I run to the set time, or should I run at the pace I've trained for. Jayde's mind was a conflicted mess.

Before she could gather her thoughts, the starter again called the field to dig in. She almost missed set, and definitely missed the gun. Once up and away she went into autopilot, her body separated from her brain and ran, just as she prepared. At the finish gates she was well over a metre behind the winner.

Still functioning on autopilot, Jayde followed her fellow competitors back to the start area where she reclaimed her blocks and left the track. Her brain only truly reconnected once she walked away from the colour tent.

Even though she knew that was the end of her racing, her mind couldn't leave the track. The false start kept playing over and over, overdubbed by Jack's voice reminding her not to do this. She had to call him.

Georgia was blissfully unaware of what had happened. Although she saw her running, her attention was well away from the track. Despite attending an all-girls school, she did have a few innocent youth group boyfriends.

This was different. The more she spoke with Nick, the more she had to say. It took both girls to break the intense connection between Georgia and Nick. Jayde wanted to leave immediately. She needed to call home. Sensing the urgency, Georgia gave her goodbyes. With his number already in her phone and an arrangement to meet for dinner that evening, this wasn't going to be a long goodbye.

The short drive back to the hotel was free of any conversation. Jayde focussed on what she would say to Jack. Georgia was planning how she was going to break it to Petra that she had arranged to meet up with Nick and his mates for dinner, and Petra was still sulking about having to entertain the dud.

The moment the car pulled to a stop, Jayde's door was open. With her phone at her ear, she headed out the driveway and down the road to the park where her day started. Jack answered after more than a few rings.

'I did what you said not to do, I broke, and they pulled me a metre.'

In her mind she had just ruined their plans. Jack had to balance his response between the demanding coach and a concerned grandad. He recognised the need to quickly settle her anxiety. 'False start penalties are immediate, they don't impact your mark for the next event. More importantly what was your time.'

'Three one-hundredths below round one.'

'Good, exactly what we need, well done!' Jack was relieved; she had kept her composure and stuck to the plan. Jayde's angst disappeared; the plan hadn't been damaged.

Making small talk just to hear his voice, Jayde asked, 'How are things at home?'

Feeling the same way, Jack wanted to hear about the town and The Gift. Like Tenterfield, Gilgandra was always a great event. Pulling the phone away from her ear, she walked back to the motel emotionally lighter. She could now get back to her friends.

CHAPTER 17

The fall

Jack leant over to return his phone to its usual spot on the counter. He was feeling good; his plan was developing well. At this rate, Jayde would be ready for her Gift showdown at easter. With his mind filled with future nuances and variables of his plan, he didn't realise his good leg hadn't moved.

He barely stumbled before losing his balance. With nothing to break his fall he hit the tiled floor hard, his hip, ribs and shoulder bore the force. Intense pain flooded the right side of his body. He was struggling to breathe, let alone scream for help.

Even if he could, there was no-one to help. Scott was pulling an extra shift in the taxi and Gillian was grocery shopping. Unable to move, barely breathing, Jack was helpless.

Gillian pulled into the driveway, parking the car on the flat section before the gate. She double checked that the handbrake had fully engaged before giving the horn a quick 'beep, beep'. Gathering the overloaded bags from the backseat she backfooted the door shut and headed to the front door.

With her arms occupied, she was grateful that Jack was at home. Hearing the 'beep, beep' he would open the front door, giving her clear passage to the kitchen.

However, this time there wasn't the familiar sound of Jack's limping footsteps. Frustrated, Gillian reluctantly put the groceries down and rummaged through her handbag for her keys. Swearing under her breath as she moved down the hallway to the kitchen, Gillian was not expecting to see her father lying motionless on the kitchen floor.

Jack moved his head ever so slightly as he heard the piercing scream. She screamed again, this time with a strange level of delight. Fumbling for her phone, she struggled to dial triple zero.

They could hear the siren wailing in the distance before she hung up. Having seen a punter or two in the same state, Gillian knew how to test for stroke. Holding his head gently, she said, 'Dad, I need you to smile'. To her relief both sides of his mouth moved.

The paramedics quickly took over and began their acute trauma examination. Monitoring equipment gave them his vital stats, while the oxygen mask assisted his shallow breathing.

Helpless, Gillian was forced to stand and watch. The limit of her influence was to reassure him that everything would be alright. Once the morphine took effect, Jack was carefully placed on the stretcher ready for transport.

Thankfully the restrictions that would have prevented her from riding with Jack had been lifted. Under lights and sirens, they backed into the ambulance bay in no time. Age and injury afforded him the highest priority, and he was wheeled directly into triage for immediate assessment.

With the few words he could get out from under the oxygen mask, he told Gillian, 'Do not call Jayde'. He didn't want her to feel pressured to rush home. He was safe and about to get all the help he needed. His priority as always – Jayde.

Before the ambulance officers could finish their handover, a team of doctors and nurses were assessing Jack. The bad two, stroke and cardiac arrest, were eliminated quickly, but one of the nurses noticed a considerable difference in the size of his lower legs.

Results soon began to form a more sinister picture as to why Jack fell. His good leg by now had swollen to nearly twice its normal size. The cause, deep vein thrombosis.

By itself this can be treated with a high level of success. But as part of the procedure with this diagnosis, Jack had a chest x-ray to check his lungs. The image it created displayed a shadow, a considerable shadow, a cancerous shadow.

Before he was moved from emergency, a more detailed picture of his immediate and long-term health concerns was formed. The acute damage – a broken hip, three cracked ribs and a torn rotator cuff. His hip required immediate surgery, but the more concerning issue in his lungs required deeper investigation. The doctors relayed their preliminary prognosis to Gillian, who sat there alone and numb.

Handing over the cab, Scott was finally able to sit and comfort his wife. They sat for hours in the waiting room. Their thoughts bounced from Jack to Jayde and the implications this would have on them both. Each would need support; how could they do this with their current workload.

Gillian's concern wasn't the broken bones; despite his years these could heal. It was that fearful word cancer that repeatedly bounced around her brain. She saw the look in their eyes and read the tone in their voices when she was sitting in the consult room. Her instincts told her more bad news was on the way.

* * *

Keeping himself busy folding the washing, Scott was relieved to hear Jayde's key entering the lock. Meeting her in the hallway she could see from his eyes something was wrong. Before he could finish, she dropped her gear and was heading for the car. The drive to the hospital felt twice as long as her trip home.

Scott found a space to park the car. It was a solid ten-minute walk. On-site hospital parking was hideously expensive as he found out when he and Gillian finally left last night. No matter the situation, Scott taught himself to always be aware of his money.

'Come on dad, get moving,'

Running may well put him in the bed next to Jack. Working sixteen hours a day gave him little time to work on his fitness. The briskness in her walk was already making him short of breath.

Gillian had been focussed on this moment for hours. She had to prepare Jayde for what she was about to see. 'Your Poppy is a very sick man, he's had surgery on his hip. They are keeping him sedated to allow his body to rest after the operation. He has a breathing tube and wires everywhere.'

Nodding with acceptance, Jayde only took in half of what was said, she just needed to see him.

Once suited in the hospital blue gown and mask, and her hands suitably scrubbed, she was allowed in. Although she thought she was prepared, nothing was further from the truth. Here was her Poppy, laid flat with countless wires and sensors stuck and draped over his body.

His stomach wore splashes of surgical iodine and heavy bruising. His breathing tube was held in place by the most vibrant white tape. Worst of all, his eyes had been taped closed. Jayde had never seen her Poppy looking so vulnerable. Despite having his noticeable limp and a slight frame, he was her superhero. You never see a superhero like this.

Visiting patients in the ICU was limited to fifteen minutes, and several of those evaporated with the initial shock. Jayde held his noticeably aged frail hand. Looking intently at the contrast between her hand and his, she began talking, just like they did when she came home from school.

This time it was about Gilgandra, the girls, the boys, and the race. Before she knew it her time was up. Walking away was harder than the initial shock.

Back in the waiting room, Gillian and Scott were sitting patiently. They were trying to hold a brave face, but when they saw the shock on her face, tears began flowing like water out of tap. For Gillian, there was so much more behind her tears; she knew these would not be the last to flow for her dad.

The trip home was uneasily silent. This small, close family riding in the darkness, each consumed by their own thoughts. Unfortunately, life as they knew it would have to continue. Work as always was their priority. For the first time in years Gillian took a day off; she needed to be there when Jack was brought out of his sedation.

Jayde insisted, 'I'm coming to'.

Knowing what was ahead, Gillian refused. The doctors warned her tomorrow was not going to be easy.

* * *

The Hardys woke as normal. Scott and Jayde went through their morning routine. Gillian wished she was doing the same. Her day was going to be anything but routine, and she knew it.

Before leaving, Jayde asserted, 'I'm visiting Poppy after my shift'.

Assuming the hard conversations would be done, Gillian agreed. Scott would have to rely on text messages and the occasional phone call to keep in touch. As always, he had two jobs to maintain.

Jayde arrived for her shift ten minutes early. After being away for a few days, she liked to re-orient herself to the café. Kahlil was pleased to see her. She was good with his late morning locals who liked to chat. Having Jayde usually meant another coffee. Kahlil was up for anything that would help increase his daily sales.

* * *

Jayde did her best to keep her mind focussed on her job. Struggling through the early morning rush, she didn't have a chance to be distracted. That was until Thomas arrived for his morning tea, she felt an overwhelming rush of emotion as he walked through the door.

Tears flowed as she stepped away from the counter and ran towards him. All he could do was brace for impact and then hold her as hard as he could,

'He looked so helpless.'

* * *

Gillian arrived at the hospital to discover Jack had been brought out of sedation and was about to be transferred onto the ward. Walking into his new room, Gillian was joined by several doctors. She recognised Dr Tran and Dr Bradley from yesterday, the other two were Dr Prasaad and Dr White, specialists in Oncology. Dr Tran the orthopaedic surgeon went through yesterday's procedure and the one scheduled for Jack's shoulder once he was physically ready.

He also explained the acute and long-term prognosis and plan for Jack. It was clear the doctors had consulted prior to this meeting; this was the prompt for their diagnosis. The mass detected on the x-ray was cancer; there were the tell-tale signs of pulmonary fibrosis at the base of his lungs. Given his age and the likelihood of exposure to asbestos their agreed diagnosis, mesothelioma.

Jack confirmed his exposure to the carcinogen. 'Before the war I worked with asbestos, doing all the things that are banned now.'

Gillian prepared herself for this, but when Dr Prasaad and Dr White went into the finer details her brain went into overload. She was struggling to process what was being said but nodded along with each statement and treatment option like she was in complete control.

Dr Bradley has seen this before and knew that as treating physician it would be his job to repeat this again once her brain was ready.

Jack listened intently to all that was said. He immediately understood the implications and was processing how this would

123

play out, especially for Jayde. When the doctors told him he should expect anywhere between twelve to twenty-four months to live, his face didn't alter in its expression.

Dr Bradley had seen this before with ex-military men, especially those of Jack's vintage. They accept and process information like it is an order; there are no questions, they acknowledge everything as fact.

The son of a Vietnam Vet and serving in a conflict zone himself, Dr Bradley had already taken special interest in this case. After what he and his fellow soldiers received on their return, Dr Bradley wanted to ensure Jack was given the respect and dignity rightly afforded anyone who served his country.

Dr Prasaad and Dr White exited the room. Walking down the corridor they prepared to deliver the same gruesome news to another patient. They learnt to refer to people and patients and their sickness as conditions, distancing themselves from the emotional burden these conversations could have.

Dr Bradley made time to stay behind. He knew there would be a need to provide more detail. 'Jack, from what we can see, and what the research in this area informs us, you have cancer of the lungs caused by exposure to asbestos. The typical time from diagnosis to death is up to two years. There are some experimental programs you may be able to get into, but at present there are very few specific treatment options that will reduce the growth of the tumours in your lungs.'

Gillian's brain returned to the room now she was able to process Jack's diagnosis. The colour drained from her face when she was able to comprehend his limited life expectancy. Like Jack, her immediate thoughts were for Jayde.

Dr Bradley had to excuse himself; he was required back down in emergency. Before leaving, he whispered to Jack, 'I'll pop past again later today or tonight, there are some more details we need to go through'.

Both Gillian and Jack thanked him as he left the room. Dr Bradley always found this peculiar. Patients who had just received the most devastating news always thanked their doctor as they left the room.

Gillian and Jack sat in silence, both processing what had just happened. Gillian was distracting herself by sending a text to Scott. He was expecting bad news, but two years; this was a whole lot worse than expected.

This was not the sort of message that warrants delivery via SMS. Scott felt sick, he should be there, but again the need for money kept him away. Gillian's '*Boys of summer*' ring tone broke the silence. This ring tone always made her smile. It reminded her of those wonderful days spent on Cronulla beach with her dad.

Today the smile was forced. It was Jayde. 'How's Poppy? What did the doctors say?'

'Poppy is awake and talking. He's out of the ICU and on the ward.'

Gesturing with his good arm, he caught Gillian's attention, whispering, 'No more, don't tell her anymore'. He didn't want the word 'cancer' to enter their conversation. Like the SMS to Scott, this was not the news to be shared over the phone. Jack had to tell Jayde himself in person; he needed to see her face and she needed to see his.

He did have one message, 'go to training'. He needed her to maintain the rage. Now more than ever he knew this would be their only shot at redemption.

* * *

Despite the obvious distractions, Jayde moved through her drills and reps with relative ease. Thomas was again left buckled over clutching for breath. With a month until her next event she was back in a building phase, where intensity was replaced by repetition. These weeks were tough and long, and her visits to the hospital would be reserved to the early evening twilight hours.

* * *

Gillian was physically and emotionally exhausted when Scott arrived. Working through lunch, he traded his usual recuperation time for time with Jack. Catching each other between things was their way, doing it for so long they developed their own language, a blend of rhyming slang and abbreviated blokisms. Gillian slumped in her chair, observing the two men she loved the most chatting in their own special way.

Both had to concede pride at different times, but they never let that get in the way of being good men who became great mates. Seeing them together brought joy to her heart, then reality joined the party. *Everything now has a time limit*, she thought, and once again, her heart filled with sadness.

Jack could see that she was exhausted. 'You're done, go home and get some rest, I know what I have to say.'

'C'mon, I can get you home before the afternoon changeover,' Scott said.

Watching Gillian and Scott walk through the door arm in arm, Jack was glad he hadn't pushed Scott away when he'd had the chance.

Still feeling the after effects of surgery, Jack managed to get a little kip in before the orderly brought dinner, baby food for adults. He was hungry. but the taste and texture of this mush soon stifled his desire for food.

Jayde entering the room lifted his spirits. Watching her walk across the room, he could see her inner athlete, strong and confident, traits he knew she would need beyond The Gift.

A seat had been placed on his good side. Moving towards it, Jayde was stopped by Jack's faint, husky voice. 'Not before you give me a huggle.' For many years she would not go to sleep until she had her Poppy hug, or huggle as she termed it. Relieved to hear his voice, she happily obliged. Traditionally, their huggle was a rough hug given with purpose and vigour. Tonight, it was the opposite; gentle, soft and most of all loving.

Breaking the embrace, Jayde sat forward in the chair, not letting go of Poppy's good hand throughout the process. As she settled, Poppy in his croaky voice asked, 'How was your day?' Truthfully, he had no interest in the coffee shop; his focus was on what she did at Bradfield Reserve.

'I broke Thomas again, plyos, ten 150s at 23 secs and 2 fitness circuits.'

Breaking into coach Poppy, he needed to know more of the specifics. 'Were all the 150s at 23 pace?'

Proudly, she replied, 'Yes, a couple snuck half a second or so under'.

'Good, and how were the legs?'

'Great at the start, towards the end I was running in mud.'

Still searching for details Jack asked, 'And now, how are they now?'

Shaking them in the chair, Jayde said, 'Yeah not bad, I did what you said, a few pieces of watermelon after warm-down'.

Maintaining his strict coaching persona, he said, 'Good, now you know what I want tomorrow?'

Her instant 'Yes' gave him confidence she was not about to drop her intensity and focus.

Taking a deep contemplative breath and letting his head sink deeper into his pillow, Jack couldn't put the next conversation off any longer. The time had come for him to bring her up to speed with everything that was wrong with him. 'Jayde, these injuries aren't the only things wrong with me right now. When the docs took an x-ray of my chest, they found something, something very bad, cancer. Asbestos cancer.'

Jayde sat frozen, unable to speak.

'They've told me I've got about two years.'

No teenager has the emotional intelligence to process this quickly. Again, the rug had just been pulled from beneath her.

Jack knew this was the time that he had to enforce the importance of keeping to their plan. 'Pinky, promise you will keep up the training.'

Reluctantly she hooked her pinky finger with his. This was their most sacred bond, and though it wasn't her priority she would honour their accord.

The visitor bell sounded, Jayde stood and gave Jack another gentle huggle. When she broke the embrace there was a sizable stain on his shoulder. Not wanting him to see her tears she turned quickly and left the room.

Although he couldn't touch it, he knew it was there. The gravitas of his diagnosis hit him hard. It was nearly twenty years since tears welled in his eyes. Watching Jayde disappear into the corridor, the stain on his shoulder widened.

* * *

As the ward was beginning to enter the end-of-day procedures, Dr Bradley came and sat beside Jack. He felt compelled to tell him his real prognosis. Before he was able to start, Jack needed to know, 'You ex-military?'

Dr Bradley nodded his head. 'Medical Corps. Served in the peace-keeping force in Timor.'

Jack gave the special nod, the one that expresses mutual respect. Jack knew serviceman to serviceman he was in good hands, honest hands that would give it to him straight no matter what.

In a direct yet compassionate tone Dr Bradley laid it out for him. 'Six months is the best you can expect. The cancer would have most likely metastasised and due to the surgery on your hip and the DVT, treatment options will be limited.' Dr Bradley maintained his steely military persona as he outlined what Jack would expect over the coming months.

This news did not come as a shock; he had seen this scenario play out too many times with other Vets at the club. They would be given a date and then not too long after it would progressively get smaller and smaller until years turned to months and in some cases mere weeks.

He appreciated Dr Bradley's honesty and advice to get his affairs in order early before the cancer really took hold. Not having a great deal to pass on, there was only one affair that required attention.

Respecting the frankness and honesty from Dr Bradley, Jack let him know, 'I need to make it to Easter'. Not willing to divulge too much more, he said, 'There is an important family event which I have to be here for'.

'It's possible.'

Realising the time, Dr Bradley had to say farewell. His parting words resonated deeply. 'Set that date in your mind, and tell yourself through every minute of every day that you will make it. It's amazing what the power of the mind can do.'

Dr Bradley promised to call in again soon, either professionally or as a friend. Jack whispered these words as he drifted off to sleep. These would become his mantra through to his terminal breath.

CHAPTER 18

Mates

Wanting to keep Jack's spirits elevated, Jayde kept training. She prioritised each session to be the most important aspect of her day. Rather than being put to shame once again, Thomas gladly accepted the role of cameraman, using the video function on his phone to record all the key elements of her session.

These would be replayed at the hospital later that night. This video flash instantly became the highlight of Jack's day. He would watch, analyse, and give advice, using this vital information to recalibrate times and tasks for the next session.

His voice gave away his excitement as he commentated everything he saw. Seeing the impact, Jayde was more motivated than ever. Revenge and Victoria were fast becoming a secondary thought.

Once the word got to the Vets community, Jack, or Hobbler as they knew him, was never short of company. His mates would visit through the day and leave the afternoon and night for family. These guys were his brothers to different mothers. He could talk to them in ways he never could to his family. Right now, Jack really needed to talk.

First in line, his best mate and club President, Bert, or Boomer as he was affectionately known. Boomer was one of those salt of the earth guys, a great bloke with a thunderous voice who always made time for his mates. Especially those who had served.

Jack and Boomer shared an unbreakable bond. They had been conscripted together, and saw action as members of 7RAR, Jack in the flanking 1 platoon with Boomer in the sweeping 2. Both received wounds in Operation Ballarat, Bert's minor and early in the battle, Jack's life altering not long after.

Back in civilian life, they remained the best of mates through good times and bad. Jack was best man celebrating Boomer's first marriage, godfather to his first son and stood by him as his marriage broke apart.

Good to his word, Boomer stuck by Jack throughout all his post-war troubles, taking him to problem gamblers and drinkers' meetings. When he lost his licence, Bert thought nothing of driving out of his way to grab him and take him to the clubhouse. It was undeniable, their bond was strong and once again today, Jack was going to lean on his best mate.

As Club President, Boomer had made this visit many times before, walking into a room where a brother-in-arms was now a dead man walking. This time it was different, though, this time it wasn't just a mate, this was Hobbler, his best mate.

Men like Jack and Bert were no strangers to facing death, accepting it made it easier to sleep at night. Back home, life took over and the constant consideration of your own mortality faded until it was a distant memory.

Bypassing the pleasantries, Boomer threw it out there. 'How long?'

'I'm fucked, six months at best.' The heaviness of these words lingered.

'Damn, that's a bastard'

Jack nodded. 'The family still think it's two years, I want to keep it that way.'

Bert sighed and nodded his head, accepting his mate's request.

'Bloody hip, shoulder and DVT in my good leg limit treatment options, but what can you do?' The words hung with a pungent odour.

Changing the topic, Jack broke the awkward silence. 'Hey do you remember the surgeon from Vung Tau? That tall streak of duck shit, with the pointy nose and massive Adams apple. What was his name?'

Both men sat there racking their brains until Bert broke the silence. 'Bailey? Nah, wait Bradley, Ernest Bradley.'

'That's right, I reckon I've got his son as my doc. He's the spitting image of old Ernie.' True to his name Boomer bellowed, a deep thunderous laugh, its infectious resonance washed over Jack.

Before he could reach the end of his first 'ha' Jack froze; the pain shot through him like a lightning bolt. The wince on Jack's face halted Boomer before he could really get going. Doctors claim laughter is the best medicine, but today this wasn't true for Jack.

'Sorry mate, I should have known better.'

'No dramas, I quietly chuckled too when I pictured him.'

Looking at Jack, Bert noticed his expression shifted from pain to seriousness. There was more he needed to say. 'Boomer, it's not me I'm worried about, it's Jayde…'

For the following hour, Jack went into explicit detail about the victimisation and brutality Jayde had experienced over the past 12 months, culminating in her trying to swing from a rope. Jayde was like a surrogate daughter to Bert. His first marriage gave him two sons and his second nothing at all.

Understanding the influence this little girl had had on his best mate, Boomer's primitive protective fatherly instincts were aroused. Without her, he would have buried his best mate long ago.

'I've got a plan, but I need your help.'

Bert signed on, committing to playing his part.

The two old warriors had one more mission. For the second time in recent days a tear welled up in Jack's eye as he said, 'Boomer, I need to make sure my girls are ok.'

Bert, wiping his own tears, nodded vigorously in agreement.

*　*　*

Jayde was joyful as she walked down the corridors to Jack's room. An early finish at the Grey Ghost, followed by her track session, gave her plenty of time to sit with her Poppy. As she rounded the last corner, she walked straight into the chest of a rather large hairy man.

'I'm so sorry, I didn't see you.'

A voice that deep could only belong to one person, Uncle Bert. Jayde leapt forward with her arms outstretched. 'Uncle Bert.'

Bert welcomed her hug with outstretched arms. She loved her Boomer hugs. His big powerful arms, and oversized belly made for a tight embrace. His long biker beard would tickle the back of her neck making her giggle and squirm. Although Jayde didn't laugh or squirm today, she still felt comforted by his embrace. Today's hug was tighter than normal as emotion took the better of him.

Bumping into Uncle Bert added to her positive mood. She had a surprise for Jack, a new, or in this case, second hand phone. The fall shattered the screen of his mobile, leaving it almost unusable. Thomas had just upgraded his and was only too happy to pass on the old one.

Her mission was to teach him how to face-time. For an old bloke he caught on quick. Jack was incredibly grateful for The Gift. Now more than ever he cherished every moment with his granddaughter.

Not wanting to get too sentimental, Jack changed the subject back to running. 'How was training today?' With no footage he hung on her every word, absorbing every morsel of information. The coming weeks were going to be heavy for Jayde. Three events in two weeks, travelling across three states. Fortunately, Thomas had been granted his annual leave and was able to join her for this epic conquest.

Jack needed to prepare her for events down south. Unlike the other states, on-course betting was allowed. The bookies' arena, or the bull pen as its referred to, is a hive of activity, punters dropping bets, bookies calling out odds, spruiking new customers. For the first time, Jayde's name would appear on their boards, accompanied by her odds. For a newcomer, this can be an unwelcome distraction.

'Your name will be down the bottom of the board with everyone else at long odds. Now this is important, Thomas must drop a few bets, a few blueys will do, ten on the favourite to win and the same on you for a place. He needs to make it look like yours is a stab in the dark, and it must be with a few bookies and not at the same time. The second and third bets need to be placed when it's busy.' Nodding her head, Jayde gave the illusion she knew what he was talking about.

'The bookies need to hold some money on you. This will help at The Gift.'

Jayde's phone burst to life just as he finished. Thomas was waiting in the drop-off zone. A quick gentle huggle and she was gone.

Having nothing else to do but think, Jack continued to play his plan over and over in his head. *Up till now it's gone off without any significant hitch, she's done everything I said. She just needs to get through the Christmas, New Year races, then there's The Gateway, Temora, Goldfields and then The Gift.*

Not being able to write, Jack had to carefully file every element in his mind. If he's careless, he becomes a juggler with too many balls in the air. Lose one ball and Jayde's opportunity could fall.

While on a break, Dr Bradley popped his head in for a quick visit. Habitually, he reviewed Jack's charts and his vitals, and all looked fine.

He took particular attention to the notes at the bottom of the page. It was time to get Jack moving. Gone were the days of weeks and weeks of infirmary. 'Physiotherapy starts tomorrow, and heads up, it's going to be painful, but it's a necessary evil if you want to get moving again.'

Having survived his childhood, basic training and a war, hard work and physical pain was something he had the emotional fortitude to deal with. As he was about to walk through the door,

Jack hit Dr Bradley with a question that stopped him in his tracks. 'Are you related to Dr Ernest Bradley?'

Perplexed he spun around. 'He's, my dad. How did you know that?'

'He operated on me in Vung Tau in 67. He saved my leg and what was left of my nuts and knob.'

Caught short of time, Dr Bradley said, 'I've got to run, but I'll be back later'. He needed to know more.

* * *

The lights on the ward had been dimmed for quite a while before Dr Bradley returned. It was ok, Jack wasn't anywhere near sleep, he rarely was. Fifty years on and he still feared the stillness of the night. Jack was more than happy to sit and talk the night away, even if it was to recall the day that changed the course of his life.

The detail of his memory was astounding; men, movement, positions, weapons, and sounds rattled out of his mouth like it happened yesterday. His description of his wounds blew Dr Bradley away; entry and exit points, size of shrapnel and the damage it caused rolled off Jack's tongue with the ease of a shopping list.

Once the firefight was over, Jack's memory faded. He can remember being evacuated to the LZ and parts of the flight back to Nui Dat. From there it was almost blank until the hospital ward in Vung Tau. Morphine not only numbs the pain, it also sedates the memory.

It was at Vung Tau where Jack was fortunate to cross paths with a very young, brash Dr Bradley Senior. Jack was one of several men wounded that day. His wounds, though not life-threatening, were significantly life-altering. He needed a surgeon with skill, precision along with a liberal dose of confidence and arrogance. At first glance these were not appropriate adjectives to describe the young doctor.

However, once in the theatre, he was an animal, dogged and determined in his approach, utilising techniques that seasoned surgeons would leave alone. If you were wounded in 1967, you prayed Dr Ernest Bradley was on the business end of the scalpel.

'I had shrapnel wounds of varying sizes concentrated up the length of my left leg and through my groin. The worst affected areas were the back of my lower leg, bum, and genitals. The mortar round exploded just behind me while I was up on one knee firing. My leg could be saved, but the same couldn't be said for one of my testicles and a portion of my penis. Your dad concentrated on saving my leg before doing the best he could for my remaining meat and one potato.'

The following day, Jack was able to meet the gutsy surgeon who saved his leg and pecker. With nothing else to do, Jack observed how the other doctors made their way through the ward by reading charts and talking to the nurses before engaging in limited conversations with the wounded men.

Dr Bradley Senior was different. His rounds could take hours as he sat and talked with all his patients. He gave what was most valuable to these men – time. Jack noticed how each would perk up as he approached and smile when he left.

A strident fan of professional running, Dr Bradley recognised Jack immediately. He was standing in the crowd the day Jack's chest broke the tape and remembered with vivid detail the commotion which followed.

Although it should have been the other way around, Dr Bradley was starstruck in Jack's presence and wanted to know everything about that coveted race from the winner's perspective.

Before leaving his care, Jack satisfied Dr Bradley's hunger for almost every detail. It was abundantly clear from Dr Bradley's curiosity that he believed in the romance of The Gift. Jack came close telling him about his swindle but caught himself in time. This part of his victory was best kept to himself; it was better for everyone to keep the illusion alive.

This walk down memory lane was only broken by a nurse quietly making her way through the ward performing her scheduled observations. Back in the present, Jack looked at Dr Bradley. 'I can see the apple doesn't fall far from the tree. There's a lot of your dad in you. Sitting here now with you is almost the same as sitting with him back in Vung Tau.'

These last words sat heavy in Dr Bradleys heart. From a young age all he ever wanted was to be just like his dad. Dr Bradley Senior was an adored and respected local GP who gave great care and service to his community. Everyone knew him and felt safe in his care.

He was a great doctor and dad and there was not a day go by that he didn't miss him. Hearing these words right now, so close to the anniversary of his passing made him smile with a heavy heart.

Looking down at his watch to centre himself, it told him it was exceptionally late, and he needed to go. Before exiting he looked back at Jack. 'Hey from now on its Marcus, for you Dr Bradley should always be my father.'

Comfortable he was in the best hands, Jack was able to grab a bit of shut-eye before being woken with the next round of observations. Today, like so many years ago, he would have to learn to walk again.

CHAPTER 19

Surfside

Victoria stood patiently waiting to board her flight to Adelaide. Airports are one of the few places where the public share space with celebrities. Today she was someone to be noticed. A recent underwear campaign placed her on high rotation throughout traditional and social media. Her amazingly toned body covered by thin straps and a minimal amount of lace was irresistible. Her image was so faultless it almost made you forget the brand being advertised.

Brand Victoria was now recognisable right across the country. Selfies with her newly found fans only fuelled her already inflated ego.

Her schedule on landing? Check into the hotel before meeting Gregore at the track. Waiting for her at the counter was a little surprise; daddy had upgraded her to an executive suite. There was no way his princess was going to share.

At the track, Gregore agreed to a meeting with Scott Palmer, a commission-based scout with contacts throughout the US college system. He had a solid track record of placing athletes. Victoria would be the first he recommended for the prestigious Ivy League. Like Gregore, he'd been patiently waiting for an athlete with her potential and profile to come along.

High nineties in her HSC suggested she had the academic aptitude, and with a few more top line performances on the track, it would be an easy sell. As a gesture of appreciation, Scott would allow Gregore to attach his resumé. Coaching jobs in the states were difficult to obtain, especially from Australia, and were often the last steppingstone before national team appointments.

Victoria exited her chauffeur-driven sportscar, another luxurious treat from daddy. Walking onto the track she noticed Gregore talking with a man she didn't recognise. Taking a moment to admire her stunning marketable features, Scott shook Gregore's hand and exited before she reached them. He would leave it to Gregore to break the news she was on his radar.

Performance management was Gregore's forte, athlete management was not. As Victoria approached, he gave it to her straight with a bit of GST regarding his involvement. 'That man was Scott Palmer, US college scout for Ivy League schools. I made meetings with him to talk about you.'

The last part was his exaggeration. It was Scott who made the meeting but presenting it this way made him the hero, and heroes always get the girl. Unable to control her reaction, Victoria dropped her bag and gave him hug.

Not accustomed to this type of affection, but also interested, Gregore gladly accepted. Wanting to reciprocate, with his arms pinned all he could do was move his hands onto her hips and bum, drawing her closer to his crotch, thus allowing her to feel his excitement. After just enough of a tease she let go. *That should keep him working hard for me.*

* * *

Christmas this year for the Hardys was celebrated on Christmas eve by Jack's bed. Jayde spent Christmas morning with the McLoughlin's. By late morning she set off with Thomas on their two-week adventure.

Jayde and Thomas were heading for South Australia. Their trip would take them diagonally through New South Wales and across the Hay Plain. It would be a solid two-day drive before the hand brake would be pulled in the South Australian capitol.

Jayde could use this time to complete the remaining hours needed for her licence. Thomas was just happy to be away, the last month or so had been brutal. Long days and difficult customers had put his patience to the test. Spending time with Jayde was the recovery he needed.

*   *   *

As they were checking into their hotel in Hay, Victoria was lining up for the 100m final in Adelaide. A bold decision by the promotor to run a Christmas Day event had paid off. The grandstands and outer areas were full of families looking for some late afternoon entertainment.

Her performance was exceptional, placing second in a photo finish to the current Australian Champion Chloe Spinner. Her time was a new personal best and her first Olympic B qualifier.

In the media zone, several reporters were impatiently waiting for Victoria. The US story had leaked, and they all wanted to know where she could be in twelve months. The source of the leak, a high-profile Sydney-based PR firm.

Scott Palmer was furious. He had dealt with the media many times in the past, but it was always on his terms. Being stung cold for a comment was not how he did business. Despite his ambiguity the story still made late-night news bulletins as well as breakfast television and radio. News feeds and social media were alive with posts and comments about the story. Victoria Livingstone was becoming a household name.

As a potential new high-profile queen of the track, the power brokers in Athletics were keen to keep her around. While she was running for them there would be media, and media, whether it was hers or theirs, equated to cash in their coffers.

Scott had his suspicions as to the origin of the leak and made a mental note; *all future correspondence will be treated with the appropriate level of confidentiality.*

Few sprinters and middle-distance runners left Adelaide after the meet; their hotel rooms would remain occupied for another few days. Their motivation to stay was the Surfside Gift, the first category one event of the season. The SAAL resisted the move to integrate, leaving their headline men's and women's races standing alone.

Taking advantage of this unique situation, Jack put two targets on Surfside; run under thirteen seconds and make the semis or better. Still off her novice mark, this was going to be a challenge.

* * *

Jayde and Thomas arrived at their hotel mid-afternoon on boxing day. Her body stiff and sore, she needed to find a park to roll through some light sprints. A quick google search revealed just what she needed only a kilometre or so down the road. Her warm-up was sluggish, her legs were heavy. It was important that she run this out today to be fresh tomorrow.

It was during her third run through that the fluency of her stride was broken by a small hole hidden under the cover of grass. The tell-tale 'What the fuck!' was followed by the distinctive hop and ginger skip strides that signalled something was wrong.

Thomas, also removing the stiffness of travel, was jogging laps on the opposite side of the oval. Not seeing Jayde run into his view, he looked back up the oval and saw her walking in circles, limping on one leg. He knew something was wrong and opened his stride.

When he arrived, Jayde was swearing like a trooper. F bombs became nouns, verbs, adjectives, and conjunctions. Somewhere through tirade of blue language he was able to ascertain she had 'twisted her fucking ankle.'

Despite the seriousness of the situation, Thomas had to look away and gather himself. Hearing Jayde swear with such fluency had engaged his sense of humour.

Gathering her breath and composure, Jayde tested the level of support her ankle was able to provide. To her surprise it was more than she expected, but would it be enough to run tomorrow. This was the start of three must-do events; withdrawing was not an option.

Thomas's years of first aid training told him to get her off the oval and back to the hotel. Here she could begin the rest, ice, compression, elevation regime that would give her the best chance to run tomorrow.

* * *

Fresh from her dazzling run, Victoria was face down on her massage table receiving a leg and back massage. Her naked body was barely concealed by a folded white hotel towel. Her coach Gregore made it his business to oversee the process.

Since becoming the next great hope in Australian Athletics, she was the lever to the next big move in his career. Holding such importance, he wasn't leaving anything to chance. He monitored everything to ensure his and her success.

He also used this time to feed his inner desire, positioning himself carefully to take advantage of the reflective power of a glass, catching glimpses of areas of her body that should only be seen by a doctor or a lover. Cognizant to his hidden agenda, Victoria was happy to oblige.

* * *

Jayde woke with a level of anxiety and apprehension that took her back to those horrible last weeks and months at MAGS. She nervously sat up in bed and placed her injured foot gently on the carpet. Testing its strength and the level of pain, she pushed her foot into the floor with ever-increasing pressure.

To her astonishment, there was virtually no discomfort. Buoyed, she stood and moved around the room. Again, no pain. Sensing movement in the room, Thomas woke from his normally deep sleep. Rubbing his eyes, he looked up to see her running on the spot. For once, could luck be on her side.

* * *

Feeling optimistic, her joyous mood was halted in its tracks. A series of life-sized banners created a virtual tunnel of featured athletes from the gate to the track. Jayde froze in front of Victoria, eyeballing the inanimate figure, the distinctive cold rush of adrenaline charged through her body. Fight or flight, her preference was obvious.

Since Jack's fall and diagnosis, Jayde had given little thought to Victoria. This banner was a stark reminder of why she was here. Instinctively her fight mechanism had been evoked. Thomas could see rage building and stepped between her and the banner.

Seeing his face softened her building rage and brought her back to Jack's plan. He had warned her about this reaction. *'Redemption could be gained quickly but it will be nothing compared to the one which was coming on Easter Monday.'*

Jayde reminded herself, *The Gift is where it will hurt her the most.*

* * *

On the track, the junior kids were going through their paces. Parents lined the fence screaming encouragement. The outer ground had its usual array of food stalls and a jazz quartet providing entertainment. There was a vibrant, positive atmosphere with reminders everywhere of the history and nostalgia of the event.

Black and white images and a brief biography of past winners were plastered on banners throughout the outer ground. Meet officials paid homage to the roaring twenties origins of the event with bow ties, pin-striped jackets, and straw boater hats, while members of the crowd gladly dressed in their best from the roaring twenties.

Having no jurisdiction once he crossed the border, Steve Paterson was invited to Surfside in a technical support role for ProRun. The first interstate user of ProRun, the SAAL insisted a technical assistant be on hand to deal with any possible issues.

The first of the big four, Surfside was an ideal event to prove the full front and back of house capabilities of his app. Six hours east in Warrnambool, Dave McPharland was testing the premium package. Comparing the performance to his trusted methods, he was testing the validity and efficiency of the app. If all worked to his advantage, he would be ready to open his cheque book. The first Victorian race was only days away and The Gift only three months later, he would take any advantage over his competitors.

Unknown to Dave, Steve added another algorithm. This one produced a positive, neutral or negative correlation for each lane. Data from each race was captured, compared, and compiled in real time. Powerful information to anyone with the right permissions.

Jayde checked her phone; it was time to collect her colours and head to the warm-up area. Of the twelve heats in the open women's event, Jayde was running in the second. Looking at the program, she could see Victoria was drawn in the eleventh. She should be well clear of the track before Victoria raised one of her most recognisable assets in the air.

Heat one was run and won; twelve point eight five seconds broke the tape. Jayde knew that if needed she could easily match this time. The first three runners from each heat were guaranteed advancement to the next round.

Setting her blocks, Jayde sensed a commotion in the warm-up area. Victoria had entered the arena. It was like royalty had entered the track. The event froze as she assumed her trademark flirtatious pose. A quick wiggle of her tits and hips along with a wave to the crowd and the event could resume.

Jayde kept her head down and reset her focus. Top three and thirteen seconds. She was called to dig in, set, raising her hips, and rocking forward on her shoulders. Her legs pushed back into her blocks, her muscles ready to release like loaded springs on the crack of the gun.

The familiar sharp crack came, and she was away. Driving her legs in shorter chopped strides, before raising her head and hips and opening her stride. The accentuated flick of her right-hand evidence of the effort she was putting in.

At the finish line, she had placed second, perfect. Her time was 12.93 seconds, smack bang on Jack's time. Jayde quickly left the track and went back to Thomas. She had no interest in watching any of the remaining heats.

As predicted, Victoria won, setting the fastest time, 12.74 seconds, a metre or more ahead of her handicap. Jack was right; track runners make poor pro-runners.

Jayde needed to contest two more rounds before day one was wrapped. The original field of twelve heats was reduced to nine and then six. It was vital that she remained within the top three throughout these elimination rounds.

Her round two was superb, equal second in 12.86 seconds. She was delighted with the place but was concerned with the time.

A quick call to Poppy settled her nerves.

The last race of the day was the most difficult; like many in the field she was fatigued. Multiple races combined with waiting made for heavy muscles. Compensating, Jayde broke her warm-up down to the essential movements only. At the end of her final run-through, the stiffness finally dissipated, and she was ready to race.

As she was moving from the warm-up area to the start line, it happened; they finally crossed paths. There would never be a better chance than right now. This wasn't a poster, this was the entitled bitch that caused all the hurt and pain at school, trolled her online, had her fired from the kindergarten and nearly made her swing from the end of a rope.

The violent portion of her brain ran the algorithm; by the time anyone could get near them Jayde could have at least four maybe five good solid right punches into her. Her left-hand clasping her head and neck, pinning her in position for maximum damage. Full blooded right upper cuts would be the punch of choice. She could feel the cold rush building in her veins.

Thankfully, the calming, soothing voice of Jack entered her head before the adrenaline, tempering the ever-increasing anger.

Jayde could clearly hear him telling her, *channel your anger into the track.*

When they were close enough for comments to be made without others being involved, Victoria muttered something, but Jayde, oblivious, walked by without any reaction at all. No-one ignores the future Queen; standing with her insult, Victoria was left fuming.

Jayde settled into her blocks and waited for the starter to call 'set'. Once again, her legs were ready to explode. The gun set her in motion, and anger worked well for Jayde. Her race was on point, third in what they would describe as a competitive time. *Jack will be ecstatic; I'm running tomorrow.*

Anger, on the other hand, worked against Victoria. Her beautiful flowing stride became choppy and unbalanced. The whole race was a fight between her body and mind. Placing fourth she had to rely on being one of the next six fastest if she was to run again tomorrow.

Rattled, Victoria quickly gathered her belongings. For the first time, she didn't want to be the centre of attention. Sitting adjacent to her driver, a relieving ping announced she could re-set and run again tomorrow. Tonight, she had other business to attend to; angry fingers would once again waken the haters and trolls.

*　*　*

Petra and Georgia both contacted Jayde to let her know what popped up on their feeds. Thomas could not believe what he saw, having managed to move through school and university in a way that never drew attention like this. He knew about it through his friends and contacts, but this was the first time he was part of it. Through association he had been injected into this cauldron of discontent.

This could be a game changer in their relationship.

For the next hour Thomas sat and listened to the events of Jayde's life from taking up the scholarship at MAGS to now. The bullying and harassment, systematic and enforced abandonment by the school. Losing her job at the kindy and the foiled attempt at her own life. He was numb.

Jayde continued. There was a reason for her running. The redemption she desperately desired would come at The Gift. Jayde explained how Jack had won it and how she was going to use the same tactics to do the same in a few months' time.

* * *

Victoria woke from a deep relaxing sleep. As always, she quickly brushed her hair and prepared for her first snap of the day. Today she would utilise the early morning sun with the view across the beach and water. Her night gown would be sheer enough to show a tantalising silhouette of her naked body.

She set her phone on the selfie stand, and four attempts later she had the shot she wanted. Standing at about forty-five degrees it reflected the alluring shape of her bum and the perkiness of her tits with the transparent material falling freely from the tip of her nipple. This would most certainly keep all her followers wanting more.

Once posted, curiosity took her over. A quick review of her socials revealed the deep impact of her late-night online activity. Everyone piled on. There were so many tags and posts there was no way she could read them all. One, however, did grab her attention, #BCH61.

From what Victoria could see, BCH61 was a sporadic follower who had a serious hatred for Jayde. Her post didn't follow the normal expansionist pile-on trend. This one was more personal and had some real venom behind it. The language used was also deeper and more sophisticated than would be expected from her audience.

It didn't take too much thought to work out who this could possibly be. Her sinister smile and an incredible sense of self-satisfaction was only broken by the rapping of knuckles at her door. It was her masseuse, and Gregore. Feeling empowered,

Victoria turned towards the massage table and dropped her night gown. Instinctively the masseuse turned away, but the same couldn't be said for Gregore.

*   *   *

Jayde arrived at the track with plenty of time to settle and prepare for her race. Thomas found a coffee and a quiet space; he needed time to process his inclusion in these shenanigans.

Jayde opened the ProRun and confirmed her intent to run. Lost in his own thoughts he didn't see her move off to collect her colours and head off to the warm-up area.

Relaxed after her early morning massage, Victoria collected her colour and was parading in the warm-up area when Jayde arrived. Her intention, confrontation, buoyed by the benefit of the crowd, their eyes gave her confidence and security.

Street smart, Jayde was mindful of Victoria's tactics and avoided any close contact. She knew Victoria's pre-race preparation was always as close to the crowd as possible. She stayed well within the optimum range for phone cameras. The infield side would be her security.

Reviewing data from yesterday's racing, Steve noted lane two was fastest, running three points above its stated mark. His algorithm compared a runner's expected time, taken as a figure from their mark to their actual time, and then converted to a point rating. The rating from each race is then compiled to provide an overall score, with one point equating to the standard quarter metre increment of the handicap scale.

Protecting himself, he was the only one who knew the correlation between the points and the track. It was never noted, written, or logged; Steve believed this was his insurance should anyone have the need to dig deeper into the various functions of his program.

He needed subjects for his experiment, at least two for a reliable data set. The first would have his advantage applied for both the semi and final, the other the semi-final only. He needed an event with a better speed variation as well.

The men's event was running too close, and in any case, they had three rounds to go. Statistics reminded him that it was highly unlikely an athlete would receive the same lane three races in a row. Two was possible, three could raise questions that he didn't want to answer.

This left the women. With two rounds to run it fell neatly into his parameters. Now he needed athletes. Steve looked through the start list on his phone. Victoria's name jumped out immediately; she was the race favourite and set the fastest time yesterday. Her data could easily validate his algorithm.

More importantly, placing her in the fastest lane would almost guarantee the win, benefitting his mates in the SAAL and in turn his own organisation at Easter. A female athlete of her stature competing for the historical double, Surfside then The Gift, would be a promotor's dream. Added to this, the strong possibility she could be the first outright female winner of The Gift. The media reach would be unbelievable and just at the right time.

Media and naming rights deals were both up for negotiation at season end. The coverage a scenario like this would generate would be astronomical, gifting him some heavy bargaining power. Best of all, this would all occur at the start of his tenure, silencing those on the committee who believed he had risen well beyond his own level of incompetence.

Scanning the field, another name stood out, Jayde Hardy, the rookie Bill confronted back at Tenterfield. Since losing the CEO role, Bill had also lost his title as Dad, it was first name basis now. Feeling like he owed her more than his apology, she became the second subject of his covert experiment.

As instructed, Jayde set her blocks in lane two. Jack had been clear about the time to run. *'As quick, but no faster than yesterday.'* Jayde implicitly knew how to run a mid-twelve eight. Places were not important. Time was all that mattered.

Settling into the crouch position, she followed the starter's instructions. Her run felt like it was on point. Her stride was fluent and consistent, her hips and shoulders well positioned. She could almost predict the time down to hundredths of a second. Placing second she fulfilled Jack's second instruction.

Official notification came with a ping on her phone, along with her time, 12.73. 'What the fuck!'

Where the hell had that come from? She ran plenty of twelve-sevens at training and that did not feel like a twelve-seven. Alarm bells were going off in her head. Poppy's instructions were clear; do not go faster than yesterday, she needed to find a quiet place to call Poppy.

* * *

Victoria set herself in the blocks, head down, faultless bottom high in the air, shapely legs waiting with anticipation for the gun. Crack and she was away. Yesterday's poor performance was quickly forgotten. Victoria flew down the track and broke the tape in twelve six one. Steve was ecstatic, his program worked. Both girls ran exactly three points faster than their mark.

Reviewing footage Thomas sent from his phone, Jack was aware of Jayde's overperformance. Evaluating the short and long-term implications this could have, he determined it wouldn't be too costly. His plan was still alive.

Jayde found a quiet space and made her usual facetime call. His first words were, 'It's all ok. You would have had to run that time soon anyway.'

'Are you sure? What about the final?'

'All's good, but no faster.'

His words soothed her anxiety. Hanging up, Jayde was glad Thomas gave Poppy his old phone; she really needed to see his face today.

There was a considerable gap between the semis and final for the women, enough for Victoria to return to her hotel, back to the comfort of air conditioning and a shower.

Jayde, on the other hand, found shelter with Thomas under a tree.

*   *   *

As the bottom quadrant of the sun was kissing the horizon, the two adversaries lined up for the final. ProRun had sent Jayde into lane seven, and Victoria, incredibly, was drawn in lane two. Steve's algorithm indicated it had moved close to a four-point advantage. The crowd fell silent as the starter called the field to their marks.

Local news crews focussed all their attention on the athlete in lane two. To their delight, in just over twelve and a half seconds Victoria was crowned the winner. Her signature tit and hip jiggle was tantalising. Meet officials and sponsors all lined for their photographs, the royal blue winners sash sat perfectly across her body.

Jayde, along with the rest of the finalists, left Victoria to her celebrations. Watching the final on his phone, Jack was ecstatic. Jayde's run was on point, seventh place in a low twelve eight.

Sitting in the corporate area, Steve was chuffed with himself; his intervention was an irrefutable success. His understanding of technology handed him the power of influence.

Feeling the familiar vibration against his thigh, Steve slid his phone just proud of his pocket. The message from Dave McPharland affirmed there would likely be a return on his investment; *meeting tomorrow 1pm in Maryborough, bring a pen!*

These last words boosted his already positive mood. With Dave on board, the others would sign on soon after.

Apart from more athletes, a big difference between the country and city races was the post-race function. In the country it was simple; meet at the nominated pub and let the night flow from there. In the city it was a designated themed event.

Everything Surfside was linked back to the roaring twenties. Men wore pin-striped and check patterned suits with bow ties and braces, while the ladies stunned in their flapper and fringe dresses.

The swing orchestra had the crowd until Victoria entered the room. Her dress was amazing, bespoke just in case. It was hard to determine which accentuated the other, Victoria in the dress or the dress on Victoria. Either way it didn't matter. She willingly lapped up the attention, comments about her dress, her win today and the rumours about her potential move overseas. Everybody wanted a selfie and a chat.

The word from Sydney; oblige. This was a golden brand building opportunity; Victoria and her stunning dress would be a social media sensation.

Jayde's treat for making her first final – a pub schnitty and salad.

CHAPTER 20

Maryborough

Jayde checked the room one final time before closing the door. Despite being new to travel, she was paranoid about leaving anything behind. Thomas was confident that he had collected and packed everything, and was waiting near the car.

Knowing there were eight hours of driving ahead, he took the opportunity to move, stretching his back and legs. Once clear of Adelaide, Jayde would again take the wheel. Today would be the last day he needed to sign her log.

Steve Paterson was several hours up the road. Setting his cruise control to a law-bending hundred and seven, he presumed there were a few kilometres per hour up his sleeve before catching the eye of any eager highway patrol officer. There was no way he was going to miss this meeting. With Dave onboard it would be an easy sell to the others; bookies will never give away an unfair advantage.

Signing Dave wasn't Steve's only business in Maryborough. There was also his role in the Highland Gift on New Year's Day. This was the opening event for the Victorian pro running season. An easy category two event, it was always a good way to start their season.

Steve as chairman would oversee the event, ensuring all elements met the high VPAL standards. After Dave signed, he had a logistics briefing, which he planned to conclude well before Bill and Adam arrived. The last thing he needed was Bill reminding him how it was done. If Adam follows his instructions this should not be a problem.

*　*　*

More comfortable behind the wheel, Jayde was able to hold a conversation and drive at the same time. It wasn't long before the conversation returned to running, remembering Jack had a special task for Thomas at Maryborough.

'Jack wants you to drop a few bets on me with a couple of the bookies.' Using his terminology, she continued. 'A blue swimmer or lobster, place only not the nose. Don't drop them at the same time, and preferably when the bull pen is busy.'

Raised in part by a tradie grandad who didn't mind a punt, he was familiar with betting and betting terminology.

*　*　*

Bert and Ken, another of Jack's brothers from the Vets, were heading southwest towards Maryborough. They were on a recce for Hobblers Ride. Their plan? To head south past the Victorian boarder, then west picking up some of the Kelly's Trails and onto Stawell.

Maryborough was being assessed as a potential place to stay. Ken, a mad Scotsman, was up for the ride the instant he heard the race was part of the towns Highland Games. Bert's plan: encourage as many within the club and any other affiliate clubs to join them on the ride. Jack's plan was dependent on strong numbers.

Steve pulled into Maryborough with time to spare. Opening his laptop, he checked to see that the electronic contract was open and ready to sign. Unable to check in until after two he went to the coffee shop and ordered his standard macchiato and Turkish melt.

Before the order arrived, Dave joined him at the table. With a quick gesture the order was doubled. Steve struggled to hold his enthusiasm throughout lunch, the deal wasn't signed just yet; he was anticipating some minor negotiations before the stylus ran across his screen.

Steve and Dave had been associates for a long-time. Their common ground professional running, accordingly, was the catalyst and focal point of their conversations. Both tested each other, trying to get the inside word, Dave to help set his book and Steve to investigate how the markets were running. Names were thrown up, previous winners, new up and commers, old stalwarts. It was only a matter of time before they mentioned Victoria.

After her recent win at Surfside and her inclusion in the Track Classic series Dave contended she would be the one to watch in The Gift. 'I expect she will limit her program to two of the three remaining category one events, Yarra and The Gift. Goldfields might be an option but an outside one at best.'

With the nod of his head Steve agreed. Victoria was their pick for The Gift.

With their appetites satisfied it was time to get down to business. Steve anticipated this to flow without too much fuss; the product was too good to refuse.

Maybe he would have to bend a fraction on his initial start-up price, a point he was willing to concede to get this deal across the line. What he didn't expect was a counteroffer. Dave wanted to be more than a client. Like a boxer who just took a shot he didn't see coming, Steve was back on his heels. *Where the hell did this come from?*

Dave McParland was more than a country bookie. He was a savvy businessman who had an eye for opportunity. He jumped on crypto early and was currently sitting on a small fortune in various currencies. Diversifying, he was an early investor in the twenty-four seven gym market.

Now the owner of four gyms in various regional centres, he had a solid income stream that he was looking to invest. Always ahead of the curve, he could see the imminent demise of the on-track bookie. Internet gambling combined with streamed race coverage equated to fewer punters at the track.

At the current rate of decline, he estimated there were only two or three years before the overheads to run his on-track bag would outweigh its earnings. Online would barely sustain his lifestyle, but this program offered an income stream that could offset the loss from his on-track bag.

Dave researched the potential reach for ProRun and saw opportunities well beyond its current scope. Some had already been factored into Steve's projections, others had offered new possibilities and markets, especially in combining professional running and off-track betting.

Viewing this as the future for him in this sport, Dave had tried unsuccessfully to gain the permissions required for off-track betting in all pro-athletics events in Australia. Many of the state authorities were keen, but regulatory and infrastructure issues were always the sticking points.

ProRun, with its event management structure and ability to link with external betting agencies, was the missing piece to this puzzle. The program would be easy to audit to ensure everything was above board and meet all requirements of the various Gaming and Racing Authorities.

Gambling would occur through third party organisations. Add in live streaming and they would have a profitable, marketable product to offer all the Australian professional running organisations. Beyond grass tracks he saw massive potential for Gift format events in swimming, handicapped events that use time delay on the blocks as the mark.

This was a cash cow just waiting to be milked.

Serving an apprenticeship under his father, the original owner of the McPharland bag, he was constantly reminded; the key to business is knowledge. Utilising some trusted contacts, he gained powerful, intimate knowledge of Steve and his current financial situation.

It was not good. He was behind, both personally and with his business. The fancy car he drove was leased and he was struggling to maintain the payments. Money was continually shuffled from one debit to another.

To many, the chaos of this business operation, combined with household spending far exceeding current income would be enough to send them packing. However, Dave recognised within this economic madness was his opportunity.

His initial buy in, a twenty per cent share for fifty thousand dollars, followed by an option to buy another twenty five per cent after two years. The second figure was to be determined as a function of the current market value.

Dave knew this cash injection would provide Steve with some much-needed liquidity. Under the arrangement, Steve would continue to hold the balance of power; Dave would provide capital and more importantly connections to see ProRun reach its full potential.

Realistically this figure should have been up near six figures. Knowing he held the upper hand, Dave was confident in his low-ball offer.

Steve in his current financial predicament couldn't afford to say no.

Dave opened his computer; the screen had been split. On the left was the contract, on the right was an electronic funds transfer waiting for Steve's BSB and account number. Dave's contract was significantly more substantial; drawn up by his lawyer it contained much more detail than a simple three optioned usage agreement.

Without any access to immediate legal advice Steve was left to review the contract himself. Compiled in legal language he could barely understand, he did his best to comprehend the implications of each line.

The clause which detailed the provision of full disclosure raised alarm bells with Steve. Should he mention the checky IF statement in the randomiser. Although technically not illegal it would certainly raise ethical questions which he may find extremely difficult to answer.

Pondering the consequences of this disclosure, Steve determined it was too early in their partnership for such an ethically challenging conundrum.

Reviewing his own circumstance there were some irrefutable facts; *initial forecasts of remaining liquid to late February or even early March are optimistic, the holiday period is costing me more than I budgeted. The wife and kids down on the surf coast are draining me.* Each night he would check his accounts. Soon he wouldn't have enough debt to shuffle to cover their lavish lifestyle.

He was at least another month away from any substantial money. School subscriptions wouldn't start until mid-February and despite being confident there was no accurate data about just how big the uptake would be with the bookies.

The remaining professional running bodies in Queensland, Tasmania and Western Australia had agreed informally to terms but with no official purchase requests there was no telling when he would be issuing tax invoices.

Figures, sums, and scenarios were bouncing around Steve's head as he attempted in vain to grapple with the enormity of this situation. Could he afford to give away some of his business, especially at this price. However, more importantly, could he afford to turn it down. Realty hit Steve like a punch in the face.

With a reluctant, shaking hand Steve guided the stylus across the screen, his signature sealed the deal. Seconds later the desperately needed funds were released and on their way to the nominated account. ProRun was now in a partnership. The deal would be finalised later with a celebratory single malt or two.

Driving the short distance to the track gave Steve a chance to digest what had just happened. Rather than sadness and regret, he felt a huge sense of relief. By the morning there would be fifty thousand dollars in his account. He would transfer enough into his personal account to cover costs, and the remaining would sit with the company. From this he could service much of his business and personal debt. His wife and family could continue to live the life he struggled to afford.

The logistics meeting was a waste of time. The organising committee ensured they were ready for racing. Suitably impressed, Steve gave the VPAL endorsement.

* * *

Bert and Ken rumbled into town under the late afternoon sun. A couple of old bearded blokes on Harley's used to turn heads, but nowadays it barely raised an eyebrow. Parched from a solid day in the saddle, the two old mates quenched their thirst with a few pots before checking into their accommodation at the pub.

* * *

Jayde and Thomas approached Maryborough from the opposite direction, the baking afternoon sun making it near impossible for her to use the mirrors. Blinded from the reflection, she had a near miss with a stock truck.

Mumbling, 'about fucking time,' Jayde couldn't hide her relief when she saw the sign for their hotel, as always, simple and on the outskirts of town.

Needing some me time, Thomas was happy to sit in the cool comfort of their air-conditioned room and catch the last session from day four of the Boxing Day Test. Australia was chasing the final three wickets to close out the test a day early.

Utilising the flat hotel carpark, Jayde kept her suppleness with a few rhythmic drills and run-throughs. Effective for what she needed, it wasn't ideal; the reflected heat from the black bitumen was overwhelming.

Returning to the room with a solid layer of sweat, Jayde headed straight for the shower. Caught up in the action on the television, Thomas barely noticed her walk by. When she emerged from the bathroom naked, she had his undivided attention.

* * *

Concluding all his business for the day, Steve was checking into his room at Kelly's when the familiar message ping rang out from his phone. It was Adam, he was in the carpark. Reluctantly, Steve went out to help, returning with an armful of bags and a whining old man. 'That's the last time I'll set foot in that car. I don't know how I'll do my job tomorrow.'

The trip up from Melbourne in Adam's WRX was nowhere near as comfortable as the Range Rover. Stiff suspension combined with a racing bucket seat wrought excruciating pain on Bill's back.

Steve dropped Bill and his bags off to his standard double room before taking his own luggage up to his king balcony suite. If Bill wasn't grumpy enough from the trip, this demotion to a standard room above the bar only added to his angry state.

A massive tightarse, there was no way he was going to dig into his own pocket for the upgrade. Add some booze and the night could get very interesting. Steve made a mental note; *assign Adam to Grandad watch.*

* * *

Bert and Ken returned to the bar and settled in for a few more pots. They found a quiet space away from the locals and begun talking about the potential itinerary for the Hobblers Ride. Tomorrow, ride out to Stawell and take a close recce of the town. It was only about an hour in the saddle, so they could afford to settle in and enjoy the country ambience.

* * *

As promised, Dave met all three generations of Paterson's at the bar. He ordered everyone a drink before settling around a table not too far from Bert and Ken. Dave, a keen observer of people, noticed the two elderly bikers. Their long beards and platted ponytails made them stand out.

Growing up in an era where the presence of bikers usually meant trouble, he kept a wary eye on these two. After hearing Ken's unmissable thick Scottish accent, he settled, figuring they were just two punters up here for the games.

Bill's mood lightened at the same rate Dave shouted drinks. This reminded him of when he was the man, and he was taking full advantage of the hospitality. Brought up in surroundings where respect for your elders was demanded, Dave gave Bill all the respect afforded a man of his age.

It was a pity this didn't continue once Dave said goodbye. If Bill wanted anymore, he would have to reluctantly dive into his own pocket. Last drinks were called and progressively everybody took their last mouthful before returning to their rooms, home or to the last trading pub in town.

*   *   *

The ride to Stawell was easy. Nice open country roads, easily accessible by all riders in the club. There were six options which could be utilised if needed.

Assessing the reaction of the locals, Bert quickly determined he would need to formulate a plan for the club to enter and move about town. The thunderous sound of a large group of Harleys would surely attract unwanted attention. Anonymity was essential to their success.

The boys rode past Central Park, the home of the Grampians Gift. It was a beautiful traditional country sportsground with several entrances. The turn of the century grandstand stood tall and proud square to the cricket pitch.

From his research, Bert was able to pick out the distinctive features of the ground and the surrounding streets. Seeing these with his own eyes would make planning that much easier and precise. He wasn't going to leave anything to chance, Hobblers Ride deserved nothing less.

CHAPTER 21

Heatwave

New Year's Eve celebrations were generally tempered in Maryborough. The influx of fit, competitive runners generally ensured an orderly night throughout the town.

Revellers could still find company at any of the hotels and there were the customary informal fireworks shows up and down main street, as the end of the countdown heralded the beginning of the new year.

Jayde and Thomas enjoyed the peace and seclusion that came from being on the outskirts of town. Their countdown was delivered via the coverage from Sydney Harbour. Like always, the moment came and went, and nothing really changed. Jayde always made a point of making a New Year's wish, and this year all her thoughts and wishes were for Poppy Jack.

* * *

Jayde rose with the sun for the first day of the new year. Not far down the road was a small industrial estate. The roads were vacant and smooth, just what she needed for her pre-race ritual.

The sun was barely above the horizon and the temperature was already climbing. The forecast was not favourable, stinking hot, not good for athletes, or people dressed in kilts. Jayde walked back to the room in a lather of sweat. First stop, the bar fridge. Her mouth demanded cold water then a shower.

*　*　*

As he was pulling the handbrake, Jayde reminded Thomas, 'Don't forget Poppy's instructions, drop the bets when the bull pen is busy'. Reaching into her bag she offered him the few notes Jack had provided.

Shaking his head, he refused to take it. 'I can cover it. Jack can save his cash for another day.'

It was a festival of tartan inside the ground. The pipe band was in traditional kit, the officials were in kilts and white polo tops, while many in the crowd created their own Aussie / Scottish fusion – kilts adorned with trucker's singlets and an Akubra hat. It was an acquired taste, but given the anticipated sweltering temperatures, it demonstrated the fluid line that exists between form and function.

The day began with the traditional march past by the various country pipe bands. For many in the crowd the unmistakable, ear-piercing shrill of bagpipes so early on New Year's morning tipped their hangover from tolerable to terrible. The pipes started early and wouldn't finish until well after the last race.

Can bars began trading early; demand was met by supply. Most punters figured it was better to stay drunk. Bookies assumed their place in the bull pen. As in the bars there was a steady trade, as people looked to get their New Year's bets on while the odds were at their best.

Thomas positioned himself on the fringe of this mayhem. He could both hear and see what was happening. Seizing a busy moment, he dropped a lobster on the second favourite and a tenner on Jayde. The bookie, Dave McPharland, was only too happy to take these bets; roughies were bread-and-butter money for his bag.

Jayde confirmed her entry online before setting off to collect her colours. As she was entering the track, Bert and Ken arrived at the ground. Ken was in his element, with kilt, singlet and biker boots he blended straight in. First stop, the can bar followed by the bull pen.

Jayde's first race came around quickly. Her run was solid, easily placing her in the next round. Looking back towards the bookies' boards, Thomas noticed that her place odds had moved from thirty-three into twenty-five to one. Race two followed a similar pattern. Jayde ran well, keeping her time down in the low twelve-eight range. This was good enough to make it into the semi-finals.

Again, Thomas took note of her odds; they had crept in further, eighteen to one. It was time to drop another bet. This time with Dave's main competitor Paddy O'Reilly. Going rogue, Thomas broke Jack's plan and dropped a bluey on the win and lobster on the place. Paddy was smiling as he wrote out the ticket.

Ken and Bert were beginning to feel the effects of beer and excessive sunlight. Ken's shoulders were scalded by sunburn. Although the beer was masking the pain, it would be a different story later tonight, and especially tomorrow with his leathers on the bike. Entering the bull pen again they dropped some more on Jayde and the favourite for the win.

Jayde lined up for the semi. She could feel the sun scalding the back of her legs as she rose into the set position. The heat dissolved her sharpness. Crossing the line last, it was her worst run of the season. Not wanting to hang around in the heat, Jayde looked at Thomas. 'Let's get out of here.'

Leaving the ground, they sought shelter under the shade of a tree while the air conditioning in the car made it possible to travel back to the hotel. Thankfully, there was a small pool at the end of the carpark that was protected by a shade cloth. She didn't even bother to change into her costume; running straight from the car she sought instant relief in the water.

* * *

Back at the track, Bert and Ken had some winnings to collect. As expected, the favourite, Chloe Spinner, got up for the win. For the tenner they dropped on, they collected eighty back. Not enough to cover the can bill for the day.

Steve Paterson also had a win; between events he convinced another three bookies to subscribe to ProRun. He anticipated sales to climb quickly as the word about his product moved from the bush to the city.

There was a mass escape after the final. Everybody needed to get out of the heat. Steve, Bill and Adam headed straight to their rooms for a quick shower. Then it was down to the bar for the post-event celebrations. Steve would once again hold the lion's share of attention.

Bill was in the mood to get drunk. Dehydrated from standing in the sun, the beers took affect much earlier than usual. Unlike last night with Dave, he struggled to get an effective word in anywhere.

Even Adam in his first year was receiving more attention. Pushed beyond the limits of the fringe only encouraged him to drink more. It wasn't long before Bill's conspiracy theory surfaced. He watched Jayde today with careful eyes. He analysed every detail of her face, body, running style, walking style, mannerisms, the way she spoke, who she spoke to, with absolute precision.

He even spent time in the VPAL archives, scrolling through old records, looking for a name that would jolt his failing memory. Just like his first encounter in Tenterfield, nothing.

Without any substantiated evidence, Bill began warning anyone who would listen about Miss Jayde Hardy from St Marys. Thankfully for Jayde, it was taken as the gibberish mutterings of an old, washed-up drunk. It wasn't long before Adam's night was over; he had to put an old man to bed.

Steve, on the other hand, was relishing being the centre of everyone's attention. He hadn't felt this happy and relaxed in quite a while. Despite the insufferable heat, the event was a resounding success. Participant and crowd numbers were strong, which gave him confidence for the rest of the season, but more importantly, ProRun had performed without a hitch.

Reports from Dave were very positive regarding real time data. He was able to frame markets and set his odds faster than all the other bookies. The time advantage he had was noticed, providing the critical evidence he needed to interest subscribers.

On the one hand, Dave knew he was giving away a significant advantage. On the other, as part owner of the program, his eyes were on a bigger prize.

Throughout the day, Dave pondered a means by which he could maintain his speed advantage. Using the odds feature located in the premium package, Steve could add his unique own code that combined this data with his odds formula to automatically calculate and post his updated market. He figured with his partner's programming ability this could be done without too much fuss. He wanted it tested and running before Frankston in three weeks.

Most critically, it must be fully trusted before The Gift. Adding to this time advantage, Steve saw the opportunity to fully automate his system. He would lose the bookies' board and move to a digital platform. Flat screens at the track along with his own app would advertise his updated odds instantly, giving him more time to concentrate on his customers.

The morning broke to many sore heads. Most of the committee and several volunteers were back at the track early pulling down the infrastructure that is unique to pro-running. It would be another year before much of this saw daylight again.

Runners, coaches and out of towners were packing their bags and handing in their room keys. Again, the coffee shop was the place to visit before exiting the town. Thomas collected their morning cups of pick-me-up, while Jayde remained safely hidden behind the heavy tint on his windows. Deep into Jack's plan, there was no way she was going to risk another encounter with a Paterson.

Jayde had one more event only a few hours up the road before heading back to Sydney – the Denni Dash in Deniliquin. Before embarking on their adventure, Thomas went online. Dennie was their longest stop, and although it had some interesting features, he couldn't see anything substantial enough to make him want to stay for a week. He accepted this trip was all about Jayde and her running, but he also needed something that was about him, something that incorporated his favourite thing, the water.

Peter and Marge, aware of his predicament, offered him a solution. They would help book a houseboat on the Murray River. There were some great midweek deals online and they would be driving right past the dock at Echuca.

* * *

Bert and Ken fired up their bikes and headed north-east. Their plan was to travel as far as Holbrook, about five hours away. Short of dodging bullets in Vietnam, these were going to be some of the toughest hours of Ken's life.

Still in reccie mode, Bert wanted to check out the direct route home. Should Jack's plan come off, like in sixty-six, everyone involved would need to flee town and get to safety as soon as possible.

CHAPTER 22

Murray River

Jayde was delighted to sit in the passenger seat. She was physically and emotionally exhausted and didn't need to think about the road. Up to yesterday, she had executed Jack's plan flawlessly, her times and places were all in his prescribed range. Her only blemish, the false start in Gilgandra.

However, the tirade she copped from him after the race was something she never expected. *'Do you think this is a game, we agreed at the start total execution, my job in this partnership is to think, plot and plan, yours is simple, just do it!'*

He had no interest in hearing about the stifling heat and the minor sunstroke she suffered; to Jack these were petty excuses and *only losers find excuses*. This last comment cut the most; Jayde never thought she would ever hear her Poppy call her a 'loser'.

In that brief facetime call, Jayde caught a glimpse of Jack as he used to be, the gambling Poppy Jack her mum grew up with. This Poppy scared her.

Only after Jack got a call from Boomer did he appreciate the intensity of the heat Jayde had faced yesterday. Embarrassed by his behaviour he had to call her immediately and clear the air.

Feeling the vibration, Jayde slid her phone out of her pocket to see who was calling. The bright letters *Poppy* made her heart sing. She touched the green button immediately. Before she could greet him he broke into his apology, 'I'm sorry, ugly Poppy paid you a visit yesterday, I should have realised you did your best. Are you ok?'

Comforted by his concern, she said, 'Yeah, I'm good, spent the rest of the day in the hotel pool. I feel better today'.

'I've been thinking about your race. As far as I can see it won't hurt anything. All the times were slow, anyway under-performance is better than over-performance. Call me before the dash, love you, be safe.' With that Jack hung up. Long conversations were becoming harder for him to maintain; his lung function was starting its inevitable decline.

Lost in her thoughts, Jayde hadn't realised that Thomas had pulled off the highway and was following the road down to the river. When he touched the brakes a bit harder than usual, she was jolted out of her distraction.

Past the carpark a kit garage masqueraded as an office, beyond that a wharf with several houseboats tied to their moorings. Confused, she looked at Thomas, who said, 'I've booked us a few days on the water'.

Initially, Jayde was apprehensive. Jack's plan had them staying somewhere on the outskirts of town, using the time to train. However, after her performance yesterday and his outburst she was more than a bit over running. Crossing paths with Victoria and enduring more of her abhorrent behaviour reaffirmed her commitment to taking the bitch down.

But a few days on the water with Thomas, away from everything related to running, was precisely what she needed to purge the negativity of Maryborough. She would tell Jack about this deviation once she returned to Sydney.

Knowing this was Thomas's time, Pete and Marge splurged, booking a boat that was well beyond the needs of a young couple. For Jayde, this was the most opulent experience of her life. The boat came with a master stateroom and two guest suites, a massive kitchen, dining, and lounge area that flowed out onto sheltered rear deck.

Understanding the importance of being prepared, Thomas ordered food and drinks online which were delivered well before they reached the dock. Anne the owner gladly packed them away to allow Jayde to feel the full luxury of houseboating.

No stranger to boats, Thomas was confident behind the wheel. Growing up in the shire, his summers were spent surfing, on patrol at the beach, or on the water cruising around Port Hacking.

As they pulled away from the dock, Jayde struggled to hide her excitement. She explored the boat as Thomas navigated his way down the Murray. With a maximum speed of just over four knots, he was going to be here for a while. Anne pinned several nice spots on the GPS to tie up to for the night. For holiday time the river was relatively quiet. An occasional ski boat or jet ski came past at speed, but other than that everything else was moving pretty much at their pace or slower.

The first mooring was taken; three houseboats had rafted up to form a floating mansion. Kids were happily jumping and playing in the water while their parents sat together enjoying drinks on the back deck of the last houseboat.

The second mooring was free. Thomas was delighted; he was done with driving and skippering for the day. Utilising his experience, he skilfully manoeuvred the boat to a point directly over the buoy and was able to tie off in a flash.

He could now relax. The heatwave that had hit them in Maryborough had not moved, making the outside air both hot and dry. His plan, cool off in the river, then either chill out on the back deck or retreat to the air-conditioned comfort of the lounge.

Once the sting was out of the sun, he could teach Jayde how to paddleboard and then take advantage of the spa on the back deck. Peeling back the cover he was thankful the water wasn't blisteringly hot. To his delight, it was warm at best.

All over Thomas's plan, Jayde was stripping off to get into her bikini when he walked into the master stateroom. The sight of her naked stopped him in his tracks. He had seen her before but not like this. Her silhouette against the sheer curtains was something to behold and he took the time to appreciate every aspect of it.

Her body had changed since they had met. She had dropped a size or two and was now beginning to look strong and toned. There was eye-catching definition in her arms and legs, and a distinct flattening of her tummy. She was smoking hot.

Startled, Jayde spun around. She could see from the look on his face that he had been checking her out. The quiet timid little girl from the tough suburb was now developing into a strong confident woman. Comfortable in her body, she knew who she was and what she wanted. At this moment that was Thomas. The water could wait; she had other business to attend to.

*   *   *

With his recent liquidity, Steve indulged, generously giving himself the morning off. Sitting peacefully under an umbrella with fresh barista coffee and his favoured poached eggs and smoked salmon, he had time to quietly reflect on the events of the past forty-eight hours.

Slicing the yoke, feeling like a surgeon making the first incision, Steve savoured the orange flood. Sprinkling pepper, his mouth was primed to tuck into the first tantalising bite.

As the fork was about to transport the first serving to his mouth, his phone uncomfortably buzzed to life. It was Dave, his new business partner. He considered letting it go, but dodging calls this early in their arrangement would not set a good precedent.

Reluctantly, he brought it up to his ear. To his relief, Dave was short and to the point. 'I want a special function added to our program that only I can access. I want to go fully digital; no more bookies' board, your program and my formulation will combine, my odds will shift automatically. I also want a Dave McPharland app where punters can view these odds. I'll give you my odds formulation and data. I want it ready for Frankston.'

Without any option to refuse, Steve agreed. His relaxing breakfast and morning off were destroyed. The eggs and coffee were no longer at peak temperature. The best he could do was to shovel and gulp them down and get back to work. His business partner, like his family and the VPAL, now owned a good portion of his time.

*   *   *

Victoria flew back into Sydney, still basking in the glory of her win. Several women's magazines approached her agent looking to secure a profile story. The standard media bidding war followed until there was an eventual winner.

Not having a strong enough profile to warrant the full cover story, she was assigned a title lead, occupying the bottom left corner cover. A stylish, sexualised picture was included. Between her recent undies campaign and this magazine article her profile was growing exponentially. Regularly papped, photos of her at events, in the street, or shopping, were fast becoming regular features in the Sunday social pages.

Her agent constantly reviewed invitations for all manner of social and charity events. It was Bethany's job to select which were in Victoria's best interest, and make sure the right photographers were informed to exploit the opportunity. Victoria had quickly risen through the Infinity.PR ranks to become one of their top ten clients.

*   *   *

Boomer and Ken pulled back into Sydney sore from two long days in the saddle. As they approached the merge between the M5 and M7, they broke their side-by-side formation.

Veering left, Boomer acknowledged Ken with a slow nod and with that they went their separate ways. Boomer's kick stand would hit the concrete in about ten minutes. Ken on the other hand had more than an hour to go before he could call it a day.

Bert parked his bike and headed straight for the fridge. His taste for the refreshing pleasure of a cold beer on a hot day returned with a vengeance. Grabbing a long neck, or in his vernacular, a *king brown*, he headed for the kitchen table. Hobblers Ride had begun its path to fruition. Before he knew it, there were pages of notes and diagrams, along with three dead browns just out of arms reach.

His next step was to convene a meeting with the Vets executive and travel committee. The proposed tour needed ratification. Coming from the Pres, this shouldn't pose a problem. The only sticking point, the accommodation arrangements once they reached Stawell.

A key feature of club rides was being together on the road and then meeting up for a drink at night. Each was as important as the other. But Hobblers Ride wasn't going to be a typical club ride; necessity dictated things would need to be different.

Once he had what he needed on paper, he sent the text, *meeting at the clubhouse: Wednesday night. Agenda – proposed easter ride. All to attend.* Within minutes all confirmed.

* * *

Bert followed his usual path through the hospital, knowing intuitively where to turn left and right. Coming through the doorway he was pleased to see Jack out of bed, perched in a chair by the window. Despite his valiant effort, recovery was slow.

Bert strolled into the room, exercise book tightly rolled in his right hand. Before his presentation tomorrow night, he wanted to review every element to ensure there were no mistakes. He tossed the book into Jack's lap. 'Let's go through this,' he said before turning to grab another chair.

Jack opened the book. Flicking through the pages he was speechless. This was beyond impressive. Bert's appreciation for the finer details of the plan combined with over thirty years in logistics made his presentation a work of art. 'Boomer, this is incredible!'

After gaining Jack's approval, Bert knew that tomorrow night phase one of Jack's plan would be complete. Phase two: access cash.

CHAPTER 23

Dene

Jayde stepped off the houseboat with renewed vigour. She was feeling great. Four days on the water went way too fast, but they had the desired effect. Getting away from the stress and focus of running allowed Jayde and Thomas to enjoy the moment and each other. Mornings were spent putting to a new location, afternoons were enjoyed basking in the sun and water.

The stifling heatwave had finally moved on, leaving pleasant dry summer temperatures. She mastered paddleboarding, using it as her training each day, her arms and core had a good workout while her tired legs had some welcome relief.

These four days had affirmed what Thomas had felt for a while; this girl was special. Even though she was young it was hard for him to see a future that didn't have her in it. Not wanting to frighten her, he kept this to himself. Anyway, she had other far more important things occupying her mind.

Anne was happy to see her boat back in one piece. She didn't usually hire boats out to young people, especially one of this luxury. Several expensive and time-consuming experiences in the past made her very cautious of this demographic.

Only after Brad agreed to a five thousand dollar bond did she confirm the booking. Thomas, aware of his father's commitment, ensured the boat was spotless before pulling into the dock. Anne went from bow to stern looking for any evidence of damage. To her disappointment, the boat was the same as when it had left the dock. The extra five grand would have really helped after her other three rented boats returned yesterday with a significant clean-up bill.

Families were her bread and butter, but they weren't without risk. Unsupervised children can be unbelievably destructive. The carpet cleaning bill would be barely covered by their bond. From their flippant attitude on the dock, Anne could foresee this matter was going to end up with the sheriff or in the small claims court.

Back on dry land, Jayde's thoughts quickly returned to running. Deniliquin was only an hour or so up the road, Mathoura about halfway there had what she needed. A nice big sports ground on the edge of town. She had to get running again.

Four days off freshened her legs, and now she needed fatigue.

Jayde was tired but relieved when she returned to Thomas. He was enjoying the cool comfort of a large Coolabah tree. Red in the face and dripping with sweat, she could feel the cool water flow from her mouth down into her stomach. Mission accomplished; workable fatigue had returned.

Their first night in Deniliquin was strangely uncomfortable. The bed was a double at best and after the king on the houseboat it felt like an infant's cot. Throughout the night the young couple's elbows and knees were bashing and bumping into each other.

Thomas was relieved to hear Jayde's alarm. She would leave, giving him the full bed for at least an hour. With no park or quiet estate nearby her routine followed the precedent set back in Tenterfield. Squats, stationary sprints, and lunges should do the trick. The concrete floor absorbed most of the noise. What was left didn't bother Thomas. After last night he could sleep through a cyclone.

Using the comfort of the hotel room to check in, the letter icon within the app flashed, alerting her to a new message. Quickly casting her eyes over the document her heart skipped a beat, her handicap was being placed under review.

Startled she woke Thomas, his eyes darted from side to side as he moved down the page. The more he read, the higher her anxiety climbed. Replaying each race, apart from the false start she had run to Poppy's plan. *A review of my handicap, how could this happen?*

Thomas lowered the phone. His heavy concerted look had vanished, replaced with a happier expression. 'You skim read this, didn't you? It's your handicap review before being upgraded to a registered athlete. It's what you've been waiting for.'

Jayde's anxiety settled. She only had Yarrawonga and then Temora before she would be upgraded to a categorised runner.

* * *

The Dene Dash was like Tenterfield, run and done in a day. Jayde mowed through the heats with relative ease, her times comfortably within Jack's tight range. Thomas again found himself in the comfort of a large Coolabah tree.

With a dry breeze blowing and their hotel within walking distance, Thomas decided a mid-afternoon beer would be the perfect antidote to quench his dry palette. Jayde laughed. 'Beer so early. Looks like you're getting used to country racing.'

He just raised his beer and nodded, country style.

Jayde's performance in the semis was bang on, fifth place, right on Jack's time. Expecting to be done for the day she prepared to leave the track. Before she reached the gate, her phone pinged.

As first reserve, she got a call up. There was a withdrawal; ratified hamstring complaint. Thomas had the time to sit back and enjoy another cold beer.

Confident in what was required, Jayde didn't need to call Jack for advice. She did anyway, just to hear his voice.

The final was nowhere near as flamboyant as Surfside. The master of ceremonies did his best to pump everyone up for one last race. Dry dusty wind and repeated races took the edge off the crowd and the finalists.

Yesterday's heavy track session was playing havoc with Jayde's legs. She was struggling to get them moving effectively. It was quite possible this the race may be her slowest run of the day. Thankfully, the Stewards appreciated the affect a full day's racing has on performance. Consequently, they were leaner in their assessment as the shadows grew longer.

The race itself was rather uneventful. Jayde followed her start procedure to a tee. Midfield out of the blocks she maintained this position to the hundred metre mark. The back markers disadvantage was now negated, they blew past her and, struggling to maintain form, she crossed the line over a metre behind in equal last.

All things considered her time was ok, only marginally outside that set in the semi-final. Leaving the track, she was confident Jack's plan was exactly where it needed to be.

* * *

Jayde and Thomas spent their last night on holidays enjoying a Thai dinner at the pub a few blocks away from their hotel. Both were sad to see their time together end, but they were ready to go home, Thomas to continue his traineeship and Jayde to see her parents and Jack. This was the longest she had ever been away from her family, and she was beginning to feel homesick. Most of all she really needed a Poppy huggle.

CHAPTER 24

Manipulation

As Jayde and Thomas were driving back into Sydney, Victoria was once again at the airport preparing to fly, her destination, Hobart. Moving through the airport, she noticed considerably more mobile phones pointed in her direction. Flattered, she took her time moving from check-in to the security gate.

Heading towards the zone that differentiates passengers from the public, she gave her phone a cursory glance. Pre-occupied by her magazine shoot prior to arriving at the airport, she forgot to remove the silent setting. Bethany was desperate to make contact. A salvo of missed calls and a text did their best to get her attention, *Gregore sacked, inappropriate pictures of you on his phone. Call me NOW for details.*

The images were discovered after a complaint was made to the Institute from a South Australian sports masseuse. He cited concerns about potential mobile phone camera usage during a routine massage. Gregore's phone was seized and investigated.

A recent messy, historical claim that played out heavily in the court of public opinion made the Institute cautious and proactive when it came to athlete welfare. They would not be caught like that again. The evidence was clear and compelling. Thankfully, the images had not been shared. With the phone in their custody, the Institute had confidence these images would never get into the public domain.

Answering her phone, Bethany's instructions were clear. 'Don't go through security, press crews are on their way. We don't care if you knew or not, play innocent, your key word *violated*. Emphatically state you were completely unaware of the images. This will be great for your profile.'

Following Bethany's instructions, she left the line and headed straight for the women's toilet. Time to check her look and practise her serious, distressed face. Making faces into the mirror reminded her of Mrs Jacobson's year nine drama class.

Satisfied she had nailed the look, Victoria took a moment to check her voicemail. Waiting to be accessed were several messages from Megan O'Donoghue, Director of the Institute of Sport. The last in this series was delivered in a far more serious tone. Apart from a tacit apology there was a warning; the story had leaked. As part of her damage control protocol, Megan left her private number and an open invitation to call at any time should she need support.

Again, the leak could be traced to a Sydney-based PR firm.

Within minutes, the first media crew arrived, and for the next half an hour Victoria put on the performance of her life. She kept to script, denying any knowledge of the pictures, despite knowing full well Gregore had taken them. Although it was technically true that she didn't consent, she didn't complain when she heard the distinctive photograph sound. Victoria knew these images would make him work harder for her, and she was ok with that.

Sitting at the pointy end of the plane, Victoria had about two hours reprieve from the media or any unwanted prying eyes. The flight crew were well trained in how to deal with celebrities and gave her the space she needed. They had their own stories about unsolicited attention; too many had been up skirted, making shapewear a standard piece of flight apparel.

With her welcome space she was able to text Bethany, whose return message read; *perfect, keep it up*! She also took the time to send a text to Megan acknowledging her message and the Institute's offer of support.

Considerate of the politics surrounding this situation, Megan replied, *Victoria, Thank you for your reply. The Institute reiterates its position of support for you. As a high-performance team we are committed to working collaboratively to resolve this matter and return your focus to being Australia's premier female sprinter.*

The word *collaboratively* handed her the ability to give back to an old friend.

Matt Bellamey was still coaching, and she had always worked well with him. This was the opportunity he needed to take the next step. He had gained his level two coaching certification and was in the process of upgrading to level three. The text was simple but effective; *Gregore has been sacked, would you be interested in his job?*

Before the plane landed, the Institute issued their own press release. Stating; *A sprint coach has been immediately dismissed for possessing inappropriate images of an athlete on his mobile phone. A thorough forensic investigation has given us confidence the images were not shared and subsequently were not in the public domain. The athlete in question has been offered support and the Institute will work closely with them to resolve this issue.*

Although no names were used, it was widely known which athlete and coach this press release was based upon.

Before walking up the skyway, Victoria took the time to again check her look and practise her sombre face. Like in Sydney, it mirrored the emotion Bethany wanted her to convey.

As she reached the top of the elevated ramp, the familiar message ping rang loud from her phone. It was Matt; *let's get the band back together.*

Local media gleefully picked up the reporting. A scandalous event with national interest, this was the story many junior reporters were hoping for, one that could showcase their talent and get them off the island and into a bigger newsroom. They tailed Victoria from the airport to her hotel and then onto the track, each trying their hardest to get more tantalising details about the pictures. To Bethany's delight, she stuck to the PR script. Her social media accounts were loaded, full of messages of sympathy and support.

In an instant she was a high-profile voice for the murky world of digital images and consent. Bethany was overwhelmed with calls and inquiries from all manner of media organisations requesting cover stories and feature pieces. Brand Victoria was now embedded in the vernacular of the nation.

Reacting quickly to this shift in focus, Bethany sent a message; *Don't play the victim anymore, that side of the story has been exhausted. If you want continued attention embrace being the advocate for changing consent laws and the use of digital images. Call me for content and key words.* Using her talking points, Victoria was able to say all the correct things in front of the camera. However, she knew the truth and it was far from what she was portraying.

In spite of opportunistic distractions, Victoria was able to shift her attention back to the track. Her final provided huge media coverage, and her first win of the series only added to the story, now lauded as a shining example of youth resilience.

The Hobart leg of the Track Classic series had never received so much attention. Secretly, the sponsors and organising committee loved it; their event held the highest ratings and widest media reach for the Track Classic series so far.

* * *

Back at her hotel and away from the media, Victoria demanded Matt be appointed as her coach. With no room to negotiate, Megan was amenable, her focal point was to placate her star athlete. Come Monday, a media release would announce Matt as her new coach, embracing the strength of their previous bond, heralding a new beginning and future success for both athlete and coach.

The media went through its typical cycle. Throughout Friday and into Saturday, Victoria held their attention. Come Sunday her story was taking the odour of yesterday's news. It wasn't until Monday's media release that the story grew legs again.

Victoria was the talk of the town. Everybody had an opinion and for the better part it was all on her side. Jayde sat by Jack watching the television when her vexatious story flashed before their eyes. Begrudgingly, Jayde sat through the torture of Victoria presenting herself as the victim.

Jack could feel the temperature within the room rise the further interview went. When Victoria said that she would become the advocate for respectful use of technology, Jayde nearly exploded. Looking across at Jack, there was nothing but rage in her eyes, 'What a fucking hypocrite, after all the shit that bitch put me through. How dare she claim to be little miss innocent.'

Jack sat there stunned, but also impressed. Not only did she know what a hypocrite was, but her passion to defeat Victoria hadn't dwindled. Looking directly at Jack, her expression shifted from pure rage to a steely determined gaze. 'You know what Poppy, when your plan works and I win, I'm going to show everybody just who the real Victoria is.'

As the bells rang, heralding the end of visiting hours, Jack handed Jayde her training plan for the coming week. Yarrawonga was two weeks away and The Gift just over twelve. It was time for her to go back to heavy hard base work.

Three months would give her time to add some strength and then sharpen up. So, it would be back to the Bradfield Sports Ground morning and night for a lot of pain. Seeing how Jayde reacted to the television, Jack knew she was up for the challenge.

CHAPTER 25

Gateway

Three days prior to Yarrawonga, Jayde finished work early to meet her driving instructor in the carpark. Typically, Angela would be calming nerves and pumping up confidence. However, this wasn't needed, her student knew she was ready.

'Next time I see you, you'll have your Ps.'

With a hint of arrogance, Jayde replied, 'Yep'.

Three quarters of an hour later, Jayde was trying her hardest to hide her smile for the expressionless licence photo.

* * *

Yarrawonga was a solid eight hours driving, nine or more when rest stops are included. Now legally allowed to drive, Jayde was happy she could finally offer her friends a break from the road.

As they approached the border, Jayde gave Jack's instructions for them at the track. 'Your job is to progressively drop cash on me, five for the win and ten for a place. Between the two of you get to every bookie and not at once, spread it out over the day. I'll give you the cash when we stop.'

Not completely sure of what she said, they both nodded in curious agreement.

* * *

Dave McPharland was also on his way to Yarrawonga. This event was important to the bookie community; it heralded the push towards The Gift at Easter. There was good money to be made as it attracted most of the top line runners. Entries for The Gift always opened the week prior, so runners used this as their benchmark for the important second half to the season.

Officially it was known as the 'Yarrawonga Gift', but to those in the game it was the 'Gateway Gift'. Not because the town was situated next to one of the few bridges dividing Victoria from New South Wales, but because winners of this event often went on to win The Gift. Winning Yarrawonga opened the gate for the greatest glory at the end of the season.

Traditionally The Gateway was good for his bag – big crowds with plenty of punters willing to speculate on mug runners they knew nothing about. For Dave, this was the start of a three-month odyssey which would see him travel to almost every corner of the state.

Between the mid-week country racing and the VPAL events on the weekends he would be lucky to spend more than two consecutive nights in his own bed. This was his season. Although his investments provided a solid income, these twelve weeks were pure profit, his play money and holiday fund all in one. Like many Victorians, Dave migrated north for the deepest month of winter and his philosophy was simple. More money; more fun.

Sitting behind the wheel of his Mercedes he was excited. He lived for the madness of the Bull Pen, sprucing punters, calling out odds, exchanging cash for betting tickets, riding the excitement of each race. He couldn't wait, this was his world, and he loved it.

He was also excited about his special feature hidden deep within ProRun. His business partner had delivered; Frankston had been a roaring success. His odds shifting automatically with the ebb and flow of the event, reacting in the blink of an eye to athletes as they progressed through the rounds.

This sneaky, hidden algorithm also contained an exposure function, adjusting the odds relative to money being held. Too much money held at long odds can be very dangerous, and events like a Gift can prove troublesome to effectively monitor. Throughout his apprenticeship, his dad reminded him incessantly about the importance of exposure, especially after he was taken to the cleaners in 66.

Dave had another reason to be excited for Yarrawonga; this would be the first event live-streamed to his own YouTube channel. He had sent out push notifications to all his clients about the coverage and was now anticipating an upsurge in online bets through his app. Leveraging Steve, he brokered a sweet deal for the online rights to cover the event.

In return, he would pay a modest upfront fee as well as a percentage of any advertising royalties. His only other expense, a simple crew and commentator. He held high hopes this new venture would entice many of his thoroughbred clients over to pro-running. A diversified client base would be another selling point should he decide to get out of racing altogether.

* * *

All three generations of the Patersons arrived in town early and were going through the pre-race audit. While Steve was completing the grounds inspection, Bill took the time to review the start list. Scrolling through the pages of entrants, one name immediately stood out, Jayde Hardy – St Marys.

Why his finger stopped on her name still perplexed him, but he was in no doubt, something about her made him uneasy. He remained convinced there was more to this girl than met the eye.

With a proportionally higher grade of competition, Steve was interested in seeing how the female athletes would perform as the standard grew throughout the day. Technically, the handicap system should have provided an even competition, but during the later parts of the pre-competition audit Adam discovered there was an anomaly between the men's and women's handicaps.

There was a small but notable discrepancy in the time and mark scale. As he highlighted the handicap marks for both twelve and thirteen seconds, it was evident that a calculated error had been carried through the women's scale.

Picking up the two printed scales, Adam went to find his father. 'Dad, you need to see this.' Looking at the highlighted marks on both pages, Steve could see that the female athletes were at a two-mark disadvantage.

Looking at the date mark in the bottom right corner, Steve traced this document back to the days when Grandad Reg introduced female events into VPAL fixtures. Unfortunately, Reg was no longer around to clarify how this error came to be. Steve's only trusted link back to this time was his dad.

Scanning the track, he saw Bill standing alone, eyes fixed on what looked like the start list. Walking over, he thought carefully about how to approach this conversation. Although he knew what he had to do, discovering why this anomaly existed would help him develop an appropriate solution. With his right index finger stuck on the name J. Hardy, St Marys, Bill barely noticed Steve was standing next to him.

Finally catching his attention, Steve forgot about any graces and went straight for the answer he needed. 'Bill, Adam did a quick audit of the handicaps and discovered a problem. The male and female handicaps are not the same. You were there when Grandad formulated them, did he give you any idea why he did this?'

Catching him in a rare thoughtful moment, Steve willingly got the answer he needed from Bill. 'Reg was a staunch traditionalist and never wanted women racing. So, there was no way he would allow the fastest time of the day to be held by a female. His solution was simple, diddle the handicap system to prevent this from ever happening. He figured there would never be any direct comparison between the male and female handicap scales. Apart from a few members of the select committee, no-one ever knew this fix existed.'

Knowing his grandfather well, Steve assumed this piece of late twentieth century male chauvinism was at the heart of this swindle, but hearing it roll so effortlessly from his dad's mouth made it just that bit more abhorrent.

Recognising the potential for brand damage, Steve quickly called together a private sub-committee to deal with this issue. They would convene in his suite prior to dinner. As CEO he would head this investigation, along with Neil Barker the new handicapper and Tim Brown the handicapper's assistant, two men Steve knew he could trust.

The AI function in ProRun predicted that all female athletes would be eliminated in the round of thirty-two. Not wanting to be drawn into an unfair event process, it was determined all female runners would be granted a quarter meter lift.

The computer modelling suggested this should have been half a metre, but an alteration like this would raise too many questions and, in any event, he was a Paterson, and he had Reg's DNA running through his veins.

The new marks would be posted to all registered female athletes via ProRun, with the following message: *Mid-season review, quarter metre lift*. Appropriate minutes were compiled, signed, and countersigned before being logged into the VPAL system.

As for the athletes, the assumption was simple; they only complain when their mark is pulled. Steve was supremely confident there would be no questions or complaints.

Jayde was now running off five and one-half metres. The effect on her time would be small and didn't require any significant changes to Jack's plan.

Georgia struggled to contain her excitement; Nick was making the drive south-east to join them. Since their meeting in Gilgandra, barely a day went by without them catching up online.

Petra felt comfortable with the group expanding to four. An even two-two split meant she would not feel like the spare wheel. A relaxing bistro meal full of chat continued back at the guest lounge of their motel.

Conscious she was racing the next day, Jayde excused herself early. Not long after Petra did the same. Finally, Georgia and Nick had some private time. They sat in the lounge chatting till the early hours of the morning. Realising the time, they headed back to their rooms. Holding hands, Georgia froze in front of his door. Taking a deep considerate breath, she said, 'do you want me to stay?'

'Yes.'

Closing the door behind her, Georgia began to unbutton her dress, and lust claimed sovereignty over her moral compass.

* * *

As always, Jayde's alarm pierced the early morning silence. The room was still dark and beyond the curtains the sun was yet to reach the horizon. Stretching her arms and rubbing her eyes, she noticed one of the beds was noticeably flat. Petra mumbled something when the alarm rang so she knew who was missing. Smiling, she knew where Georgia was.

As Jayde was quietly escaping her room, she heard a door quietly close nearby. Startled, she froze for a second. It was vital that no-one saw her, especially in her training gear. If she was seen, serious questions would be asked that had the potential to derail everything.

Thankfully, it was Georgia trying to get back to their room. Equally shocked to see Jayde, she also froze. Both girls needed their little secrets to remain exactly that, a secret.

There was a silent acknowledgement of each other as they passed. Jayde headed towards the street, to a new estate under construction not far up the road that was quiet and secluded. Precisely what she needed.

Georgia snuck into her bed and tried to catch a few hours' sleep. At Nick's door she had felt assured, but now she was overcome with guilt. Years of conditioning by her family and her school had just been abandoned. It was a decision that could never be reversed. There was way too much noise in her head. Sleep would have to wait.

Petra was still sleeping as Jayde returned from her pre-dawn race day ritual. Georgia raised her head; it was clear she had been crying. Fearing something sinister had happened, Jayde rushed to her side. Quietly, she allowed Georgia to explain what led her to be in Nick's room.

Whispering, Georgia said, 'I don't know what came over me, but I couldn't walk away. It just seemed right.'

Jayde took a deep relieving breath; it had been her choice. Intuitively, she appreciated the origin of these tears. At MAGS, sex education was presented from an abstinence perspective. It was real fire and brimstone stuff, everything from the dangers of disease and pregnancy to the teachings within the bible.

Fear and anxiety were their biggest weapons. Jayde could only imagine what it was like for Georgia, indoctrinated with this all the way from kindergarten. She could feel the guilt pouring out in the stain of tears forming on her shoulder. Cradling her friend, Jayde sat there in silence, letting her cry.

*　*　*

Petra begun to stir as Jayde made her final preparations to leave for the track. Now licenced, she could use Georgia's car. Early rounds, especially with popular events like the Gateway, were laborious, a repetitive series of races with one intent; eliminate the weakest.

Confident she would be there later in the day, Jayde told the girls to stay away till late morning. Jack's instructions were clear; no bets before the third round. Money on a roughie too early can also raise suspicions.

As Petra stretched her arms out from under the covers, Georgia made a quick dash for the bathroom; she didn't need her to see her like this. The last thing she needed right now was Petra's moral sanctimony, force-feeding her more guilt.

189

Nick and the girls arrived a few heats before Jayde's second round, each with their own variant of hot happiness in their hands. The trio staked their place under a tree not far from the finish line.

As Jayde was rolling out of her second run-through, she noticed that crazy old magpie from Tenterfield following her every move. Rather than feeling intimidated, she felt reassured; he still hadn't made the connection. Judging by his dumbfounded expression, she was confident he never would. Anyway, if he got too close, she could always make a complaint.

Her second-round race went to plan. She placed third, stopping the clock at the higher end of the range set by Jack, fast enough to keep her racing. With her job done, her mind moved away from the track; she needed to check on Georgia.

It seemed a ham and cheese crepe and a double shot flat white settled Georgia's emotions. She was coming to terms with her decision, but still didn't quite know how to react around Nick. Speaking quietly to Jayde, she asked, 'You've been through this, what do I do now?

Without hesitation, Jayde replied, 'Things haven't changed, you two have been inseparable since the day you met in Gilgandra. If anything you've become closer.'

Reassured by her friend's words, Georgia gave Jayde a big hug. Before they broke, Jayde had one last question, 'You were safe?'

Nodding her head, she whispered, 'He used protection'.

*　*　*

Immediately following Jayde's race, Bill attempted to file an under-performance motion against Jayde. His contention: she chopped her stride from the eighty-metre mark. He knew for the process to proceed it had to be supported by at least one other track marshal.

Using all his cunning, he lent on his grandson. Leveraging the family connection along with his grandson's inexperience, Bill had the support he required. His next step, inform Harry Wallace the Chief-Steward and Neil Barker the VPAL Handicapper. These two men were then required to undertake an independent review of Jayde's performance.

Thankfully for Jayde, the racing violation process had been amended and now required video assessment prior to any athlete being informed of an under-performance violation. This protocol was introduced by Bill almost a decade ago to protect VPAL from frivolous or vexatious claims.

Steve walked into the Stewards' room as the video was being replayed for the second time. The first run-through was embarrassing for Bill; there was no evidence of her stride changing. Steve leant in and took time to watch another replay, immediately concurring with Harry and Neil that there was no conclusive evidence of her stride altering. Bill's motion was dismissed, and Jayde would remain racing off her allocated mark.

Pissed off beyond belief, Steve fought to hold his words. A person in his position could not be seen or heard verbally abusing his own officials, even if they were family. This would have to wait for a private moment tonight. Bill knew what was coming, but Adam really was none the wiser. For now, he said, 'We have an event to run, both of you back to your posts'. Steve needed them out of his sight.

Once the room was clear, he grabbed his laptop and moved behind the bar. He needed to find a quiet space to check how ProRun was performing. In the fortnight or so after Maryborough, he had signed up nearly all the on-track bookies, and several who would only appear at the three category one events.

Sales had outperformed his most ambitious predictions. ProRun was making him money, money that he had to share with Dave. He knew Dave had stung him on his price, and he didn't like it.

ProRun was faultless in its delivery. It was by far the most complete package ever developed for this style of event. Organisers loved it because it took care of all their race day logistics. Runners were equally impressed with the quick reliable information sent to their phone while the bookies appreciated the combination of live and historic data.

Dave was cashing in on his odds feed. New odds were flashing up on his screens instantly after the completion of each round. Dave's bag and online service was seeing more attention than ever.

Checking he was alone, Steve opened his section of ProRun after two rounds data was showing lanes four, five and seven were all running at a three-point advantage. It was time for him to ensure at least one female qualified for the final. Computer analysis may have predicted an all-male final, but it didn't account for his sneaky algorithm.

Chloe Spinner was the highest profile female athlete and was immediately added as Steve's number one runner. Still pissed off at Bill, Jayde was added as his back-up.

* * *

Back on the track, the running was intensifying. The anticipated round of thirty-two – four heats with eight runners. The top two in each race automatically booked their place in the final. The remaining two places would come from a repo charge round. All fourth and fifth placed runners had the opportunity to race off and gain their place in the final.

Drawn in lane five, Jayde's run was exceptional, 12.66sec a new season record. Passing through the gates in fifth place gave her another race to run.

To everyone's surprise, Chloe Spinner ran a blistering 12.42sec, placing second and, most importantly for the VPAL, automatically qualifying for the final. Steve checked the results and was quite chuffed with himself; *This proves beyond doubt; the Patersons can have control over the outcome of any VPAL race.*

Jayde was both excited and apprehensive to call Poppy with the news. 'I came fifth in the semis, fastest time this year, 12.66, but I get to run again in something called a repo charge round. What's that?'

His plan was for Jayde to get to the semis but not any further. Jayde had never heard of repo charge rounds and with all the other planning in his head he had overlooked telling her anything about them.

Remembering this was the race for the quickest losers, Jack quickly ran the scenario and all the permutations he could think of through his mind. Nothing came back that was alarming. In fact, if anything, it worked well for Jayde. 'Repo charge is the chance for the fastest losers to get into the final. This is good, it helps our plan.'

* * *

With her bookie duties complete, Petra volunteered to facetime the race. Jack was happy with Jayde's form, style and pace. Making this round would give her more top-line racing. Knowing it would take a mid to high 12.4 time to gain entry in the final he was confident that this would be her last race at Yarrawonga.

Racing this late in the day would put her name at the periphery for bookies and punters, exactly where he wanted it to be. Her odds would remain long, but she wouldn't be a stranger. Knowing a 12.6 would put her at the back of the pack, he gave her permission to push a little harder, a high 12.5 was the target.

Jayde was settled as she knelt to push her feet back into her blocks. She was going to enjoy this race. Even though she was being moulded into a Pro-runner her origins were always back with match racing. Having regained control of her emotions, Georgia was back in Nick's arms. Petra was distracted with her new cinematographic role; everyone had their place and was happy.

The starter ordered the runners to 'dig in,' and soon after, Jayde was up and running. This was by far the fastest race she had ever competed in. As Jack predicted, the winner broke the tape in 12.44 seconds. Jayde was at least three-quarters of a metre behind in 12.58 seconds. Her racing was now over, this was her most successful failure.

Damien Olgonovski, a seasoned runner from Geelong, took out the final in just under 12.4 seconds. Chloe Spinner passed through the gates just under half a metre behind Damien as the AI model had predicted.

* * *

As promised, Steve caught Bill and Adam before they could escape to the safety of their rooms at the pub. His words were short and to the point. His eyes found Adam first, and in a low tone he said, 'You're forbidden from signing any official documents unless you get permission from me. Stand on the track and learn, that's all you need to do. Now piss off and stay out of my way tonight!'

With that, Adam willingly disappeared down the hall. He needed a cruiser or two to settle his nerves.

With an uneasy calm in his voice and demeanour, Steve turned to face his father. The shift in tone blindsided Bill. He was anticipating a barrage that could be measured on the Richter Scale. That's how he would have handled it. Shifting tack, Steve took the time to ask, 'What's making you so neurotic about this girl?'

Bill's expression changed, feeling he had finally been shown some respect. His usual arrogant scowl softened, leaving him the most vulnerable he had been since Emma walked away two decades ago. The only problem was, he couldn't pinpoint the root cause of his concern.

The frustration this was causing him was clear, and you didn't need a sphygmomanometer to see his rising blood pressure. His ears had moved from being their usual crimson red to almost purple, his lips began to quiver, and his hands had a noticeable shake. For the first time Steve saw his dad for what he was, an old man.

Steve had never seen Bill in such a state. After a deep breath or two, it was Bill who became the aggressor. He looked Steve directly in the eye. 'A lifetime in this game has taught me to trust my instinct and my instinct says there is something up with this girl.'

Steve took this as the chance to go on the attack himself. With a raised voice he put the conversation to rest. 'Once you get some evidence then we can do something, until then stay away from Jayde Hardy. Do us all a favour and stay in your lane. You're the old fart who reminds us of what has been, beyond that you have no power.'

Having no hard proof, Bill had to wear this. Before turning away Steve reminded Bill about their adversary on the VPAL board. 'If Stan gets wind of this, he and his cronies can push for a no-confidence motion in you and therefore me, forcing a vote which could push us out forever.'

Taking some long soothing breaths, Steve regained his composure and was ready to take his place at the post-event drinks downstairs. For the first time in living memory, Bill didn't feel like a drink. He turned the other way and went back to his room.

CHAPTER 26

Nothing to chance

Bert was having one of his regular logistics meetings with the clubs Road Captain Phil. Hobblers Ride had been sanctioned and a call went out to all members to see who would be interested. Bert saw no need to reveal the full intention of this trip. He knew when the time came, they would be there for their mate. For now, it was presented as a chance to support Jayde and ride some classic parts of the Victorian countryside.

As a matter of respect, Bert contacted Doug Wales, his counterpart in the Victorian Chapter. Doug had heard of Jack's plight through the grapevine and was saddened to think another of his comrades was on his way to the grave. Doug had met Jack at several Vet events and took a great liking to him. He and some other boys from Victoria wanted in on the ride.

Phil stared at the growing list in front of him. With the four from Victoria the numbers were beginning to swell to over forty. Sensing the need, Bert brought Phil up to speed about the true motivation for this ride. Phil felt honoured and privileged to be involved.

Jack had been an inspiration to him on his own journey away from alcohol. Up to his retirement Phil had been a career military man. He enlisted as regular infantry, his action, the Middle East. His final years were in supply, where he oversaw operations both locally and overseas.

With both men rooted in logistics, Jack couldn't have had two better qualified men on his side for this operation.

Recognising the enormity of the task ahead, both agreed they needed to develop a system that allowed them to control as many movements as possible while they were in town. There was no doubt in their minds that forty plus bikers would attract some attention.

Members were informed early that due to the popularity of the Grampians Gift their accommodation would be spread throughout the town and district. As each rider registered, Bert or Phil would quickly search availability online then reply with a nominated venue. They would then make their own booking either over the phone or online.

Bert or Phil would then wait for confirmation and add them to their list. Every hotel and motel in the region populated their spreadsheet; four cells below awaited names.

Word spread north to the Brisbane chapter. Several northern brothers sent a request south; *we want a spot on the ride*. Their plan, meet the main group at Yass, making it a road crew rapidly approaching fifty riders.

*   *   *

Bert handed Jack a printout of the rider list.

Looking at the number of rows, Jack noted, 'Fifty Harley's in two-by-two formation will attract unbelievable attention.'

Boomer in his settled deep tone reassured him. 'It's already sorted. Phil and I have it all under control.'

Implicitly trusting his best mate, he made a mental note; *ride logistics are covered, Boomer is all over it.*

The next order of business, cash. Jack needed cash. He had a few thousand in savings, but his plan required much more than this. His only assets were an old car and his prized Harley, but the right buyers could fetch him somewhere around ten grand each.

The car was easy, it could be sold tomorrow. Boomers' eldest son Wayne was a mechanic, and years ago he had made Jack promise that if he ever wanted to sell it, he would gleefully take it. Jack gave his price to Boomer, and it was done.

His bike on the other hand was his pride and joy and he wasn't prepared to just let it go. Ideally, he would have passed it on, but neither Gillian or Scott rode and there was no way he was letting Jayde anywhere near it.

As it was in good condition, he was confident he had enough time not to rush, and anyway he had a few options he wanted to chase before opening it up to strangers.

*　*　*

After nearly four months of being in the same room, Jack's body clock had adjusted to hospital life. His traditionally poor sleep pattern was made worse as he woke in preparation for the three and six am rounds.

His stomach would rumble at seven, twelve and five, followed by nausea at eight, one and six. This was one aspect of hospital life he couldn't get accustomed to, the food. It was always cold and it either clogged him up or drained him out. Jack joked with Boomer as lunch was being served, 'I would happily have army chow over this shit'.

Jack was a shadow of his former self. His pyjama pants were a comfortable fit when he fell, but now the elastic in the waistband was barely doing anything at all. Anxiety about exposing his damaged genitals was becoming an uncomfortable bed fellow.

Bert sensed the distress this was causing his best mate; his constant checking was verging on obsessive. Boomer read the situation well, grabbing new pyjamas and trackie-dacks two sizes down from Jack's usual size.

Always the joker, Boomer tossed Jack his new kit. 'You lose any more weight and I'm going to have to shop in the kids section.'

Appreciating the humour, Jack laughed, although it really wasn't a laughing matter.

Bert hated to see his best mate wither away before his eyes. Along with the clothing he brought Jack's favourite junk food, cheeseburgers and a coke. He figured a few cheesies would help to keep some meat on his bones, and neither the sugar nor the fat would do him any damage now. Apart from Boomer' s company, Jack really looked forward to his burgers and soft drink. Famished, he would almost inhale them.

* * *

Down at the reserve, Jayde was deep into another flog session when she had an idea to see what sort of time she could push out. Using a tape measure Thomas kept in his car, she did her best to measure fourteen and a half metres back from the hundred metre mark. Thomas used the stopwatch function on his phone and did his best to give start instructions from the finish line.

Jayde ran a blistering 12.38 seconds. Even with an accepted margin of error this was smoking fast. Jayde bounced her way through the rest of the session. She knew when fresh this would be even faster.

* * *

Jayde's buoyant mood continued as she strode down the corridor to Jack's room. She couldn't wait to tell him the time she had just run. The curtain was drawn, and she could hear the familiar voice of Dr Bradley.

Jayde stood quietly and listened. Cold shivers shot down her spine, the words were clear: significantly reduced lung function and anaemia.

After what felt like an eternity, the curtain was pulled back. Jayde had to quickly find the positive mood she was in when she entered the room. She had to keep the promise made many months ago; *no tears, no sorrow, there's not enough time to waste on that stuff.*

Startled, Dr Bradley gave a louder than usual, 'Hi Jayde, how long have you been there?'

Still composing herself, she mumbled, 'I just got here'.

Once the curtain was cleared, Jayde went straight to her Poppy and gave him a huggle. This had become soft and gentle; today her grip was measurably tighter.

When she finally let go, both tried to hide wiping tears from their eyes.

Lifting the mood, Jayde announced, 'I did a test run down at Bradfield today, and midway through the session I dropped 12.38.'

It had the desired effect. Jack's mood skyrocketed. 'A 12.38 off your 5 and a half mark, that's fantastic.' The Gift was only eight weeks away and there was still work to be done, but this reinforced she was on the right track.

Jack knew any time in the 12.3 range would traditionally get a place in the final. She needed to get this down to the mid to high 12.2's to guarantee victory. The hardest thing now would be to mask this speed.

In this sport you can't run dead. For the next hour he spoke to Jayde about some subtle changes to her training program. In the days leading into Temora and Ballarat, she would do some of the hardest, heaviest sessions of her life.

CHAPTER 27

The Golden Gift

The trip to Temora was pleasantly short compared to her recent races down south. Jayde was becoming all too familiar with the features and conveniences offered along Hume Highway. Her body had become accustomed to the regular stops for fuel and food.

She was beginning to get jittery twenty minutes out of Yass.

The Golden Gift was one of only a handful of category three events on the calendar. A small purse and competing against the newly manufactured category one, the *Yarra Dash* in Melbourne attracted a small insignificant field.

For Jayde, Temora was the ideal event. It was the last race she needed to qualify as a categorised athlete. Jack set out his usual careful schedule for her performance and was waiting with anticipation for the facetime call from Thomas to see her run.

Holding the lowest categorisation, VPAL gave Temora minimum priority. A single, low ranked official was sent as their delegate. Adam was not impressed with having to drive over six hours north. Steve saw this as his penance for his indiscretion in Yarrawonga.

Jayde breezed through the heats and semis with times in the mid-12.5 range. She was the fastest ranked female in the final, surprising given the intensity of her training session less than twenty-four hours ago. She was still within Poppy's time range, but only just.

There was only one other runner, a middle-aged man from Griffith, who was slightly faster. He was barely half a chest ahead of Jayde at the tape. Jack could tell from his stride and the strain in his neck that this guy was at his limit. Seizing the opportunity, he told her, 'I want a 12.5 flat for the final'.

The time was on the faster side of his master plan, but it should put her in the frame to win. With permission to open out a little more, Jayde was in complete control from the moment the starter's gun sent the finalists down the track. At the finish gates Jayde was a clear half-a-chest in front. She was never happier to be blessed with C cup boobs.

Thankfully, she watched with interest the end of the race process. Turning back towards the finish gates, the chief steward presented her with the winner's sash. In the past this would have been draped over her head, but now due to the hangover effect of Covid and the litigious risk of inappropriate touching, Jayde was left to crown herself.

Standing behind the large novelty cheque she posed for the obligatory photographs with the different dignitaries and sponsors. In her right hand, held in a vice-like grip, the actual winner's cheque, five thousand dollars, Jayde had never been so close to this much money in her life.

After collecting her blocks and bag, Jayde headed towards Thomas. It seemed everyone wanted to congratulate her. Overwhelmed, but gracious, she politely acknowledged each person for their praise. Her smile was like a child's at Christmas, pure and innocent. Thomas had never seen her smile like this before, and he hoped to see it again.

Jack already knew the result when Jayde finally called from the safety of Thomas's car. While at the track she was public property and there was no way she would make this call with so many people around. She was both anxious and excited at the same time.

Excited about the prizemoney, but anxious, she asked if this damaged her overall goal. Jack was quick to dispel her anxiety.

'The Golden Gift was always a small-town race, to the Magpies it will mean nothing. You needed a win to take the attention away from you at The Gift. No first-up winners have worn the Grampians sash. Relax my girl, it's all part of the plan.'

These were the words she needed to hear; now she could truly savour her first win.

* * *

The Yarra Dash was the newest of the category one events. It didn't have the history and prestige of The Gift or Goldfields but what it did have was an enticing bounty which lured athletes from all over the country.

Steve Paterson was in his element, his days crammed full of racing and media commitments. With Victoria in the field, it moved from a race to an event. Ticket sales climbed exponentially, more media applied for passes, and the host network for The Gift set aside an hour's programming on one of their minor channels.

Dave McPharland was incensed. Although he still held the rights to broadcast through his own online channel, his viewing and online takings would take a hit. At best, his online venture would barely break even this weekend.

Victoria was coming into the weekend full of confidence. Victory in a new meet record told her Matt was doing his job. With a little help from his algorithm, Steve would ensure the VPAL didn't miss out on their piece of the Victoria publicity pie. With her ever-growing profile, they could make this year's Gift the biggest in the event's history.

The media attention at the end of the final was off the charts. Her stunning win was the lead sports story on all free-to-air and subscription networks. Like Jayde in Temora, Victoria was presented with the winner's sash and offered to the crowd.

Rather than accept the sash following the new protocols, she dipped her head forcing Steve to awkwardly put it over her shoulder. Moving at just the right moment, she gave Steve a solid brush of her right breast. Stunned, Steve pulled back quickly. Victoria gave him a little wink before waving to the media and the crowd.

Victoria's photographs behind her novelty cheque were an array of pre-rehearsed moves and gestures. She spent weeks with her media team and in front of her mirror perfecting the look. The actual cheque was given to Steve to hold until her performance was over, after which it was thrown in her bag only to be found days later in an almost un-bankable state.

* * *

Jayde was sitting in the passenger seat of Thomas's car as they headed home along the Hume Highway when Victoria's victory interrupted her thoughts during the sports report on the radio. Up until now, Jayde had been contemplating what she could do with her winnings. Front of her brain, buy a car now she had her licence, a car made a lot of sense. She could forget about catching buses to visit Poppy or get to training.

Looking online while Thomas was driving, she saw that five grand didn't buy you much in the current second-hand market. Catching a glimpse of her phone Thomas could see she what she was doing. 'Hey if you're looking for a car, I might be able to find you a better deal.'

Her interest instantly prickled, she asked, 'How?'

Keeping his eyes firmly on the road he went on. 'You know the old lady next door, Mrs David, she failed her oldies' driver's test and had her licence taken away. She might do you a good deal. Her car is old, but it's been looked after. God knows she owes me something, I've mown her lawn for years for nothing.'

Jayde had seen the car many times, a little yellow Toyota Starlet parked under the carport. She could picture herself behind the wheel. Excited she leant across the console and gave him a quick kiss on the cheek.

Arriving home as the sun was setting, Jayde burst through the front door. Dropping her bags and blocks at the door she went looking for her mum and dad.

They were both out the back. Scott was up to his arms in grease and muck trying to get his car ready for rego. Gillian was inside the car pumping the brake pedal as Scott tried to bleed the line. Mumbling and swearing to himself in frustration, Scott missed Jayde coming out the back door and down the path to join them.

Popping his head inside the passenger window he looked at Gillian. 'I can't see it getting past rego, between the brakes and fuel injector issues, as well as two new front tyres, it won't pass. It needs to go to a mechanic! With the bills this month we can't afford it.'

Trying to get a gauge on how bad the situation was, Gillian asked how much the repairs would be. 'Probably two to three grand'.

In her own despondent tone, she gave her reluctant reply. 'I guess we'll have to dip into the house account again; we can't live without your car.' Once again, their dream of getting out of the rental trap was that much further away.

Jayde could hear the frustration and despair in her parents' voices. She heard this conversation too many times, wishing she could offer something to help. Today she did; help was in the small piece of paper in her right hand.

Breaking the awkward silence, she said, 'Take this,' offering her winner's cheque. Confused, Scott looked down at the piece of paper now in his hand. Gillian leant across the console to investigate what he was holding.

'How did you get this?'

Standing a little taller, Jayde replied, 'It's my winner's cheque from Temora'.

Scott knew bits and pieces about her running but had never really paid attention to the details.

'What, you won this by winning a running race?'

'Yes dad, the races I've been going to are for prize money. Take it please, I want you to have it.'

His voice abandoned him as he was overcome with emotion. He couldn't have been prouder of his daughter and her generosity; however, it was just another reminder that no matter how hard he tried he always came up short in providing for his family. His male pride took another big hit. Wiping tears from her eyes, Gillian rushed from the driver's seat to give her daughter a hug.

* * *

From her penthouse suite by the bay in Melbourne, Victoria prepared for her traditional post-event selfie. Her hair and make-up followed the tone set by her stylist. The spot was selected to take advantage of the Melbourne sunset and the reflective power of glass.

She dropped her robe, carefully placing the Yarra Dash and Surfside winners' sashes across each breast. After several different poses, she had the picture she wanted. There was just enough side boob showing to make it stylish without being overtly smutty, but if you looked carefully at the reflection on the glass balustrade there was a subtle view of her naked bottom. She knew this detail wouldn't be missed by her followers. Sending the picture to Sydney for approval, Bethany quickly gave the thumbs up emoji. This was a blitzkrieg image to be dropped at once on all her social media accounts.

The associated comment would vary depending on the platform. The more conservative sites were given a simple *two down one to go* tag, while on the wilder ones it was more like *what will the third sash cover.*

Within seconds her followers were posting comments. By the time Victoria returned to her room after the post-race function, she was pushing over a million views.

206

CHAPTER 28

The proposition

Jack was sitting up in bed chatting with Boomer about the next part of his plan. Final numbers were set; thirty-eight riders plus a few in cars in the main group and another bunch of ten leaving early on Good Friday.

Boomer and Phil carefully worked through how to manage so many riders. Once across the Murray they would progressively break into smaller groups, taking different routes to their accommodation. The thunder of one arriving would settle well before the next hit the outskirts of town. Club colours would be removed, replaced by day-to-day riding gear.

In another sign of solidarity, most of the travelling pack agreed to remove their biker plaits and beards. As a sign of respect to Hobbler, and the effects of his disease, each donated their locks to cancer patients. To anyone paying attention they would look like a bunch of blokes going through a loud and expensive mid-life crisis.

With travel sorted, Jack could focus on part two of his plan, redemption.

Boomer was holding the cash Wayne paid for the car. Jack insisted he pay cash; he needed the notes. His only other asset was close to sold. Before leaving, Marcus popped past for his usual quick chat. Holding a leather jacket and helmet in his arms, his quick visit turned into a sit down as they chatted about riding and the bikes they owned.

Jack discovered Marcus had a passion for the classics. His restored Triumph Truxton café racer was his pride a joy. Jack could see from the photos on his phone that Marcus would challenge him for a 'show and shine'. Not having a brag book on his new phone, Jack's only picture was on his home screen.

'What a beautiful ride. I've always wanted a thumper.'

'You could always buy mine; I won't be needing it.'

'Get me some more pics and I'll have a chat with the minister for finance.'

Accommodating the request, Boomer used the hidden spare key to grab a handful of photos. Even after standing for months it only took a quick wipe before it resumed Jack's famous sparkle.

* * *

Jayde was taking orders at the counter of the Grey Ghost when she received a ping on her phone. Quickly glancing at the screen, she could see it was from ProRun. *It must be my handicap.*

Pushing her phone deep into her pocket, she continued working. On her way out the door she remembered the ping. Opening ProRun, she saw there was the familiar number one over her message icon. Skim reading through the letter she finally came to what she needed; her mark was set at five and three-quarter metres.

Stepping into the obscurity of the footpath, she immediately rang Jack with the news. 'They've set it, five and three quarters.'

'Good news, that's where I thought it would land.' He was hoping for an even six metres, but this was workable. 'Now we know what we are working with, get down to Bradfield, there's still more work to do.'

* * *

Marcus sat down with Bert and Jack. 'I've got good and bad news. The good news, my wife agreed to buy the bike.' His offer of ten thousand five hundred was accepted without hesitation.

'The bad news, your lung function and VO2 stats have dropped again. You'll now need oxygen permanently.' As he fitted the nose piece he spoke to the nurse. 'I want a small oxygen tank and nose kit fitted to Mr Hill's wheelchair.'

Jack felt better once the oxygen was flowing. He was able to speak without losing his breath. Arrangements were made to pay and pick up the bike. As with the car, the money was to be paid in cash.

Using the cover of the bike pick-up, Marcus asked to speak to Bert in the corridor. Doing sums in his head, Jack was happy to let them go.

'I've got a proposal; one last road trip for Jack, down to Stawell for The Gift. Through my connections around the hospital we can access transport, and the support he needs. Coby, an ex-army nurse down in emergency, has volunteered to join us.'

Bert stood there trying hard to comprehend what Marcus proposed. He knew their connection was strong, but this was extraordinary.

Before he could ask why, Marcus continued. 'My father tried for years to get me to go with him to The Gift and for whatever reasons I never did. Since his passing I look back now and regret I missed that opportunity. Jack will not be here next year. I missed it with my dad, so I'd like to share it with Jack and his family.'

'It sounds fantastic, but it's not my decision to make.'

Checking the message that just buzzed on his phone, he said, 'I've got to go, can you talk with Jack?'

Sitting down in the visitor's chair, Boomer respected Marcus's request. 'The doc has offered to take you, Gill and Scott to see Jayde run in The Gift.'

Jack's reaction mirrored Bert's. He was stunned. His initial reaction was yes, how he would love to be there when she broke the tape. To share that moment, how could he say 'no'.

Then his scheming side kicked in. Would him being there be enough for Bill to finally make the link between himself and Jayde. He was in a conundrum; the emotional side was saying *yes*, and logical side was saying *no*. Looking back at Boomer, he said, 'mate give me a day or so, I'm going to need to think carefully about this'.

Knowing what was at play, Boomer acknowledged the request with a nod of his head.

Jack had no trouble lying awake throughout the night contemplating all the different implications of the problem. His dad's words rattled around his brain; *there is always a solution to any problem, you just needed to think hard enough to find it*. He must have flipped twenty times between yes and no before the solution finally came.

With a few more hours of deep thought, he had a workable plan that would allow him to see her run, while not give anything away until it was too late. The most critical element, Jayde; she must not know anything, her approach must not change.

* * *

Marcus quickly called past as he was conducting his early morning rounds. 'Bert spoke to you about my offer to head south for The Gift. What are you thinking, yes, or no?'

With a husky 'Yes' Jack gratefully accepted his offer before adding his own special conditions. Logically these didn't make sense. Marcus realised there was so much more to this for Jack than just seeing his grand-daughter run. Intrigued, he couldn't wait for Easter Monday.

CHAPTER 29

Goldfields

Jayde had one final event before her showdown at The Gift, the category one, Goldfields Gift, in Ballarat. This would be her only chance to race off her new mark before Grampians. She needed to recalibrate her feel for this distance. There was a danger that she could potentially run too fast too soon. Added to this was a shift in her training, her focus; speed, her power phase was over, it was now time to sharpen up. This shift would also change the feel she had for her allocated times.

Once again Thomas assumed his position at the finish line, phone ready in stopwatch mode. Jayde set in her blocks waiting for the crack of the toy cap gun in his other hand. Hearing the sharp crack, her drive leg pushed hard against her blocks. Her first fifteen metres was proof of all the hard power work she had put in over the past six months. Her shoulders rose and her stride opened.

Thomas stood at the finish line in total awe. Her action was both powerful and elegant. He could clearly see her leg and arm muscles working in unison to propel her down the track. Her trademark right hand flick had softened in its intensity and now almost flowed evenly with the rest of her body. Lost in this majesty, he almost forgot to press stop as she burst through the finish line.

Not having a large roll out area Jayde had to make a rather sharp left or right turn to avoid crashing through the picket fence.

This was good practice, the finish line at The Gift has the same problem. Struggling to catch her breath she made her way back to Thomas; his eyes were fixed on his phone.

Jayde popped her head over his shoulder to get a look at her time. Her high-pitched scream penetrated deep into his left ear. Startled he dropped the phone, Jayde scrambled to pick it up. She needed to see that time again, 12:21 seconds.

'Send it to Poppy, send it to Poppy!'

Rubbing his left ear, Thomas took his phone and grabbed a screen shot before sending it off to Jack. Within seconds, the facetime request burst to life on his phone. It was hard to tell who was more excited, Jack or Jayde. After a quick warm-down and stretch, Jayde left Bradfield Sports Ground brimming with confidence.

*　*　*

Victoria was also at the track preparing for her next race. On hand she had her coach, masseuse, dietician, physiotherapist, bio-mechanist, and sports psychologist. Apart from Matt her coach the rest were window dressing; they were superfluous to her needs on the track.

But having an entourage gave her status; it reinforced that she was the queen in waiting. After each rep or run through they would take turns pampering her ego. Matt knew he may set the agenda, but he was by no means in control.

As Jack predicted, Victoria didn't enter Goldfields. It was too close to the nationals, and she was desperate to hold the mantle of fastest woman in the country.

Scott Palmer contacted Matt, re-opening discussions about the US College scholarships. This time he didn't muck around with the usual pitch, he simply presented a time, '11.10 seconds and she's in.' This would set a new Australian record. Having a better understanding on how Victoria operated, Matt kept this to himself. He didn't want a repeat of the circus that occurred in Adelaide.

Functioning more like her PA he fielded a call from one of her desired shoe companies. They were interested in stitching up a deal prior to the National Championships. Frustrated by these distractions, he quickly referred it to her PR team.

Less than twenty-four hours later she was decked out head to toe in their apparel and was booked in for her first promo shoot later in the week.

Matt saw the 11.10 as an achievable, and her success would be his success. Her gold medal could open opportunities; he could quit his current job and chase his true passion, coaching. On current form it was possible, but she would need ideal conditions. A tailwind just under the legal two metres per second would be enough.

As a coach he was entering dangerous territory; looking for answers that were beyond his scope of influence. Before his thoughts went any further, he heard the voice of his father and mentor; '*coach what's in your control, leave the rest alone.*' This prophecy grounded him; he needed something that would show her she had that extra tenth of a second.

Thinking deeply, he remembered a technique his dad used back in the day, overspeed training. Closing his eyes, a vivid memory returned. He was standing next to his father at a soccer pitch when a group of athletes thundered by. He remembered looking up at his dad as he said, '*Look at their legs Matty, see how fast they're going. The hill is teaching them to run faster.*'

Going deeper into the recesses of his brain he remembered reading about an overspeed technique that didn't require a gentle slope. It was one of those which came in and out of vogue with coaches, but for what he needed it may just work.

With his thoughts rapidly expanding, he remembered it used belts and a pulley, along with a few other accessories. Then came the spark he needed; he was positive something resembling this was in a bag at the back of the gear shed. Come tomorrow, Victoria was going to feel what it was like to run 11.10 seconds.

*　*　*

Jayde sat by Poppy's bed leaning forward intently listening to her instructions for the Goldfields Gift. Since going on the oxygen his voice had changed. It no longer had his usual deep resonance; it was now softer with a higher pitch. He also carried a noticeable wheeze as he gasped between his words.

Talking left him fatigued, his sentences were short and to the point. His instructions, 'make the semis, run a high 12.3, it won't hurt your mark anymore'. He kept the last part to himself; Goldfields is more about your odds.

*   *   *

Ballarat came alive for the Goldfields Gift; it was as if Sovereign Hill burst its gates and took over the town. Ladies dressed in fancy crinoline and corset silk dresses with gloves and wide hats, while the men varied between the formal top hat and tails or the miners' high leather boots, cotton shirt and waistcoat, a reverent tribute to the heritage of professional running right down to the winner's bounty, a ten-ounce gold bar.

Jayde knew what to do once she got the Ballarat, but getting there was proving to be a much bigger issue. Thomas, having put in leave for the popular Easter long weekend, couldn't take any more time off, and her parents, as always, were booked up with their own work, and the girls were back at university.

Just as she was about to give up and withdraw, Boomer came for his daily visit. 'What's with the long face?'

'I have to pull out of the Goldfields Gift, I can't get there.'

'Easy, I'll take you.'

He had planned to head south before The Gift to catch up with the Victorian boys anyway, and to help her he would drive, not ride.

'Thanks mate. I don't know what I'd do without you.'

*   *   *

214

Doug nearly walked straight past Boomer as he stood in the outer section, adjacent to the bull pen. His thick biker beard trimmed into a neat goatee and his long plait gone was replaced by a number two clipper cut all over. Doug couldn't remember a time when Boomer looked so neat.

Getting in early, Bert had already dropped a twenty on Jayde for the win, and he slipped another to Doug to do the same with Dave McPharland. By the end of the day, each of the oncourse bookies were going to be holding varying amounts of money on Jayde for the win or place.

Jayde did her job, moving through the heats with relative ease. Her times were consistently in the low 12.4 range, smack bang in Jack's comfort zone.

As she was running, Bert brought Doug up to speed with the Victorians' part of Hobblers Ride before carefully handing over an envelope containing fifteen hundred dollars in a range of green-, yellow- and orange-coloured bills. Acknowledging his understanding with a handshake, Doug turned and disappeared into the crowd.

*   *   *

Jayde rolled out of bed with her alarm as the sun was meeting the horizon. Her first race wasn't till late in the morning, so she had plenty of time to complete her pre-race routine. Bert booked their accommodation; it wasn't as secluded as Jack or Jayde were used to. Without any other options she was left to go through her routine in the safety of her room.

Not long after she had emerged from the cold shower there was an anything but a gentle knock on her door. Quickly pulling on her running gear, she opened her door to find Uncle Bert fully dressed. 'I'm taking you out for breakfast.'

Casting her eyes to her now unappealing pre-race combination of long-life milk and Nutragrain sitting on the bench in the kitchenette, she gladly accepted.

Steve sat several tables across from Bert and Jayde quietly enjoying his coffee and bagel in the early morning sun. Today was one of those days he had circled in his calendar months ahead of time. He really enjoyed Sunday racing; all the numpties were in their cars heading out of town, leaving only the fare dinkum contenders.

Racing would be tight, so he and his team needed to be on their toes all day. Looking at his phone, he could see lanes three and five were running a clear two-point advantage. It would be hard work for the rest of the field to negate this advantage. Having no need to use his special algorithm, Steve decided the process should be as intended; organic, allowing the best sprinter a win.

The real highlight for him was presenting the gold bar. As a way of managing his stress and acquiring some extra income he took up amateur prospecting. Walking through the Victorian bush, swinging a coil and scratching the dirt, had done wonders for his physical and mental health. After turning up a few decent pieces he was most definitely bitten by the gold bug. Holding ten ounces of gold would be like the best sex he ever had.

* * *

Bert found his place near the bull pen. He had a few more bets to drop before calling it a day. Jayde gave him a kiss on the cheek before heading off to collect her colour and warm-up. She wasn't used to seeing him with smooth cheeks; she missed the tickle of his beard.

Not able to facetime, Bert recorded each race before messaging it to Jack. Jayde's run in the quarters was beautiful. She pushed hard through the line; equal third, automatically qualifying for the round of thirty-two. Watching the race for the third time, something in the back of the shot caught his eye.

An old steward on the side of the track wasn't scrutinising the race, he was focussed purely on Jayde. Wanting to know more he sent a text to Boomer; *first magpie from the starter, get a picture.*

Not long after, a near flawless image of Bill Paterson popped up on Jack's phone. He couldn't control the wide smile that spread across his face. He still hadn't got it. Whispering to himself, *'You had no idea what was coming in 66, and you have less of an idea now!'*

Jayde dropped a season best 12:38 in the semi-final, and in a blanket finish she was somehow awarded fifth place. With no repechage round, Bert and Jayde could get an early start on the long trip home. She was excited that her next trip down the Hume would be for The Gift.

CHAPTER 30

Coronation

There was a sense of anticipation throughout the SOPAC track as Victoria lined up for the national women's final. She breezed through the heats, switching off and coasting well before the finish line.

Her semi-final required a little more effort. In absolute control, Victoria stopped the clock at a scintillating 11:14 seconds. Chloe Spinner was strategically placed in the other semi-final and qualified only 0.02 seconds behind. Could the master hold off the apprentice? This was showdown everybody wanted to see.

Despite beating Chloe several times in the Track Classic series, she was still the national champion. Victoria needed this to be the true queen of the track. Both their times were fast, and there was no doubt the final would be even faster.

Not since that famous four hundred metres twenty odd years ago in the stadium next door had there been so much expectation on one race. Media crews and reporters jostled for prime position as the starter called the runners to their marks.

Matt stopped his pacing. From the time he gave his final words to Victoria till now, he was replaying everything he had done to get her here. He was confident that all that could be done, had been done.

He knew she had the speed; she just needed to find that extra per cent or two to get this done. Matt was hoping the scholarship news he dropped on her at the warm-up track would be the catalyst she needed.

From the call 'Take your marks' complete silence fell over the crowd.

'Set' echoed through the stadium.

As all eight hips rose and locked in position. The zephyr of breeze that was meandering up the straight increased in intensity to become a light wind.

The crowd erupted on the crack of the gun. Victoria was in complete control from her opening strides, opening a metre advantage before they hit twenty metres.

From here her acceleration took hold and her lead pushed out to nearly three metres by 70m. In the final thirty metres, most athletes struggle to hold their terminal velocity and begin to decelerate. Not Victoria. Her speed remained solid. The breeze that was pushing her continued to intensify.

Matt froze on the landing adjacent to the finish line, sweating bullets as he felt the zephyr turn into a tailwind. It had to be close to a red flag race. Victoria blasted through the finish line, stopping the clock at a scintillating 11:09 seconds.

The crowd erupted; she was now the undisputed queen of the track, marking her coronation; a new national record. Having no timing displays anywhere in her rollout area, Victoria had to crank her neck a long way to see the scoreboard in the opposite corner of the track.

Her amazing time was being shrouded by a series of tacky animated fireworks. Unable to contain her excitement, she bounced around screaming 'Yes, Yes, Yes!'

Photographers swarmed to capture her raw emotion.

While everyone in the stadium was going crazy, Matt turned his attention to the lone track marshal positioned just off the track. Sitting there in his chair behind the wind gauge, he had the power to ratify her amazing performance or cancel it depending on what the machine told him to do.

A green flag and she would be off to America, then the Olympics, and he would abandon his daily grind and move into full-time coaching. A red flag, she stays in Australia, and he remains in his nine to five.

The reading was in, following the instruction on the LCD display. The marshal leant forward. Matt's eyes fixated on the flags, his lips muttering, *'Please be green, please be green'*. The suspense was killing him.

'YES!' Matt made everybody in the stadium aware the race was legal.

Collapsing into his seat, he needed a moment to absorb what had just happened. He had done it! He could now add the open national title and record to his CV.

Under the instruction of the meet officials, Victoria was already parading herself back down the track, bee-lining towards the ground announcer. Between questions, she struggled to stand still, and of course, with every wave came her signature tit and bum shimmy.

Scott Palmer pushed his way to the fence, tossing her a black and orange tigers cap. Sitting it stylishly on her head she publicly announced that this was likely the last time they would see her run in Australia for quite a while.

After taking all manner of selfies with her new fans, Victoria finally acknowledged her coach with a quick wave. That would be all he would get from her today. Her training program saw them reunite on Tuesday at the SCG. Access to this most hallowed turf was courtesy of one of daddy's clients, who happened to be a board member on the trust.

Not seeking the limelight, Matt decided it was time to leave. Walking anonymously through the crowd, he received congratulatory handshakes from only a handful of athletes and coaches. They appreciated the role he had played in her success. It was a unique challenge to pick up an athlete mid-way through the season, especially one like Victoria.

Breaking into a striding walk, Megan caught him before he disappeared. 'What you did with Victoria was nothing short of amazing, she's a complex athlete. I heard you completed your level 3 accreditation recently, is that correct?'

'Yes, my certification was confirmed two weeks ago.'

'Good, we can work with that. Are you prepared to undertake level 4 if it can be arranged.'

'Of course.'

'From this can I take it we have a memorandum of understanding.'

Struggling to hide his smile, he said 'Yes!'

Handing him her business card, she replied 'Call me first thing Monday morning, I want this wrapped up before lunch. The press release needs to be out to catch drive and the six pm news.'

Matt nodded. His second call on Monday would be to quit his job.

Victoria, on the other hand, was gleefully captive. She had her press conference and mandatory drug test to complete before she could leave. The reporters' questions focussed heavily on the issues caused by Gregore and her new move to America.

Bethany invested hours in preparing her until she had mastered the art of fake sincerity, and the press lapped it up, comparing her to other great Australians who overcame adversity before achieving success. Not once did she publicly thank Matt; as always, this was all about her.

Once clear of her press obligations, her phone didn't stop ringing or pinging. It seemed everybody she had ever met was calling or texting to offer their congratulations. Her socials were in meltdown; fans and followers watched, commented, and shared her race, press conference and the few sneaky blogs she was able to record and post from the track.

There was no doubt, she was the hottest property in Sydney, and everybody wanted their piece. Bethany was already fielding a multitude of requests for her company at events over the coming week.

Following her instructions, Bethany did her job, booking Victoria up as much as possible. Andre, the owner of Infinity.PR knew with her pending scholarship that they only had a small window of opportunity before she would be out of sight, and out of mind. Infinity.PR had to cash in quick.

Preparation for The Gift played second fiddle to her media commitments. She was forced out of bed early for interviews on morning television, followed by podcasts, photoshoots, and cover stories. Training was crammed into a very tight window in the afternoon before she was whisked off to a socialite function that wouldn't break before the change of day.

Victoria was where she always expected to be, in demand. Adding to her appeal was a new boyfriend, Rhys Polkington, a rising soapie star who had his eyes firmly set on Hollywood.

They had met several weeks ago in Bethany's office, where she floated an idea that would benefit all three parties – a tantalising, manufactured relationship. Victoria and Rhys were the hottest singles on the Sydney social scene, ad combining them into a couple would mean the crossover reach would be unbelievable.

What started as a relationship of convenience soon blossomed into something else. They were young, in demand, superstars. It was only a matter of time before things turned physical.

They were acquaintances with benefits. Couple selfies attracted followers from one to the other. Managing their posts carefully, never double dipping, their images and comments were always deliberately fresh.

When not on set, Rhys was known as a party boy. He revelled in hanging out with the who's who, doing his best to hold the reputation as the hardest player. Dropping pills, doing lines, partying throughout the night and well into the next day kept him at the top of their wanted list.

Paparazzi were aware of what he was up to and respectfully gave him a moment to clean up or hide any evidence before taking their snaps, and in return he always made himself available for a pose. It was a symbiotic relationship that no-one wanted to abuse.

Not willing to give up the intense feeling of her victory, Victoria, with the encouragement of her publicist, wilfully embraced the party lifestyle, feeding off the adrenaline created in just over eleven seconds on Sunday afternoon. Although her mind was willing, her body was not able. She was not match-fit in this world of late nights and endless flutes of champagne.

Drinking well beyond her threshold was hitting her harder and earlier each night. Rhys, noticing she was getting stumbly, pulled her aside. He didn't want his night ending early because she was shit-faced within the first hour.

Guiding her into the wheelchair toilet, he took a little packet of white powder from his pocket. Utilising the underside of his phone he carefully created in a thin line before handing her a small drinks straw. 'Snort this, it will keep you going for a while.'

Sitting through endless drug seminars with the institute, Victoria knew this was inexcusable, but the combination of alcohol and coercive encouragement shifted her sensibilities. Taking the straw, the line of prohibited white powder evaporated, her endorphin-induced high was instantly replaced by another. The rush was amazing, but unfortunately this wouldn't be the last time she visited the wheelchair toilet during the night.

* * *

Meanwhile, Jayde was at Bradfield Sports Ground each day going through her final preparations. Her speed was on, and she was beginning to feel razor sharp. In the best shape of her life, she was ready physically and emotionally for both The Gift and Victoria.

CHAPTER 31

Complications

Bert called a last-minute meeting for the Vets travelling south on Hobblers Ride. Arriving early, he arranged the room into the configuration he needed.

Taking his time, he neatly placed forty or so large white envelopes with each rider's club name emblazoned in thick black texta on the tables adjacent to where he and Phil would be speaking. Safely hidden behind the seal were the instructions to Jack's eternal peace.

A few minutes later, the large room was full; punctuality was a key feature of this organisation. As road captain, Phil opened the meeting. 'Welcome everyone to Hobblers Ride, a unique ride to support a brother and his family.'

Standing tall, Bert took over. It was time for him to reveal all aspects of this special ride.

Although most were familiar with Hobblers' story, Boomer covered it again; their service together, Jack's difficulties with alcohol and gambling, what it had cost Gillian, and his devotion to Jayde. For some in the room, it was a reminder of their own post-war struggles and for others it was inspiration for the life they were experiencing now.

'Like Phil said, this trip has been named Hobblers Ride. It's dedicated to our mate Jack, our brother in arms who won't be with us for much longer.' His deep booming voice quivered on the last words.

Taking a deep breath and gathering his composure, Bert continued. 'In your package there is another itinerary, each is unique, set up only for you. It will tell you what to do and when to do it. There is also cash, this is Jack's cash; proceeds from his bike and car, and is to be bet as instructed. Jack is going all in so DO NOT deviate from your plan. Hobbler, Phil and I have spent weeks putting this together; we want the money on without any unwanted attention. Angus has confirmed there's nothing illegal here, you're just placing a bet or two.'

Taking a considered breath, Bert used his position of authority to make a captain's call. 'The winnings will be given to Hobblers family. We all know he's done it tough with money, so we're going to help. Whatever is in your package I want you to double it. The logistics of when and where stay the same.' His authoritarian tone made it clear that this was not a point of negotiation.

'We meet back here on Tuesday after the ride. I'll need your cash and the betting slips. Hobbler will need proof of where the cash came from. Now if you want to drop something on yourself do it online. No one bets their own cash at the track. There will be bars at the track, enjoy a beer or two, but don't get loose. We have a rare opportunity to send Hobbler off with his soul at peace; appeasing his sins, knowing his girls will be ok. That's our mission, we will see it done.' Stepping back, he gave the floor to Phil to continue with his riders' briefing.

'We will ride to the border under normal formation, and once at the rest stop just before Albury, we will stow our colours and ride in everyday leathers. From Albury onwards our operation begins. We will break into smaller groups, taking different routes.'

Sipping some water he continued. 'Our intent is to make as little noise and grab as little attention as possible. The only race that we will see as a group will be the final. We have something special planned for this so look out for a text message on Sunday night. Any questions? Now look at your itinerary, study it, know it!'

Bert stood again, and with his anointed tone of authority he decreed, 'Take extreme care with your plan, do not leave it lying around in your room or take it out in public. Secrecy is the key to our success, do not fuck it up!' With that he stood back and quenched his dry throat with a sip of beer.

*　*　*

Kahlil and the oldies at the coffee shop wished Jayde well as she finished her shift. They had watched her evolve over the past six months. Starting behind the counter as an overweight, quiet, unassuming girl, she was now a confident, toned, powerful woman, comfortable in who she was and what she could achieve.

Her confidence was infectious. Looking up as she walked out the door, Kahlil's intuitive sixth sense told him she was on the cusp of something special, and mouthing a small prayer he sent her his blessings.

It was his turn in the punters club he had formed with his gaggle of elderly ladies. A few good weekends had pushed their account to just shy of five hundred dollars. Mavis, the self-appointed leader of the group, approached Kahlil. 'After quick consultation, we propose you put everything on Jayde to win The Gift.'

'Funny you say that. I was thinking the same thing.'

*　*　*

Jayde kept to her usual post-work routine – a final visit to Bradfield Sports Ground for a short, sharp session, then over to the hospital for her final instructions. As she came striding through the doorway, Jack reflected on her transformation. Forever grateful he was there to help her rebuild and to empower her to believe in her own self-worth. No matter what the result, she could proudly hold her head high. The darkness that had engulfed her had been vanquished by a bright empowering light.

However, winning The Gift would ensure the brightness of this light would last a lifetime.

He was proud of his granddaughter, from that first morning he kicked her bed she did everything he had asked and more. His last wheezy instruction was 'Show them what you've been hiding.'

*   *   *

Stawell and the wider Grampians district were enjoying the cathartic calm before the storm. The last of the beer trucks rolled out of town, and coffee shops and bakery storerooms held kilos of extra beans and boxes of specialty milks, while cool rooms were burgeoning with fresh meats and produce.

The town had three days to cash in; profit from this weekend would sustain the service industry until the tourists returned for the bushwalking and climbing season in spring.

Steve checked into his suite while the hotel carpark was still empty. He wanted to check and double check everything; it was essential this year went off without a hitch. It was a rare double first, the first under his leadership and the first unrestricted event since the dreaded pandemic.

The extent of Steve's power in Stawell abruptly ended at the barbed wire fence that protected Central Park's sanctified turf. Beyond this barrier he was influential without any appointed authority; partnering with Mayor Wayne he was able to expand his zone of influence.

Politically, this informal union worked for both men, each able to extend their reach, banking credit they could use as capital both electorally and in the boardroom. Steve's overpowering, fastidious manner was fast becoming a source of frustration for Wayne and the local committee. They were the custodians of The Gift, and appreciated the responsibility they had to both the athletic and local community. Each stood to benefit from its success and as such no stone was left unturned.

Wayne breathed a sigh of relief when Steve was forced to make his apologies. Antoine Greene, a medal-winning member of the American 4x100 metre relay team, was in Melbourne on a

227

pre-season training camp. Hearing about The Gift he demanded entry.

Last-minute requests like this weren't anything new. VPAL had a process ready to go that dealt with the unique opportunity a runner like this provided them. International athletes attract extra attention and extra coverage both locally and overseas. Up until the pandemic The Gift was gaining traction on the world stage. A handicap race with a rich chequered history and an enticing purse, those whose egos appreciated the influence of the handicap saw it as an interesting challenge that could be a lot of fun.

Antoine would not be categorised as a fun athlete. He was narcissistic, loud, and obnoxious. Controversy was his wingman, and his chequered career included numerous sanctions for misconduct, as well as a four-year ban for doping. On appeal, his legal team used a dubious defence based on ambiguous testimony and had this reduced to two.

Upon his return, he managed to curtail his narcissism enough to become an Olympian. Qualifying as the fifth member of the coveted 4x100 relay team, he was sacrificial, his job simple, to get the team to the final, then watch as the number one team claimed gold.

Silently sitting at the far end of the press conference, he received his medal from the team manager. Taking it from the royal blue velvet-covered box, he suffered the indignity of awarding it to himself.

Burdened by resentment, he took to blogging, stirring up trouble with unfounded claims of racism and preferential treatment. Polarising in his politics, he carried a large and vocal audience, one which extended deep into continental America. Sometimes you must dance with the devil to create an empire.

Under VPAL's classification, Antoine would be unfairly defined as a novice runner. Using a rarely used sub-clause, he was immediately upgraded to established athlete status. His performances set him as the backmarker, running off the full Sheffield distance of one hundred and twenty metres. The issue for VPAL was that his true handicap placed him at one hundred and twenty-one and a half metres. If allowed to start with this advantage, the result would be a fore gone conclusion; Antoine by over a metre.

Steve had to think quick, or this year would be a farce, and the brand damage could take years to repair. Locals didn't mind if a high-profile blow-in won, but they did demand a fair contest.

Sitting in his hotel room, Steve racked his brain, reviewing the laws and by-laws which governed The Gift. The solution was simple; adjust all marks out by the discrepancy Antoine created, but the provision that justified this radical adjustment remained hidden.

He did have the *Discretionary Lift* clause which was specifically available for The Grampians. This clause allowed the handicapper to lift marks by up to four graduations. It was essential he find another rule or clause that would negate Antoine's remaining half-metre advantage; Victoria's hopes for her third sash depended on it.

He could utilise his lane identification program, modify the algorithm to run in reverse; meaning Antione would be allocated the slowest lanes. Never used in this way, it wasn't tested and therefore couldn't be trusted.

Also, an audit by Gaming and Racing could highlight a discrepancy in the repetition of lane allocation, sparking interest for further investigation. He needed another ruling which could justify the additional two marks.

Steve was now reaping what he had sown. In his haste to take what he believed was his, he forcefully pushed three decades of corporate knowledge out the door. Bill knew the VPAL constitution, rules for racing and the handicapping regulations inside out. He was particularly familiar with how clauses and sub-clauses could be interpreted and manipulated.

Out of time, Steve had to swallow his pride and make the call. He knew before hitting the bold green button on his phone this advice wouldn't come cheap. After the way Bill was dethroned, there was no way he would give away his knowledge for free, especially after what was said in Yarrawonga.

To his surprise, Bill freely handed him the solution. 'Quickly convene a handicap review panel, then utilise the rate per metre rule, providing the justification for lifting the field by another one-half of a metre.'

However, there was sting in the tail of this solution. 'The panel would need to meet immediately, vote and publicise the changes. The bookies need to be informed before the Call of the Card and Calcutta tonight.'

Mid-afternoon on the eve of a long weekend, getting hold of the right people would be difficult, and getting them to the office or online would be near impossible.

Under VPAL rules, a minimum of three members were required to form a panel, two of whom must be members of the executive committee. Fortunately, Neil the handicapper was still in Melbourne. A quick text and he could be online within minutes.

As the CEO, Steve had the power to convene and chair this panel, and as an operational life member, Bill could be invited as the third participant. His acceptance came with the expected cost.

His request, rights; he demanded full Stewards' rights.

Appreciating the origin of Bills motivation, Steve immediately knew where this was going to land; Jayde Hardy. Agreement would put her firmly back in his sights, and once again Jayde faced the prospect of being cannon fodder in a larger political game.

The meeting was over in minutes, the facts were presented, Bill proposed the use of the rate per metre scale and Neil the handicapper accepted the recommendation with Steve's endorsement.

Neil promptly typed the minutes before issuing a brief statement on ProRun.

* * *

Dave McPharland was sitting in his hotel room preparing for the Calcutta tonight when the message pinged on his phone. Lifting handicaps had implications on his book. He needed more clarity, and scrolling through his phone book he found Steve's number.

Getting straight to the point, he said 'What's this bullshit you've dropped on us.'

'Settle down, it's a full field lift based on the new backmarker, short of a stride or two everything should be the same.'

Comfortable with this concise explanation, Dave continued to check his market. Victoria and now Antoine were set as favourites with an opening margin of five to one. Jayde's odds shifted slightly; her status, an outsider at forty to one.

CHAPTER 32

Round one

Petra and Georgia were happily making their way down the Hume Highway towards Yass when a large group of motorcycles appeared in the rear vision mirror. Keeping left and slowing slightly the girls were happy to let the large group pass.

Sitting in the passenger seat, Petra took note of their patches; Veterans Association Motorcycle Club. Feeling a little shaken by the experience, she turned to Georgia. 'I hope they're not going the same way we are.'

Chuckling to hide her own trepidation, Georgia agreed.

Nick and Andrew were also heading south. Following the route down the centre of New South Wales, they would meet the girls at the motel. Nick was excited to spend some more time away with Georgia. Their relationship had grown since returning to university. In their limited free time, they would get together as much as possible, either on campus, at his dorm or at her house under the strict supervision of her parents.

Jayde and Thomas arrived early and were waiting for everybody to join them. Even after their lengthy drive she felt amazing. This was her time to shine.

* * *

Coming down from the previous night's party, Victoria slept through her alarm. Woken by the beep of her chauffeur's horn she frantically ran to the bathroom to get herself ready. Looking in the mirror, she struggled to find her usual glamour.

Three beeps later she finally emerged. Her charter flight was booked for a 12pm take off and she had at least a one-hour drive across the city to get to Bankstown Airport. Her driver would have to fracture a road rule or two to get her there in time.

Tyler her masseuse would be her only company on this flight, Matt was at Sydney's larger airport preparing to board his own flight, a well-deserved family holiday on the Gold Coast.

With minutes to spare Victoria was escorted up the stairs before taking her seat. The small six-seater plane had a flight time of just over an hour and a half before touching down in Stawell. Enough time for a quick nap and foot massage.

* * *

Dave McPharland set his stand in his traditional position next to the entrance of the backroom of the Town Hall for the Call of the Card and Calcutta. He enjoyed this night; it was a prelude to the next three days, when good money here usually equated to better money at the track.

The weekend was looking good, and there was plenty of money in the room. Two years of restrictions brought everybody out to play. Using the concealment of activity, the Vets surreptitiously went about placing their initial bets. At the first call of the card, Jayde was sitting at forty-to-one for the win and half that for the place.

Word from the auditorium was that the Calcutta was also bringing in plenty of money. Punters were all in for Victoria and Antoine, both being auctioned for well over three-thousand dollars. This year as a post-Covid bonus, the Calcutta offered a ten-thousand-dollar winner take all prize.

Crazy Ken purchased Jayde for a mere two-hundred and twenty dollars, putting her true value at forty-five to one. Dave always used these values as a method of cross-checking his market. With Victoria and Antoine sitting at a true three and a third to one, slightly under his five, he went to sleep that night believing his book, as always, was bang on the mark.

* * *

Saturday morning came and Jayde woke rested and joined her friends for breakfast in the café across the road. A flat white and a warm almond croissant helped her settle into the day. Opening heats didn't start until midday, leaving her plenty of time to relax and prepare.

Using ProRun, she was able to check-in from the comfort of her room. Her plan; to grab a quick piccolo and sip it as she walked down to Central Park just before eleven, collect her colours and head straight into the warm-up area.

The walk would be good, allowing her to loosen up and settle her nerves. Her mission; move through her two heats and progress to the semis on Monday.

The athletes' entrance was on the opposite side to the main gates. She could hear the familiar sounds emanating well beyond the small grandstand that blocked their view of the track – the crack of the gun, the cheer from the crowd and the commentary from the ground announcer.

Standing for a moment she imagined what it would be like just after quarter past three on Monday when it would be her name that escaped from the confines of the ground.

As quickly as it came the thought was lost. The pragmatic side of her brain pushed her back to the here and now. She had to perform today, two heats, and then she earnt the right to dream further on Monday. Holding this sentiment, she gave Thomas a quick kiss and disappeared.

* * *

From the start of the day, the Vets moved in and out of the famed wrought iron gates. Drifting with the natural motion of the crowd, their collective presence remaining veiled.

Bert stood on the edge of the bull pen, the sentinel to Jack's bequest. Should he suspect the bookies were onto their fix, he could save what was left of the cash and get his members out of harm's way. His trusty dark wrap around biker sunglasses gave his eyes the concealment they needed to execute this vital role in the operation.

His trust in his brothers was not wasted. They were inconspicuous, moving through the madness of the betting arena without causing a ripple.

Jayde's odds were still at their pre-race best. Over a quarter of Jack's money was now resting in the bottom of a bookie's bag. Not every dollar was dropped on her; combined favourite and roughie bets were a good ruse. The illusion was working a treat; her odds were yet to shorten.

* * *

Receiving her colour, the organisers handed her a reminder of how she got here; maroon, Poppy Jack's favourite colour, the colour he served under. The rich, deep, dark colour reminded her this was a fighting colour, one which demanded the best from whoever wore it.

Stopping herself from becoming too sentimental or superstitious, she balanced her thoughts before striding through the gate into the warm-up area. It was time for the real Jayde Hardy to stand up.

In her own zone, Jayde didn't realise or care that Victoria had entered the warm-up area. The same couldn't be said for the crowd. There was a distinct increase in buzz as she moved through her own pre-race routine, stopping sporadically to acknowledge their support with her signature shimmy wave.

Not accustomed to being the support act, Antoine pulled out his best showman theatrics; strutting, flexing, stretching; no matter what he tried the crowd had their favourite. His bullet-proof ego took a heavy blow.

Petra, Georgia and Thomas staked their place on the small grassed knoll adjacent to the thirty-metre mark. It was not the best location for a facetime call, but unlike the same location further down the track, it wasn't shoulder to shoulder, and here it was easier for Thomas to keep Jayde in the shot.

Nick and Andrew slipped down to the Bullpen to drop a lobster or two on Jayde before her odds drifted in. Stumbling upon a can bar on their return they grabbed half a dozen draughts, two for themselves and two for their new mate Thomas.

The girls each held a beer as Thomas made his obligatory facetime call to Jack. Focussed more on getting the best view, he didn't pay attention to the small image being returned from Jack's phone. A more astute analysis had the potential to scuttle his final surprise.

Jayde set her blocks to the new mark of seven and one-quarter metres.

Her body felt amazing as the starter called 'Runners dig in'.

From this instruction onwards, Jayde had complete trust in her ability to perform. Her head was free from times and places, taking her back to running as she knew it, fast from gun to gate.

Set, rolling her shoulders, and raising her hips, her drive leg loaded and prepared for release. Thomas aimed the camera on his phone in her direction. The crack of the gun was the cause, and the powerful release was the effect. Jayde was away, her drive phase was impeccable, she had power to burn.

Pushing up and raising her head, shoulders, and hips she accelerated quickly to her top speed, her right-hand flick refined so that only a discerning judge would be able to pick it. There were only two runners ahead of her as she passed through the seventy-metre mark. With each stride she was making ground.

As she passed through one hundred metres she pulled alongside both runners who were now running dead even. Backmarkers were now making solid ground; Jayde could hear them coming and kept her form tall and strong.

The gates were approaching fast, and the backmarkers were approaching faster. Jayde was now leading. There was less than five metres to go when one backmarker came up on her shoulder. Blasting through the gates, Jayde had to make a quick swerve to the left to avoid heavy contact with the fence.

Looking over her shoulder she was delighted. Her lane was awarded second place, and automatic qualification for the next round in two hours' time.

Victoria lined up for her heat. Although not completely run in, the track was showing signs hardening up. Victoria's mark had been lifted by the standard one and one-half metres, but this was then reduced due to her recent record-setting Australian Open title. Her net gain was three quarters of a metre, giving her a start position one metre behind Jayde.

The distinctive call '*Runners dig in*' was analogous to a conductor raising his hands to an orchestra, and almost in unison a cluster of mobile phones were held aloft, thumbs quivering over the record button. 'Set,' the gun rose in the air, like the baton striking the upbeat. The sharp crack of the gun was the downbeat. Thumbs swiftly flexed, initiating several thousand recordings of the same event.

Following in the footsteps of his father, Bill found himself behind Victoria's lane on the call of set. Absorbed by her beauty, his whole body shuddered with the crack of the gun. Victoria powered through the gates to finish half a body in front. Her roll out was deliberately aimed to the left and ended at edge of the grandstand where she gave her customary titty, bum wave before making her way back to the start area to collect her blocks.

Exiting the track, Victoria was mobbed, her new admirers crowding for selfies. When you're the Queen, you must keep your subjects happy.

Antoine was infuriated by the lack of respect he was receiving. How could this young attractive girl who wasn't a blip on the international stage steal his limelight. He was an Olympic gold medallist; that alone should make him the undisputed headline act for this hillbilly event.

Lining up as the favourite in the last heat, he doubled down on his theatrics, flexing his legs and shaking his arms before settling into his blocks. Rising slowly into the set position he was doing his best to dictate his terms.

The starter, not fazed by his antics, pulled the trigger the moment his hips locked into position. Struggling out of the blocks, he took several extra strides to get into full flight. Once up and striding, his class took over. His action was elegant and graceful. His powerful arm action drove his leg speed.

Antoine was forced to sprint for the full 120 metre Sheffield distance, something he was not used to in an opening round. By the time he pushed through the finish gates his pedigree accounted for each runner in the field.

Strutting with renewed arrogance, he headed back to collect his belongings. Although his mannerisms exuded confidence, his mind called it quits. Full throttle handicap racing wasn't his forte. He liked coasting through the heats, only opening into full race mode for the semis and final. Before the sun moved any further in the sky, Antoine was relaxing with his manager in the backseat of his chauffeur-driven Bentley, regretting his decision to force his way into this farcical event.

Jayde made her way anonymously through the crowd to reunite with Thomas and her friends. Appreciating her unassuming temperament and Jack's instructions, their celebrations remained very restrained.

Acknowledging their congratulations in the same unobtrusive fashion, she dropped her bag and blocks at Thomas's feet before giving him a quick kiss. 'Give me a few minutes, I need to call Poppy.'

Looking around the crowded oval, she searched for the best location to make the call, not for secrecy, but so she could hear his voice. Tucked up behind the historic grandstand was a beautiful nineteenth century rose garden, an ideal location for a quiet conversation.

Jack was delighted to hear her voice, although it was a bit more difficult with the noise of the diesel engine and wheels rolling on the rough country asphalt.

Unlike Thomas, Jayde quickly noticed the change in background noise. 'Where are you, it sounds different.'

'They've given me a treat today, some time outside in the sun not far from the main drag.'

Accepting this as plausible Jayde moved on. 'I'm through to round two.'

Pretending like as though this was the first time he had heard this, he replied, 'Well done! Keep your focus, you need to be there on Monday.'

Jayde could hear the effort he was putting into this conversation, so for his benefit she reluctantly cut the conversation short. 'Poppy, I need to eat before the next round, love you, see you on Tuesday.' With a sense of guilt, she tapped the red call end button on her phone.

Standing alone in the Rose Garden, Jayde was struck by a white rose that was almost in full bloom. It reminded her of the rose bush Poppy had planted when she was a little girl. He cared for this plant like he cared for her, pruning and cultivating it, ensuring he gave it the best opportunity to grow.

Selecting the most radiant blossom, he would carefully cut it, strip the bottom leaves before placing in his mother's smallest vase. Returning from school, Jayde found this exquisite little surprise waiting in the middle of her dressing table.

For the next few days, her bedroom was filled with a subtle fragrant scent.

After a few days the scent would fade, and the petals wilt. Poppy would whisk it away, saying, 'best to remember it while it was in full bloom, not when it's withering away.'

In a cold burst of reality, Jayde understood the gravity of Poppy's condition. He was the rose that was about to be taken away. Given his recent rate of decline, it dawned on her that he didn't have years or even months; he had weeks at best.

Without warning, a stream of tears flowed freely down her cheeks.

Looking past this rose, she could see another just about the bloom. In a day or so it would open to show the world its full beauty. On Monday she would do the same. Not thinking, Jayde snapped the stem below the bud. This rose would follow her to victory.

CHAPTER 33

Round two

Warming up at The Gift is comical. Athletes are free to move between events, but they must stop and crouch when a race is underway. For those unaccustomed to this formality, it looks like the world's largest game of red light, green light.

For the athletes it was frustrating. They are creatures of habit, each following a regimented process to ensure peak performance. This staccato, stop-start process can be enough of a hindrance to cause an early exit. Under Poppy's instruction, Jayde trained for this and was able to find her speed without any frustration at all.

Out of curiosity, Steve snuck a quick look at his very private section of ProRun. There was no need for intervention yet but noticed lanes three, five and six were beginning to show a small advantage. Running in the third heat, Jayde was drawn in lane five.

In the warm-up area prior to the first race of round two, there should be sixty-four runners bobbing up and down and competing for space. Counting heads there was only sixty-three. Their last-minute headline had vanished.

Meet officials scrambled; this was not a good look to have a backmarker and a short-priced favourite disappear. Within minutes they had their answer; he had abandoned the event. There was a groan of disappointment as the announcer projected the news to the crowd.

The bookies scrambled for clarification. When was he officially scratched. Under VPAL betting rules, any money held before scratching must be refunded in full.

Steve consulted with his executive team and determined scratching was made official prior to the commencement of the second round, so all money held must be refunded.

The bull pen was sent into chaos. Cash was going on at the same rate as being handed back. Bert saw this mayhem as his opportunity, dropping another thousand or so with several bookies. This was outside Poppy's plan, but Bert was confident that with all the pandemonium, it would go unnoticed.

Victoria was heading towards the start line when she heard that Antoine was a late scratching. Her stride, already full of arrogance, grew bolder as she realised she was now the stand-alone favourite. History was within her grasp, the first person to win the triple treat, Surfside, The Dash and The Gift. She could leave Australia with nothing else left to achieve.

As expected, racing became tighter in the second round. Victoria was called to *dig in* in the first heat. Giving the crowd her usual tease, she performed her seductive shimmy before settling in the blocks. Set, rising quickly to gain maximum power, and then the gun.

Her form was spectacular. Blasting through the finish gates a full chest ahead of her competition, she was the first to qualify for Monday's semi-finals. Knowing this would be the result before she took her marks, Victoria had time to plan her post-race celebration. Rolling out to stop in front of the bull pen, she gave the punters some serious food for thought.

Jayde set her blocks in lane five, and on the call of 'Set,' her body braced for release. Her reaction to the gun, sublime. She was up and away in a flash. Her race was fantastic, pushing through the finish gates in equal first; mission complete, she had gained automatic qualification for Monday's semi-finals.

As an automatic qualifier Jayde, attracted more attention when she left the track. Random punters congratulated her as she moved towards her friends. These weren't the only ones who took note of her run. In codgers corner behind the start line, Bill Paterson was gifted a new perspective on Miss J Hardy from St Marys.

Steve had a new appreciation of how this position behind the blocks gained its name. Apart from running out of a lane, which was virtually impossible due to the knee-high white rope dividers, there was nothing to adjudicate. Any old bugger could do that.

Seeing Jayde disappear down the track, right hand lightly flicking outwards at the end of her arm drive, took him back nearly half a century to this very spot. Standing and staring down the rope tunnels he had a flashback to his racing days when he was dressed in his traditional running whites, navy blue cotton racing singlet with the elastic neck, arms, and waist. Standing at the marshalling point behind the one-twenty-yard mark, he was watching the heat ahead line up on their marks.

He could see the runner in his lane settle himself in rough, beaten, old blocks. On the call of set, all three strands of hamstring muscles stood out and the unmistakable bulge of his calf muscles were flexed and waiting to pounce into action.

He felt the shockwave of the starter's gun, and could see that the power release from this man was incredible. Bill could clearly see him disappearing down the track, with a powerful stride, strong arms, stable hips, and shoulders. Then something odd caught his attention, like somebody clicking their fingers in your face; his right hand flicked awkwardly at the end of each arm drive.

The vivid detail shocked Bill, it was so strong and clear, like it happened yesterday. Just as his ailing memory was about to reveal the mystery runner's face, the shrill blast of the starter's whistle revealed his first tangible lead into the origins of this mystery bolter from Sydney's west.

Rather than annoyed he was relieved. Now he had something concrete to work with. His racing days at Central Park spanned a decade, his involvement in the event was many more. The parameters of his search had just narrowed significantly.

* * *

Jayde exited Central Park as soon as she could. She wanted to be back in the quiet of her hotel room before calling Poppy with the good news. Deep into their third shout, Nick, Andrew and Thomas decided to stay on at the track. Petra and Georgia, bored with running, joined her for the short walk back.

Appreciating the difficulty, Jack had had earlier in the day, Jayde timed her call to coincide with her mum's usual late Saturday afternoon visit. If he was struggling, she could act as the amplifier.

Jack answered within a few rings. His reaction to her news mirrored his excitement from earlier in the day. Knowing they only had limited time, she rattled through his checklist of important details, only being interrupted once.

'Where did you say he was?'

'That silly old bugger was at the top of the track, behind the start.'

'You bloody beauty, he can't do anything from there!'

His elation was abruptly interrupted by a fit of heaving coughing. She could hear her mum in the background, tapping and rubbing Jack's back and encouraging him to sip some water. Not wanting to create more discomfort she brought their conversation to an end.

His crackling wheeze with each breath was a constant reminder of the frailty of his condition. But this cough was something new; it was deep and uncontrollable. She could picture his reddening face and bulging eyes as he struggled to gather control. Little did she know there was a sizable amount of blood embedded in the tissue that was used to cover his mouth.

Thinking about the rose she picked earlier in the day, she gently removed it from the front pocket and placed it carefully on the makeshift dressing table above the chest of drawers.

As she put her phone next to the rose, tears rolled freely from her eyes; she really needed a huggle.

CHAPTER 34

Sunday

With their thirst up and no more racing, Nick, Andrew, and Thomas followed other likeminded punters across the road to The Gift Hotel. Before Thomas knew what he had got himself into, the shout had moved from beer to rum.

After the fourth or fifth shout of the vile sugary brown liquid, Thomas was shitfaced. Stumbling his way through the main bar he was spotted by security, and with gentle precision they carefully redirected him through the main doors and out into the street.

Nick and Andrew soon joined their new mate on the pavement; security had a simple rule, one out, all out. The punchy influence of the rum hadn't kicked in. Without causing a ruckus, the boys stumbled their way home. It wasn't till he put his head on the pillow that the true effects of mixing beer and spirits kicked in.

The room began spinning at a gut-churning rate. Having enough sense to know where this was going to end, Thomas made a bee line to the safety of the bathroom. Jayde did her best to sleep through the sound of rum and beer being recycled.

* * *

Easter Sunday was full of rest and relaxation for Jayde. A lay day for Gift competitors, she had no need to visit Central Park. Her quiet breakfast with the girls, followed by some light run throughs at the park down the road, would give Thomas time to wake from his alcohol-induced coma.

Thankfully the remainder of his day was a gentle mixture of coffee and Netflix.

Penance for the other two was a brisk walk into town for a casual look around. Standing inside another homeware shop, overwhelmed by the competing scents of sandalwood and lavender, Andrew turned to his best mate, and said, 'Fuck this'.

Abandoning this informal aromatic hangover cleansing, he headed down the arcade. Time to go old school – a pie and coke. His metacognitive response was so positive, he decided to double down on this classic remedy.

*　*　*

Victoria woke in her usual glamorous fashion. Carefully styling her morning post she gave her fans a shot of her lying on her pillow in a silk slip. The camera was angled to catch the perkiness of her breasts. Her post was simple; *Dominate Saturday, rest Sunday, win Monday.*

Pete her pilot was booked to fly back to Sydney to pick up Rhys. Bethany wanted him there to jump the fence and hug Victoria when she won. The media reach for both would be off-the-charts.

Apart from the other events at The Gift racing, there was not a lot to do in Stawell on Easter Sunday. Apart from the photo opp the following afternoon, Victoria was looking forward to seeing Rhys. She was in the mood for some afternoon delight. That was until her phone pinged, his message cutting and short; *Partying hard, don't send plane.*

Seething, she announced with venom that her relationship with Rhys was over, citing a breakdown in trust and commitment. Within minutes, it was trending across tabloid pages and sites. Posts flooded her pages; everybody wanted to know why.

Sitting in his room, flicking through his own socials, Tyler sensed opportunity. Grabbing his massage table and bag he knocked on her door. 'Do you need a massage?'

Craving attention, Victoria gladly accepted. Setting up more than just his table he carefully positioned his mobile phone as Victoria gently nestled her face into the terry towelling covered opening.

Tyler began his treatment in his usual professional manner, removing any residue from yesterday's racing. Seizing the opportunity when he was focussing on her back, shoulders and lats, his hand conveniently slipped, brushing a good portion of her right breast.

Revenge sex is always dangerous. Although it feels good at the time, there is always the debris of guilt and shame. Rarely experiencing these emotions, Victoria felt empowered; she wanted sex, and it just happened to be with someone else.

* * *

Bert and the rest of the Vets moved in and out of Central Park with clockwork precision. Everybody played their part. Roaming seamlessly among the crowd, no-one paid them a second look.

Progressing to the semi-finals, Jayde's odds moved into twenty-two to one. A savvy punter could see she was still offering good value. Progressively, another bundle of Poppy's wallet was dropped into various bookie's bags.

Dave ran a check on all his bets. He was always careful not to be caught long on his deals. Focussing on the top ten runners, he was re-assured his position was safe. Mug money dropped on hackers with long odds was given a cursory glance. No-one in the past two decades had won with Saturday odds over twenty to one, and with Victoria in the field, Dave didn't expect this to change.

Leading into the last day of racing, he was holding anything from a few hundred to a couple of thousand for a win or place on each of these mugs. This was why he loved The Gift; one winner from one-hundred and twenty-eight starters, the odds were loaded in his favour.

Dave gleefully printed slips for Jayde and the other remaining twenty-somethings; bright, crisp, vibrant notes filled his bag. This would be his play money when he ventured north for the winter.

*   *   *

Jack was happy to be exhausted as they pulled into their overnight stop in Maryborough. Marcus carefully planned the trip south. Saturday was a full day of travel, Sydney to Albury, while Sunday moved them within spitting distance of The Gift.

Strapped down with his chair, Jack was able to take in the everchanging view. Marvelling at how the landscape had changed without changing, the fields of sheep and wheat were reminders of the days he had spent running up and down the same patch of road.

As he cast his eyes from one side of the car to the other, he caught a glimpse of Gillian and the expression of wonderment she wore. She had the eyes of a five-year-old, capturing all she could as the window presented her with a fresh new vista to enjoy.

Watching her joy, sadness filled his heart. This was the first time Gillian had experienced the vast beauty of the Australian countryside. As a little girl, holidays had been a luxury well beyond their means. His sadness soon turned to shame. He pictured Gillian in her tiny, almost threadbare, school uniform, enduring accounts of her classmates' adventures from coastal paradises such as Forster and Mollymook. What highlight could she share was running under the sprinkler as she tried to avoid the bindies in the backyard.

He felt ashamed, and reaching forward he gently placed his hand on her arm. As she turned, he whispered, 'I'm sorry'.

Confused by this random apology, she replied, 'It's alright'.

Jack appreciated every aspect of the hotel room. There were no beeps or buzzers, no snoring, or check-ups throughout the night. There was just beautiful, peaceful, silence. For the first time in months, he had a mattress that gave him comfort, not just support. His usual insomnia was replaced by blissful, restful sleep. Jack woke refreshed and ready for the last leg of their journey.

CHAPTER 35

Day of days

Easter Monday was VPAL's day of days. Media trucks arrived overnight and set up for the day's broadcast. The ground staff applied their final cut and roll to the track, and everything was positioned for a great day of racing.

By mid-afternoon, another runner would have their name attached to the highest paid running race in the nation. For those fortunate enough to still be racing, they had a combined twenty-four seconds of full-paced effort to get their name on the honour board and fifty-thousand dollars in their bank account.

Bert woke early. Despite all his careful planning there were still a few elements which needed his attention. First was the text message he warned everyone was coming. In this, he spelt out very carefully the plans for the day; where and when they were to meet and when to don their colours.

Jayde slept comfortably deep into the morning. Her semi-final wasn't until midday. She had time to catch breakfast with her friends. Sitting there enjoying the last few sips of her coffee, Jayde thought deeply about her past twelve months. Her scholarship, that horrendous race and the MAGS response. Victoria, with her harassment and victimisation. Losing her job and the scuttled attempt at her own life. Her Poppy wrapping his arms around her and giving her hope. The bitterly cold and stinking hot days on Bradfield Sports Ground. Meeting Thomas, travelling around the state and country with him and her two best friends.

Recounting these moments, Jayde knew none of these would have occurred without her Poppy. His genius brought her to this moment. His desire for her success didn't waver, even during times when he could have been excused for focussing on his own issues.

Today was the day she would repay him. With no limits or boundaries, she could finally show everyone just how fast she can run.

* * *

Steve stood in the Stewards' room, pigeon-chested delivering his impassioned maiden Easter Monday speech. Many in the room had heard versions of this before, only from the mouth of a different Paterson. 'Today we showcase our sport to the nation. The Gift is the jewel in our crown. Many people don't know about professional running, but they know The Gift. Our job today is to ensure they remember this race. You know what to do, get it done!'

Implicitly knowing his position and role, Bill sat in his favourite chair disengaged from Steve's uninspiring ramblings. Quietly sipping his morning coffee, he sat there staring at the honour board. His eyes focussed on his decade competing in The Gift. Like checking the door twice before leaving the house, Bill ran through the names once again.

For the most part, he could match a name with a face. However 1966 always came up empty. He certainly remembered the controversy. He had stood in this very room with his coach, arguing there had been a fix. The asterisk behind the name J. Hill, Lidcombe reminded him that this race remained refuted.

His mind travelled back through the filmstrip of his running career. He knew he had seen Mr J. Hill from Lidcombe before, somewhere up in the Murray events. Memories about this mystery man began flooding back. He was known as a plodder, someone who was always around, but never noticed, good enough to work his way past the heats.

The filmstrip kept playing, returning to the vivid memory from yesterday and that hand flick. It had to be him; his action mirrored that of this blow in Jayde Hardy. Finally, he had his man. Now he had to find the link.

His gut was right. She was trouble, and there was a good chance another stitch-up was about to happen. He needed time to investigate, but he was minutes away from marching out into the biggest day in the professional running calendar. From that moment there would be precious little free time before the final. His only hope, Victoria; she could stop history from being repeated.

*   *   *

Victoria woke relaxed. Her daily routine began as always with a message to her fans and friends. Predicting the day's events before they happened, Victoria announced that she would be the first athlete in the modern era to win the triple treat.

By the end of the day, I will have the RGB, Red, Blue and Green sashes. Her selfie showing the blue and green sashes waiting for their partner. Many of her fans couldn't care less about what was in her hand; they were more interested in the shapes and colours coming from under her semi-opaque silk gown.

*   *   *

Dave McPharland was excited. Easter Monday racing was by far the best day of his season. Virtually every race was a final and each had its own unique market. He had reviewed his book the previous night and checked them against his ProRun algorithm. His position was strong.

Most of the money held on Antoine shifted over to Victoria. He liked when the short-priced favourite won. His payout in relative terms was considerably less and, most importantly, the money he made from the other runners was measurably more.

His predictions put her at least a half metre ahead of the field, and her odds crept in further to an unenticing one and one tenth to one. Only Muppets took these odds; for every dollar on, your return was a measly ten cents.

*   *   *

Jayde could hear the captivating sounds of racing as she approached the athlete's entrance. The crack of the gun was followed by the ever-building roar as the race drew closer to its conclusion. Then the cheers as winner cut the tape.

These sounds excited her; today come three-fifteen, these would be for her.

*   *   *

Victoria was the first to run. Normally the favourite would be allocated the last race to help build tension, but this year Steve decided it would be better to reverse this process. He wanted her locked away as soon as possible.

She didn't disappoint. A blistering effort had her two marks ahead by the end of the race. Her post-race celebrations met everyone's expectations and were already trending before she collected her blocks. Holding no interest in the other three races, Victoria quickly exited the track.

Drawn in heat three, Jayde was glad to see her leave. Setting up her blocks, she looked down her rope-defined tunnel. She had learnt a little about lane quality, and her lane looked and felt fast. It was firm and flat under foot. She would not have to be worried about lumps, bumps, or rolls on this track.

As the starter called 'Runners dig in,' details of the other lanes were discarded by her brain; all she could see was her single lane, one-hundred and twelve metres down to the gates. 'Set,' and her body loaded ready to explode. Her start was fantastic, then there was the distinct crack of a second gun. Her impeccable start was in vain.

As she rolled down to a stop, her brain connected back to her body, and fear shot through her body. Did she cause the false start. If so, that would cost her a metre. In a quality field like this, that could be impossible to overcome. Poppy's plan may fall short by one race.

Her heart skipped a beat as the flag official briefly paused at the end of her lane before stepping over the rope. The distinctive rush of relief flooded through her veins. She had thirty seconds to get back into race mode.

With a few deep breaths and a stationary sprint, she was back in the zone. For many athletes, any break can ruin their race. They lose sharpness and sit in the blocks, while others take advantage and pick up an early metre or two, making them nearly impossible to catch, let alone beat. Thankfully, she had developed the physical and emotional intelligence to withstand this distraction. Her start was as impressive as before, and she gained early ground on the field.

Leading into the gates, she was under attack by one of the backmarkers. As they burst through the gates, the Stewards and finish camera couldn't separate either runner, and the race was declared a dead heat. Both runners would progress to the final.

Ecstatic on the inside, Jayde maintained her calm demeanour. She still had another race to win before letting her emotion go.

As her position in the final was confirmed, Bert reached for his mobile phone; *she did it, see you soon.*

* * *

The final was just under two hours away and Jack was just under an hour and a half in Maryborough. Jack, Gillian, Coby and Marcus were already on the move when Boomer's confirmation came through. Thomas's facetime call had set them in motion. Not wanting to disappoint his mate, Jack replied, *You bloody ripper.*

Next, inform his brothers it was time to bear their colours. Progressively, they were to take their place in the crowd. A few of Jack's closest mates would form an unofficial honour guard for Hobbler and wheel him through the famed wrought-iron gates.

Jayde made her way out of the athlete's zone and into the general admission area. Walking through the crowd, she was no longer inconspicuous. Random punters congratulated her and wished her well for the final. The walk to her friends took considerably longer than expected.

Eventually she made it. Petra and Georgia rushed her. There was no need to inhibit their excitement. Their wild, loud congratulations brought the attention of those nearby, who also joined the celebrations.

Nick and Andrew gave their best country salute; a considered nod of the head as they raised their beers. Thomas stood back and captured the excitement with his phone. Celebrations paused while he give her a congratulatory kiss.

Excusing herself from the gathering Jayde made her way back to the seclusion of the Rose Garden. She knew Poppy would already know about the final, but it was important she told him. It was only fitting, given the work he did to get her here.

Before she had the chance to open her favourites, her phone burst to life. Unknown number; *if it's important, they'll leave a message.*

Seconds later, the anticipated voicemail alert popped onto her screen. Figuring this was safe, she dialled her message back. A familiar voice greeted her; It was Miss Morrison. 'Jayde, I saw your brilliant run to make the final. My thoughts and prayers are with you, best of luck. Win and show the stuffy MAGS community what you were capable of.'

Jayde remembered the encouragement Miss Morrison had given her, challenging her to chase her dreams. Right now, this was her dream, and following her mentor's advice, she was going to turn it into reality.

Buoyed, Jayde returned to her reason for this solitude.

Jack soaked in every word as though it was the first time he had heard about it. In his whisper quiet voice, he gave her his last piece of advice. 'Now you show them what you can really do!'

While in the quiet of this garden, Jayde had her own business to attend to. For the first time since returning to running, she called her dad to let him know she had made the final. Sitting behind the wheel, bored shitless, he was delighted to hear her voice.

Never having time to understand the nuances of professional running, Scott was happy to listen as she described her rise to the final. Moving his taxi up the rank to be the next available, he was about to end the call when Jayde hit him with an unthinkable proposition. 'I'm on for the win, take whatever is left from Temora and get it on me.'

After what had happened with Jack, Scott made a conscious choice to never bet. 'What do you mean?'

'Withdraw the money, go to the TAB and get it on me.'

'How, I'm on shift?'

'Take a break, park the cab, whatever. Please trust me, but you need to do it soon, the final's on just after three.'

He knew there was seven hundred left after he had paid for his car and Gillian's trip with Jack. This would cover their upcoming electricity bill, giving them breathing room for the insurance renewal at the end of May.

Sitting behind the steering wheel, Scott was conflicted. He trusted his daughter, but it was gambling that condemned him to this seat. Now she was asking him to willingly engage in the activity that took so much away.

Rationalising the conundrum, Scott was able to find a way to follow his daughter's instructions without betraying the promise he made to himself all those years ago. It was her money, and she could do with it what she wanted; he just happened to be in the best position to make it happen.

*　*　*

With his conscience clear, he parked the taxi and headed off to find the nearest ATM and TAB. Walking through the doors, it was clear he was outside his comfort zone. Television screens with races, commentary and odds adorned each wall.

The visual stimulation was overwhelming. Several standing tables were placed strategically to embrace the action from the big screen. A diverse cross-section of the local community stood transfixed, holding tickets, hollering pointless encouragement to a horse race in a place called Morphettville.

Beyond the big screen, he could see footage from The Gift, and the panel reviewing the field and their odds for the final. Jayde's odds had shortened further; at fifteen to one she was still a rank outsider.

Scott had to take a second look; he couldn't believe his daughter's name was on the screen. Standing behind a rather large hairy man who was in desperate need of a long soak and a good blast of deodorant, he waited for his time at the counter.

The cashier was stunned; traditionally this was a small wager outlet. Following the responsible service of gambling protocols, she asked Scott to confirm the amount before validating the process with the duty manager. Finally, after several minutes he placed his first bet.

Taking his ticket, Scott went and stood at the only remaining table, his eyes tracking back to the coverage from The Gift.

Sensing something was on, several locals joined him. If there is one thing that can be said about TAB dwellers, they are a friendly bunch. Before Scott knew it, he was chatting away with half a dozen new friends.

Noticing he was only focussed on one screen, they began to question his interest in The Gift.

'My daughter is in the final, and she says she's on.'

Inside information, now that's a rarity in here, and trusting their new buddy's tip, each scrambled to get his own piece of the action. Now everyone had some skin in the game, there was a real sense of anticipation as the clock eased towards the three-fifteen start time.

Feeling the familiar vibration in his pocket, Scott checked his phone. It was Santo, the owner of the cab making his usual check-in call. Feeling like a teenager jigging school, Scott hit the red call end button. He would deal with Santo later. A dummy fare or two from his potential winnings would keep him from getting the boot.

CHAPTER 36

The Gift

Each of the eight finalists moved through their preparations in their own unique way. Supremely confident, Victoria combined her pre-race routine with a sequence of stretches and wiggles that kept the crowd and internet entertained.

Chloe Spinner had her game face on and ignored everyone. Brandon, the second favourite, was doing his best to intimidate with his spectacular strength and speed.

Dave McPharland quickly checked his position for the final. There was the usual frenzy of last-minute bets as everyone looked to get on a winner.

His program glitched, and he was caught long on J. Hardy, St Marys. It failed to shorten her odds in-line with the money being held; she was still holding at twenty-to-one. Combined with the bets taken from her opening odds, Dave was exposed well beyond his acceptable level of risk.

Concerned but not worried, he calmly reviewed the situation. Since qualifying, Jayde went from the lowest backed finalist through to the third highest while still carrying the longest odds. 'Why?'

Reviewing the field, this was Victoria's race to lose; even with her pre-race adjustment she was off the most competitive mark. Brandon would also be there in the mix, and Chloe had a point to prove.

Satisfied the odds remained stacked in his favour, he remembered the words of his father. 'If you are caught long, mitigate however you can, protect your position, and minimise the risk.'

He still had one more ace up his sleeve. Scrolling through his contact list he stopped on his recently acquired business partner.

There was no obscurity in his message. *'Caught long on J. Hardy, do what you can.'*

Feeling the vibration in his pocket, Steve snuck a look at the loaded message, 'What the fuck!'

This was hard evidence he had coercive control over the outcome of races. If the Gaming Authorities ever subpoenaed his phone, this would initiate an investigation, ending with him in serious trouble. At best it would cost him his job and reputation, at worst a criminal conviction and time behind bars.

Notwithstanding these legal factors, he still bore the scar from their deal. Dave had duped him, coming to his meeting with a pre-prepared contract then low-balling him with his offer.

On the verge of the biggest race of the season, Steve was caught in a dilemma; this was his business partner, and loyalty had to be the bind that underpinned their operation. However, the unbalanced way this partnership formed continued to cause consternation.

He needed time to think. Excusing himself, he went to spend a penny.

Sitting on the shitter, he was torn. Dave had kept him afloat long enough to witness the potential of his creation. The school uptake exceeded expectations, and cashflow was no longer a problem. However, a portion of this had to be handed away, profit that should have stayed in his pocket.

The more he thought, the angrier he got; Paterson's Curse, as his grandfather Reg called it, kicked in. Enveloped by the purple ire, he settled on his response to his partner's request.

Looking at his phone, he could see lane five was holding a clear two-point advantage. With a sinister grin on his face he uttered, 'Fuck you Dave, I hope she wins!'

Doubling down on his *fuck you,* he placed Victoria into lane two, which under his system was running at a 0 rating.

Along with the other seven finalists, Jayde was escorted to the parade area positioned just to the outside of lane eight on the sixty-metre mark, directly in front of the historic federation style grandstand and front entrance.

Protocol dictated that each athlete would be presented to the crowd before receiving their lane. The parallels to the Betty Cambridge Cup were overwhelming. Jayde sensibly kept her acknowledgement as lowkey as possible. The same could not be said for Victoria. This performance was one of her best.

As Victoria was embarking on her provocative seduction of the crowd, Jayde saw several men wearing Poppy's colours. They were moving away from the track and heading towards the front gate. Her heart sank Wouldn't it be great if he could see her race. Looking away, she needed to steady her thoughts.

Subconsciously, her eyes darted back to where she saw the men in their biker vests. They were slowly walking back into the ground, and looking deeper she recognised some of the faces, Uncle Bert, Kenny and a few others. A wave of happiness fell over her. If Poppy couldn't be here, then this was the next best thing.

They were walking carefully in a straight line, shoulder to shoulder, heading down the concrete path towards the front of the grandstand. As they entered the concrete concourse, Bert, Ken and the others parted, leaving a small space which was quickly filled by a slender figure pushing a wheelchair.

Focussing on this new detail, Jayde struggled to hide her excitement. Her wish had come true! Poppy was here with her now. She had to blink several times to make sure that what she was seeing was real, and wait, who is that pushing him? 'Mum!'

Leading into the race, she was ultra-confident that there was another gear left in her. Having Poppy and her mum there confirmed this. This was going to be the performance of her life.

Steve stood at the front of his team of Stewards for the pre-race formalities. Bill and Adam occupied the last two spaces on the fringe of the group. Acutely aware of their station in this process, Adam stood tall, knowing he would progressively make his way towards the centre of this shot. Bill stood defeated. He was on borrowed time, and before too long he would be pushed the other way, out of the frame altogether. Holding his position, Bill's eyes also scanned the crowd. He needed something to take his attention away from these stodgy formalities.

Looking around, he recognised some old foes from his running days, and others he might consider calling friends and several sponsors which he brought into the event when he was in a position of power. None of these people held any interest for him; they were about as boring as these tedious proceedings.

Running his eyes further around the crowd, something grabbed his attention. Several bikers moved aside to reveal a man being pushed in a wheelchair. Bikers were not generally associated with this event. He had seen a few over the years but never this many together.

As his eyes adjusted to the distance, the details of each person began to take shape. It wasn't until he focussed on the man in the wheelchair that a ghost from the past appeared. This was the face he had been searching for, this was Mr J. Hill from Lidcombe. Like everyone from his era, his face displayed the scars of time, but this was undeniably him.

As the announcer concluded the athlete's call and commanded the field to the start line, Bill looked across to Jayde. She was yet to move; she had steely eyes directed at the man in the wheelchair. Then it happened, the evidence he needed, a frail, quivering thumbs up. His instincts back in Tenterfield were right, Miss J. Hardy was a sandbagger.

He had to think fast. What reason could he use to stop the race?

He knew from his previous attempt that Steve would never entertain the idea, not on the evidence of a name, face, and a thumbs up. Broadcasting had to run to time, contracts and sponsorships depended on this. His position on the track made it virtually impossible for him to apply any non-compliance or anti-competitive charges.

He was snookered, with no cards to play, so he had to accept what will be, will be.

*   *   *

Silence fell across the ground as the starter called, 'Runners dig in'.

Feeling like this race was already won, Victoria gave her last titty, bum wiggle before seating herself in the blocks. Jayde moved into the same position with much less fuss.

The call 'Set' echoed around Central Park. In unison each athlete rose, loading, ready to release.

The crack of the gun brought everyone to life. Athletes exploded out of their blocks and began their straight-line dash to glory. The crowd roared to life with a level of noise that had not been heard all weekend.

Jayde's feeling in the warm-up area was mirrored on the track. Her first ten to fifteen metres exuded power, and she had already pulled a metre on the field. Her lane was fast and responsive, and raising her head and hips out of the power phase she opened her cadence and stride. Accelerating quickly, she was pulling ground on the front marker.

Victoria, on the other hand, had been left in the blocks and was struggling to find form. Jayde continued to accelerate, each stride drove her faster and closer to the finishing gates. Blasting past the front marker she was now the clear leader.

The ground announcer couldn't believe what he was witnessing as the race blew through the eighty-metre mark. Victoria's long, elegant stride was struggling to make any ground on Jayde.

By ninety metres, Victoria had found her form and was beginning to take back some of the ground she lost. With only thirty metres remaining, did she have enough track to make up the deficit.

The rest of the field was now covered, Chloe Spinner was committing the sprinters' first deadly sin; overstriding, falling behind every time her foot hit the ground. Brandon the second-favourite and backmarker was gone; his dodgy hamstring couldn't stand the pressure.

Flying through one hundred metres, Victoria's stride began deteriorating. Her races usually stopped at this mark, so the additional fourteen or so metres would be a struggle. Jayde, on the other hand, had trained for these glory metres her entire campaign.

Jack's voice ran through her head. *'Track runners go out the backdoor once they pass the 100m mark.'* Jayde made her final effort, and with eyes sternly focussed on the finish gates she hit that extra gear. Battling to maintain her form, Victoria looked to her left, where Jayde's lead was opening further.

Dave McPharland could see with less than ten metres to go that this race was run and won. Turning away from the finish gates, he already knew this was about to become a very expensive day.

Jayde was about to make history, not only becoming the first female to win the open Gift, but also by the widest margin. There was no way Victoria was given the fastest lane. His request had fallen on deaf ears, the player had been played.

Jack was in awe of Jayde's performance. He could tell early in the race she was going to be hard to beat. By the half-way mark, he knew the race was in the bag, and resting deeper in his chair he savoured every stride.

She was majestic in her action, her hips and shoulders were stable, her arm and knee drive were both fluent and powerful, and her heel recovery minimised any unnecessary movement. Her only blemish technically was that tell-tale right-hand flick at the end of her arm drive. Jack revelled in this one single flaw; it was his flaw, and he loved it.

Luckily, the brakes were activated on Jack's wheelchair as Gillian's reaction moved from proud and encouraging to hysterical, loud, and rambunctious the closer her daughter came to the finishing gates.

Marcus and Coby stood back and enjoyed the spectacle both on and off the track. On all the excitement, Marcus felt a tinge of sadness. He now understood the lure of this event. It was his inaction which prevented him from sharing this with his dad.

Scott and his new mates were screaming all manner of expletives and encouragement at the big screen, louder and more animated the closer Jayde got to the finish gates. He could barely feel the slaps on his back as it became obvious that she was on her way to victory.

Keeping his emotions in check, Bert stood straight and tall. Although controlled on the outside, he was hysterical on the inside. His giant heart pounded as Jayde shot past his vantage point.

With a satisfying deep breath Bert felt immense pride; he had helped his best mate and granddaughter accomplish such a phenomenal feat. Throwing some numbers into his phone, he roughly calculated how much they stood to earn from this win. This was a life-changing day for the Hardys.

Bill stood in his allocated position staring down the track, frozen in disbelief; history was repeating before his eyes. Typically, it was impossible to pick the winner from codgers' corner. However, today was something special; even from the worst position on the track it was clear Jayde was well ahead.

Standing there, Bill's right hand sub-consciously began to undo the shiny silver buttons on his sacred black and white sports jacket. As the third button popped through the eye, Bill could see the tape strung taught across the finish line suddenly go limp.

Jayde had done it! She broke the tape a clear three metres ahead of Victoria and the rest of the field. As the broken sections of tape turned quickly into streamers that had lost the gravity-defying effect of wind, Bill's prized Steward's jacket beat them in hitting the ground first.

Bill had no interest in being on the track anymore. All he wanted was one last beer in his favourite chair.

Jayde continued running well past the finish line, making a sharp left arc she headed straight towards Poppy and her mum. Traditionally, members of the winner's squad would be storming the track, surrounding their victor, jumping up and down with delight.

Jayde had no squad; she only had her Poppy. Scaling the picket fence, she headed to where he was patiently waiting in his wheelchair. As she approached, he gave her a quivering double thumbs up. The smile on his face was pure joy.

Struggling to control her excitement, she had to quickly remind herself that he was a seriously ill man. Stopping in front of his wheelchair, they shared are special moment of silent adulation. Unable to hold back anymore, she crouched and gave Jack the most loving, special, soft huggle of her life, whispering in his ear, 'You're the best Poppy!'

Once again, a rare single tear rolled out of Jack's eye.

The television cameras followed her as she made her mad dash into the crowd. The commentary team, still in a state of shock, were struggling to find material to keep up with the images going live to air.

They were all baffled by the ease with which she had decimated the field, and it wasn't long before comparisons were being made to the 1966 Gift. Capturing Jayde and Poppy together, sharing that special post-race moment, would have been much more powerful had they known this was the embrace of two Gift winners.

Before Jayde could break the embrace, Jack held her ear close to his face. In his whisper quiet voice, he said 'You did it. You worked hard and you did it. Now go and enjoy it!'

Jayde gave him a kiss on the cheek before turning her attention to her celebrations. She wanted to continue celebrating with her mum, Thomas, and friends, but there were important formalities that needed her immediate attention; the famous red sash and fifty-thousand dollars.

Heading back down to the fence, she received countless congratulations and pats on the back from those nearby. Vaulting back over the fence, she could see and hear Victoria remonstrating with Steve, shouting in his face, 'She cheated, she had to cheat to beat me, I'm the national champion, I own the Australian record, there's no way this fucking bitch is faster than me'.

Mobile phones and the television crew dialled into this confrontation; her voice was clearly audible to anyone in the front rows. The production team, captivated by her outburst, missed hitting the dump button, allowing the expletive to be broadcast nationwide.

Maintaining his dignity and composure, Steve gave Victoria some valuable racing advice. 'See the series of white flags? That means the race was legal.'

Victoria's fury turned on Jayde, and she screamed over Steve's shoulder, 'I should have spat in your lane again, you bogan bitch.'

Could today get any better? This was an irrefutable admission, proof Victoria had done it. Before Victoria realised what she had said, footage was trending social media.

Several Stewards stood in front of Victoria, linking arms to create a virtual wall, keeping her at bay from the rather informal presentation ceremony. Tradition dictated that both the sash and winner's cheque were handed over without any significant pomp and ceremony.

Steve offered Jayde the sash while Antony presented the fat fifty-thousand-dollar cheque. Jayde accepted both with glee and happily posed for photos with the official party. Her smile was priceless; it bore the joy of accomplishment and redemption.

Stepping in to get the first interview, Dan the on-ground reporter struggled to land on where to start. Should he open with her dominating performance or go straight to the juicy, scandalous post-race blow up.

Under instruction from his producer, he led with her dominant race performance. Stock questions; 'How do you feel?'

'When did you know the race was yours?'

'Tell me the emotion you felt when you crossed the line.'

Each question was building to the meaty part of the interview, Victoria's post-race shenanigans.

He had one last question before his strategic shift. 'Who did you jump the fence to see?'

'My Poppy, Jack Hill.'

His name bamboozled Dan. As a former competitor and Gift winner, he was familiar with the urban myth that was Mr J. Hill of Lidcombe. Reacting to this outrageous news, Dan took the initiative. 'Could you take me up to meet the myth that was the 1966 winner.'

'Let's go!'

The cameraman and sound guy had no way of scaling a picket fence, so the group headed to the nearest gate before strategically moving through the crowd. His producer, keeping up with the play, barked orders down Dan's earpiece. 'Slow down, get the low-down on Victoria now. Then focus on Jack.'

Following these instructions, Dan kept interview rolling as she walked beside him. 'Can you explain that extraordinary outburst by Victoria and the end of the race?'

'That goes back to Year 12 and the Betty Cambridge Cup, when she spat in her own lane, then blamed it on me. I was thrown out of the event, trolled online, bullied, and victimised at school. After school she continued to troll me, getting me fired from my job as a teacher's aide. Grabbing some rum and rope I went very close to not being here. Thankfully, my Poppy got to me, inspired me with his story and here I am.'

Dan couldn't believe his luck; he was just gifted a juicy scandal, along with interviewing a gift ghost. His earpiece was full of chatter as the producers shifted their scheduling to accommodate these tantalising tales.

Kneeling beside Jack's wheelchair, Dan introduced himself before shaking his frail hand. 'What an absolute pleasure to meet a Grampians myth, Mr Jack Hill, winner of the 1966 Gift.'

Jack, aware of his frail voice, nodded his head.

'That was an amazing effort by your granddaughter today, you must be proud?'

Trying his hardest to speak beyond his whisper, he said, 'Too right!'

'Jack, your win in 66 has remarkable similarities to your granddaughter's win today. Tell us your family secret.'

Taking a moment to think and get his breath, Jack decided to have some fun. 'Preparation, we learnt how to prepare for this event.'

Laughing, Dan kept playing along. 'Two winners in the family, who gets bragging rights at home?'

Keeping the banter going Jack replied, 'I won it first, so I'll let you work it out.'

'After your win in 66 you vanished, and from then all manner of theories surfaced about why you left. Can you clarify for our audience what happened?'

Jack's happy Poppy face shifted, and his voice returned to a whisper, and with a noticeable quiver he replied, 'National service in Vietnam. I was wounded in the Battle of Suoi Chau Pha. Nerve damage in my leg removed my ability to run.'

Dan gave reverence to Jack's chilling explanation. 'I know it wasn't said enough then but thank you for your service.'

Bringing Jayde into the shot, Dan threw back to the commentary team. The broadcast continued reviewing the performance, the post-race shenanigans, and the interview with Jack. There was so much to unpack the team struggled to cover everything in the remaining programmed timeslot.

Recognising the importance of being the first to break this news, the production team kept Dan's earpiece channel open. Their instructions; get verbal agreement for an exclusive interview.

Using his confidence and charm, Dan escorted Jayde back through the crowd, chatting to her as only another winner could. Through the conversation he dropped their proposal. 'My network wants to hear your story, we want to know about you, Jack and your relationship with Victoria, they're offering a fifty-thousand-dollar retainer.'

Without a moment's hesitation, Jayde accepted; she wanted to tell her story and to get fifty k; amazing. In a manner of minutes, her family's fortunes had been turned on their head.

Jayde headed back to the start line to collect her belongings under a chorus of congratulations. Waving and smiling, her brain was buzzing. What would she do with one hundred thousand dollars.

The next phase of Hobblers plan rolled into action. Boomer's men moved conspicuously through this area, entering empty handed and leaving with handfuls of cash. He sent the call to wear colours as a message to the bookies to keep their muscle away.

Regaining his thoughts, Scott was also waiting patiently in a queue with his new mates to claim his winnings. He dropped seven hundred on the win at odds of fifteen to one. Before he could complete the equation in his head the cashier was handing over nine thousand dollars, cash.

He was stunned; he had never held such a fistful of cash in his life.

Aware his cab was standing still; Scott farewelled to his new mates and went back to work.

CHAPTER 37

Payback

Collecting her blocks and bag, Jayde afforded herself a moment to absorb what had just happened. Casting her eyes around the fence line, seeing the crowd, and feeling their energy, she wanted to remember this life-changing moment forever.

Satisfied, she headed for the exit point in the athlete's zone. Waiting patiently adjacent to the gate were several Sports Integrity officials. As the Gift winner, Jayde was automatically selected for a drug test. Until she peed in the jar, she was to stay within the confines of the athlete's zone, a chaperone following her every move.

To keep its clean sport sanction, two other athletes from the final were also randomly selected to provide a urine sample. Victoria and Dylan, a seasoned runner who placed fifth, were the athletes required to remain until their specimen jar was full.

Still reeling from her post-race explosion, this was just another source of frustration to Victoria. The last thing she needed was delays and a shadow following her every move.

More concerned about getting Pete ready to fly her back to Sydney, Victoria paid little attention to the details on her declaration form. Her signature verified that no traces of performance enhancing or illicit drugs would be found in her system.

* * *

Bert left his post to help Jack back to his transport. The honour guard which welcomed him to the ground grew in numbers for his exit. Mates who collected his winnings and members of the public created an informal corridor as Gillian and Marcus pushed Jack towards those large wrought iron gates.

Parking adjacent to the famous gates, Coby waited for Jack to arrive. Despite the elation and adrenaline of victory, the reality was he was gravely ill, and this excitement had exhausted him. Marcus gave him a quick once over before locking his wheelchair in position. After his interview with Dan, he was a popular man, and punters from all over came to offer their well wishes.

Jack felt like royalty as he waved to acknowledge their attention. Before closing the door, Boomer leaned into the van. 'Got a big surprise for you tonight, see you up the road.'

With that he closed the door and headed back into the track. Surprised and intrigued, Gillian looked to Jack for an answer, but his lowering eye lids told her this could wait for another time.

Their plan was to head north as far as Holbrook, just over five hours up the road. Jack and Bert figured this would be far enough away to keep out of the clutches of any repercussions that may come their way.

The rest of the touring group would head off in different directions, some directly north, some west, then north, like Jack back in the day, and others came along the main thoroughfare. Each was booked to stay in different locations, and only when they were back in Sydney would they meet again.

* * *

Bill sat back in his favourite chair, sipping away on his favourite Draught beer. There were still half-a-dozen races remaining on the program and he was scheduled to be on duty for all of them. With alcohol in his system, he instantly removed himself from the roster. He had no intention of picking up his jacket and going back out onto the track. He was about to use two words no-one thought possible from a Paterson, 'I quit.'

Dave McPharland was stuck in the bull pen; the steady precession of punters holding winning Gift tickets appeared never ending. Payouts on twenty, fifty and hundred-dollar bets at ridiculously long odds soon depleted the cash reserves in his bag. Acutely aware of the reputational and brand damage he could suffer if he did not return all winnings, Dave always carried a sizable cash reserve. Only a couple of times in his career had he been forced to dip into this safety net. Today he was concerned that what he was holding may not be enough.

Sensing this was not a random occurrence, Dave began to look more carefully at the movements of people within the bull pen. Punters were moving here and there, getting their last bets on, or collecting from earlier in the day. However, he noted a regular stream of punters in biker vests he had paid were lining up to collect their winnings from his competition.

Concerned, he decided to carefully follow the next person in this kit who presented a winning ticket. A large, behemoth of man in Vets attire happened to be this next customer, the same man he saw in the pub in Maryborough at the start of the year.

For the next hour or more he followed Bert as he moved in and out of the bull pen. Each time he entered he collected handfuls of cash from another bookmaker. Dave estimated this massive human being was holding somewhere between sixty to seventy thousand dollars by the time he finished. Dave knew he and his compatriots had been taken to the cleaners and there was almost nothing they could do about it.

*　*　*

Finally, after what was the longest day of the season, the last race was run and won. Dave, Paddy and the other bookies could now close their bags and call it a day, a very bad day.

Normally, they would pull their boards down, give a farewell nod and head off. Comradery wasn't a word usually associated with this group of men. However today they stood together as one, each in possession of a very empty bag and a head full of questions.

Paddy pointed out what Dave already knew. 'We've been swindled out of a swathe of money by a cunning, devious, well-orchestrated plan.'

Dave wanted answers and he wanted them now. Taking Paddy with him, he stormed into the Stewards' room.

Steve, along with his team of men in black and white jackets, were enjoying a well-deserved cold beer. Though scattered throughout the room in their own groups, there was a common theme to their conversations, the unprecedented Gift.

As Dave made his way across the floor an uneasy silence fell over the room. This was a sanctioned space, accessible only by those wearing the official attire.

All eyes were trained on Dave as he made a beeline for Steve. 'What the fuck do you call that? Do you have any idea what today has cost us?'

'You're bookmakers, you're the punters, punter. Some days you win, others you lose. I'm figuring today you lost.'

'You're fucking right we lost!' quipped Dave. 'Guess how much that race cost us?'

Continuing to control his reaction, Steve replied, 'I don't know, but if you're in here I guess it's a fair bit'.

'A fair bit, try over a million dollars combined.'

The extraordinary amount nearly drew all the oxygen from the room.

'You, me, us, we have been played,' Dave said looking briefly at Paddy. 'What was the term you used? Swindled, we've been swindled. I want to see her data, how the fuck was the granddaughter of the most infamous Gift winner off seven and a quarter metres.'

Never in the history of VPAL had such information been shared and there was no way Steve was going to set a precedent here. In a more defensive tone, he looked Dave square in the eyes.

'You know our process is valid, she was off the correct mark, you just fucked up with your odds.'

This politician style response only added fuel to Dave's fire. He was now on the point of no return. 'You could have stopped this; I gave you the warning.'

The odour of these words hung in the air like a rancid fart, giving those in the room a chance to digest what had just been said. Stan and his close allies waited with bated breath for Steve's retort.

In his typical deflective style, Steve ended the conversation. 'I'm offended by your accusation and will not dignify it with a response.'

Dave knew he was on the rough end of Steve's square up. He had swindled Steve earlier in the year and now Steve was making him pay. There was a reason Dave's bag had longevity. He never let anyone get one over him. With the message on his screen, Dave held his phone out for all to see.

Not satisfied that this message had done enough damage, Dave dropped another bomb before leaving the room. 'You know what, business partners usually work together.'

Steve stood there, mouth open, ready for his brain to send a witty or sarcastic reply, but none came; his brain already admitted defeat.

These words hung longer and harder than his first. Those early words were a tacit allegation, these new ones were hard proof. Steve had violated clause eighteen of the constitution. No member of the executive or organising committee will hold an interest or partnership with an affiliated or sanctioned betting agency.

Stan sat back in his chair taking copious mental notes. Come the post-season board meeting he would immediately push a no-confidence motion on Steve and his team.

Like all dynasties, their time came to a spectacular and devastating end. With his greed and unsatiable need for power, Steve ensured the Patersons' generational hold over the VPAL would end with him. Adam had just been denied his birthright, the chance to overthrow his father.

A sip or two away from the bottom of his beer, Bill sat quietly through the shenanigans. He had unofficially relinquished his affiliation with VPAL when his prized jacket hit the hallowed turf a few hours ago. This shit fight, despite having different players, held the same premise to the one he was involved in over half a century ago.

While they argued, Mr J. Hill and Miss J. Hardy were far away, holding both the answers and the cash.

Bill could have rightfully rubbed salt into Steve's wounds by reminding him of their conversation back in Tenterfield. It's certainly what Reg would have done to him. But what would that achieve, the Paterson name was already in tatters?

Instead, for the first time in his life, he had respect and admiration for someone other than himself. Acknowledging this in his own special way, Bill looked up to the honour board, focussing on 1966 J. Hill, Lidcombe and raised his beer.

CHAPTER 38

Scotch on the rocks

Bert and Kenny rumbled into Holbrook with just enough time to catch dinner before the town shut down for the night.

Today was Jayde's day and worthy of a celebration. However, tonight was Jack's night. Acutely aware of his prognosis, he was in no doubt that this was the last meal he would share with his family and friends. Tonight, his all-time favourite; a Chinese banquet.

Since his diagnosis, his sense of taste and smell had progressively weakened, and only the strongest flavours and scents would tingle his taste buds. But tonight wasn't about the food; tonight was about sharing precious time with those he loved.

His only disappointment was that Jayde hadn't arrived yet. She was due soon; her drug test took longer than anticipated. Two races left her dehydrated and the knowledge that she had to pee in full view of a stranger kept the urge at bay for quite a while.

Knowing Bert was holding some serious cash, Jack instructed him to offer the owners an extra five hundred cash to stay open until his party was done. More than their night's takings, they were happy to oblige.

There was a loud cheer as the lady of the moment finally entered the restaurant; celebrations could now begin. Every laugh and cheer were music to Jack's soul. As the last courses were being loaded onto the lazy Susan, Jayde leant across and gave Jack another of their special huggles, whispering 'You're amazing' in his ear.

In his soft voice, he replied, 'Revenge feels good doesn't it?'

Smiling, Jayde agreed. 'Poppy, it was incredible, her meltdown was next level, and the best thing is that it has already gone viral. According to Georgia, it already has more hits than mine.'

Looking at Poppy, they shared another special moment, uncontrollable laughter. This was good and not so good for Jack, as it induced a nasty coughing fit, only alleviated when Marcus increased his oxygen.

As the last of the dishes were being polished off, Boomer took his turn to sit next to his best mate. He couldn't hold his surprise any longer. 'Need to let you know how much you've won.'

Curious, Jack mouthed, 'Five-hundred k or so. Remember we did the sums.'

Struggling to hold his excitement, Boomer said, 'Bit higher mate, everyone doubled the bets, so by tomorrow night you'll be holding over a million in legitimate cash.'

'Bullshit!'

'Nah Hobbler, no bullshit, tomorrow night we'll collect it and lock it away in the safe at the clubhouse. Your girls will be ok.'

It took a moment for the enormity of this to sink in. Looking at Gillian, he was now able to repay the investment she had made in him. Deeply embedded guilt lifted from his conscience; he was now comfortable with his fate.

For the first time in nearly two decades, Jack felt like a drink. Leaning over to Boomer, he asked him 'Grab a Scotch on the rocks for the both of us.'

Shocked at his mate's request, Bert called the waiter. Jack's first sip was like his sobriety never happened. It was smooth and delicious. Sitting back in his chair he let the sweet, complex flavours dance around his mouth.

Wetting-the-bet was the final act of his swindle, finishing on a gambler's dream, trumps after going all in on his last throw.

His legacy wouldn't be remembered for what he took, it was now about what he gave.

* * *

Victoria touched down in Sydney well before the first course hit the table. Her focus, get home as fast as possible. Paparazzi, reacting to an anonymous tip, waited in front of her parents' Darling Point mansion. Grabbing as many snaps as possible, they made the short distance from the car to the front door feel like a mile.

Brittany waited for the pings to appear on her phone. The candid snaps now strategically entered the social media news cycle. The reprehensible behaviour and stunning admission would ensure astronomical view and share numbers. Profiles are manufactured on good and bad news.

For the first time, Victoria was trying to get out of the spotlight. Her social pages were in meltdown, vile, obscene, disgusting comments overloaded her inbox, and fans and followers morphed into haters and trolls.

Closing the door on these predators, Victoria looked around, and as usual, the large house was cold, barren, and empty. Her parents were out, dinner or drinks at the Yacht Club. Their return, hours away and even then, they wouldn't be in any state or mood to listen to her problems. They never did. Their parenting philosophy was give her everything she wanted, then she couldn't complain.

What she wanted and desperately needed tonight was their love. Alone and afraid, the world that was so recently at her mercy just turned and was tearing her apart. Shutting everything off, she curled under her doona, and cuddling one of her many pillows, she quietly cried herself to sleep.

* * *

Jack pushed as long as he could. Recognising the tell-tale signs of deep fatigue, Marcus and Coby suggested they get him to bed. One by one, Jack's special people congratulated him and wished him goodnight. Gillian and Jayde waited patiently, they wanted to go last.

Sharing a special group hug, Jack was desperate to share Boomer's unbelievable news, but the family wasn't complete. Scott earnt the right to hear this life-altering news first-hand. Acknowledging their love, he whispered, 'My beautiful girls, I'll see you in the morning'.

Kenny and Bert were holding well over a hundred thousand dollars in cash and had no interest in kicking on. Covering the bill and the promised extra, they gave their goodnights and headed to the safety of their hotel room.

Bikies or not, they were still old men who would struggle to defend Jack's bounty. Thomas, still reeling from the hideous effects of rum two days ago, was happy to see everyone call it a night.

Jayde and Gillian strolled back to the hotel, still buzzing. In a tick over twelve seconds their world had changed. Walking and chatting, Jayde saw a different side to her mother. She wasn't burdened with finances and organisation; she was free to be a mum.

'Hey, I just remembered, that TV guy who interviewed me after the race, he offered me fifty thousand to do an interview with them next week some time.'

Gillian was gobsmacked. "Wait, what, you just made another 50K, are you kidding me, you have one hundred thousand dollars!'

'Mum, I want to share this with you, you and dad, half. Maybe that could get dad out of the taxi or you a car. Whatever, it's yours.'

Or it could be the deposit they had been struggling to find for so many years.

'Once I've done the interview, I'll give them your account details and they will transfer the money direct to you. Easy.' Her tone and expression indicated this was not to be denied.

'Before you do anything, let me run this past dad.'

Gillian couldn't wait to call Scott. His shift in the taxi would be over soon. Kissing Jayde on the cheek, she said, 'Thank you, I better ring dad.'

Walking to the far corner of the parking lot, she hit the green call button. 'Hey darling, how was work?'

'Unbelievable. Jayde called before her race and forced me to drop the remains of her Temora money on her for the win. I'm sitting here with just under nine thousand dollars cash in front of me.'

'That's amazing! I've also got some news to pass on from Jayde. She's accepted an offer to do a television interview next week, her story with dad and the Victoria saga. It comes with 50K payment, and she wants us to have it.'

'Bullshit, she wants to give us fifty thousand. What about her? That could set her up. She could be a teacher, not just a teacher's aide.'

'I know, I was thinking the same, but she was adamant. I think we say 'yes' to half. With your nine and another twenty-five we would be back on track.'

'Absolutely, we can't take it all, it's too much.'

'She's gone inside, I'll tell her in the morning, See you tomorrow. Love you.' Gillian walked back across the bitumen, her head spinning, *Thirty thousand, that's a five per cent deposit on a six hundred thousand dollar property. Maybe we could look at a two-bed unit.*

Tonight, Gillian's dreams would be filled with how to best use their new fortune, not what they had to do to make it.

CHAPTER 39

Atone

Victoria's social media woes had gone from bad to worse. A sex tape emerged overnight and was trending as the hottest property on the internet.

Creative editing kept the perpetrator's face out of shot. Extending beyond social media, it featured every half-hour on morning television. This mainstream coverage only fuelled the public's curiosity, and Victoria's PR team was in overdrive trying to mitigate the damage.

* * *

In Holbrook, Gillian and Jayde woke to their own tragic news. Some time before the sun rose Jack's stoic battle with mesothelioma ended.

Taking refuge in Thomas's arms, Jayde sobbed.

Gillian, holding her emotion gently knocked on Bert's door.

'Give me a minute. I just need to get dressed.'

Pulling on his jeans, he took a moment to prepare himself for what awaited on the other side of the door. Drifting off to sleep he had had a horrible premonition; he saw a change in Jack once he knew his girls were safe.

He had fought the good fight, stood toe-to-toe with this insidious disease, hung in for as long as he could. Knowing they were secure, he lowered his gloves, submitting to the inevitable knockout blow. This was a loaded fight; mesothelioma was never going to lose.

Wiping tears from his eyes, Bert whispered farewell to his brother in arms. 'Rest long my friend, you leave us with a clear conscience and peace in your soul.'

Marcus and Coby were able to use their medical expertise and connections to handle the formalities when someone passes outside of a hospital.

Aware that saying goodbye before the body is taken away is a vital part of the grieving process, Marcus took both Jayde and Gillian into Jack's room. Lying in his hotel bed with the blanket up to his shoulders, he gave the illusion of sleeping peacefully.

The vital nasal oxygen tube was no longer making its familiar circuit from the neckline up and over his ears to finally rest under his nose. It was neatly rolled and placed over the valve.

Pulling the two side-table chairs up to the bed, Marcus started the process. 'Hey Jack, I got your two precious girls here, and they've got their own special things to say to you. From me, I'm going to miss our nightly conversations. You gave me such an insight and appreciation of my dad. Thanks for allowing me to join your last adventure, and don't worry, mate, your baby will be safe with me.'

With that, Marcus stood to attention and raised a stiff right hand to his eyeline, honouring both the man and his service. Lowering his hand, Marcus looked at Gillian and Jayde, and nodded his head before quietly leaving the room.

Jayde and Gillian reflected on the important part Jack had played in their lives. 'I remember seeing you for the first time, a strange man in a soldier's uniform with a funny limp. I was scared but then I got to know you and love you. I will never forget our special days on Cronulla beach. We would extract every ounce of daylight before returning home, and I would fall sleep in your arms on the train, waking only to change at Central, then the short walk home.'

'I know you had your demons, and given the circumstances, you did the best you could. I was so proud of you, giving it all away for me and my family. I loved coming home, knowing you were there with Jayde. Rest in peace dad, you've earnt it.'

'Poppy I've never known a day without you. I loved coming home and telling you about my day, you were always so interested. I always knew you would be there for me, even in the garage when everything seemed too much, you were there. You held me, then helped me move away from that dark place. I am where I am now because of you. I love you, Poppy.'

With tears streaming from their eyes, Gillian and Jayde hugged. A gentle tap on the door broke their embrace. It was Marcus; the Funeral Director had arrived, and it was time for Jack to go.

News of Jack's passing spread through the Vets community, so the ride back into Sydney was now a memorial ride. Groups gathered and rode in formation. Their planned meeting tonight to gather Jack's winnings would also be their first chance to raise a glass in honour of their mate Hobbler.

Taking his last sip of coffee, Scott stood next to the kitchen sink in his high-vis outfit, ready to quickly wash the cup and head off to work. His phone, tucked in one his many pockets burst to life. *That's strange, who rings at this time of the morning?*

Frozen with grief, his first instinct was to get to his family as fast as possible, but he was stuck. There was no way his shit-box would get him anywhere near Holbrook; it would be on the back of a tow-truck before Moss Vale.

Gillian and Jayde wouldn't reach home till mid-afternoon. Dressed and ready to go, he did what he always did; went to work. Working straight through without any breaks, he could leave early and be at home to meet his family. Only then could his grieving begin.

* * *

Bert opened the clubhouse late Tuesday afternoon, straightening a few chairs, and checking the fridge was stocked until he was satisfied they were ready for the start of Jack's farewell. Progressively, members of Hobblers ride gathered, handing their cash and receipts directly to Bert before grabbing a drink to toast their fallen comrade.

As expected Jack was the centre of all discussions. His personality, his exploits with 7RAR, his dedication to his families, both here and at home, his reclamation, and The Gift. This tale moved quickly from fable to legend.

By night's end, the oversized clubhouse safe struggled to house the mound of cash.

Tomorrow, Bert would have the honour of presenting Jack's legacy to his family.

* * *

Early in the planning process, Bert had brought Angus Masters to the hospital to speak with Jack. Angus, the club's solicitor, helped maintain the legal requirements of a motorcycle club, ensuring it remained registered and on the right side of the law.

He also offered his services to members and their families at mates' rates, his two most popular being conveyancing, and the creation of wills. Should his plan come off, Jack was going to need a will.

As sole beneficiary, Gillian would receive all financial assets, including any cash or bank credits which fell under his name. He also decreed his body was to be cremated, and his remains to be placed in her care.

His final request? His ash was to be scattered wherever Gillian saw fit. He was very specific that he did not want to be kept in an urn or placed in a cemetery. He wanted to be free.

Opening the safe, Bert saw the life-changing loot standing tall in neat piles, each providing the pathway to a new chapter for the Hardys. Placing two envelopes on top of the safe, he quickly changed the combination and closed the door. Even though he implicitly trusted every member within the club, he knew cash like this could test the loyalty of the most faithful ex-soldier.

Satisfied with its legitimacy, Angus placed the money in his trust, thus enacting the provision of probate. After six weeks Gillian, Scott and Jayde would never have to worry about money again.

*   *   *

Anxious, Bert fussed about the clubhouse, straightening stacks of chairs, sweeping the already clean floor, and wiping down the benchtops in the small kitchen and bar area. He was like a child on Christmas eve, full of anticipation, so keeping busy kept him distracted.

Hearing the distinct sound of a car that was struggling to perform its duties pull into the compound, Bert took one last look around. Catching the picture of Jack with his beloved bike on the wall, he stopped and in a soft, deep voice he spoke to his mate. *Come on Hobbler, time to change your girl's lives.* With that he made his way to the front door.

Gillian and Scott were operating on autopilot, the stifling effects of raw grief weighing down their thoughts and movement. Bert gave Gillian one of his engrossing hugs, his powerful arms and torso somehow gentler and more refined. Not satisfied with a handshake, Scott was on the receiving end of one of Bert's famous embraces.

Gillian figured this meeting had something to do with the club and their involvement in Jack's farewell. She was expecting Bert to give her the money he was holding from the sale of the car and motorcycle. They had enough cash from Scott's win to cover a basic funeral, but the extra would allow them to indulge in some special touches.

Taking Gillian's hand, Bert led her and Scott through the main room and into a small lounge and office area. Three seats had been strategically placed in front of an open cupboard door that concealed a substantial safe. Two crisp white A4 envelopes sat on top.

Bert gestured to Gillian and Scott to sit. Handing Gillian the top envelope, he said, 'Call me when you need me'.

Opening the envelope, Gillian found a letter addressed to her, it read;

'To my beautiful daughter,

Thank you. Thank you for sharing your family and life with me, but most of all thank you for saving me. If it wasn't for you and your ultimatum there was no way I would have survived, let alone lived for so long with love and joy in my life.

Although I didn't deserve it, you made me a part of your family, tasking me with the most important role, raising your daughter. I cannot express how I have rejoiced seeing both you and Jayde grow. You are an amazing, selfless, loving mother and wife.

I hope you can forgive me for my poor behaviour as a father when you were a little girl. My choices of drinking and gambling stole your childhood. For that I cannot say sorry enough. I will forever be embarrassed and ashamed that I was an absent father.

That day you willingly gave away your dreams to save me was without doubt the lowest point of my life. From that day I have lived with shame and guilt that my only child gave up everything for me. It tore me apart to see what I had done to you and your marriage. Although I never said this to you, I have always felt that I caused the stress which resulted in you losing baby Hannah.

There is so much that I need to atone for. I hope the money Bert will show you allows you, Scott and Jayde to find and enjoy the life you wished for so many years ago.

I fondly remember our days down at Cronulla, playing in the sand and surf, using every bit of daylight. I also remember what we used to say before leaving; 'the waves will always be here, rolling in and out'. Once all this is over, take me to Cronulla, and let me roll in and out at our happy place.

Love forever
Your dad, Jack.'

Wiping tears from her eyes, Gillian handed Scott the letter. Casting his eyes over the neat script, it wasn't long before he was using his sleeve as a makeshift handkerchief. So many emotions and memories were stirred up in one short letter.

Intrigued by his reference to money, Gillian called Bert.

Punching in the code, Bert's heart was racing. He knew what this moment would have meant to Jack. Not having the suppleness of a young man, he rose slowly from his kneeling position. The towers of cash on each shelf revealed their identity at a sluggish pace.

Finally, the full contents of the safe could be seen and appreciated. Speechless, Gillian and Scott sat glued to their chairs; from that small office the space/time continuum froze.

Bert broke the silence. 'Gillian, this is legal and it's all yours.'
'What? How?'

Sitting in the spare chair, he said, 'You know how Jack controlled Jayde's times at each event, this was done for both her running and betting handicap. His plan was to get her fast enough to win and long enough to make big money for you.'

Still struggling, they said, 'Where did he get the money?'

'He sold his car and bike. On that ride to The Gift, his money was split, and everyone had instructions on how and when to bet. That's 1,245 million dollars sitting there in front of you. It is legal. Angus the club solicitor has made sure of that and soon enough it will be all yours.'

'Are you telling me we're millionaires?'

Adding more detail, he said, 'You will be in about six weeks. Angus, following the instructions in Jack's Will, has put this in his trust and in six weeks after probate has finished it will be yours, no tax, no fees, all yours.'

Taking the letter back from Scott, Gillian read it again.

Seeing Gillian was lost in her thoughts, Bert gave Scott the other envelope. 'This is a copy of Jack's Will. From what Angus said it's straightforward.'

Nodding his head, Scott put it on his lap.

Having no need to keep the safe open any longer, Bert stepped forward and placed the precious money back into the safety of darkness. The next time it saw the light of day it would be Gillian's.

Moving back out into the main room, Bert welcomed Angus and Brian, the club's celebrant who handled most of their funerals. For the next hour they sat and confirmed all the arrangements for Jack's farewell.

CHAPTER 40

Thunder

Jack's funeral was full of all the chrome, leather, and thunder associated with a biker's farewell. His mates wore maroon T-shirts under their vest and patch as a mark of respect to their fallen comrade.

His bike was parked adjacent to the entrance of the club, with his helmet on the bars and his patch across the seat. In his own dedication, Marcus had the 7RAR pig airbrushed across the top surface of the fuel tank, while on the rear guard, his regimental badge with 'Hobbler' and his service number were neatly scripted below.

Jack arrived in the back of a hearse surrounded by an honour guard of Harleys. Pulling up to a stop, Kenny the guard leader removed his left hand from the handlebars; raising it in the air he made a circular motion with his wrist.

The booming sound of thunder bouncing around the compound was deafening. Then, with a clench of his fist, there was silence. The bikes shut down in unison.

Newer, younger members of the club assumed the privileged positions as pall bearers; those who served with Jack were well beyond this type of physical exertion. For the next hour, he was remembered for the man he was and the life he lived. Tough men were reduced to tears as they learnt more about the struggles and triumphs of the man they knew as Hobbler.

Jack's exit was as loud and thunderous as his entrance. The haunting howl of a lone piper playing the 7RAR's slow march *My Home* ushered the pall bearers as they carried Jack to his final journey.

As his coffin gently rolled into the back of the hearse, Kenny gave the signal for the parade to ring out the dead. The deafening tenor of a dozen Harley Davidson throttles being opened and closed in no particular order, sent a message to heaven; their brother was on his way.

Thomas, standing with his family, was mystified by the solace and respect dedicated to Jack by his brothers. This was one element of society they never thought they would have any involvement with. Peter had missed his call up in the ballot by a single day. Understanding that this could have been him, Peter felt a strong connection to Jack and felt privileged to be here to pay his respects.

Before joining Jayde, Thomas snuck a quick look at his phone. There was a message from his best mate Nate; *check the news*. Opening the news app he saw the headline, 'Queen of the Track Tests Positive'; quickly skim reading, he realised this was something Jayde needed to see.

Standing by her side, he was able to catch a quick moment between condolences. 'Check this out,' he said handing her his phone.

Seeing the headline brought a smile to Jayde's face. Scrolling down, Thomas took her to the critical part of the story. *Victoria Livingstone's A sample taken at the Grampians Gift has tested positive for a substance of abuse. Under WADA and Sport Integrity guidelines the penalty for this offence is an unconditional three-month ban. Dana Westcombe issued a statement indicating they were reviewing their support, while Australian Athletics and the Institute of Sport were yet to officially comment.*

Jayde could not believe what she was seeing, especially today. Poppy meticulously planned her takedown. However, this was something else, this exposed Victoria's vile, unconscionable character to the entire world.

Athletes like her could handle being known as a 'bitch', wearing this as a badge of honour, but being known as a drug cheat, that was something altogether different. Forever more there would be a stain over her running career.

* * *

In Darling Point, Victoria's life was crumbling before her eyes. Sport Integrity made her aware of the positive result only hours before it went public. Sponsors were publicly questioning their ongoing support. Scott Palmer was much clearer in his private message; *the Tigers have terminated your scholarship.*

As part of due process, she held the option to challenge the findings, relying on a variation in the B sample. With the regular visits she made to the toilet with Rhys, she knew there would be no change in the result.

Her only option; admit to using cocaine.

Her PR firm had gone past damage control. They were now trying to distance themselves from the controversy. Her sex tape was damaging enough, but with the swift and public arrest of the perpetrator, they were once again able to turn a negative into a positive.

But this, this was irrefutable scientific evidence; in the court of public opinion, she was a drug cheat. No spin, no matter how strong, would bring her back into favour. Protecting her would mean throwing their future Hollywood superstar under the bus. By mid-afternoon, Bethany was given the directive; *remove her*!

Separation was delivered by a brief and impersonal text; *Under the terms of your contract, Infinity.PR wishes to invoke clause 11. From this moment Infinity.PR will NOT represent you in any capacity.* No regards or sign-off, just 'you're gone'.

The haters and trolls were having a field day. News of her situation was being viewed and shared at an astonishing rate. Public commentary and memes progressed from the disgusting to the vile and disgraceful. Anonymous scum offered advice on what and where she should go next. It seemed everyone who had an opinion felt compelled to share it.

Celeste Ferguson weighed into the ongoing commentary, stating, *'In light of the recent scandals, it is important to note Victoria Livingstone does not represent the values of a Swinton House girl. The school has forthwith removed all references or images of Victoria Livingstone. We wish to inform the alumni and wider community she will have no representation as a Swinton House old girl.'*

Brand Victoria was no longer a tradable commodity.

*   *   *

After several hours of talking, Gillian was exhausted and ready to go home. She gathered Scott and Jayde before saying goodbye to Bert and Kenny, asking them to extend this to the rest of the lads who were settling in for a rather large night on the cans, toasting their mate and brother. Nodding, Bert helped the family leave without any fanfare.

Driving home, Jayde checked her phone. Petra and Georgia provided a constant commentary on the very public execution of Victoria. Screenshot comments reminded her of how she suffered in those days and months following the IGAA carnival.

Looking at the screen, the satisfaction she had felt earlier curiously vanished, replaced by an even more powerful emotion; empathy.

CHAPTER 41

Redemption

Life for the Hardys ramped up as the day approached when they could access Jack's towers of cash. Plans were well under way to make that long-held fantasy a reality. Borrowing most of Jayde's winnings as a deposit, Gillian and Scott secured their dream unit in Cronulla; a spacious two-bedder only a few blocks back from the beach.

Still with a considerable balance, they splurged, purchasing two new cars. Never again would Scott be forced to play in the engine bay when it came to registration. Thomas spoke with his elderly neighbour and negotiated a fair price for her little runabout.

Apart from the standard changes to address that follows any move, the Hardys had to find new employment. Gillian was able to transfer to one of Isaac's new centres one suburb over in Woolooware.

Scott, on the other hand, had to find a new job. With years of experience, he was quickly picked up by a custom trailer manufacturer in Taren Point, remarkably in a section of the old Davies factory where Jack had worked before his job was shipped overseas.

With a heavy heart, Jayde spoke with Kahlil. Moving out of the area left no opportunity to stay under his employ. She wanted to thank him personally; he showed faith in her when she needed it the most.

Her last order of business was to farewell her ladies. Sad to see her go, they knew her recent success opened opportunities that had to be pursued. Her parting gift for Kahlil and the ladies was a sizable balance in their punters-club account.

Dan and the network were saddened and disappointed when they heard of Jack's passing, but there was still a juicy story sitting there waiting to be explored. Arrangements were made, locations selected, and dates were set aside; people wanted to know her story.

Researchers for the production team discovered very little on Jayde. There were her handful of races in the state school system, the infamous Betty Cambridge Cup debacle, and the past six months of events in the professional league. She was an unbelievably rare find, a pure natural talent, hidden within an astonishing story.

This intrigued Dan, himself a former Olympic runner and Grampians winner, who wanted to know more about her motivation and training. Jayde gave Jack credit for everything. Without giving up his plan, she told him about how he set her training and how she would use her phone to record sessions for him to review.

'So let me get this right, you trained alone, here at Bradfield Sports Ground, under the guidance of a coach, Jack, who was in hospital. That requires incredible commitment and motivation, what gave you that drive?'

Taking a deep contemplative breath, Jayde looked at Dan. 'Initially, my deep hatred for Victoria, for what she did, not only on the track but afterwards, trolling me, getting me fired, pushed me into the darkest of places where I thought my only option was to end it all. After the embarrassment and the shame she caused, I needed redemption. I needed to prove to myself I was better than that. However, after a while hatred fades. Hearing Dr Bradley talking to Poppy one day about just how sick he was, my Poppy became my driving force. I wanted to run and win for him.'

Picking up just how low Jayde had become, Dan asked for clarification. 'So you actually considered self-harm.'

'Yes, after being told for months by people you don't know you should kill yourself, it starts to become an option you consider. I had parents stop their cars as I was walking to school and hurl abuse at me. One lady even got out of her car and tried to take my coat and hat, saying I wasn't worthy of the MAGS uniform, and behind the gates I was ignored. Months after leaving school, Victoria posted a picture of me in my childcare uniform along with one of the many videos of my IGAA blow-up with a horrible tag line, it went viral, and I got fired. Feeling like this moment would never leave me, I decided the only way out was for me to leave everything. Thankfully for me, my Poppy caught me in time, counselled me, gave me direction and I'm here, happy, safe, and talking to you today.'

Ensuring he maintained the public safety requirements for broadcasting, Dan added the contact details for lifeline and other support services.

'Speaking of Victoria, what do you make of the recent controversy surrounding her?'

This was the money-making, scandalous, dirty part of the interview. The producers hoped Jayde would take the bait and dump all over Victoria, joining in with the mob, putting the boot in while she was down.

What they got was beyond expectation; compassion. 'I was brought up to treat people how I would like to be treated. I could relate to the hurt and isolation she must be feeling. Having total strangers tell you you're worthless and your life is not worth living, no one deserves this. Sure, she made mistakes, but I'm also sure those who feel free to offer their opinions have made mistakes themselves, and they're not being held to the same account. I reached out to her the other day; you know what, why don't you ask her yourself.'

'She's here?'

'Yep, just over there pretending to use the fitness equipment.' Standing, Jayde made a gesturing motion.

Dan could not believe what was happening. Victoria had shut herself off, hiding from the public and the media. He might have missed interviewing an urban myth, but getting the current queen of scandal, this could propel him from part-time to full-time sports journalism.

With no preprepared questions or research as a support, he would have to wing it, using his instincts to tell how and where to go with his questions.

'Well, this is an unexpected surprise, you've had a tumultuous week, how are you?'

'I'm ok, I've had plenty of time to contemplate how and why I got myself in this position.'

Picking up the shift in her tone and expression, he could see and hear this was not her usual overconfident, cocky, brash persona, this was honesty and vulnerability.

'Let's deal with the elephant in the room, the positive test, what can you tell us about it?'

Owning her actions, Victoria responded. 'On the night before leaving for The Gift I was at a function where I used cocaine. I should have known better. I'm not attributing blame to anyone, I did it, now I'll pay for it.'

Not expecting contrition, Dan had to think quick. 'There has been some significant fallout from this, where do you go now?'

'In a sporting sense, I've lost everything, my opportunity in America, my position in the Institute, my coach, and my sponsors. All I can do is sit out my three months and then rebuild. I've still got the speed, I'm not a drug cheat in that sense. As a person I need to use the time to learn and grow. This past week I realised who I was; nasty, manipulative, bitchy, not very endearing traits. I will return to the track, hopefully better for the experience.'

'Jayde was very clear about her feeling towards you. If you can, give us some idea of how this intense rivalry began?'

'I guess I can say this now I'm officially expunged as a Swinton Old Girl. Before the final for the Betty Cambridge Cup, I was summoned to a private conference with Ms Ferguson. She was adamant that I win; it was my duty to her and the school. Fiercely proud of my school colours I was easily influenced. I listened to her plan, executing it perfectly on the track. It had the desired effect; removing Jayde and gifting me the win.'

'Coming from a sprinting background, I know there's all sorts of tough talking and strutting around, but this is next level, this is premeditated deception.'

'Oh, it gets better. Through connections I will not name, I was made aware of the motivation behind her demanding I do this horrible, disgusting act; a bottle of wine.'

'What do you mean a bottle of wine?'

'Apparently, there has been a long-standing bet between our schools, an expensive bottle of red wine for the winner of the cup. I also heard Ms Ferguson shared it with the board of directors at the Foundation Day Dinner.'

'That's why my principal Ms Cockington-Hardy told me I had cost her bigtime, and she would make me pay.'

This was unbelievable. It seemed there was no end to the complexity of this story.

Continuing, she said, 'Up to the point I was punched it wasn't personal, I've never been hit before and when I did that's when I made it my mission to get revenge. I'm not a fighter, so I took to social media to vent my anger. I had no idea of the consequences of my actions and nor did I care.'

Her honesty was brutal. 'Seeing Jayde at that coffee shop and recognising the colours within the logo, I knew I could get her into some serious trouble, so without any conscience I took to social media again. I have to take responsibility for being the antagonist in this horrible affair.'

'Ok, I can now understand the different perspectives, motivations and reactions at The Gift, but answer me this, how in such a short space of time did you get to where you are now, sitting here comfortably next to each other?'

As the instigator, Jayde took this question. 'I heard about the positive result at Poppy's funeral, my boyfriend showed me the news feed on his phone. I remember thinking karma's a bitch isn't it. But, then as my friends sent me screenshots of disgusting comments, my happiness disappeared. I remembered what these did to me, they made me feel isolated and ashamed. On the way home in the car I decided I wasn't going to be part of the problem; I wanted to be part of the solution. After a text message or two, I got her number and gave her a call, we chatted and here we are.'

'You don't know how much I needed that call. Nothing said about me was positive, traditional media, social media it was all forcing me into that place I put you. Your first words, *are you ok?* were so empowering, they gave me the strength and motivation to push on.'

'So, let's look down the road, where will you both be in a year from now?'

Continuing with her humble approach, Victoria gestured for Jayde to address the question first. 'Well, my family and I have just put a deposit on a unit, so I'll be settling into coast life. I'm going to start my studies to become a teacher. As for athletics, I think my days on the turf are done. After my win I will have lost my competitive mark, so I'm going to return to hard track racing. I've linked up with a sprint coach that operates out of Sylvania Waters.'

Jayde gave Victoria the nod. 'I'll be in the second year of my law degree and back on the track. I've also linked up with the same coach, and I'm looking forward to the two of us pushing each other throughout the year and delivering a gold and silver medal at next year's national titles.'

For her humility, brand Victoria regained a small amount of lost ground.

*　*　*

Both Barbara and Celeste watched in horror as their actions and behaviour were aired on national television. At no part did either Principal get portrayed in a positive light. Pictures taken from their school websites accompanied the story, removing all anonymity, and both ladies noticed the look of distain they received as they moved through their daily lives.

Each was ordered to face their board of directors to explain their reprehensible actions. Neither walked from these meetings still under the employ of their school.

Jayde, on the other hand, was an instant hit. People were drawn to the authenticity of her story and the honesty with which she portrayed it. Most of all, they loved her integrity; people wanted to know more about this formerly shy girl from the west.

She accepted more opportunities to tell her and her Poppy's stories. Her financial future became more secure with each interview.

* * *

Down in Melbourne, Steve Paterson was given notice of an extraordinary executive meeting. There was only one item on the agenda; depose him!

Crunching the numbers, he realised the no-confidence motion was going to get up. Bill had already moved on and he advised Steve to do the same. In the short time since relinquishing his ties to VPAL, he noticed a significant shift in his outlook on life.

He felt the huge weight of tradition and expectation lift. Finally, nearing his seventieth birthday, he felt free. He could now see the toxicity of VPAL, how it controlled every element of your life, destroying anything that competed for your attention. Family, friends, marriages, it consumed them all. It was an unsatiable attention-seeking master that knew no bounds.

For the first time in decades, Bill sat with Steve and spoke to him as a father should, with love and vulnerability. Calling Adam to join them, together as a family they made the decision to walk away. Steve would offer no contest to the motion and resign; Adam would relinquish his position and with that the reign of the Patersons ended.

* * *

Dave McPharland was reported to the Victorian Gaming and Racing Authority for the comments he made in the Stewards' room. The investigation was rapid and pointless. Dave received a letter of caution for his outburst, allowing him to continue to operate without restraint.

CHAPTER 42

Serenity

The day finally arrived when Angus could release Jack's winnings to its rightful owner. Gillian arranged for a secure pick-up to take it the short distance from the clubhouse to the bank, where it would be counted before being deposited into her account.

Almost immediately, the money for their new unit, cars, and repaying Jayde was transferred out. Fearful of being hacked, Gillian wanted the major amounts out fast. The remaining money was spread across various short- and long-term investments. Gillian never wanted to go back to the financial woes of living pay cheque to pay cheque.

Their new unit was the size of the old three-bed fibro shack they had just given up renting. The building was only a few years old, but to the Hardys, it felt like it was brand new.

Gillian collected Jack's remains the same day they moved in. His urn stood lonely on the new side table just near the front door. Looking through her fresh new unit, Gillian had to pinch herself to believe this was real.

Each room was like a picture out of the home magazines she used to sneak a look at while waiting to be served at the supermarket. How life had changed. But there was something missing. She couldn't quite put her finger on it, but there was something extra she needed to complete their transformation.

The unmistakable message ping from her phone broke her concentration. It was a message from Jayde; *close your eyes.* Gillian could hear Jayde's keys enter the lock on the front door, and following her instructions she closed and covered her eyes.

Hearing the door close, what a surprise awaited her. Opening her eyes, Gillian was presented with Jayde holding a picture frame. Focussing on the image it contained, she saw the unmistakable image of Jack on his Harley, the same one featured on the wall of the Vets' clubhouse.

However, it wasn't a picture, it was a painting, a beautiful soft, enduring painting, which captured the essence of Jack's character perfectly. That was it, that was what she needed to complete the new home. Wiping tears from her eyes she hugged her daughter. She knew exactly where she wanted to hang it, above the side table that was holding his remains.

Jack's urn stood proudly under his portrait while Gillian waited patiently for a picture-perfect summer Sunday. Taking it to the beach, the family spent the day relaxing on the sand and swimming in the surf.

As the shadows from the Norfolk Island Pines extended across the beach and kissed the waterline, Scott ventured up into the mall for some fish and chips, just like Jack did if he had a win with the nags.

Sitting on the beach, eating fish and chips, Gillian, Scott and Jayde all thought about Jack.

Once the battered dinner was finished, and the shadows blended with the light, Gillian reached into her beach bag and stood. It was time to let Jack go.

Holding hands, they waded waist deep into the surf. Standing at the edge of a gutter, Gillian looked skyward. 'Dad, this will always be our special place.'

Unscrewing the lid, she gently upended Jack into the moving water. In a soft voice, Gillian repeated their last words before leaving for home. 'The waves will always be here, rolling in and out, be free Dad, rest in peace.'

The three stood solemnly watching the light grey plume make its way out to sea. Breaking into smaller sections, some rolled in with the waves and others continued their journey into deeper water.

With tears in their eyes, Gillian, Scott and Jayde left the water knowing that whenever they needed time with Jack, all they had to do was walk to the end of the street, sit on the beach and watch the waves lap the shoreline.

About the Author

Stuart McLean is a high school teacher who lives works on the southern fringe of Sydney.

He has a wife and three active children who through their representative football commitments provided an abundance of time in carparks and grandstands to complete his first novel.

In his life before children, he was a decathlete and pole-vaulter who spent countless weekends on the track at Sydney Olympic Park.

Studying his undergraduate degree at Sydney University, he was exposed to the carnival that is gift running.

The pageantry and theatre of handicap racing left an indelible mark on his conscience.

Overlaying this with his twenty-five years of educating teenagers through an ever-increasing myriad of complexities provided the impetus for 'The Swindle'.

Stuart has a Bachelor of Education – Industrial Arts as well as a Graduate Diploma and Master's degree in health and physical education, and is a recipient of Sporting Blue in Athletics from Sydney University.